HADVARIAN HEIST

Age of Azuria Book Two

BETH BALL

ALSO BY BETH BALL

Age of Azuria (in chronological order)

Aurora: An Age of Azuria Novella

Song of Parting: An Age of Azuria Novella (preorder before release on
February 9, 2021)

Buried Heroes: Age of Azuria Book One

Story Magic: An Age of Azuria Novella (forthcoming, 2021)

Hadvarian Heist: Age of Azuria Book Two

Forest Deep: Age of Azuria Book Three (forthcoming, 2021)

Published by Grove Guardian Press

Edited by The Blue Garret

Cover design by 17 Studio Book Design

Ebook ISBN 978-1-952609-06-0

Paperback ISBN 978-1-952609-07-7

Hardback ISBN 978-1-952609-08-4

groveguardianpress.com

To my dad
For all the fantasy worlds we've shared
& for showing us how to create and follow our own path

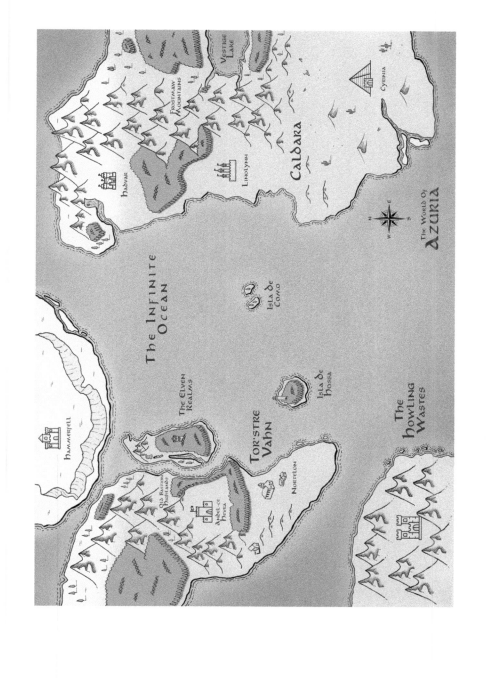

PROLOGUE

Y vayne pulled aside the mists that separated the planes of life from one another. Disturbed spirits swirled through the ether. More than a century had passed since her last visit to the Shadowlands. But as the ancient conflict rekindled and the war began anew, they would need allies.

Besides, Apollo owed her a favor.

The guardian turned slowly at her approach through the dark corridors of his dwelling. His black wings hissed as they trailed across the stone floor. "The one who travels through mist has come to see me at last."

Yvayne stared into Apollo's golden eyes. "Certainly you know why I am here."

Darkness swirled around the borders of the circular stone courtyard. The pathway she'd traversed to stand before the guardian had disappeared the moment she stepped into the chamber. Flashes of light danced through the murky shadows around them. Apollo's servant spirits, the vulpine, whispered. They were surprised by her return.

"I had expected you to come sooner." Apollo's voice rumbled out across the courtyard, unimpeded by the black leather mask that concealed the entirety of his face save for the glowing eyes.

"I have many pressing matters to attend to in Azuria. You are well aware of this." Yvayne stretched her fingers, willing herself to be patient. He would agree to help her, eventually. It was only a matter of how long it might take. And of what he decided he wanted from her in return.

Apollo's boots clicked on granite stones as he approached her. The corners of his eyes crinkled as he smiled from behind the mask. "I hear your thoughts while you are in my realm, Yvayne. You fear what I will ask of you."

"Your requests have been unreasonable in the past."

The spirits hissed all around her but stopped as the guardian raised his fist for silence. "Mistress Yvayne comes to us for aid," he said to the darkness, cupping the bottom of her chin in his hand, "and we are here to help, are we not?" Yvayne's eyes flashed, and the guardian chuckled. He released her and stepped back. "How is your new pet? The garnet-haired druid? Is she indeed one who has returned?"

She scowled in reply. "We shall see." There was no need for the guardian to be informed of the entirety of the situation. He needed only to know enough to be prepared to intervene should the tide turn early. "Lucien's spirit has been sent back to this realm. At the very least, I need to know when he leaves."

"And at the very most, dear Yvayne?"

Her teeth ground together in irritation. It had been foolish to expect a more reasoned response from the self-assured guardian, insulated in his dim domain.

She could turn that to her favor, though. Yvayne raised an eyebrow, her eyes flickering over the powerful being before her. Apollo rolled his shoulders back beneath her gaze, sending ripples down the thick onyx feathers of his wings. "You could actually exert yourself and try to stop him."

Laughter echoed up from behind her, cascading around the room as it grew in volume. A trick of the chamber's acoustics. Apollo shook his head, his unseen smile brightening his eyes. "What an intriguing idea, but I think not. I won't be swayed so easily this time around."

"Do you find this a change from your actions before?" Yvayne crossed her arms, scolding herself for traveling here first. She still had allies among the Brightlands fae. Even reasoning with the angels would have been less tedious than this.

"No need to bring them into it." Apollo's eyes narrowed.

So he truly was observing her thoughts. "Name your price, and I'll be on my way."

"I'm surprised you think so little of me, Yvayne." The guardian tucked long arms behind his back, pacing in a circle around her along the borders of the room. "You see, I have already begun to play."

"Play?" A rush of cold flooded Yvayne's senses. What had he done?

Apollo chuckled again, the heels of his boots grating across the floor. Yvayne pressed her shoulders down, steeling herself against the hair that rose down the length of her neck. "One of your flock is of great interest to me. A certain saudad with hazel eyes."

A torrent of violet flame erupted from Yvayne and streaked across the room at the guardian. Apollo waved his hand and brushed it aside, sending the fire to sizzle harmlessly in the surrounding shadows.

Green and copper eyes reflected the light of the flames back to her. Apollo's fox-servants tilted their heads in interest.

He knew interfering with the saudad was forbidden.

"She is only half saudad," Apollo whispered, reading her thoughts.

A growl flickered in the back of Yvayne's throat. "Persephonie is no concern of yours." She turned to go, but a strong hand reached out and seized her shoulder. Her body went rigid at his touch, and he leaned down, the sides of his jaw grazing her pointed ear as he spoke.

"You forget with whom you are dealing," Apollo whispered. "I wish her no harm. Why are you so quick to assume we must all follow Lucien's cursed path?" The guardian slid in front of her, his wings outstretched to stop her.

Lucien had destroyed more than the two of them could ever express. But he was right. Not all guardians were doomed to the lich's corrupted fate.

Apollo, intrigued by her thoughts, raised his eyebrows, his black-gloved fingers drumming against one another. "I have my own promises to maintain, Mistress Yvayne." He sighed and lowered his head. Yvayne struggled against his spell's hold. The guardian waited for her mind and limbs to calm before lifting his eyes to hers. "Allow me to offer the girl a measure of protection."

His spell loosened to allow Yvayne to speak. "Protection?" She frowned. "So that you can do what?"

He swept a gloved hand to the side as though his proposal were as simple as an acorn stretching limbs out through air and earth to become an oak. "I might please Cassandra, to begin with." A second flash of golden eyes. "And I think you'll agree it would be nice to have the fates on our side."

Yvayne pursed her lips. There was more he neglected to say.

Apollo raised a gloved finger. "But if that's not enough for you, I have an active interest in the fate of the city." He leaned his masked face against his glove. "The outlaws specifically."

Yvayne stepped back, breaking the last vestige of his holding spell. Why would he have allied himself with the few remaining natural casters in Andel-ce Hevra? "You cannot be serious."

His golden eyes glittered.

Yvayne frowned. "Why?" How was she going to tell Persephonie's father of the guardian's plans? This news would devastate Cassian. But the saudad would not easily allow his daughter to part from his side. He knew as well as any the severity of the stakes taking shape around them.

"I made a promise to help the band of outlaws in the city for my own reasons that are"—the guardian squinted up at the shadow ceiling—"mostly benevolent. What do they call themselves? The Untamed?"

Yvayne stepped closer to the guardian. "Help them how?"

Apollo shrugged and retracted his wings to resume his pacing. "I promised survival, what else?"

Yvayne drew herself up to her full height, her eyes even with Apollo's covered lips. "Survival is not enough." A circle of purple flame erupted around the two of them, locking them together and keeping the vulpine beyond the guardian's grasp. "Are you going to actively help them against the entrenched powers of the city? The Council of Andel-ce Hevra is influential enough to send a werewolf pack to destroy an entire druid conclave. Do they have any idea of Lucien's involvement, of his twisted forces strengthening the council's foul roots? What they're truly up against?"

The guardian chuckled as he glanced down at Yvayne. "No, *they* do not. But I do." He reached toward one of her dark blue braids, and she fought back the urge to smack his hand away. Apollo was too used to his charm allowing him free rein with the denizens of Azuria. She had a longer memory than they.

But she'd also seen his grief when they failed to prevent Alessandra and her minions before. How was she to remind him of that and convince him this time would be different?

"That's not good enough, and you know it," Yvayne said. She'd start with an appeal to his pride. "Your followers in the city think of you as a guiding spirit. Someone to help them." She narrowed her gaze. "And here you are, playing tricks."

Apollo flinched. She had hit a nerve. Good.

Yvayne crossed her arms over her chest. "Why are you intervening, then? And tell me, exactly, what your intentions are for Persephonie and how you're going to help her in the city."

"Or what?"

The flames stretched higher, turning from violet to black. They wrapped around the stone columns that stretched into the shadow space around his sanctum.

The smirk fell from the guardian's expression. "I've no desire to allow Lucien free rein in Andel-ce Hevra. He deserves a challenge at the very least. Which, I surmise by your presence here, you are not prepared to pose, or at least not yet."

She lowered the tongues of flame slightly. "And what of Persephonie?"

Apollo lifted his chin. "I'll send a vulpine to protect her."

Yvayne nodded. "And . . ."

The guardian ground his teeth together. "And I'll make sure that she and her mother do more than survive."

"Hmm." Yvayne scowled, considering. How long ago had their last conversation of this sort been? Apollo had been more pliable in the earlier rounds of the cyclical war, less inured to the separateness of life as a guardian.

He had come to stand by her side as the last war's final cadences reverberated through her chest, when she reached forward to close Rowan's bright green eyes. Yvayne's tears had fallen as beads of ice as she draped the elf's hands over her heart space and removed the shepherd's amulet from her chest—the amulet Iellieth now bore. "Now you know what it is to live as we do," he had said. "Though your path is different, Yvayne, it too is one you must walk alone." His half-smile had tugged against his dark lips. "But those who walk as we do, from one age into another, cannot help but hope for what we can never have."

For the present, she would set the terms of his interference. Perhaps he might be drawn into the larger conflict from there. "You're not to speak to Persephonie."

He inclined his head.

"Or to appear to her in dreams."

One eye shrunk as he grinned. "As you wish."

"And tell whichever vulpine you're sending that she'll have her hands full."

Apollo laughed, his eyes brightening. "Of that, I have no doubt." He caught her hand in his, giving her fingers a gentle squeeze. It always amazed her how quickly the guardians' emotions could change. "Thank you," he said softly.

"There's one other thing."

Apollo peered down at her, curiosity flickering behind his gaze.

"If there comes a time when she needs to leave the city or be returned to her people, you'll take her if I cannot."

Apollo folded and unfolded his wings, maintaining his stare. A cool breeze ricocheted across the circular chamber.

"Lucien has returned to his full strength." Yvayne's voice was clipped and cold. "The girl could be a target if he grows desperate enough. If you won't stand up to him, or at the very least watch his movements, I'll have little choice in the matter. And that leaves her and the others vulnerable."

The guardian's arms crossed. "I can sense him, but—"

"No." Yvayne shook her head. "This is not a game, Apollo. We do not know that this opportunity will present itself again."

Apollo shook off Yvayne's reprimand and his own hatred of their old enemy to affect overconfidence once more. "I'll keep a sharp eye."

"See that you do." *He nearly destroyed us before. Who's to say he won't succeed if he tries again?* There was no need to voice the warning aloud. "I will be watching you as you watch her." It was Yvayne's turn to smile. "Perhaps she'll pull you in deeper as I cannot."

Apollo's jaw stretched the bottom of his mask but clamped back closed.

"And in the meantime, I have more allies in mind." Yvayne brushed aside the black and violet flames, striding toward the swirling smoke where she knew a door would appear.

Apollo's voice caught her shoulder, asking her to wait before crossing the threshold. "Which ones?"

She glanced back, her own eyes flashing. "Who do you think?"

The guardian threw his arms into the air. "The Brightlands fae? You cannot be serious! They're not going to intervene."

Yvayne grinned. "You did." Her foot stepped through shadow onto the stone pathway beyond. Spirit guardians and the Brightlands fae had a long-standing rivalry. Apollo would do what was required if it prevented one of them from interfering in what he considered his own territory. She could stop and warn Cassian on the way.

The guardian had been right in what he told her before. Near-immortals couldn't help but fall for the vibrancy of those they watched, however unwise it was to do so, however much pain they would live with from that moment forward.

It seemed that he had forgotten, but it was something she knew better than most.

CHAPTER 1

L inolynn's pale silhouette faded against the shimmer of the Infinite Ocean and an azure sky as Iellieth, Marcon, and Quindythias made their way to Red's Cross. Quindythias alternated between grumbling at the pace of their travels by foot and regaling them with stories of his daring past deeds. Marcon qualified these tales of bravery and added a few, more modest accounts of his own, painting a picture for her of the long-lost time of the heroes.

"And that's why they call me the Blade of Bastion," Quindythias said with a shrug. The elf skipped off, outpacing Marcon's easy stride beside her to examine the leaves of the willow oak.

Marcon grinned. "Of course, what he's leaving out is that the moniker began as a defamation campaign by Alessandra's puppet government in the city and was not actually intended as a compliment."

Quindythias spun around, hand clutched to his chest. "Marcon! How can you say such a thing?"

The champion shook his head. "I'm only telling her the truth."

"Are not." Quindythias stomped. "Iellieth, don't listen to him. He's just jealous that after I saved Bastion and had to sneak out, I became the most popular champion in Respite instead of him."

"Is that so?" She raised an eyebrow as she glanced at Marcon. If he didn't let up the teasing soon, Quindythias would pout for the rest of the evening.

"No one slips past armies of guards like you do," Marcon conceded.

Quindythias harrumphed his victory with a nod and darted off into the trees to demonstrate his abilities. He spent the twilight hour sneaking up from behind her and pouncing.

As dusk fell, Marcon gestured to a small copse of trees off of the road that stretched from Linolynn to Red's Cross. "I think we should rest here for the night, lady."

"Unless we want to travel by starlight," Quindythias added.

"Hmm"—Iellieth smiled—"as tempting as that would be . . ." A yawn interrupted her clarification.

Quindythias draped his arm around her shoulders, and they followed Marcon to a cluster of trees. "You'll get used to the travel after a while. Not everyone can adapt quite so well as Marcon has to keeping up with me, but I have hope for you."

Iellieth turned her head to hide her amusement from Quindythias. He took laughter that he hadn't intended to create quite personally. "Your faith is much appreciated."

Marcon called back to them through the trees, "Quindythias, leave her alone and help me set up camp."

The elf stopped, halting Iellieth's progress forward as well, and mock-saluted his friend. With a quick turn and a wink, he scampered across the remaining patch of field to Marcon's side.

The minor moon, in a waxing crescent, cast a soft orange

glow across the inky sky, her sister a silvery white, waning just above her.

Once more, she pictured Katarina handing Mamaun the black rose she had grown, an apology, she hoped, that ran deeper than words. What would Mamaun have said in return? Was she angry that Iellieth had left in the middle of the night? Would Mamaun forgive her for what she had said—that she had failed to protect her daughter, had failed to care? However true it was, she need not have said it. But what would it take for her mother to understand?

Iellieth sighed and glanced down at the dark blue-green grasses around her feet. Strands of tiny white flowers had grown in a circle around her, winding their way across the tall, thin blades and weighing them down. She shook her right foot, freeing it from the flowers' embrace, and extricated herself from the self-made sanctuary.

"That will happen if you let it," Mara would have said. "Emotions and energy build, but they need to move. If not, given time, their waters will overwhelm the dam and break through, bringing cleansing life to the dry beds downstream."

A cold hand gripped her heart, and Iellieth shut her eyes against the vision of her druidic mentor, surrounded by a wreath of green flames. A soft whisper from the earth beside her caught her attention. Careening to the side, its large, petaled head staring up at her, a single black flower blossomed by her foot. Iellieth wrapped her arms around her waist and hurried ahead into the clearing.

"Lady, is everything alright?" Marcon's eyebrows creased as he watched her arrival.

"Yes"—she managed a half-smile—"I was just . . ." She shook her head. "Just thinking about something. Do you need any help with camp?"

"We're nearly finished." He kept one eye on her while continuing to stack wood beside the fire.

Iellieth kept her expression blank. *Please just believe me, at least for now.*

"Ready, big guy," Quindythias announced suddenly, catching them both off guard. The elf leaned back on his heels, grinning up from behind a perfect pyramid of sticks that he'd arranged for their fire.

Marcon squatted down next to his friend, his broad silhouette contrasting with Quindythias's narrow frame. At the third sharp click of flint on steel, a shower of sparks fell onto the kindling and caught. The fledgling fire sizzled. Marcon bent lower, his olive-toned hands pressing into the dark earth of the space they'd cleared beneath the leaves. The runes along his hands danced from dark to light in anticipation of the fire, just as Quindythias's arcane markings celebrated the kiss of the wind. Marcon breathed life into the flames, and the fire roared to life.

The fire's chatter soothed her as they ate their bread and dried meat. Marcon's baritone rolled beneath the dry crackling and warm rumble, and Quindythias's sharp-voiced stories and exclamations accented the lulling rhythm.

Iellieth pulled Mara's shawl around her shoulders as she fell asleep beneath the gaze of the stars and Quindythias's watch. He would wake Marcon partway through the night, and Marcon would wake her just before dawn.

※

A MUFFLED CRY YANKED IELLIETH FROM SLEEP IN THE MIDDLE of the night. The fire had burned down to glowing embers. Quindythias lay splayed beside her, his chest rising and falling with an elbow draped over his eyes.

Iellieth sat up, searching the trees for Marcon. His sword and shield rested beside Quindythias, but he wasn't within the copse's close embrace.

A branch cracked in the woods, and she sprang up, sparks of energy dancing at her fingertips. Iellieth ran toward the sound, ignoring the sharp prods of twigs beneath her stockinged feet.

Her eyes adjusted to the obscured light of the copse, her elven vision clarifying the darkness. *There*. A dark shape writhed in the darkness before her. She darted closer.

A narrow-shouldered figure in a black cloak struggled, shadows sweeping toward their body around the trees' peaceful silhouettes. Elbows stuck out from beneath the billows of the dark cloak, the figure's hands pulled back tight in front of their chest.

As she drew closer, a choking gurgle reached her. The figure jerked to the side, revealing a feminine curve beneath the cape and Marcon half-kneeling in front of her, a garrote tight around his neck. His shoulder muscles bulged as he tried to pull away from the attacker.

"Marcon!" Iellieth shouted. The sparks in her right hand erupted into a ball of flame, streaking toward the cloaked form. She willed her strike to set the woman's body ablaze.

Marcon's eyes widened, bright in the darkness around them, and he strained harder against his attacker. What power did she possess to have Marcon in such a position?

Iellieth froze as the woman locked burning red eyes on her. Ashen skin glowed, cracked with blazing embers, beneath her hood. She hissed, rows of yellowed teeth gnashing.

Iellieth shrieked as the sensation of frigid, slithering worms engulfed her skin. Chills ran up and down her spine as she shook the feeling off. She sprinted forward, shouting to the trees for aid. The Druidic chant poured from her lips as sparks flew around her. "Branches burn, leaves entangle, above roots' walk, maim and mangle."

Limbs shot toward the woman, striking at her arms and face. She pulled back harder against Marcon's neck, breaking his skin. The champion gagged, trying desperately to wrench himself free.

Iellieth growled her chant again, the druidic energy flowing freely through her body. The incantation burned the back of her throat. Peridot fire smoldered behind her eyes. Roots slithered in the earth below, whipping out at the woman's feet, entangling them. A sharp crack echoed through the copse as one of the roots snapped her knee to the side. The woman's screams pierced the darkness. Her hood fell to her shoulders as she threw her red gaze up to the sky. Hair with the crumbling texture of ash slumped over her shoulders. Thick black burns had scarred their furious tendrils across her throat and chest. Moonlight simmered against her flaky gray skin. She clutched her scalp, wriggling beneath the incandescent glow.

Another branch caught around her throat, and she released Marcon, forced to focus on her struggle against the trees. The champion fell forward onto his knees, coughing and clutching his neck.

"Maim and mangle." Iellieth's voice clawed at the back of her throat. The forest quivered with energy that leapt from tree to tree, their spirits resolved to root out the intruder.

Branches wrapped around the woman's wrists and pulled, further snaps echoing through the woods. The red eyes fixed on Iellieth and exploded. A rushing force caught her in the chest and threw her backward. Her spine crashed into a tree, and she fell to the ground.

A roar erupted all around her, drowning out all other sound. Had Marcon recovered? Or had the woman broken free? Iellieth dug her fingers into the earth, gasping for breath, unable to make her muscles comply. She had to finish off this creature of ash and shadow.

Crisp air streamed through her lungs. She gulped it down and sprang up from the wet forest floor.

Marcon drew his hand back. The woman's nose was a crushed mass of burning coals across her face. Her jagged smile stretched wider, and blazing eyes looked from Marcon to Iellieth and back. "What an interesting twist," she wheezed. Her head tilted sideways as her blazing eyes fixed on Iellieth. "Goodbye for now." Her sizzling cackle filled the trees.

Iellieth clasped her hands over her ears at the piercing laughter. Black smoke coalesced around the woman. The wind in the woods lifted a shield around Iellieth, swirling through leaves as the dark being battered branches. With a final whoosh and faint cries of delight, the woman's body melted to shadow, a dark silhouette flapping away against the twilight.

She vanished in the vast expanse of the sky, and Iellieth ran over to Marcon. He winced and swayed back, staring at the empty hand that had clutched the creature's cloak. The other hand reached for the bloody gash across his neck. "Lady, I . . ." Marcon's eyes rolled back, and one of his legs gave way. She leapt forward, catching his side as they both toppled to the ground.

"Oof." Her thigh struck a root. She clutched his shoulders and gently laid him back. The laceration on his neck was eerily similar to the creature's glowing-coal lips. Iellieth closed her eyes against the thought. *"Elenai."* Her fingertips grazed the cut. Lavender sparks flickered over the wound, knitting his skin back together.

Marcon shivered and his eyes fluttered open, finding her face in the umbral dark of the woods. He opened his mouth to speak, but his body tensed at a crashing sound tearing through the trees. The champion shoved himself up, thrusting his torso between her and the approaching danger.

Quindythias's lanky form burst through the trees, moonlight glinting off the curved daggers in each of his hands. He stopped short, breathing quickly, when he saw the two of them. His shoulders sagged for a moment. "There I was, sleeping when I heard you scream—wait." He sheathed the daggers and ran forward, peering at Marcon's neck. "What happened?"

Marcon's jaw twitched in response. He turned away from both of them. Quindythias peered at Iellieth, waiting for an answer.

"A woman . . . made of ash, fire, and shadow attacked Marcon in the woods." The stone line of his jaw jutted out beside her. "I-I don't know what she was . . ."

"A revenant," Marcon growled. "A vengeful spirit."

"One returned from the grave," Iellieth whispered. Rumors of such creatures had trickled across Caldara, ancient legends that originated in the Frostmaw Mountains. "But how—"

Marcon shook his head. "Not how. Who."

CHAPTER 2

"So this vengeful spirit attacks in the middle of the night, but you don't know who she was?" Iellieth walked close by Marcon's side the next morning as they continued toward Red's Cross. He'd said very little when they returned to the campsite, and she was certain he had only pretended to sleep once he finally agreed to lie down for her watch.

"That is correct, lady." He stared straight ahead.

Quindythias shrugged and made a small pushing gesture behind Marcon's back. She should keep trying.

"Did you recognize anything about her?" Iellieth shuddered at the memory of the ashen visage with glowing red eyes. "Or is that not possible given her transformation?" Surely he would have remembered someone from his past whose looks were so distinctive and frightening—something terrible had happened to her in the interim.

Marcon sighed and rubbed his hand along his jaw. "I did not recognize her, though if her identity becomes apparent to me, you will be the first to know."

Iellieth crossed her arms against Marcon's chilly tone. There was no cause for him to be angry with her. He might have died if she hadn't heard him and intervened. She traced a thumb across the golden tines of her father's amulet. While it made sense to *assume* that Marcon would return to the amulet if something that drastic occurred, they had no way of knowing that for certain. Perhaps somewhere in Azuria, there was a record of guidelines for former champions bound to amulets, but until they came across it, she saw no reason to take rules around death and regeneration for granted.

Scattered pebbles in the pressed-dirt road crunched beneath their feet as the silent party of three traveled through the early morning mists. Their first day out from Linolynn, the landscape had changed from flat to rolling hills. The knolls grew on their second day of travel, and this morning, the path increased in elevation still further as they reached the foothills of the Frostmaws.

They stopped in the early afternoon to rest beside a clear stream. Quindythias searched the shore for rocks to skip across the surface of the water.

Marcon scooted closer to her and cleared his throat. "Lady, I apologize for the way I spoke to you this morning." His elbows rested on raised knees, and he locked his gaze on the stationary drape of his hands in front of him.

Iellieth bit the inside of her lip before she spoke. "I am relieved that you're alright. Truly, that was a terrifying way to wake up." He still wouldn't look at her. "But I don't understand why you are still upset now. The spirit left, didn't she?"

"What is to stop her from returning?" Marcon scowled. Finally, he turned to her. "What's to stop her from trying to harm you, lady, if and when she does return?" Shimmering gray crystals burned behind his eyes.

Iellieth's fingers trailed the outline of her amulet. The woman had vowed to return, but why was she attacking them?

Had Lucien, the dark mage who destroyed her conclave in search of Iellieth, sent this revenant? Or was it someone else?

Marcon interrupted the wave of questions that rose with the tide in her mind. "The one Yvayne sent us to speak to, perhaps he will know more about this as well."

Iellieth laid her hand on his forearm and squeezed gently. "I'm certain that any friend of Yvayne's is well informed."

She jumped as Quindythias's face appeared between her and Marcon.

"Who is this Yvayne person?" He tilted his head and looked back and forth between them. "More importantly, if she knew where I was this whole time, why didn't she come get me? Or why not tell you to wake me up and then Marcon?" Quindythias pursed his lips, already revising the history of his new adventure.

⚜

LATE IN THE AFTERNOON OF THEIR THIRD DAY, THE PATH wound up the side of a modest peak, granting them a view of the lush, forested foothills. Iellieth gasped. "Look!" She stood on her tiptoes and pointed ahead. There in the distance, the outline of a city appeared over the tree line.

An hour before sunset, they arrived on the outskirts of Red's Cross. The city's architecture resembled that of the Earth and Water Wards in Linolynn, a mixture of whitewashed clay, wooden structures, and brick edifices. The streets were orderly, and there were plenty of signs to guide travelers to the city center.

Many of the merchants were packing up for the day, and Iellieth struggled to pass through the streets crowded with mule carts and milling townsfolk. The rows of booths led uphill toward a towering stone building named Western Station.

Structurally, the station resembled a large manor house, but the center had been opened up for commerce, and the citizenry of Red's Cross wandered around the open-air spaces, some arm-in-arm, others sharing drinks with friends. Iellieth climbed the gray stone steps leading into the central market, Marcon and Quindythias a few paces behind her.

"Excuse me." Iellieth raised her hand to catch the attention of two guards stationed in the center of the indoor plaza. They wore crimson doublets with a copper-spoked wheel across their chests that, she gathered from the posted maps they had seen, represented the city's layout. Behind the pair of guards, a self-important, finely dressed man sat at a wide wooden table strewn with documents. "We are newly arrived in town and would like to discuss scheduling an audience with Master Red."

The guards turned to the man seated behind the desk. He pursed his lips and twirled his feather quill. "And who is it that requests this meeting?" He glanced between her, Marcon, and Quindythias, his eyes lingering on the runes that crossed the champions' skin.

"Lady Iellieth Amastacia and . . . her companions." She gave a sharp nod and drew herself up to full height.

"What a treat for us, to host nobility from our neighboring kingdom." The steward leaned back in his chair, crossing his arms behind his head. "I recall receiving a writ from the king several weeks ago indicating that such a noblewoman was missing and, if discovered, should be immediately returned to the court." His eyebrows rose. "Shall I call for the nearest patrol, or might you be someone else?"

"That writ—"

Quindythias slid forward and wrapped an arm around her waist. "Such a clever man, this one. Much smarter than the document supervisor of . . ."

"Penshaw," Iellieth whispered, naming the next closest town.

"Penshaw!" Quindythias waggled a finger at the man behind

the desk. "Very well, sir, most astute, we bid you good day." He tugged at Iellieth and pulled her away from the guards and steward. Their eyes lingered on her back as she and the champions disappeared into the crowds milling about the station.

She wriggled free of his grasp. "Quindythias, why did you—"

He waved his hand. "Don't mention it. Happy to help."

Iellieth sighed, casting her eyes up to the arched ceiling. There was so much more to teach him about the world he'd just reawakened into, yet he remained oblivious to any apparent gap in his understanding. "But now—"

"That man wasn't going to help us." He shook his head and draped an arm around her shoulder, leading her down the crowded halls of the marketplace. "Speaking of, allow this experienced connoisseur of the adventuring life to pass some hard-earned knowledge to you, someone who is very new to our trade." A wide smile flashed across the elf's face. "Don't tell anyone, besides myself and Marcon, anything more than they absolutely need to know."

Iellieth squinted up at him. "But what about—"

"No." Quindythias pirouetted in front of her and bent at the waist to drop his eyes on level with hers. "Only what they need to know." His features scrunched as he contemplated the ceiling over her head. "And maybe not even that much . . ." He stood tall once more. "Let's grab a drink, and then we can practice on new guards in the morning."

Marcon chuckled softly behind her, and Iellieth spun around. "It's not funny. We need to find Red, and he . . ." She dropped her hands.

"He is himself, always, lady. Quindythias means well, I promise."

"I believe you. It's just . . . hmm, very well. Let's see about some food that isn't dried rations, and then we can inquire after lodgings."

Each of the taverns inside the station had a unique atmosphere. One was brightly lit, full of storytellers and entertainers, another dark, with sombre music and hushed conversation, and a third, the one they were closest to, boasted a full musical ensemble.

Freshly baked bread called to her from the far end of the market. Her stomach rumbled, and she laid her hand below her ribs to quiet it. "Let's try there." A sign with two bulging eyes jutted out into the hall: THE WIZENED GNOME. It glowed with warm lantern light, and the patrons inside dined on buttery dinner rolls that they washed down with large tankards of dark beer.

She led them over to one of the tables near the far wall, and Marcon signaled the bartender for their first round.

A tottering tray started making its way toward them, carried about waist height with no figure visible beneath it. The tray slid onto their table, and the gnome toting it appeared. "Here you are, lady and gentlemen . . ." His tinny voice faded as he stared at Marcon's shield, gazing from the top of it to the man it leaned against. The gnome gasped and waddled forward, leaning to get a better look at himself in the shield's reflection.

His small hands reached up and clawed into Marcon's arm.

"Gah!" Marcon's chair flew back as he stood, taking a few stumbling steps away from the eager gnome.

The waiter's mouth dropped open, and his giant eyes blinked rapidly, trying to clear his vision. He tilted his head to the side. "Marcon?"

CHAPTER 3

Passersby swirled around Persephonie on the streets of Andel-ce Hevra, going about their daily affairs. She breathed in the mingling perfumes from their hair and clothes and the aromas from the spice sellers down the street. Any number of people around her might know where her mother lived—they could even be friends. This latent possibility, of friends waiting behind the faces of strangers, always struck her upon arrival in the ancient city. She knew all of the saudad in her muster, yet here, she knew only her mother and a few acquaintances Esmeralda'd had over the years. Persephonie wasn't even certain where in the city Mama lived, though she'd visited enough times to guess where she should start her search. Most of the time, Mama invited her with a specified day and place to meet, but she could manage without that. At first, Datha had protested when she expressed her wish to spend a few weeks with her mother, believing it too dangerous a time to be separated, but as he and her brothers were sheltering with the rest of the saudad muster in the Brightlands, she convinced him to allow her a visit.

Her father would have prevented her had he known about the visions, but she'd kept them to herself. Well, almost . . . but her former partner Velkan guessing at what Cassandra had shown her wasn't the same as her revealing the portents of darkness and calamity to Datha and causing him needless worry.

Heads turned toward a flash of bright red fur that streaked past above the crowd. Their curious murmurs stopped abruptly as the shouts and clatter of guards rose in the distance. The populace scattered, seeking shelter from the city's enforcers. A fluffy tail, the tip of which darkened to the same deep auburn-brown of her own hair, splashed through the aqueduct overhead, spraying water as it fled.

Persephonie dodged through the shoppers in pursuit of the fox. Someone would need to defend the poor creature from the guards or help it escape. Her half-skirt caught on the breeze, heeled boots clicking over the cobbles as she tried to catch up with the frightened creature.

"Let me help you," she called in Queran, the ancient language of the forest. Still the fox charged away. She tried again in Druidic. "I can protect you."

The bushy tail swished against the static of the city air, crackling with its excess of unused magic. Two large, erect ears and glittering amber eyes peered down at her from overhead.

Persephonie held out her arms. "Jump!"

Fox spirits had always played an important role in her life. Mama said she'd never seen so many in one person's tarot readings. Almost every spread she drew for her daughter involved the furry embodiment of the suit of wands, foretelling a life of magic, passion, and fire. They often appeared to Persephonie on her travels with the saudad, a flame flitting through the foliage or a dancing shape formed in the clouds.

The fox tilted its head, considering. Sharp white teeth

flashed as the creature mewled. The shouts and clanging of guards drew closer.

"Hurry," Persephonie called.

The citizens of Andel-ce Hevra gave her a wide berth, averting their eyes. An anxious fog hung over them, growing heavier as the guards neared.

The fox flicked its tail, and beads of water trickled onto the street below. It propped its fuzzy paws on the edge of the trough and leapt down, small wet feet and legs immediately soaking Persephonie's blouse.

"Away we go," she whispered. Persephonie tugged the shawl from around her shoulders over the fox's quivering body and dashed down an alley.

"Girl"—a gruff voice called from an open doorway three buildings down—"in here." A large man stepped out from the doorframe, waving her inside.

Persephonie sprinted toward the figure, glancing up to smile her thanks before she darted inside.

"In the back," he murmured.

Low lanterns glowed against the shiny tabletops scattered across the tavern's stone floor. A few patrons glanced in her direction before returning to their drinks.

Persephonie walked across the bar with her head high as Datha had taught her—"It decreases the chance that someone thinks you're somewhere you don't belong, especially when that's precisely where you are." Her father always delivered his best advice with a wink and a pat on the head.

She tried to slow her breathing and whispered a soothing *shh* to the bundle draped over her chest. The swinging door to the kitchens glowed warm against the tavern's dim light. She glided behind the polished wooden bar, leaned her back against the door, and slipped inside.

"Pardon me, miss"—a tenor voice rang out in accented

Torstran—"ought you to be here?" An androgynous half-elf blinked at her, lips pursed.

"I, erhm, you see, there was . . ."

The half-elf jerked back as the fox popped its head up from beneath the scarf. "A beast!" they cried, stumbling away.

"It is alright." Persephonie held out her other hand. "It won't hurt you."

The heavy wooden door swung open, and the gruff man who had helped her appeared. Dark brown eyes studied her from beneath thick brows. "She's alright, Tess," he said with a glance at the half-elf.

They stayed several feet back from Persephonie but calmed, straightening their apron.

"Girl, this is my chef, Tess. I'm Otmund, and I own the bar here, the Green Owl."

She inclined her head first to Otmund and then to Tess. "I am Persephonie." She smiled and held up the fox, seeing as she did so that it was a vixen. "And this is . . ." Shimmering spheres of amber stared back at her. "Juliet."

"You look awfully familiar," Otmund said, peering at her. "Have we met before?"

"I am certain that I would remember you." The kitchen's worn counters and black iron lanterns provided a soothing contrast to the glare of the streets outside.

"Do you have any relatives in the city?" Otmund peered over her shoulder as Juliet went to investigate the stove. "See that she doesn't eat anything she shouldn't, Tess," he said, jerking his chin in the fox's direction.

"Yes, my mother is here, Esmeralda Arelle." She squeezed her hands together behind her back. "Do you happen to know her, Mister Otmund?"

He scowled. "Arelle . . ." The tavern keeper scratched at his beard, the hairs crackling beneath his fingers like the rustle of dried leaves. "She wouldn't be one of *them* now, would she?" He winked at her and then rubbed the bridge of his nose.

Persephonie looked down. Depending on where they traveled, she and her people were received as an unwelcome *them* of some kind, and her mother often fell into this category as well even though she wasn't a saudad by birth. But feigned ignorance was safest in circumstances such as this. "I am sorry, Mister Otmund, I do not know who you mean. I have just arrived in the city."

"Otmund is fine." He leaned closer to her, dropping his voice. "Is your mother one of the Untamed? The outlawed natural magic users running around the city."

Persephonie's eyes widened. Her mother had learned druidic magic from the conclave to the north, the one Yvayne said had been destroyed by werewolves. It was no secret that the Council of Andel-ce Hevra despised magic derived from the natural world and those who channeled it. But she hadn't been aware of her druidic powers being forbidden altogether, and she had never heard of the Untamed. Was this the source of the foreboding visions Cassandra had given her regarding her mother? "I do not think so. Who are these Untamed? And why are they against the law? Have they done something wrong?"

Otmund gestured to a small room off the kitchen with straight-backed wooden chairs around a small table. Along the walls were shelves full of bundles of dried herbs and lumps of rising sourdough. Her stomach growled at the warm mix of aromas. Otmund picked up a pitcher of wine and two goblets and followed her. "I figured you might be unaware of the Green Law, given, ahem . . ." He coughed, indicating her colorful ensemble and the flowers braided through her hair. "Didn't want to judge unfairly, but you don't look like you're from here." He rubbed the back of his neck, hiding a pink flush.

"I am not from here." Persephonie bit down on her lower lip.

"What is this Green Law?" Otmund seemed like he wanted to help her, but she needed to be sure.

"They've had statutes against nature-based casters for some time," the tavern keeper explained, "but writing it is one thing, enforcing it another. The council means it this time, though, after what happened." Otmund frowned. "No natural-based magic is to be cast inside the city of Andel-ce Hevra." He raised an eyebrow, waiting for her reaction.

Persephonie wiggled on the worn wooden seat. Otmund had brought her in away from the guards, and his warnings didn't carry the tenor of a reprimand or threat.

Her eyes brightened. It was a test, of course. "If I were, perhaps, of a similar persuasion as these Untamed, where would I hide out in the city?"

Otmund's bark of laughter echoed across the kitchen. "I see that you're catching on already." He chuckled, pouring wine for her and for himself. "Most of them are in the Sessorium at the edge of the city, others in Holdenfield. You'll find a rare few in City Center South."

"And where are we, here right now?"

"Calaboro, near the intersection with City Center and City Center South." He paused to watch as Juliet strutted into the room, tail held high and swishing. "Speaking hypothetically, as we are, I don't condone all of the Untamed's methods, but there are plenty of others like me in the city who believe the council has gone too far this time, and we agree that the Green Law is harsher than it needs to be."

Persephonie added this Green Law and the Untamed to the collection of things to discuss with her mother. No wonder Cassandra had sent her here.

Otmund leaned his elbows on his knees and looked back at her. "I've a way of getting in touch with them if you like. Would that help you locate your mother?"

"Do you really? Yes, I am certain that it would." At the worst, contacting the Untamed would tell her where Esmeralda wasn't and, at best, where she was.

The tavern owner sat back at her excitement, but his expression lifted into a smile.

"Thank you so much, Mister Otmund, that would be wonderful."

He waved Tess back over, shaking his head. They scowled but pushed off of the doorjamb and walked over to Otmund's side.

"Send word to our contacts, eh? We'll get this one and"—he indicated Juliet with his thumb—"the fox sorted. Tell them one of their own has washed up in the city and needs to find a place to land."

Persephonie scratched the short fuzz between Juliet's ears, much to the fox's delight. Soon, she and her mother would be reunited, and Esmeralda could help her make sense of these visions and what they foretold.

CHAPTER 4

Marcon gaped at the gnome, eyes wide, and Iellieth sprang up to stand between them.

Two guards burst from the kitchens, and one extended his hand toward Marcon, muttering under his breath. Marcon's shoulders began to creep up toward his ears, his muscles struggling against an unseen force.

"Wait, please," Iellieth urged. Sparks crackled from her palms. She could stop at least one of the guards if she had to, but it would create quite a scene for those nearby.

The gnome, lips pursed, squinted at his guards. "You two, stop that." He shook his head and went over to pick up Marcon's chair. "Here you are." He grunted as he raised it to standing. "And you must be Quindythias." He peered over the edge of the table at the elf. "Nothing to worry about here!" The gnome smiled at the other patrons, waving the guards away to return to their posts.

Iellieth laid a hand on Marcon's arm and asked the gnome, "Are you Red?"

"Why yes, of course," the gnome squeaked. He adjusted the

waistband of his pants. "Red Snicklefritz, at your service. Whom did you think you were talking to?"

"I-I wasn't quite sure." Iellieth crouched and lowered her voice. "Did Yvayne tell you we were coming?"

"Yvayne!" He bounced onto his tiptoes and glanced around the bar, his mouth pulled down as though, at any moment, someone would force the secret from his lips. Red gestured Iellieth closer. "Maybe we should find somewhere more private to talk." He nodded at Marcon, then Quindythias—"You know, for them"—and winked. "Follow me."

The gnome waddled off toward the kitchen as the three exchanged looks.

"Has everyone in this time taken a leave of their senses?" Quindythias whispered.

"Perhaps, but we have excellent hearing," Red called. "This way."

Large murals decorated the hallways behind the tavern's kitchen, and the gnome leading the way figured prominently in the artwork. In the earliest pictures, his beard was half the length it was at present, though an equally bright orange. The murals told of a small town's development into an important trading hub, and the final picture depicted the city from above, the streets spread out like spokes through the urban landscape.

Red stepped up to the mural and pressed his palm against one of the low stones. The brick scraped as it slid back into the wall. As it went, the bricks surrounding it followed, rolling back into a recess behind the mural like the ends of a scroll. Where the center of the city had been, a long passageway now stood open. The gnome grinned up at them once more and led them down the passage to a beautiful wood-paneled office.

"Sit, sit," he instructed, pushing the two chairs in front of his desk closer as they entered the room. Marcon gestured for her to take one as he stepped behind it and Quindythias sat beside her.

The gnome climbed into the plush green leather chair behind the desk and then onto the large wooden desk itself, taking a seat on the top.

"I can't tell you what a pleasure it is to finally meet you in person," Red said, his eyes twinkling as he gazed at Marcon.

"Uh . . . thank you, sir." Marcon bowed his head.

"Have you been waiting to meet him?" Iellieth asked. Yvayne had known who Marcon was, as had Mara, but they had spoken not as if they had anticipated his arrival but rather had recognized him when he appeared.

"Since I was a wee gnome, yes." The tips of his large ears waved as he nodded. Red groaned as he pushed himself back up, and his short legs carried him over to the bookcase beside his desk. He brushed dust off the spines and ran his fingers along the gilded titles. He seized a tome bound in walnut-brown leather and slid it gently off the shelf. The gold leaf along the spine had worn with age, but the engraving beneath the curled Gnomish script remained.

It was the same emblem of flame as was on Marcon's shield.

"The sigil of Ignis," Marcon said softly.

Iellieth gasped and leaned forward, gripping the bottom of her chair.

Red's face crinkled in a smile as he walked back toward them, his volume held out in front. "I first met Marcon in a children's tome some four hundred years ago." His voice quietened. "This volume, called *The Tales of Marcon*." He ran his tiny hand over the leather. "The stories were forgotten histories and accounts of bravery. Or at least I thought they were only stories when I was that age." His eyebrows flashed up at the man behind her.

Red held the book out, and Iellieth took it. Energy radiated from its pages, heavier and more soothing than the sparks that came to her aid. It bore the weight of its story and the love of its reader.

Her right hand shook as she curled her fingers under the front cover. She stopped and looked up at Marcon. What would it mean, to discover a story about you and your life thousands of years after you had lived? Would it bring back painful memories?

His fingertips traced the top of her shoulder. "Go ahead, lady." Marcon leaned over beside her. They would experience the story together.

One of the earliest pictures focused on his shield with the tripartite flame, Marcon screaming in rage behind it. Slouched figures cowered along the edge of the page, their gray mouths twisted and teeth bared.

The champion reached down and flipped forward. His breath caught at a picture of himself standing in front of a troupe of soldiers, all in full plate, the flames emblazoned across the chests of their armor.

"Is this your battalion?" Iellieth whispered. He nodded.

"What do you think, Marcon?" Iellieth jumped as Red's voice interrupted their examination of the volume. She had forgotten he and Quindythias were there. "Painstaking research over the course of many, many years indicated that you were a real being and not simply a heroic faery tale meant to inspire young gnomes," Red continued. "But these discoveries have not always been safe or easy to come by. Yours is a dangerous history that has been deliberately erased over time." His gaze settled on each of the champions in turn.

"We scholars of the Schism must be cautious, but the more optimistic among us"—his eyes gleamed—"have held out the hope that the work of the Shepherds might return. And that is where you come in, dearie." He turned to Iellieth, smiling.

"The Shepherds?"

"Yes! Did not Mistress Yvayne tell you? Where is your . . ." He squinted at her rings and at the crescent-moon pendant from

Yvayne that Quindythias had helped her fashion into a clasp at her wrist.

"This?" Iellieth pulled her father's amulet from beneath her tunic.

Red's mouth fell open. "My gods," he sighed, "I never . . ." The gnome shook his head. Iellieth leaned forward so he could hold it in his hands. After examining it, he raised glassy eyes to meet hers. "You bear the first, my dear."

"The first?"

"The original. The first amulet of the Soul Shepherds. The one that started their great work." He spoke faster, the pitch of his voice growing higher alongside his excitement.

Iellieth furrowed her brow.

"I've made the study of the Soul Shepherds, they whose work you carry on, my life's pursuit. I'm even an honorary member!"

"So there are others, then?" Her heart quickened in her chest. They weren't alone.

"No, not so far as I can tell." The swell of light dashed against the rocks. Red chuckled, shaking his head. "As you might imagine, the membership process was easy for me. Being the sole member, I swore myself right in." He giggled, dancing back across his desk. "I never imagined I would meet a second practicing member, a shepherd who has rescued two for the fold!"

The amulet's ruby reflected back against Red's shining eyes as his expression fell. "Many champions met an identical fate to the two here beside you, Iellieth. But our sacred order sought to discover where the enemy had hidden them away and how to bring them back. The Shepherds tethered the champions' souls to this plane that they might live again."

His shoulders relaxed as he settled back onto the desk. "Yours is the first amulet that was created for this purpose." Red glanced from her to Marcon, a small smile playing across his lips.

"How many stories do you have about handsome, heroic

elves?" Quindythias interjected. Red waved him over to the bookshelf, and they began to search.

Marcon was staring down at her, a fierce storm behind his gray eyes. Iellieth cleared her throat and ran her fingers over the familiar lines of her amulet. "Would you like to see more of your book?"

Further depictions of battles followed. They ranged over a variety of terrains and civilizations. Strange ships buoyed by floating sea creatures hung over the cities, each of which was larger than the last.

The brightly illustrated story turned dark near the end. A thick forest gave way to a narrow mountain trail. Marcon stood alone, the fallen members of his battalion all around him. He raised a flaming sword over his head, rearing back from the severed neck of a giant black dragon.

Beside her, his jaw twinged, and his hand weighed more heavily on her back.

"This is the final battle that you spoke of to me?"

"Yes, lady," he whispered.

What pain must he feel seeing this story play out? A renewal of the deaths for which he blamed himself. "And who is that?" She pointed an unsteady hand at the dragon.

His jaw ground back and forth before he answered her. Iellieth's shoulders strained against the urge to wrap her arms around his waist or to close the book. The center of her chest burned.

"Braemorn." He pulled his gaze from the book to her. "One of Alessandra's lieutenants." His eyes softened, and he turned away. "The battle with him is the last thing I remember . . . until I awakened and saw you."

CHAPTER 5

T ess led Persephonie and Juliet through the streets of Andel-ce Hevra. They passed out of the bustling Calaboro District into a more residential area. Thin stacks of apartments pressed against one another, and a cacophony of dialects and rich herbs drifted through the streets.

"What is this place?" she asked Tess, taking a long whiff as they passed a bakery selling orange cakes and dark brown breads.

A jeweler called out to her from the corner, offering to add pieces of great beauty to her collection.

"The Wayfarers' District," they answered. "When disaster strikes the smaller towns around the city, many of their residents come here for safety rather than resettling elsewhere. They bring with them their customs and fare." Tess gestured to the bakery and smiled. "It's one of my favorite parts of the city."

"It is much more interesting here than what we passed through so close to City Center." The powerful, tall buildings had been striking, to be sure, but they lacked the flavor and diversity of this space. Here, colorful blankets hung on lines above them, their handspun fibers drying in the full afternoon sun.

"I thought your mother might live nearer to the wall, but when we asked around, we were directed here." Tess pointed at a black iron railing outside a tall third-story window.

Scores of potted plants crowded the balcony, their vines and tendrils pouring over the edge in a green cascade that swept toward the second floor. Persephonie smiled. "That looks like it would be hers."

"Would you like me to walk you up?"

"No, that is alright." Persephonie gave Tess's hand a gentle squeeze. "I really appreciate you helping me to find her. And taking care of Juliet too."

Tess frowned at the fox traipsing between Persephonie's feet. "I hope she doesn't get you into too much trouble."

"Just the right amount." Persephonie scooped Juliet up and into her arms. She nodded her farewell to Tess, who drifted off into the milling chaos of the afternoon. "Shall we go and find Mama?"

Juliet's eyes shone back at her. That must be fox for *yes.*

Persephonie picked her way across the street, careful to not bump into any of the shoppers crowding the stalls of fruit and nut sellers along the sidewalk. Datha's concerns about her trip to see Esmeralda echoed above the din around her. "Remember that you cannot stay long, Sephie." He had stared down at her, pain etched around his brown eyes, more worried than he had been on any of her previous trips.

She had raised her hand to his face, resting her palm against the slight stubble of his jaw. "I know, Datha. I promise I will be careful." He had insisted she be the one to tell her brothers that she would be gone for a few weeks. Felix had taken it well, but Stefan stormed off, upset that she was leaving them after they'd endured so much danger.

Velkan had approached her then, and she had to hurry to mask her tears under the close scrutiny of his dark eyes. "Are you sure that you should be traveling to the city at this time?"

Though it had been several months since they had severed their romantic ties, Velkan retained the ability to perceive her thoughts without her having to speak them aloud. "Yes. Cassandra has shown me that I need to be there to help my mother and . . ."

"Peril and uncertainty, Persephonie." He scowled. "Cassandra has shown you visions of a darkness surrounding your mother."

Time and again, she'd seen disaster rampaging across the streets of Andel-ce Hevra, figures huddled together, animals screaming as they sprinted away from a mounted pursuit, swords gleaming. And in the middle of it all, a great fire. Her mother's voice chanted under the edges of each of these visions, beseeching Cassandra to set them on a different path.

She scowled back at him. "How do you know?"

Velkan took a step nearer. "Do you think that our goddess is silent when I speak with her about those I care for? That she shows me nothing of you when—"

"Don't." Persephonie had cut him off before he could profess his feelings for her again. For the present, her path led her away from her people. Led her here, to her mother's dark green door at the top of a pale wooden staircase.

Before she lost her nerve, Persephonie reached out and rapped thrice on the wood. She trailed her fingers through Juliet's fur and held her breath.

"Coming," an unfamiliar female voice called from the apartment's interior. An elven woman with silver skin and waves of moss-green hair opened the door, blinking at her with golden eyes. "Can I help you?" She squinted at Persephonie's layers of gem tones, her own clothing airy fabrics in earthy browns and light grays.

"I don't . . ." Persephonie pursed her lips. The other two doors on the landing were plain brown wood. Esmeralda wouldn't live there. "I am sorry. I thought that my mother lived here, but I must—"

"Sephie?" Esmeralda's voice echoed from farther inside the apartment, and Persephonie's heart quavered, chills breaking out over her skin. "Cassandra be praised, you are here," her mother exclaimed as she appeared in the open doorway. She dropped an armful of small volumes onto a brown couch as she rushed over and took Persephonie in her arms, their dark hair intermingling. "Let me look at you." Esmeralda pulled away and took Persephonie's face in her hands, her hazel eyes peering into her daughter's. "You grow more beautiful every time I see you." She took a quick step back as Juliet's head popped up between them, stumbling into the elven woman, who caught her around the waist. "And you have already made a new friend, I see."

Before Persephonie could answer, the elven woman leaned forward and whispered something into Esmeralda's ear. Green tattoos of vines and leaves wound around the length of her neck. "Why don't the two of you come inside," Mama said, gesturing to the sparse but sunny apartment behind her.

Persephonie and Juliet followed Esmeralda and the elven woman into the apartment. Mama ushered her over to the long sofa in the center of the room and cracked open the tall window Persephonie had seen from the street outside. A breeze carried in the noise of the crowds and the fragrance of the sun-warmed herbs. Plants lined the walls of the apartment as well, but otherwise, the space was curiously bare.

A white bed rested near the far wall, and Esmeralda slid around a low row of cabinets to the stove, setting her copper kettle on to boil and stoking the coals.

"I am Persephonie," she said to the staring elf, "and this is Juliet." The fox traipsed over and began investigating each of the plants in turn, clawing her way up a delicate table to sniff a blossoming sapphire rose.

"Aylin," the woman said with a nod, keeping one eye on Persephonie and one eye on the fox. The rough brown fabric of the sofa scratched at Persephonie's palms as she sat on her hands to disguise their trembling.

"I'll be there in a moment," Esmeralda called. Had her mother not been expecting her? She'd always had a sense about these things before, having an extra mat made up as well as a steaming cup of tea and a box of cinnamon cookies readied just in time for Persephonie's previous arrivals to Andel-ce Hevra.

Esmeralda hurried back over, a less harried smile on her face, and clasped Persephonie's arm as she sat beside her. "So, my darling, what brings you to the city?"

Her surety faltered. Persephonie weakly returned her mother's smile, searching for a reasonable explanation. "I, erhm, I have been worried about you, Mama. Lately"—the elf with green hair narrowed her gaze—"I have had alarming dreams that foretold of danger to you." Persephonie sighed, her shoulders relaxing now that she had confessed this weight.

Esmeralda's brow furrowed. "That is strange, Sephie. And what has been the nature of these dreams?"

The elven woman cleared her throat, calling their attention to her.

Esmeralda flushed, her smile widening. "Pardon me, I heard you introduce yourselves but"—she squeezed her daughter's arm —"Sephie, this is my partner, Aylin."

The golden eyes flashed combatively. Perhaps they had not been together for very long. Sometimes her mother's partners were nervous or possessive at first. "I didn't realize you were seeing someone, Mama. Then I am additionally pleased to make your acquaintance, Aylin."

Aylin rose, tightening the belt of her brown tunic. "You must excuse me—the others are waiting." She inclined her head to Persephonie and bent to peck Esmeralda on the lips before sweeping out of the apartment.

Esmeralda turned back to her, eyes unnaturally bright. "You will have to forgive Aylin, *cher'a*, she is . . ."

Persephonie's shoulders fell. "She is not happy that I am here."

"No! No, it's not that." Esmeralda pulled her lips between her teeth, eyes darting around the apartment before finally settling back on her daughter. "It is the timing, that's all. We have many things planned for the coming week. You know about the Hunt here in the city."

Persephonie shivered. For one week each year in mid-spring, the streets of Andel-ce Hevra filled to celebrate the overthrow of the empress who had ruled their land before the introduction of the council. They released exotic animals into the streets and chased them, slaughtering the innocent creatures when they reached the central plaza. "I was frightened that the visions portended some sort of disaster with the Hunt, Mama. That is why I had to come now."

"I am pleased you've come." Esmeralda leaned closer to her. "Aylin was only surprised, that is all. She and I have been hard at work preparing an alternative festival, for people like us."

The kettle whistled from the stove, and Mama rose to answer it and make their tea. Persephonie settled back onto the couch, calling Juliet to her side. She could confide to her mother that, a few weeks before, she had met a young half-elf whose magic would grow to be like that of the empress, though, of course, she had no fear of Iellieth oppressing others like the empress supposedly had. They hunted the animals in mockery of the empress's many forms. And from what Otmund had said, it seemed that, in subtler ways, they continued to hunt those of similar abilities.

Like her. Like her mother.

"Have you truly not seen the visions as well? I was certain Cassandra would show them to you."

Esmeralda sat across from her on a sloped wooden chair. "The city has felt darker, these last several weeks. Since"— Esmeralda pressed her palm to her heart—"you know what befell the druids, do you not?"

"I do, Mama."

Before, and for a short while after her relationship with Datha, Esmeralda had spent time with the druid conclave to the north of the city. They'd taught her to wield the magic she sensed in the world around her, and she, in turn, had taught her daughter. Persephonie had only spent a short time with the conclave, but Datha had taken her aside to grieve in private when Yvayne told them what had happened. For her mother, it was worse. The death of a community she cared deeply for, with friends and mentors alike, and one of the few places she'd ever felt at home.

Esmeralda bowed her head, struggling against the sobs that gripped her chest.

"We do not need to speak of it at present, Mama. Let us talk of something else."

CHAPTER 6

Iellieth gently closed the book of stories about Marcon and slid the volume onto Red's desk. Something struck her about the champion's tone when he spoke of opening his eyes and seeing her. She parted her lips to speak, but Marcon turned to address Quindythias and Red.

"Master Red, if I may, we've another concern." He rolled his shoulders back, an even more impressive warrior than the pictures had been able to convey. "A dark spirit attacked us on the way here. I believe it was a revenant."

Red's eyes bulged.

"You are aware of these creatures?"

The gnome nodded. "I am, though I have trouble imagining why someone would send one after you." He crossed his small arms and flexed his feet, tapping his toes together.

Marcon's flaming sword raised above the neck of the dragon flashed before Iellieth's eyes. In the illustration, he'd been surrounded by the bodies of his battalion, the lone survivor in the fight. How many similar instances had he and Quindythias endured? How much death had the two of them seen?

Quindythias crossed back over to her, and she returned her attention to the conversation at hand.

"But why would one be here, now? Quindythias and I, we've only just reawakened, and besides a few werewolves, and that mage"—he glanced at Iellieth—"we've made few outright enemies."

"And it was primarily interested in you?"

Marcon nodded. "She was, yes."

Red drew his shoulders up. "Well, I can help you there." The gnome returned to his bookshelf, searching the volumes. "It makes more sense for the spirit to have come into being before. Now where is that tome?" He craned his neck to read the spines on the higher shelf.

"Before?" Marcon prodded.

"Yes, for her to have been bound to you in Eldura." He scrunched his face, squinting at the ceiling. "Hmm, yes, it would have to be that. They are not made quickly, these beings. You see, it takes a powerful binding spell to call forth such a spirit." He turned back to Marcon. "And the incantation dictates that the spirit lasts as long as the one it has been sent to destroy lives."

Marcon's expression darkened, but the gnome failed to notice as he returned to the bookshelf.

"If she was bound to you before," Red continued in his shrill voice, "she might have slept, so to speak, while you did. But now that you've returned, the spirit has as well."

Quindythias scowled. "But I thought that if we died, or nearly died, that we went into this velvety red room he's convinced is inside her amulet."

Red brightened, raising a finger in protest as he looked at Iellieth. "Actually—"

Marcon's glare stopped him short.

Mara's discovery in the clearing flickered back before Iellieth and filled in what Red had been poised to say. The two champions couldn't be killed unless—"Unless something happens to me," she whispered.

An avalanche of heavy rocks broke free in Iellieth's mind, tumbling around her shoulders. So this was the cause of his anger earlier in the clearing. He wasn't upset with her . . . he blamed himself, his past self, for whatever had initiated the return of this cursed spirit.

Quindythias's eyes widened as he prepared to object. Marcon's jaw pulsed. A growl rose in the back of his throat, and he paced the length of Red's office, running his fingers through his dark hair. "I've no recollection of such a spirit attacking me before. I did not face her on our last charge through the mountains." He gestured at the book on Red's desk, the pictures contained within depicting more lives for which he held himself responsible.

Iellieth stepped in front of his path and laid her hand on his shoulder. He flinched but stopped. She turned to the gnome, who watched the three of them with furrowed brow. "Do these spirits have to attack, Red? She said she will return, but we've no way of knowing when?"

Red nodded while his small fingers played with a knot in his beard. "That is correct, Lady Iellieth. She will come back. But you are safe here—I have carefully warded my home and most of the city. Allow me to do some further research, and we will see what else you may expect from this creature."

"Thank you." A soreness she'd been too distracted to notice crept across her legs and shoulders, and a yawn she couldn't suppress broke from her lips.

"Might there be somewhere we could turn in for the evening?" Quindythias asked. Marcon had returned to his fierce stare, boring a hole in the book-covered walls of Red's office.

"I was hoping you would ask." The gnome sprang up and

crawled back down his desk. He used the lower handle to open his office door. "Leora," he shouted down the hall, "we have guests!" He brushed his hands together as he turned back around. "Don't let her fussing deceive you. When no one is here, she scolds me for not having more visitors." He stared back up at Marcon, smiling blissfully. "And here we are with ancient heroes."

Footsteps clicked toward them, and an elderly human woman poked her head in through the open door. "You called, Master Red? Are these our esteemed guests?"

⚜

"I AM SURPRISED, LADY IELLIETH, THAT YVAYNE DID NOT speak to you about the Soul Shepherds herself," Red said early the next morning. "Though I'm sure she has her reasons." He patted her hand. "I would have thought that after she found someone with whom to share her great store of knowledge that she would have recounted the whole of the Shepherds' noble history. Though, come to think of it, verbosity isn't exactly characteristic of Yvayne . . ."

Iellieth chuckled. "No, it isn't. But could you tell me more about them?" Yvayne had explained much in their time together, though losing Mara and breaking away from the conclave had overshadowed her teachings. "She was so worried, and we'd just escaped Lucien."

"Lucien!" Red shrieked. "Horrifying indeed." He pursed his lips and squinted at her. "I wonder . . ." The gnome scurried over to a pile of books on the low table in his office. "When you get to be my age, you have a fair share of secrets, and by the time you're *her* age . . ." Red grinned. "What did she send you here to speak with me about?"

Would Yvayne have told her more had there been more time?

And why was it so surprising that she had left the Shepherds out? Iellieth set the questions aside for the time being. "She sent us here to speak with you about your specialty, but I didn't think it was to do with my amulet. Something about a gate and a seal?"

"The planar gate?" Red's voice squeaked, his eyes flaring. "How intriguing! Do you know about it?"

Iellieth frowned. "No, I don't believe so."

"What are they teaching in the academies these days?" Red shook his head. "A query for another time." He called Marcon and Quindythias over and asked Marcon to fetch one of the burgundy-bound books from high on his office shelf.

The tome *thunk*ed onto the surface of the low table in Red's sitting area opposite his desk. The gnome had to stand on tiptoe to safely turn the pages. He found the illustration he was searching for near the midpoint in the volume.

In faded blue ink, the artist had drawn a stone circle inscribed with runes. Arcane script curved along the sides and center of the circle, but the middle was bare except for six runes, the ancient symbols for each of the elements. "It was a very secretive project," Red whispered over the text. "Very, very few knew of its working. But at the time of the Schism"—he looked at Marcon and Quindythias—"around five thousand years ago, when the two of you were split from your souls, those gifted in the arcane fashioned this magical device to protect the realms of the titans from our plane of existence. As the titans left our world, they closed the portals behind them. On our side, like a very powerful two-way lock, the mages engaged this circlet, the planar seal, to secure the elemental planes so that no one could pass from our world to theirs."

Mara had mentioned Iellieth's amulet connecting Marcon's body to his soul and said that when his enemies turned him into a statue, his soul had not traveled to Astralei like so many others. Was Red suggesting that Marcon's and Quindythias's souls were on the elemental planes, accessible only if they could reform and then break the planar seal? "And that's why my amulet is so important?" Iellieth asked. "It helps to connect their souls . . . on the elemental planes to find them, their bodies, here in Azuria?"

"Very well done." Red beamed at her. "Now, after the fall of those allied to the titans, as Alessandra stepped into her victory, the mages who survived broke apart the physical seal and divided the pieces across the remaining realms in hopes that one day, when the kingdoms stood together once more, or when the world was ready, they might be able to reassemble the seal, reopen the planar gate, and reunite with the titans. Once we rejoin the pieces of this artifact, the magic will be powerful enough to break through the lock on the planar gate."

Iellieth's head swam through the new information. How many remaining pieces might there be? What if they couldn't find them all? Would Marcon and Quindythias remain bound to her forever? What would happen when the lich who had killed Mara returned, or when the revenant attacked them again?

"Yvayne sent the three of you to me because of a secret that she and I share." Red looked down at his intertwined fingers. "She sensed Alessandra and her servants moving to collect these pieces, so it is something we have done instead. We hid them somewhere . . . unexpected." His eyes flashed, and he winked. "We lack but two, and with them the seal will be restored."

She squinted at the gnome, her brow creased. "And why did Yvayne want you to share the secret with us? If it was so important for the gate to be sealed, and then for the seal to be broken into six pieces, how do we know that it's safe to restore the seal now?"

Marcon leaned over to her. "From what we understood, lady, gaining access to the elemental planes would have granted

Alessandra the last vestiges of power that she needed to claim all the realms as her own."

Iellieth's eyes widened. "Then why—"

"That is true," Red added quickly. He folded his hands together and stared at Iellieth. "We can only assume that her plans from previous wars will take similar shape as she grows in strength. But if we can find the pieces before the dark goddess and her minions, we will have the option of enlisting the titans' aid in the fight against her, not to mention restoring your friends."

Quindythias inhaled sharply behind her. "We could travel to the elemental planes and . . . and undo the severing?" He stretched his arm out, rolling the dark runes back and forth in the light.

Marcon squeezed the edge of the desk, his knuckles whitening as he gazed at Red. "And Iellieth, the bond that ties her life to ours would be broken?" His gray eyes burned as he looked at her. "The danger over you would recede?"

Red nodded. "This is what we are hoping for, though much of it remains theoretical. I am pleased to see your enthusiasm to act." He smiled at the two champions before turning to Iellieth. "I fear that Alessandra's anxiety to assemble a planar seal of her own will only grow with the knowledge that a Shepherd has been reborn into our midst."

A spark flashed in the back of her mind. "What do you mean, reborn?"

He coughed and stammered for a moment, waving his hand. "Reappeared, Lady Iellieth, reappeared into our midst. Forgive me." The gnome cleared his throat. "Now, returning to your question, our hope is to find the final two pieces of the seal before Alessandra's servants do. It would be possible for her to reconstitute a seal of her own, but the process will be much more difficult without an original seal piece for her to work with."

The sparks simmered beneath her skin. Red was leaving something out regarding the Shepherds, but now might not be the time to press. "So Alessandra and her servants want to acquire the remaining pieces. And the others . . ."

Red smirked.

"The others are with you?" She raised an eyebrow, certain she'd guessed correctly.

"I see why Yvayne takes such an interest in you." Red grinned. "Yes, as far as I am aware, two lost pieces remain to be found. From the records, we believe that the piece corresponding to the element of darkness is located in Hadvar, and the one for the element of earth resides with the elves across the Infinite Ocean."

The mention of the Elven Realms drowned out Red's next words. Iellieth's heart pounded. Her father might be even closer than she had thought. If they could just get across the sea . . .

A squeak in Red's voice brought her back. "Most likely, the piece in Hadvar is with the royal family."

Cold water sizzled as it smothered the sparks around her heart. "Are you saying we need to go to the Hadvarian court?"

"Yes, precisely."

Iellieth swayed in her chair. Marcon caught her shoulder and knelt down by her side.

"I think we should send you there before you go to the elves as it's so much nearer," Red continued. "Your amulet, Iellieth, should react with the seal pieces and help you identify where they are. They'll be made of stone and carved with runes that resemble, well . . ." Red reached out and grabbed Quindythias's arm, pulling back his sleeve. He pointed at the gray-black tattoos against the elf's dark brown skin. "They'll look rather like this." He smiled, his expression falling when he noticed her distress.

"With the war still brewing between Linolynn and Hadvar . . ." Iellieth tightened her hands into fists. She had narrowly missed a transmigration to the northern kingdom several weeks earlier. But even though so much had changed, she still wasn't ready to return to the cold, conniving court.

"I wish the three of you could stay here with me," Red added. "But I am afraid I must send you north to Hadvar as soon as may be. You carry a magical bag, do you not, Lady Iellieth?"

She nodded and opened Mara's bag for him to see.

"May I?" With a second assent, Red reached into the bag and withdrew a thin volume of stories bound in bright green leather.

The weight in Iellieth's chest grew heavier. It was the book Mara had given her in their final days together, where the druid had recorded tales she'd gleaned from the forest. "You will add stories of your own in time, cher'a," she'd said. "The forest has a great many to tell."

Red gave her a small smile before he returned the book to the hidden recesses of Mara's bag. "Unless your need is dire, keep the piece in here. Each seal piece draws the power of its element, so you will first attract the element of darkness." The gnome held out the bag.

Iellieth took it and tucked her head through the strap, settling the bag back onto her shoulder. "What do you mean by attracting the element of darkness?"

His eyes sparkled before his expression turned more serious. "Remember that darkness itself is neither evil nor good, though it is more mysterious and, often, more alarming than the other elements." The gnome sighed. "I hope we are not too late. Shadows move swiftly beyond hidden horizons, and it seems certain our enemy is not idle in the vast reaches of Caldara. Be on your guard as you travel, and keep a sharp eye."

"We will." Iellieth knelt in front of him and took his hand.

"You've been such a great help to us. Thank you, Red. We'll be back in a week or two with the fifth piece of the planar seal."

"I look forward to it, fellow Shepherd." The elderly gnome grinned. For a moment, the thought of the dark mage and his goddess being added to the dangers of the Hadvarian court faded away, and the swirls of magic within her stilled. "You'll know what to do, when the time comes," Red whispered. "Trust your companions, and your amulet will show the way."

CHAPTER 7

Briseras narrowed her eyes against the setting sun as the last of the werewolf pack disappeared over the rise. There was still time to take out a few more. *Twang, twang.* Her shoulders kicked back as she unloosed an arrow from each of her crossbows. The barrels clicked forward, notching her next shot into place.

"Wait!" a voice cried from behind her.

One of the beasts screamed as her arrow found its mark. It crumpled to the ground.

A tall, thin young man was sprinting straight for her. "Vera." Briseras nodded to her wolf companion, who leapt up to intercept the figure.

Twang.

Her crossbow sang as another arrow flew toward the creatures, embedding deep in one of their monstrous shoulders. The target slid through the tall grasses, the body returning to human form as it settled on the earth.

Oof.

The young man fell with a thud as Vera pounced on top of

him, pinning him to the ground with her front paws. Flecks of saliva fell onto his face as she growled.

The last of the werewolves disappeared over the rise. Five still bodies littered the hillside.

Briseras sighed. Not her best headcount, but it would do for now. She turned to the man beneath Vera's paws. "Who are you, and what do you want?"

"Is . . . is it going to kill me?" His hands and voice were shaking, but he was too frightened to try to free himself from the wolf. Perhaps he had a modicum of sense after all.

"Tut, tut." Briseras called Vera back. The wolf pushed off the man's chest, eliciting another groan, and came to join Briseras in glaring at the villager.

He scooted away on his elbows but stopped as Vera's lips curled in a snarl, warning him to stay put.

"She won't hurt you unless I ask her to"—his eyes grew wider, and Briseras grinned—"which I won't, for now. But tell me, why are you trying to interrupt my kills?"

His breathing slowed and, as the panic subsided, he looked older than she'd first thought, mid-twenties, just a few years younger than her. "My partner"—he sniffed and wiped his nose on his sleeve—"he's part of the pack." The man pressed his lips together. "I have been trying to find a way to free him." He patted the lumpy bag lying on the ground next to him.

"The only freedom for beasts is in death."

"You cannot mean that." Whatever the young man carried in his bag was too heavy for him, causing him to slouch to one side as he scrambled after her. No wonder Vera had toppled him so easily.

His reproof wasn't worth a response. She picked up her pace. Didn't freedom come for them all in death? She tucked her second crossbow behind her back as she charged down the hill, pulling arrows from the quiver on her thigh as she ran and notching them into place.

"Wait for me," he called from behind her again. His heavy footfalls slowed as they approached the first body.

Briseras glanced at the corpse's head, and Vera slunk forward, ready to end its life if the lycanthrope had somehow managed to survive. The fact that a nude human body lay sprawled in the grass increased the likelihood that it was dead, but they'd witnessed enough foul tricks to take precautions.

The werewolves carried very little on their persons. Those she'd hunted in Tor'stre Vahn had kept satchels of supplies, a cloak, provisions that would allow them to survive if they were separated from their pack. But they had traveled in groups of ten or twenty. This pack was ten times that size.

"What's your name?" Briseras glanced over her shoulder as Vera sniffed the area around the body.

"Everett." He peered at the corpse for a moment before raising his eyes to the other slain bodies. "Who are you?"

"Briseras." She rose, striding over to the next body. The simplest way forward would be to track down the alpha, but she couldn't risk having a pack of this size turn on her. For the time being, she picked off stragglers.

The young man sprinted past her, arms outstretched. "James!"

She caught his collar just in time. Everett's face contorted in pain. He slung his elbow at her head and tried to wrench himself free, but she held him fast. "Are you mad?" She yanked at his coat, pulling him down the hill away from the prone form. "The venom remains in their saliva. You must be more cautious."

He sobbed and pitched himself forward, trying to crawl on hands and knees toward his fallen partner.

Briseras hissed, releasing him. Lucky for the man, Vera was

more patient than she. The wolf stood poised on the other side, ready to extinguish the corpse that was once James if he awoke.

One of her arrows poked out of the side of his neck, the blood already drying around it. A good shot. She stepped away and scanned the hillsides, ready to loose another should a situation arise.

Everett wrapped his arms around James's torso and buried his head in his chest. Sobs wracked his body.

None of the corpses stirred, and no scouts appeared along the top of the hillock. Briseras knelt down next to Everett and laid her hand on the soft leather of his shoulder. "He's free now."

Everett hugged James tighter.

Briseras went to examine the other bodies and scanned the pack's trail through the rolling valley. Where were they headed?

As Everett quietened, her raven returned, flying in sweeping circles overhead. Briseras whistled and held out her arm. Otto landed, head cocked, watching her new human companion. No, human with a faint trace of elven heritage, judging by the ears.

"Why do you keep saying that?" Everett sniffed, wiping the tears from his face. He sat with his shoulders angled over the prostrate man, as though he could protect him after death. He glared at her, eyes narrowed.

Briseras turned back to the horizon. "Why do I keep telling you that your lover is free?"

"Yes." Everett's voice was dry and scratchy.

She sighed and dropped her head back, her hood falling around her shoulders. Briseras unwrapped her cloak and tilted her head to the side as she pulled the collar of her armor toward her shoulder.

Everett gasped at the two sets of twinned white scars, the four deep punctures from the fangs.

Briseras shrugged her armor back into place. "It's not the same as what he received. But being caught between two worlds, you can never be free. He's not trapped anymore." She smirked. "You're welcome."

"And, are you . . ." Everett's mouth remained open as he stared at her neck.

"Go ahead. Ask me."

"A-a vampire?" He shrank back closer to the fallen werewolf.

"No." Ridiculous question. "How many stories have you heard where the vampire immediately reveals her true identity to the grieving young man?" She tossed her hood back up over her short black hair. "No, Everett." She shook her head. "I hunt vampires . . . or werewolves. Doesn't really matter."

How many years had it been since the attack? Its memory still flickered, a faint haze, in the spirits all around her. Malthael's fangs had sunk deep in her neck, draining her. A sharp pain in her abdomen. Darkness. Ophelia's voice chanting over her, calling her back from the spirit realm.

"You are bound now," the moss-cloaked druid had explained, "to dwell always between the two realms. In exchange for your life, you must protect those who walk in the light from the monsters as well as from the creatures they cannot see."

The milky blue silhouette of a handsome man, with a strong jaw covered with dark stubble, floated over Everett's shoulder. He gazed at the young man before her, mist swirling through his eyes. The spirit ran translucent hands through Everett's hair.

Briseras turned to give James's spirit a moment of privacy with his love. With a final kiss, he would go on to Astralei. She glanced back as Everett shuddered. The spirit was gone.

Everett slowly rose to his feet beside her. "I collect stories." He lifted the flap of his satchel to reveal several leather-bound volumes and a few thin vials of ink. "Most of them recently have been about werewolves, but there are older tales rooted in these mountains that suggest . . . other monsters." He turned back to his fallen partner, and his voice softened. "How do you know where to find them?"

A small smile crossed her face. Legends of the region's monstrosities might hold the key to explaining the pack's abnormalities, and, if she could exploit what made them unique, could make their droves easier to kill. "Let the land tell you what's important instead of deciding in advance. We're here to learn." How many times had Rajas said that to her? From Everett's sudden scowl, he found it as irritating as she had. "Let's go." She nodded toward the glade of trees beyond the next rise. "We need to gather wood for their pyre."

"And then what?" Everett clambered after her.

"Hunting."

CHAPTER 8

T he horses Red had lent to Iellieth, Marcon, and Quindythias sped their journey north. She whispered to her mare as she rode, interweaving tales of faeries and knights that she had read or overheard to calm the protest pounding against the walls of her heart. But in spite of the stories, she couldn't expel the dread the return to Hadvar inspired.

A few days' ride from the city-state, Iellieth withdrew Mara's raven from her satchel. *"Nor corveau,"* she whispered. The bird shook itself, head to tail, sending a cascade of silver flakes across her arm. "Welcome back, Edvard." Iellieth smiled. "I need you to do something for me."

The raven croaked and tilted his head to stare at her with his left eye. "Beside the Hadvarian palace is a library with three spires. Fly to the base of the central spire and look for a broad-shouldered man with dark, shoulder-length hair."

Edvard croaked again. He understood.

"Commen"—Edvard's eyes glazed over as she uttered the magical phrase. "Dimitri, it's Iellieth. Could you shelter me and

two of my friends in the library for a few days? And arrange for our entrance into the city? I'll bring a new book, I promise."

The raven nodded to her, and she supported his clawed feet as he pushed off her arm, sending the silver sparks fluttering to the earth.

"Who is this Dimitri, lady?" Marcon asked from beside her.

"He's the Keeper of the Grand Reserve, the great library in Hadvar." Iellieth sighed. With few exceptions, her only fond memories in the northern city revolved around Dimitri and his books. "I'm hoping he can get us past the guards."

Marcon nodded. "What else should we expect of this neighboring city to Linolynn? I'm surprised you're willing to go. You've never spoken of them fondly, and they still threaten war against your home, do they not?"

"I'm not sure 'willing' is the right word." Iellieth scrunched her lips together and tapped her horse's side, sending her into a graceful trot. "And you're right. Well, Linolynn threatens war against them. But there's something more than that." She took a deep breath. "The day we met, when I was supposed to transmigrate to Hadvar . . ." Iellieth slowly met his eyes. "My stepfather had planned for me to marry one of the Hadvarian noblemen against my will."

Iellieth turned away before she could see his reaction. Would it change how he saw her, as the constant barrage of suitors had soured so much of her life in Linolynn? She drew herself up in the saddle. No. The duke's schemes didn't hold sway over her any longer, not after all she'd learned and seen. She'd found a community and released the magic waiting within. "But if that's where Red says we can find the planar seal, do we have a choice?"

"Lady, I—" Marcon cleared his throat. The trees shifted away from his fierce scowl. "We always have a choice." He set his jaw and squeezed the reins, glaring down at the back of his hand. The runes across his skin darkened in response. Marcon clicked his tongue and urged his horse closer to hers. "It's important to me that you have a choice." His voice was soft. "So much has fallen onto your shoulders on account of the two of us. Are you . . . worried about this former suitor?"

Iellieth shook her head. She ran her fingers over her amulet, her ward against the memories of Lord Stravinske. Once they were in the city, perhaps she could tell Marcon what had happened at the last Festival of Renewal in Hadvar. Iellieth shivered, part of her still trapped on that icy balcony, pinned beneath Stravinske's grasp. She blinked quickly, breaking free once more. Tree limbs stretched toward her, inviting her into their embrace. Marcon's brow was furrowed, watching her. "Not anymore." She smiled to set his mind at ease.

Marcon nodded, though his jaw remained tense. "I wonder why Red has not acquired the seal piece sooner, living so near the city." He scanned the hillside to the east and the forest to the west as they traveled.

"I don't know." Iellieth frowned. "Maybe it's dangerous to have all the pieces together. He sounded a lot like Yvayne when he spoke of it and the gathering shadows." The druid had told her of waiting for a sign of some sort, that the appropriate moment had finally arrived for their next steps to shape the history of Azuria. It seemed, from what Red had alluded to and Yvayne had said, that those events revolved around her and her companions. But if that was the case, why wouldn't they confide in her whatever it was they were leaving out? Her thoughts crashed once more against the chasm of the Soul Shepherds. "Marcon, do you know anything about the Shepherds?"

"I'm afraid they were after my time, lady. Though I am thankful to know of them now." The corners of his lips turned upward, and a flush of heat rose to Iellieth's cheeks.

Quindythias shouted back over his shoulder, and Marcon

rode ahead to tell him once more that they remained a couple days and not hours away from the city.

Her mare whinnied and picked up speed, anxious to remain close to her friends. Perhaps Dimitri would know.

❦

"WHO GOES THERE?" THE HADVARIAN GUARD GREETED THEM roughly, scowling out into the gathering twilight of the crisp northern night.

"Guests of Master Dimitri," Iellieth answered, laying a heavy Elvish accent over her Caldaran lilt to disguise her origins.

"Names?" He raised an eyebrow, his gaze directed at the longsword at Marcon's side before he glanced down at the scroll before him.

Cold beads of sweat gathered along the small of Iellieth's back. She hadn't sent any secret names ahead for Dimitri to leave for them.

Quindythias swept forward and bowed with a flourish. "Lord Havastrias Shade, at your service, and these are my associates, Lilith and Colabra."

"Mmm," the guard growled, looking over his list. "Here it is, three guests of Master Keeper Dimitri Leu. Very well." He waved them through the gate, stepping aside to make way for them and their horses. "Tell the Keeper I'll expect names in the future," he called after them, his accent thicker with his raised voice.

"Thank you, Quindythias." Iellieth let out the breath she'd been unconsciously holding as soon as they were out of earshot of the guard. "I don't know what we would have done if he hadn't believed you."

The elf grinned and flicked a dagger from his belt into the

air, catching it and twirling it between his fingers. "I am certain we would have devised something." He winked at her.

"Put that away," Iellieth urged, her eyes wide. "We're not going to kill innocent people for doing their jobs."

Quindythias shrugged, turning away to study the low stone structures around them. Iellieth rose on tiptoe to peer down one of the side streets. The primary road through the city should lead straight on to the palace, but she didn't want to arrive directly before its doors unprepared.

"Have you been to this part of the city before, lady?" Marcon frowned as he appeared beside her.

"Umm, no." Iellieth bit her lip. "We've always transmigrated here before, and I was never allowed this far out into the city."

A burst of laughter splattered onto the street as a human couple in their middle years threw open a tavern door and strode out into the night.

The three of them wound through the city, occasionally passing groups of residents, but most of Hadvar's society remained indoors.

"Where is everyone?" Quindythias muttered as two elderly women crept past, casting suspicious looks over their shoulders. "I know we won't receive a fanfare welcome or anything—at least not till we find a place where people remember who we are —but I expected something more robust than this." He gestured toward the women, who quickened their pace and slipped into an alley.

Iellieth shook her head. "Most Hadvarians keep to them-selves." Katarina had spent a brief time in the city trying to make her way among its stuffy scholars. But the translator was much better suited to the ease of life in Linolynn, though she often said she wished the ocean would sing its constant lullaby a little faster on occasion to add excitement to the coastal king-dom. "The vast majority of them work in the mines beneath the city." Once or twice, she had seen the soot-stained faces and grim expressions of those emerging from the mines. The sweet song of the ocean was driven from her mind as she imagined the clamor of miners in search of riches that would benefit others. "It's very hard labor that they endure, and few of the residents truly benefit from their efforts."

"Says someone who grew up in a castle?" Quindythias smirked.

"The king doesn't subject the people of Linolynn to indentured servitude like the Hadvarians do!" Iellieth crossed her arms, more easily baited than she would have liked. The elf trotted away, pleased with himself.

"He's only teasing you, lady." Marcon's gaze was soft, though there was an edge to his stance as he studied the thatch rooftops. "And we are most grateful"—he threw a look of reproach at Quindythias—"for your expertise in these matters."

The street she'd been searching for appeared at the crossroads ahead of them, a sign directing them to the Grand Reserve up the steeper hill to the right.

"Almost there." Iellieth patted the mare's neck. She'd make sure the stable hands were well paid for their efforts and that both they and the horses received additional fare if they so desired.

They crested the hill as night fell. The three domed turrets of the Hadvarian library shone pale gold in the starlight, eliciting a gasp even from Quindythias as they stared up at the structure. The double entrance doors burst open, and a square form rolled out, a deep voice booming into the night. "Is that who I think it is?"

Iellieth squealed and rushed forward, leaning down to wrap her arms around Dimitri's broad shoulders, tears stinging her eyes. "I'm so happy to see you," she whispered. "Thank you for taking care of us."

"Oh, it is my pleasure, my pleasure." Dimitri patted her heavily on the back and peered around her, grinning as he looked back and forth between Marcon and Quindythias. "And who are these handsome fellows that you bring to my library? Have they come to join you as prospective scholars?"

Iellieth laughed and shook her head. "I'm not here for that yet, either." A warm glow spread from the center of her stomach as she recalled all the times Dimitri had suggested that she leave her noble life behind and enroll as one of his pupils. She dropped her voice. "Can we tell you more inside?"

"Of course, of course." Dimitri wheeled his chair around, leading the way into the library. "Ahem!" He coughed, raising an eyebrow at the young man stationed in front of the door who stared openly at the three travelers.

"Oh, sorry, Master Dimitri," the young man exclaimed, flinging the door open and gesturing to the four of them to walk inside.

A wide circular room opened before them, books lining the pale wooden shelves that covered every wall. A few of the older keepers and mages-in-training sat scattered along the tables in the center of the room. During the day, the chamber was flooded with sunlight from the many windows overhead, but now the mages held glowing orbs of light over the books.

"Let us stop by my office first, and you can give me this book you have promised," Dimitri said, indicating the wooden door behind a low counter to the left. "And then you can explain what transpired several weeks ago, eh?" He winked at her exaggerat-edly, referring to the Festival of Renewal she had missed.

Marcon and Quindythias added solidness to this setting, her one space of shelter in the oppressive city overrun with her step-father's would-be suitors and allies. Though their armor and ready stances certainly stood out among the careful movement and lowered voices of the Grand Reserve.

Teodric had brought her here on her first trip, a treat meant to cheer her up as the duke's schemes for marrying her off became more overt and aggressive. After Teodric had been sent away, Dimitri figured centrally in her plans of escape. The librarian had personal experience in the matter and lent whatever aid he could to Iellieth. A few years prior, his fiancée had to flee the city one autumn evening after crossing a corrupt noble family. Dimitri's eyes had grown more distant since then, but Iellieth knew he held out hope that, one day, she might find a way to return.

CHAPTER 9

The shadows lengthened along the floor as Esmeralda told Persephonie about the Untamed, her new community of natural magic users and free-minded individuals in the city. The name had begun as an insult by the council and priests, but they had taken the mantle upon themselves. A few, like Aylin, were even confident enough in the power of their collective to openly show their magical persuasion despite the threats of the city against them.

"The guardian Apollo has taken a special interest in us and our people," Mama said. "He has granted us his protection."

"But why? What do the Untamed do, exactly?" Persephonie asked. The guardian Apollo had aided her people in the past, but it was unusual for him to intervene in the daily lives of mortals without special incentive. What was almost as rare was Esmeralda's continued delight with a cause, but she had been involved with the Untamed for several months, coinciding with her relationship with Aylin.

"We provide shelter for those who need a shield from the council's firm glove." Her gaze drifted out the window as a twanging melody rose from the street outside. Esmeralda always said that stringed instruments made her think of Datha. "And, as I mentioned, we are planning an alternative celebration for the Hunt."

"That will be nice." Persephonie grinned at the idea. She had only been in the city for one previous Hunt. She and Esmeralda had hidden indoors for the second half of the day as emotions and shouting rose outside. She shook her head against the memory of the animals' screams, still unsure as to whether or not the sounds had reached her or if she'd only conjured them in her imagination.

"There is something else I need to speak with you about." Esmeralda trailed her fingers through the ends of her hair, avoiding Persephonie's gaze.

"What is it, Mama?"

"This is a busy time, these next few days, and while I am glad you have come to see me . . ."

Persephonie waited. She would not finish this sentence for her mother. Mama had to say it.

Esmeralda coughed. "This is not my home, cher'a. It belongs to Aylin. We may need to find another place for you to stay as the festival grows nearer."

A cold blade pierced Persephonie's heart. She should have foreseen this.

Esmeralda sat on the edge of her chair and reached out for her. "Cher'a, I am sorry."

Worry creased her mother's brow. This was the part of their exchange where Persephonie was supposed to tell her that it did not matter, that she was not hurt. But how could she not be? She been so quick to assume this visit might be different. Persephonie's eyes danced around the room to avoid her mother's anxious gaze. "I thought the decoration was rather sparse for this to truly be your home." She smiled as she glanced at her mother.

Mama grabbed the peace offering. "Yes," she chuckled, "Aylin's taste is . . . more modest than ours." Datha had often joked with Esmeralda that her aesthetic was more saudad than any saudad he had ever met. Many associated them with gem tones and rich fabrics because of the trade they undertook on their travels, and while this was true for some of their people, there were plenty of others, like her father, who preferred dark grays and blacks instead. But she and her mother took this assumption to a new extreme, embracing a wide array of colors and tones.

Persephonie frowned. Her mother's ensemble had changed, she now noticed. Aylin seemed to be rubbing off on her. She still wore her signature emerald sash, but her ivory chemise and burgundy leggings would have fit in with the elderly saudad women and most of the citizens of Andel-ce Hevra.

"I sensed that you did not wish to speak of your visions while Aylin was here."

She nodded. "I hope she was not upset, Mama. It is just—"

"I understand, and I will see that she does too. But now that we are alone, can you tell me what it is you have seen?"

Persephonie described the fire on the streets and Esmeralda's voice chanting prayers to Cassandra. "There was a dark figure as well. With tall black wings."

The mauve flush of her mother's copper cheeks paled, and she drummed her fingers against her crossed arms. "That could be Apollo himself," she whispered. "How long have you had these visions, Sephie?"

"A few weeks." Persephonie shrugged. "Datha did not want me to come at first, but then I started to see the danger stretching out toward you." She shuddered as though cold water had dripped down her spine. "I do not wish to be a burden, but I hope you see why I had to come."

Esmeralda pushed herself over onto the couch and wrapped Persephonie in her arms. "Of course I do, cher'a." She tucked Persephonie's head against her chest and rested her jaw on top of her daughter's head. "Why don't you tell me about other, brighter things that you have seen?"

Persephonie grinned. "I met the woman from your prophecy all those years ago." She pulled back to see the surprise in her mother's eyes. "When you and Datha went to visit *Varra Yvayne*." As evening spread her orange and indigo skirt around them, Persephonie recounted discovering the half-elf in the snow and the friendship that had unspooled from there.

"Would you like to hear more of what Cassandra showed me those"—Esmeralda sighed—"what was it, twenty-three years ago, when I first learned that you would be coming into our world?"

"Yes, please, Mama." Persephonie snuggled closer to her mother for one of her favorite stories. Juliet's ear tickled her neck as the fox spun in her lap, wrapping herself up in the fluff of her tail.

Esmeralda's bracelets jangled as she rose to fetch her card deck. The glow Persephonie was accustomed to seeing in her mother's eyes flared with the strike of the match and simmered in the candle's warm light. "It is my hope that you never tire of this story, Sephie. I hold it dear as well."

Her mother arranged her favorite deck of cards and began the chant to call Cassandra to their midst, to oversee the retelling of this, one of her most sacred encounters with the goddess.

Esmeralda's fingers grazed over the cards in front of her, the jewel tones rippling beneath her touch. "I had been having vivid dreams and identical readings for several days. They each started the same, leading to the Magician—your new friend who you met on the mountain."

"Yes, Mama. Iellieth." Persephonie squeezed her ankles tighter against herself, scooting closer to her mother and the cards.

Mama nodded as though she'd been expecting this precise name all this time. She pulled a card from the deck and turned it to Persephonie. THE ENCHANTRESS. A woman with swirls of dark brown hair, tinged red in the light, stood with her hands open above her head, her face turned skyward. Amethyst and emerald garments floated freely around her, caressing her skin, and her feet floated over the earth. An owl and a raven flew on either side of her, and the waxing and waning moons graced the sky above.

"After the Magician, my readings followed a few different paths. But one of them, following the Lovers, always led me here."

Persephonie's hand trembled as she picked up the Enchantress card, heat curling within her as she gazed at her mother's reading of her destiny.

"Cassian and I were delighted that we would bear a daughter together. And three years later, there you were. I have never seen a happier, more beautiful baby." Tears glimmered in her mother's eyes, and the warm glow spread to Persephonie's chest, forming a knot in the base of her throat. Mama and Datha expressed affection so differently. She lingered over this moment, compressing it into a golden key that she clutched to her heart.

"Your tale was one of excitement and complication," her mother continued. "In some of the readings, at first, I had difficulties separating out your story from mine and your father's." Esmeralda smiled sadly. Part of her still missed him, and Cassian's love for her mother would continue on though they chose to live apart.

"It began with the Star, followed by the Four of Wands." Esmeralda glanced between the various candles lighting the room, her eyes lingering on the three violet flames nearest her. "Your readings have always been ruled by cups and wands." Her lips twisted to the side. "I wonder where you get that from?"

Persephonie giggled. Between Esmeralda and Cassian, what chance had she had of a fortune different than one ruled by emotion and passion, especially for one destined to follow the goddess of fate?

"I have been curious to see which path you might follow. In the cards, I saw two—one guided by the Knight of Cups, the other by the Knight of Wands." Esmeralda traced the lines of Persephonie's palm, her brow furrowed.

"Perhaps Cassandra will show me the path between them, Mama." The goddess would not ask her to choose between two such vital parts of herself. But paths only appear one step at a time.

CHAPTER 10

"What brings you secretly to our city during this troubled time, Iellieth and heavily armored friends?" Dimitri's eyes ran over Quindythias's collection of daggers and Marcon's longsword and shield. "I was relieved to hear from you after your disappearance before the Festival. Your mother came to see me." Dimitri smiled at her.

"Yes, it . . . umm, it seems she was quite worried. But she knows that I'm alright now, and, since we're here, so do you." Iellieth wriggled her toes in her boots before raising her gaze to her friend's. "We had to arrive in secret because of the war."

Dimitri nodded. "I assumed as much." He leaned forward in his chair. "But, Iellieth, you must understand that it remains dangerous for you to be here." He glanced at Marcon and Quindythias and lowered his voice. "Even more than before."

Iellieth shivered. Dimitri had been the one she had gone to following Lord Stravinske's attack. He'd cobbled together a rotating cadre of young scholars and mages so that she was never alone again through the remainder of that festival. Two years later, her skin still crawled at the memory of being trapped in the Hadvarian nobleman's clutches, his unwelcome, slimy lips, and the cold terror his assault had inspired. "Is"—Iellieth cleared her throat and clutched her hands together to prevent their shaking—"is he still here?"

Marcon's gray gaze crackled beside her.

"I am afraid so." Dimitri shook his head. "He's in charge of the war efforts as well . . ." The keeper pulled his lips between his teeth, unwilling to finish the thought, but she couldn't leave it there.

She squeezed her fists tighter. "So if we're caught, it's him we'll answer to."

"That is correct." Dimitri sighed. "This whole business of the war is most regrettable. King Arontis seemed almost"—Dimitri gazed off into a corner of the room, searching for the right word —"stunned, when I saw him before his meeting with the queen." He scratched at his beard. "The king is usually such a careful man, and so sharp-eyed, nothing gets by him. Did you notice, when you were there? Or wherever it was you saw your mother?" Dimitri squinted at her, half in the room with them, half searching his memories for further clues about the strange eruption between the two sovereigns.

"I-I saw her in Linolynn," Iellieth stammered, unable to shove the recollections of Lord Stravinske from her mind. She had to focus on the task at hand. Linolynn's future—and that of her friends—depended on it. "I did not have the opportunity to see the king, though I was shocked to learn of the war." Iellieth rubbed her arms, trying to root herself in the present moment. The sparks that ran through her being had scattered. She needed them to bind together once more.

Dimitri glanced from her to Marcon. "Let us turn to gladder tidings," he said quickly. Quindythias looked up from his explorations of the books and papers on the keeper's desk. "I was not entirely alone when your marvelous bird found me, so there is another friendly face who will insist on seeing you now that you are here." The librarian grinned. "He was planning a party anyway, but, from what I hear, it is a much more ambitious affair since he learned of your coming."

"Much to his assistants' chagrin, I'm sure." Iellieth shook her head. Of course Kazi would have somehow found out about her secretive arrival. The Hadvarian socialite had a special knack for uncovering whatever transpired inside the walls of the palace, the Grand Reserve, and the Arcanium.

"Who is this person?" Marcon asked. He scowled at the door to Dimitri's office as though hostile forces who threatened their security might burst through at any moment.

"Maybe you should meet him, instead." Iellieth rose and gestured for Marcon and Quindythias to follow her. "He'll be furious with Dimitri for weeks if we delay going to see him."

The librarian waved them out, snatching his inkwell away from Quindythias on his way out the door. "I'll have your rooms ready for your return," he called.

"Lady, is this the man you were concerned about—"

"No," Iellieth added quickly, "Kazimir is my friend. I can tell you more about the other later." She shuddered again. "Kazi may have trouble keeping it a secret that we're here, but he'll have an easier time of it if he thinks he's the first to know."

"And what if we tell him he wasn't?" Quindythias turned the music box he'd successfully snatched from Dimitri's office over in his hands, distracting her from Marcon's frown.

"You'll have to give that back, you know." Iellieth raised an eyebrow at him. "And I'll let you be the one to tell him that we saw Dimitri first."

Quindythias sighed. "Fine, I'll come up with something more

interesting." He shook his head and muttered to himself as they walked, "Even my secrets are boring now. What's happening?"

"Iellieth, darling, it's wonderful to see you!" Kazimir's singsong voice echoed out across the hall.

Iellieth grinned and hurried forward as her friend glided closer, the dramatically elongated sleeves of his silk tunic nearly dragging the ground as he walked. "You as well, Kazi."

Kazimir grasped her by the elbows and planted a kiss on each of her cheeks. "You were supposed to be here a few weeks ago." He jutted his rounded chin forward. "Do you know who had been asked to design your wedding dress? And who is now left with a gorgeous green gown that no one else is fit to wear?"

"Kazi, I—"

"No." He held up a hand and closed his eyes. "I don't want to hear it."

Marcon's heavy bootsteps drew closer behind her. He would be concerned, not understanding Kazi's sense of humor.

Kazimir broke out of his affected pouting, threw an arm around her shoulder, and spun her around. "Tell me, who is this delightful new escort of yours?"

Marcon stopped short, glancing back and forth between them.

"A new beau, perhaps?" Kazi pretended to whisper, his eyes twinkling at her blush.

"Kazi, no, this is Marcon, a . . ." What would be the best way to describe him? "A traveling companion of mine."

Marcon bowed. Kazimir lifted the sides of his silk pants and curtsied.

"And this is Quindythias." Iellieth held out her hand as the elf sulked forward. She drew her eyebrows together, watching him. Why was he upset?

Kazimir scowled as raised voices bounced off the elegantly tiled halls. "What is it now?" He clasped Iellieth's hand between both of his. "Pardon me for just a moment."

With forearms extended, Kazimir strutted back toward the main hallway. After a shared glance, Iellieth, Marcon, and Quindythias followed.

The socialite scolded whomever he had encountered outside, and their voices immediately dimmed. Iellieth could only catch Kazimir's side of the conversation, and she peeked out of the large wooden doors to see him with his hands on his hips, squaring off with two young men in long flowing robes.

"I will speak to him myself, then," Kazimir declared. He glanced back and caught Iellieth watching him. "Come, dear." He waved, and Iellieth slipped out of the doors. "The things one must endure to throw an elegant fete around here!"

"Kazi, what is it—"

"An attack on my artistic rights, for starters." Kazimir spun and stomped off down the hall.

The two young men—mages, most likely, from their robes—looked at her in confusion. Iellieth took a deep breath as she parsed through a catalog of appropriate responses. Marcon and Quindythias stood behind her, ready to follow her lead. She nodded to the two of them and hurried after Kazimir.

He wound his way out of the halls of the palace and into the Arcanium, the home to Hadvar's elite school for mages and scholars. The Arcanium building continued the sweeping columns and intricate arches of the Hadvarian palace it adjoined, but it eschewed the colorful tiles and veined marble for onyx walls and cold slate floorings.

Iellieth trembled at the compressed power emanating from the walls. The school had only started admitting female students within the last decade or so. Her attendance would have been out of the question regardless, but the magic pulsing at her fingertips protested the heaviness of the contained space, as though spirits had been pressed into the very walls of the structure and longed to be set free.

Kazimir's voice bounced across the stony chamber, and he waved his arms as he spoke to an older man, who wrung his hands together and nodded with brows furrowed.

"I understand, Kazimir," the man said softly in a heavily accented, deep voice, "but you must see that what you are proposing—"

"What I am proposing is the grandest event in living memory! Everyone throws their parties in the halls. I need to do something fresh, surprising—why, we're on the brink of war! Shouldn't we celebrate while we have the chance?"

He extended his hand. "Kazimir, I . . ."

"Can we throw the event or not?" Kazimir remained just out of reach, and Iellieth waited behind his shoulder.

The older man sighed. "Very well. But please be careful and respectful of my students. I will have them help to clear out the hall and remove some of our more precious items." He gestured around the chamber, indicating a series of low pedestals that held an assortment of items and artifacts.

Iellieth's amulet glowed warm against her chest as she surveyed the room. *What had it found?* She twisted back as the man gave instructions to the two young mages he'd sent to speak with Kazimir. *There.*

A curiously shaped piece of stone rested in the center of the room. It was plainer than the others . . . and covered in runes.

Iellieth peered over Kazimir's shoulder. "Could you take me on a tour of the magical artifacts before they're moved? The displays are most intriguing."

The mages turned to her in surprise.

The older man considered her carefully. "Do I know you, my dear?"

Kazimir began to introduce her, but Iellieth cut him off lest he forget to keep her presence here a secret. "I'm . . . Lilith," she said, giving a small curtsy to disguise her moment of uncertainty as to the false identities Quindythias had created for them. "My two companions and I are guests of Master Dimitri. Kazimir has been kind enough to show us around and help us become acquainted with the capital."

A low green light glowed in the older man's eyes, and Iellieth felt her magic spark in response. He raised an eyebrow. "Curious indeed."

Iellieth's heart raced at the man's close scrutiny. Did he know she was trying to find the missing pieces of the planar seal? Would he try to stop her? She fought to maintain a neutral expression, unsure of how such a learned mage would feel about druidic magic.

"I am Master Yugo, Lilith." He placed his forearms parallel to the ground and laid one hand on top of the other, bowing deeply. "Welcome to the Arcanium."

She audibly exhaled as she smiled, and Marcon laid a warm hand on her shoulder. Her concern hadn't been very subtle after all.

"I'll need to take at least two of you back for a fitting." Kazimir shook his head. "There's so much still to do!" He squinted at the tall windows of the circular space and sighed. "So much."

"Would you like to take a turn with me then, Lilith?" Master Yugo offered her his elbow. "And I'll see you returned to your friends shortly?"

The heat from Marcon's hand increased. She laid her fingers on top of his and pressed down. "That sounds wonderful, thank you. I'll meet the two of you in Kazimir's hall. I just want to look around for a moment."

"As you wish, lady." Marcon bowed.

"I look best in blue," Quindythias said, turning his gaze from the tower's windows to Kazimir. "What are our options in terms of fabric?"

Iellieth grinned after them as they left the Arcanium.

CHAPTER 11

"Y ou there," a gray-haired sailor called.

Genevieve ducked instinctively, sure she would be removed from the wharf at any moment. Could they tell by looking at her that she was a druid? Her eyes darted after the sallow man she'd followed through the streets of Andel-ce Hevra as he stepped onto the deck. The handsome, younger man who'd been waiting for him on the dock followed just behind him. He guided the dark-haired man toward the ship with a proprietorial air, clearly someone of importance aboard the . . . she glanced again at the ship's name carved along its side, the *Amber Queen*.

What if the man with her conclave's dagger realized she'd been tracking him? Would he tell someone on the ship and prevent her boarding? Or, worse, report her to the Andel-ce Hevran guards?

"Yes, you!" he yelled again.

She straightened and pulled her cloak tighter. *He's more likely to notice you acting suspiciously if you keep acting suspiciously. Breathe. They don't know about druids who can turn into werewolves . . . you didn't either until you became the first in . . . how long did Ophelia say? Thousands of years?* Her secret inner wolf, Jade, sniffed the air, trying to discern the man's intentions. In their almost two weeks together, she'd grown accustomed to interpreting Jade's smell impressions, to trusting her inner wolf's instincts about the world around them.

"Are you hoping to come aboard?" The older man walked to the edge of the ship's railing and leaned against the banister. Jade sensed he was even-tempered and didn't pose a direct threat to their well-being.

Genevieve nodded. "Yes," she called, repeating herself more loudly a second time so he could hear her above the general clamor of the docks. How experienced did one need to be in order to join a crew?

"Well, come on, then." The man waved, swinging his arm as though the movement alone could pull her on board.

She stole a few glances at the nearest deckhands but approached the gangplank unchallenged.

"New to the waters, are ya?" The older man smiled from the top of the walkway. "Come on, you've almost made it."

Genevieve curled her fingers into fists and ran up the slanted walkway. It was only the second time she'd stepped foot on a barge, though this one was larger and steadier than the craft they'd taken downriver. How could she convince this man to allow her passage on the ship? She peered over his shoulder, but the man she'd been following had already disappeared among the bustling crew. She had to find out how he had acquired her conclave's dagger.

"Welcome aboard the *Amber Queen*, miss." He smiled. "I'm Ambrose, the chief navigator of this vessel." Ambrose bowed his head and met her eyes. "Now who might you be?"

There, she spotted him. Off to the side, the younger man in the pale blue coat ushered the dark-haired man she'd been following into a room at the back of the ship, a hand resting on his shoulder as he led him across the threshold.

"Genevieve," she answered quickly, looking away from the pair before Ambrose noticed her curiosity.

"A pleasure, miss. Have you ever sailed before?"

"Only on the boat that got me here." Genevieve's brow creased. All her hopes of recovering her conclave's dagger could be dashed here. She only needed enough time to investigate how the man had acquired the dagger and to reclaim it, and then she could resume the task Ophelia had set for her—to sail across the Infinite Ocean, find the druids in Caldara, and ask them to lead her to Yvayne. The man was waiting on a reason to allow her passage on the ship. "But I've always wanted to sail," she added. "I . . . I'm accustomed to making food for large numbers of people. Might you be in need of an assistant cook?" In the weeks before the attack, she and Mariellen had spent several days preparing the Feast of the First Thaw together. At the time, it had been a welcome respite from her training in druidic magic. Would she ever have a chance to partake in her people's feasts again? Jade's stomach rumbled at the idea of plentiful amounts of food.

The sailor laughed. "We might be. Our cook doesn't have the easiest time getting along with others. Let's see." He waved a young woman over, her shoulder-length blonde hair pulled back in braids that hung beneath her cap. "Athena, come here a moment." He smiled happily between them. "Will you escort Genevieve to meet Master Keever and see how they get on?"

The woman nodded. "If you'll follow me." Her dark blue eyes regarded Genevieve warily.

A snarl prickled along Jade's nose as a burly half-orc woman stomped over. "Ambrose, a word? Who is this?" She waved a thickly muscled arm in Genevieve's direction. The woman's green skin reminded her of Ophelia's moss cloak.

"Ah, Kriega, our esteemed first mate." Ambrose bowed his head. He rose with a thin smile pasted across his lips. "Before you say no out of hand, allow me to introduce a possible chef's assistant who's eager to come aboard."

The woman's tawny brown eyes narrowed at Genevieve. "And why are you qualified to come aboard a ship?"

Genevieve opened her mouth over Jade's growl of frustration, but the blonde-haired woman spoke first on her behalf. "As you'll notice, the docks aren't exactly crawling with crew anxious to sail under the banner of Admiral Syleste." She glanced at the docks and crossed her arms. "I wonder why that is." Sarcasm dripped from her every word, though Genevieve and Jade couldn't determine its source.

"One who owes her life to the admiral's mercy should speak more carefully," the half-orc growled. She indicated one of the deck's busy doorways. "Take her below and report back to me." A brown eyebrow rose along her brow. "I'll make the final decision."

The blonde woman's eyes shone bright with rage, but she said nothing further as she led Genevieve toward the dark staircase leading into the bowels of the ship. "Are you sure you want to be here?" she whispered as they began their descent. "I promise you, you won't find mercy beneath the admiral's flag."

She must have misunderstood the woman's initial scrutiny. It wasn't due to herself but to whomever this admiral was. "I found mercy to be in short supply on land as well," Genevieve replied. She bit the inside of her lip to drive back the memories of her conclave in flames, of everyone she loved murdered by vicious werewolves. "It's not mercy I'm seeking."

The woman paused on the stair and looked back at her. "Then you'll fit right in."

"So, Master Darcy, is that right?"

It had taken Teodric a moment to pick out Syleste's agent from among the barge passengers sailing to the coast from Andel-ce Hevra. Before they arrived, he'd debated between anticipating someone with a physically commanding presence, like Syleste herself or even Kriega, his first mate, or someone who immediately left a faint yet slimy impression. *Slimy it is*, he'd concluded, seeing Darcy's shifting, bright blue eyes. By the time they'd stepped on deck, the man's sly smile said that he'd evaluated Teodric and had moved on to analyzing the best way to bend the eager young captain's weaknesses to his advantage. *Bend away.* Darcy's being valuable enough to the admiral to necessitate such a retrieval said plenty about the conniving personage, the subtle, poisonous snake, he'd brought on board.

Teodric stepped aside to allow one of the deckhands passage into the quarter gallery with their new passenger's bags.

"Anywhere is fine," Darcy said with a wave to the deckhand. "Yes, Captain, I thank you." Syleste's agent took a turn about the room. "An impressive array of windows aboard your ship, I must say." He tucked his arms around his back and spun to face Teodric. "It would seem you've done something extraordinary to fall into the admiral's good graces. I had been expecting a Captain Steinvas, I believe?"

Teodric's stomach twisted. There were still nights where he awoke in a cold sweat, his blade poised above Steinvas's trembling form, asking to be spared. The man's blood seeped into glowing amber burls shaped like the admiral's eyes, disappearing into the polished deck wood. "We had a change in leadership in Nortelon and then set off to acquire you, per the admiral's request."

"Lucky me." Darcy smirked and returned to the windows. "And where to from here, Captain?"

"Isla de Hossa." The admiral had been adamant about her spy

in Andel-ce Hevra being brought to her island as quickly as Teodric could deliver him there. She'd acquired the remote island early in her career, and stories abounded as to how exactly it came into her possession.

Darcy flinched at his answer. He was wise enough to fear Syleste at least. Teodric doubted that half the tales came anywhere close to whatever brutal, bloody truth had actually transpired in her taking ownership of Isla de Hossa, hidden by impenetrable mist and guarded by rocks sharp as dragon's teeth. The very thought of her island sent a chill down his spine. And yet, despite having traveled there with the admiral on several occasions, he had very few memories of time actually spent on the island. There were several months of which he could recall nothing but a cold prison cell, biting pain across his chest . . . and a secret he'd wanted to keep hidden. But had he? And what had it been?

Darcy studied his fingernails as the deckhands filed out. "Is your family still in Nortelon?"

Teodric frowned. "Yes, my mother is." Why would Darcy know that?

"Still searching for Frederick, then?"

His pulse quickened. "Excuse me?"

The man glanced up, sunlight glinting off his blue eyes. "Your father, are you still searching for him?"

Teodric stared back. The twisting in his gut returned. Syleste had been plotting something by having him be the one to fetch Darcy. Had she found a way to give this man valuable information about him while he was still en route to Andel-ce Hevra? Or had she anticipated an impending change in her leadership and passed the information along to this slimy informant?

"Might I set your mind at ease, Captain?" Darcy's eyebrows flashed. Heat rose along Teodric's chest and neck. The man deliberately strode out into dangerous waters, baiting whatever lurked below. "For quite some time, it was my responsibility to know the workings of Tor'stre Vahn's diplomats and nobility. You and your family being both, of course, piqued my interest. I was grieved to learn of your father's disappearance."

That glint again, and the intonation, as though this man either knew something and wouldn't say or worse, that he'd had some sort of hand in his father vanishing. Teodric ground his teeth together. He clenched his hands, controlling their desire to wrap around Darcy's throat.

Shouts rose on the deck behind him. Kriega's voice rose above the din, immediately taking charge of the situation. Their rocky start had eased onto steady waters over the last few days. They were beginning to trust one another.

Teodric cleared his throat. "You must excuse me, Darcy." He gave a slight bow and backed toward the door. "I thank you for your concern." *Click.* Teodric snapped the door shut behind him.

⚜

"WHAT MAKES YOU THINK I NEED HELPING?" THE GOBLIN chef, who the woman named Athena had introduced as Keever, glared at Genevieve, his yellow eyes burning as though she'd tried to have him expelled from the ship to take his place.

"N-nothing. I just thought . . ."

Keever's jaw jutted forward. He snapped his fingers together, and a full roasted chicken appeared from thin air on the table between them. "Can you do that?"

"No, I can't." Genevieve struggled to arrange her thoughts around Jade's salivating. Her eyes tore across the spotless kitchen and settled back on the thin, hunched goblin in front of her. "Umm, I could help you deliver food."

Athena nodded approvingly beside her, but Keever's scowl deepened. "Are you saying that you would be willing to be *exposed* to the ravages of the sun and the sea?" His lips settled into a frown.

"I didn't think of it as . . . yes, I would. If that's agreeable to you, of course, Master Keever."

The goblin extended his small, bony hand, and Genevieve took it hesitantly. The goblin gave it a single shake before he crowed, "Aha! We have a deal." Keever chuckled to himself and ripped one of the legs off the chicken. His teeth tore through the browned flesh, and he hummed happily as he chewed, ambling over toward a tall pot on the stove as though she and Athena had suddenly disappeared.

Athena grinned and slid back toward the door. Genevieve followed. They wound through the belly of the ship and came to a long room full of three columns of stacked bunks.

"Assuming everything works out with the first mate," Athena said, "you'll be staying down here." She guided Genevieve along one of the rows and gestured to the left-hand side, near the back. "It's quieter in this corner, and you could stay by me if you like."

"That's very kind of you." Genevieve remembered to smile while Jade paced. She had never given much thought to the reality of life on the ocean. Though the sea offered her own comforts, how would a druid raised in the forest fare with weeks where the only trees she walked among were those that were dead and polished beneath her feet? Would the sunlight even strike this room at dawn? "How much time do you spend down here?"

They slipped through a gap between a middle row of bunks, and Athena led her to the corner she'd indicated. "Not a lot. I like to be above decks myself. Is this your first time sailing?"

Genevieve nodded. "Is it that obvious?"

"Only if someone is paying attention." Athena patted the spot next to her on the mattress. "I know I warned you about coming aboard a little while ago. The woman in charge of this ship, whose bidding our captain is duty-bound to follow . . ." Athena sighed. "There are dark sides to sailing aboard the *Amber Queen*, but it's not as bad as I thought it would be."

Since the attack against her conclave, a dark cloud had hovered over Genevieve. The haunted look in Athena's eyes said she wasn't the only one to have recently weathered a loss. Given time, they might be able to confide in one another about it. "I hope you're right."

She had grown disoriented on their tour below decks. Would the man with her conclave's sacred dagger be staying down here too, or would he reside in a less communal space? The lanterns creaked on their posts around the dim room, tossing light side-to-side with the rocking ship. "Assuming the first mate lets me stay, can I sleep on a lower bunk? I'm used to being on a mat on the ground . . . on land." Jade paused in her pacing to sniff the air.

Her guide laughed. "Yes, I'm sure that will be fine."

Jade's growl drowned out whatever Athena said next. The hair prickled along the back of Genevieve's neck. Jade flexed her claws. A broad, rigid frame stepped beneath one of the lanterns on the far side of the room. Glowing eyes peered across the cots; the man gave a dark scowl at the sleeping sailors and the few taking a moment's rest to read. Her fingers retracted, flexed, as her heart began to race.

"Who is that?" Genevieve whispered.

"Hallix," Athena said with a shudder. "He constantly seems like he's scheming, or watching. I think he's a relatively new addition, like us. He came over from the ship that's in charge of this one, the *Dominion*." A shadow crossed Athena's expression, but it passed as Hallix left the bunk room. "Come on, I'll take you above, and we'll tell Kriega the good news. Keever's from the Underland, so he avoids stepping onto the deck whenever possible. You'll never hear him say it, but he'll be much happier to have someone else transporting the food above decks."

A heavy scent lingered in the entry to the sleeping chamber —peat moss, woodsmoke, and the iron tang of blood. Jade sprang up and howled at her discovery, her nose pointed to the invisible moons. There was another werewolf on board.

CHAPTER 12

Early the next morning, Persephonie and Esmeralda set out from the Wayfarers' District toward City Center to try and find lodgings for Persephonie during her stay in Andel-ce Hevra. They left Juliet napping in the thin bands of sunlight floating in through the windows. Aylin hadn't returned that night, but Persephonie couldn't tell if her mother was worried by this or not.

Esmeralda's eyes darted over to a collection of people gathered around a statue in the square ahead. Her pace increased.

The statue wasn't one Persephonie had seen before. It depicted a group of priests kneeling together in prayer. The citizens dabbed at their eyes, and children laid flowers and candles around the priests' feet. "What are all of those people doing by that statue?"

"We need to keep moving." Esmeralda tugged at her sleeve, pulling her away from the mourners.

"But why?"

"Hey!" A sharp voice rang out over the crowd. "Haven't you done enough?" Rocks and pebbles crashed against the sidewalk in front of Persephonie, and she jumped back, arms outstretched to shield her mother.

"We must go," Esmeralda whispered. They ducked around a street corner as angry voices rose up behind them.

"Mama, what do they think we have done?" Persephonie raced after her mother, clutching the ends of her shawl to avoid being snared by one of the many obstacles in the city streets.

She bumped into Esmeralda's back as her mother stopped at the end of the alley, debating the best path forward. A bright green owl with large, yellow eyes stared down at her from across the street. "Here," Persephonie exclaimed, pointing at the sign for the tavern she and Juliet had sheltered in the day before.

Esmeralda nodded and ran after her. Their heeled boots clattered across the cobblestone intersection, and they ducked into the safety of Otmund's pub.

Minerva, the true green owl for whom the tavern had been named, hooted at them, swinging gently on her perch behind the bar.

"Be with you in a moment," a man's gruff voice called from the back.

"How did you know about this place?" Esmeralda turned to her, her expression obscured by the low light.

"Otmund helped me yesterday when I was trying to find you."

"Alright, what're ya having?" The dark wooden door with stained-glass panes swung open from behind the bar, and Otmund emerged, wiping his hands on a beige towel that he tossed over his shoulder. "Oh, you again." He nodded to Persephonie and raised an eyebrow at Esmeralda. "And this must be your lovely mother. I've heard a lot about you," he added with a wink.

Persephonie suppressed a sigh. Esmeralda's effect on strangers remained one of the most reliable of her mother's traits. "Mama, this is Otmund. Otmund, this is my mother, Esmeralda."

Muted voices echoed from outside the tavern, and mottled silhouettes rushed down the side streets around them.

"Trouble again, miss?" Otmund grinned as he lifted a flagon and began polishing the shiny emerald glass.

Persephonie frowned. "We encountered a problem near a statue, a monument, but we were only walking nearby. And then the people . . ." She turned to Esmeralda to explain.

"We passed by the Monument of the Kneeling Priests," Mama said. Otmund nodded, picking up another glass.

"Yes, but why were they upset with us? We cannot walk there?"

"You"—Otmund's finger drew a line through the air, pointing at her and Esmeralda—"should avoid it in the future."

He hadn't been rude like this the day before. She and Esmeralda should have found somewhere else to go.

"Red, white, or something stronger, Madam Esmeralda?" Otmund ducked behind the bartop, bottles clinking beneath.

"Red, please." She took Persephonie's hand in hers. "Come, we will explain."

Otmund gestured to one of the corner tables, thumping his foot against the door and calling for Tess on his way over. Esmeralda smoothed her skirt across her lap, and the tavern owner uncorked the bottle, pouring them each a glass.

"We spoke yesterday of the ban in the city," he began, his fingertip jamming into the wood of the table.

Persephonie nodded. He had told her that no natural magic was allowed.

"That ban was loosely enforced until several weeks ago, when someone"—his eyes darted over to Esmeralda as she dipped her chin ever so slightly—"from the Untamed created some sort of magical explosion that killed a group of acolytes who were studying to be priests of the Pantheon Supreme."

Her mother averted her eyes, searching the street outside.

"I am very sorry for the young priests, but . . . Mama, that must have been another part of the Untamed. Did you know of this?" Persephonie leaned toward her mother.

The tavern owner cleared his throat, and Esmeralda's attention drifted back to the table.

"Not all the members of the Untamed are so radical, Sephie," Esmeralda said, reaching out for her.

Persephonie jerked her hand away. "What are you saying?" This was not the clear denial it should have been.

Otmund grumbled, rubbing his beard. "Not all of the Untamed are bad, miss. And like I said, there are many of us in the city who stand by them, who support their right to believe as they wish, to practice their own magic, so long as it don't hurt anyone else." He drummed his knuckles against the tabletop.

"Those in the city who are very religious, in an official way," Esmeralda interjected, "they think that everyone who practices natural magic is dangerous. The council has them in such a frenzy, especially after Senator Ignatius made a spectacle of the druid elders." Her lips trembled, and she lowered her face, covering it with her hands.

Persephonie scooted her chair closer to her mother's and rubbed Esmeralda's back, soothing her.

"Wherever you go in the city," Otmund's rumbling voice spoke over Esmeralda's muffled sobs, "those on the opposing side of fanaticism will be suspicious of you." He took a long draught of his wine and turned to Persephonie. "I'm guessing your, well . . ." The color rose on Otmund's face. "I'm sure you look very nice for the people you're used to, but in the city, dressed like that, they'll assume you're one of the Untamed."

Persephonie glanced down at her burgundy blouse, lapis

corset, and emerald skirt. "Because of the flowers?" That's what Otmund had pointed out on their first meeting.

"Because you're different." Esmeralda's head shot up, the corners of her eyes narrowed, but they softened as she looked at Persephonie. She reached over and brushed the braid of ribbons and flowers back over her daughter's bare shoulder. "They will always resent us for that, Sephie."

࿗

OVER THE FINAL DREGS OF THEIR WINE, ESMERALDA mentioned that they were trying to find Persephonie somewhere to stay. Otmund brightened at this. If they could wait for him to check on a thing or two, he might have just the place.

The tavern keeper showed them into an eclectically decorated parlor on the third floor. "Fewer eyes up here, Madam Esmeralda," he said with a bow. "Go ahead and make yourselves comfortable. I'll be back up shortly." He gestured to the bottles of wine and carafe of water on a side table, bowed his head to Mama again, and slipped out to return downstairs.

Persephonie settled onto the chartreuse settee with stitched russet flowers and tucked her feet beneath her, the silk fabric crisp against her skin. This new wrinkle in what it meant to be part of the Untamed flapped in the corner of her mind, croaking for her attention. "This is more serious than what you told me yesterday, Mama."

"There have been a few accidents," Esmeralda said, shaking her head with her palms upraised. The bright fire returned to her mother's eyes. "I thought you were proud of me for taking on a leadership position."

Persephonie's brow furrowed. The steadiness she'd seen in her mother the evening before took on a sharper edge with this talk of something more. "I am proud of you, Mama, of course."

"Aylin is the leader of our most active faction." Esmeralda flushed as she smiled, her eyes drifting out to the window and over the brown- and green-tiled rooftops of the city. "Otmund knows more than he lets on. I suspected as much when you described him, and I was certain when he indicated that he knew who I was when we arrived." She turned back to Persephonie, her foot crossed behind her ankle, marking impatient time. "I don't want you to be alarmed by what you saw today. The Untamed have clear goals, and we've made great strides in our negotiations with the Council of Andel-ce Hevra for bringing about a more egalitarian future. Aylin always says that if we don't stand up to them, who will?" Her hazel eyes searched Persephonie's face. "They've spurned us and our magic for long enough. What we have is a gift, not something to be feared and controlled. It's well past time they recognized that."

Persephonie chewed on her bottom lip. The omens she'd seen before her arrival here, that had driven her to her mother's side, cast a shadow against the picture Mama painted now, adding a troubling, unspoken depth to the frame. "What do you mean by these negotiations, Mama? Some sort of petition?" She shook her head. The Torstran words kept sticking in her throat. "You know I am unfamiliar with the politics here."

Esmeralda waved the questions away. "No need to concern yourself with that for now. You do seem to have made quite an impression on Otmund, though."

"Yes, erhm, he has been very kind to me—"

The door behind them swung open, and Otmund came clomping up into the room, a bright-eyed fox jumping onto the last step behind him. "I believe you've been missing someone."

"Juliet!" Persephonie sprang up and ran over to her, scooping the fox into her arms. "You were supposed to wait for us at the apartment. How did you find us here?" She hugged Juliet against her chest, and the fox's tail brushed her skirt. Anything might have happened to her alone in the city.

"She's got a special knack for locating you, this one," Otmund said. He crossed his arms and regarded the three of them. "I was wondering, if I might be so bold"—he nodded to Esmeralda—"with your permission, of course, Madam Arelle . . ." He cleared his throat. "I've been short-staffed of late, and we have the Hunt coming up in a matter of days." He squared his shoulders to Persephonie. "How would you feel about working for me, while you're here in town with your mother?"

"Oh!" Persephonie's eyes widened, and she set Juliet down.

"You could even live here, or at least on the nights you're working," Otmund added quickly.

"Mister Otmund, that is very generous of you. Mama, what do you think?"

"It is a very kind offer." She flashed a brilliant smile to the tavern owner. "I know you are here to spend time with me, Sephie. Staying here would allow Aylin and I . . ." She left the sentence unfinished.

Staying here would mean she was out of her mother's way. "I do not wish to be an inconvenience, Mama." She crossed the room to stand by her mother. "And I am sure the extra money would be helpful, so that I am not another person for you and Aylin to try to feed." Esmeralda had often found providing for herself in Andel-ce Hevra difficult. Each time she visited, Datha sent Persephonie with extra coins to sneak into her mother's small store.

Esmeralda's eyes softened. "Thank you, Sephie." She clasped her daughter's hand. "That sounds wonderful, Otmund. We are in your debt."

"Anything for the cause." His eyebrows rose again, and he stepped out of the living quarters to return to the tavern below.

"So he is a member of the Untamed too?" Persephonie floated this easier question out onto the waters between them. Why would it have been so distressing for Aylin to have Persephonie stay in her apartment? Was there a deeper reason her mother wished to keep them apart? It had never been an issue in her mother's previous relationships—why now?

"More of an ally." Esmeralda swung her arms by her side as she looked around the sitting room. "But these are fine rooms you will have, and Otmund can take care of you if you need help." Her mother's eyes flashed conspiratorially. "And, if you decide that you would like to stay in the city as part of the Untamed, I believe he may have a few patrons you could keep an eye on for us."

"Like a spy?" Persephonie frowned.

"No, no"—Esmeralda shook her head—"a precaution, in case something unexpected transpires."

Persephonie nodded slowly. "I will think about it, Mama." The shadows she had foreseen were becoming clearer.

CHAPTER 13

"K azimir is a unique soul," Master Yugo observed to Iellieth. His eyes were warm as he watched them leave. "I have noticed that."

The mage looked down at her. "You are of a magical persuasion, are you not, my dear?"

"I am, sir." Iellieth helped to steady him as they descended the wide, low stairs leading to the series of pedestals that decorated the floor of the Arcanium.

"I suspected as much." He patted her hand. "I'm afraid we don't have any others like you within these walls. Ah well." He gestured to the chunk of broken stone that had caught her and her amulet's attention. "Most of these items I can have the apprentices manage, but there's one I'll take care of myself." The tendons in his thin hands strained as he lifted it from its pedestal. "Some of the other masters have been dismissive of this artifact over the years."

The amulet heated against Iellieth's chest. Thankfully her jacket covered it, and the runes on the stone didn't glow in response. "Do they not find it to be important?" Her voice warbled only slightly.

Master Yugo shook his head. "Do you read Arcane scripts, Lilith? I'm not sure how common that is for druids." He closed his eyes and inhaled deeply, his large nose extended toward her. "Your magic carries the scent of a fresh spring rain, life-giving and powerful."

Iellieth pressed her fingernails into the palms of her hands. The amulet lifted off her chest, straining against her jacket. "I had no idea it carried a unique scent. Do you, umm, can you do that with everyone?"

"My special gift." He smiled kindly, the wrinkles beside his eyes deepening. "Though we do not cater to students of your abilities here, if I were younger, it would be my great wish to do so." He turned from the center of the chamber and began walking toward the onyx wall that enclosed the room. As they drew closer, an archway appeared, opening onto a curved stone staircase.

Iellieth tried to soothe the amulet as they went, but it ignored her urgings and began to gently pulse against her skin.

Master Yugo gazed fondly at the piece of the planar seal in his hands. "The script on this stone speaks of holding fast and the turning of an age. Though it is not an attractive piece, we have used it in our coronation ceremonies for centuries. I have long suspected it holds a latent magical ability, but the others are certain I am wasting my time." The mage lifted the stone to his nose, the whistle of his nostrils filling the stairway. "But you see, many scents combine here, which indicates an object of great power. Sun-warmed earth, the smoke from a fire, a crisp spring breeze, the salty kiss of the ocean." A final inhale. "And underneath all of it, the wet stone and sharp spice of a hidden mystery, waiting in the dark."

His eyes sparkled as he looked up from the seal piece and

smiled at Iellieth. "They would have said something similar about my relationship with Kazimir, but they would have been mistaken there as well."

"What is the nature of your relationship with Kazimir, Master Yugo?" The upward turn of his lip assured her that he was looking for someone to confide in. Why else would he have brought up something so personal?

Master Yugo paused on a landing carved out from the winding stair. He leaned against the wall for a moment, resting the seal piece on the handrail. How high in the tower did he live? "Ah"—he shook his head—"I don't wish to bore you with the matters of an old man's heart."

"You're not boring me." Iellieth reached out her hands. "Might I carry that for you, and you can tell me?" She wanted to be certain it was the piece Red had described, and the mage's shoulders were beginning to sag.

Master Yugo sighed. "Thank you, yes." He handed Iellieth the stone. It was surprisingly light in her grasp, almost levitating in her hands as her amulet did against her chest. The outer sides were smooth, save the carvings, but it was broken on either end where it had been severed from the rest of the planar seal. Her amulet danced on her neck, twirling back and forth on the golden bands.

"Kazimir is young, full of energy and passion." He pushed himself up using the handrails. "But we had a quarrel a few weeks ago, and then the unpleasantness with our neighboring country erupted, and that has caused more division between the two of us."

How much would a visitor to Hadvar be expected to know about the conflict with Linolynn? She should have asked Dimitri. Had anyone else witnessed the disagreement between the two monarchs?

Master Yugo was too wrapped up in his story to notice her

indecision or her amulet's excitement. "I don't know if he found a chance to tell you about it, but the argument between the two rulers transpired just before Kazimir's event at the festival."

"Oh, that's terrible." Kazimir prided himself on his unique celebrations.

"I made the unfortunate error of trying to convince him to take a wider view of the situation." The mage smiled sadly. "He did not appreciate that very well. And since, I've been busy with preparing the young mages should war prove to be unavoidable."

Iellieth shuddered at the thought of the two young men she'd met facing off against an army of Linolynn's soldiers, tossing spells into a marching line of troops. Her throat tightened as the memory of Mara's last stand took the image's place.

"It seems I wasn't as understanding of Kazimir's personal feelings as I ought to have been. It has been difficult to balance all of the responsibilities appropriately."

"I'm sure," Iellieth said. "I know that I am new to this, but it sounds to me that you did the best you could under the circumstances."

The mage's eyes remained weighed down by sadness.

She tried a different approach. "What if the two of you were to reconnect tomorrow night, at this newly planned ball that he's working on?" Waves of energy radiated from her amulet to the seal piece. She needed to prevent him from noticing.

"That is a nice idea." His shoulders straightened as they stepped onto the final landing at the top of the tower. "I could have my best suit pressed between now and then. He would be impressed by that." Master Yugo's expression took on a dreamy glow, and he waited with her at the top of the stairs before realizing that he was the only one of the two of them who knew the way forward. "Pardon me," he said, smiling. "My room is just here. Allow me one moment."

Master Yugo approached the middle of the five stone doors

on the landing. He held his left palm outward and murmured an incantation under his breath. A light wind swirled up the stairway.

The mage exhaled as the stone ground before him, sliding open to reveal a modestly decorated bedchamber laden with books.

"If you'll set that on the ledge, my dear." He indicated a low kneeling rail that ran the length of the bare left-hand side of the room. Bright stars winked down at her through the thick pane of glass in his arched window.

Iellieth placed the stone on a flat wooden box perched in the center of the ledge. An inlaid pitcher sat beside a large crystal on one side, and a dark wooden chest with a padlock rested on the other.

The seal piece continued its tug on both her and her amulet as Iellieth pulled herself away. Master Yugo's back was turned to her while he sorted through trinkets he'd pulled out of a tall dresser. Swirls of magic emanated from various parts of the room, some deep tidal pools, others rushing brooks, but none were as strong as the seal piece's siren call. She feared her amulet would scream when they stepped out of the room, or that she would.

Iellieth laid her hands over her chest, trying to calm it and herself. They would be back, and they could take it with them then. If she asked him for it, or explained its worth, would he let her walk away with it?

Red's warning about Alessandra's desire to acquire the seal piece floated back to her. How would she know whether or not she could trust anyone?

Energy swelled around the room's stone door. "Oh, I've left you open, have I?" Master Yugo hurried forward and waved his hands at the archway. The magic stilled. "It's a little temperamental at times." He smiled at Iellieth. "Have you encountered objects like this before? Most people are more surprised." He motioned for her to join him at the doorway. Iellieth yanked herself free of the seal piece's grasp, disguising her stumbling steps as a rushed gait with mixed success. The mage raised an eyebrow at her.

"Once or twice." She smiled, thinking back to the friendly door that had led her to Marcon. "Doors especially tend to have a palpable personality, don't they?"

Master Yugo chuckled his assent. "Yes, yes, I think that's true."

Iellieth stood behind him while he resealed the door. The stone glowed blue, and the seal piece's grip broke free.

"Let's return you to your friends." The mage leaned on her arm as they proceeded back to the lower floor of the Arcanium.

CHAPTER 14

"I just don't understand why Marcon gets all the attention." Quindythias crossed his arms and poked his chin forward, clamping his jaw shut. He scowled at Iellieth from the top of his bed.

"That's just how Kazi is, Quindythias. He doesn't mean anything hurtful by it."

The elf looked away. "Everywhere we go, people fawn over him. It used to be the other way around. You'd think, as no one here has managed to remember anything important, that at the very least they could treat us both like heroes instead of pretending that I'm invisible." He slumped further against the headboard.

Marcon grinned and shook his head, denying her silent plea for help.

Would it be so terrible to lean into Quindythias's wounded vanity instead of trying to draw him away from it? She wanted to spend some time in the Grand Reserve with both of them—they might find something useful, and she was hoping to uncover more about the Soul Shepherds. But it would be too difficult with Quindythias pouting.

"I'm sure Kazimir thought you were unavailable." She leaned toward the elf, and he drew his chin ever so slightly in her direction. She smiled inwardly. This tack *was* working. "You have a . . . a very sophisticated energy, and he probably felt intimidated by that, or at least assumed that you're already involved with someone else." She bit her lip, waiting to see if he believed her or not.

Quindythias sighed. "I guess you're right. He is less subtle than my partners tend to be."

Iellieth patted his leg. "That makes sense."

"Your friend Katarina was smitten with me immediately."

"Oh." Iellieth nodded. "Yes, I'm sure she was." He had been so different than she expected when he met her and Katarina, she couldn't discern whether or not there was any truth to his assertion.

Quindythias squinted at her, trying to decide if she was being honest with him.

"They have a school here," Iellieth added quickly, "maybe you can find someone to spend time with there?"

The elf gazed up at the ceiling. "I guess that would be alright." He shrugged and sat up. "So where was it that you wanted to go this evening?"

Iellieth smiled. "The library."

Marcon came to stand behind her, now that Quindythias was no longer the topic of conversation. With his olive complexion and dark hair, he fit in well with Hadvar's rugged populace. "And what are we looking for in the library, lady?"

"For lost histories of the two of you." She skipped toward the door. With the three of them searching together, who knew what they might find? For the first time on any of her trips to Hadvar, she could spend as much time in the Grand Reserve as she wished. "Dimitri already promised to help us. He's waiting below in the primary collection."

❧

DIMITRI HAD SEVERAL VOLUMES ALREADY SELECTED FOR THEIR perusal, and he and Quindythias quickly became mired in a discussion of erased histories and how cultural memory shifted over time.

Marcon glanced through one of the tall stacks Dimitri and Quindythias had left in their wake in the center of the room.

Iellieth appeared at his shoulder. "There's another intriguing phenomenon occurring in the Grand Reserve tonight." She peeked at the volume, but she couldn't read the Dwarvish script he had been perusing.

"I spent some years as a diplomat to the dwarves in my time," he explained. The book clicked shut in his hand, and he set it carefully on the stack, leaning back against the table as he turned to face her. "What is this exciting event you speak of?" The gray in his eyes was the sun-touched tip of a wave before a storm.

"Here, come and see." Iellieth caught Marcon's hand and pulled him after her to the winding stairs that circled the lower library floor. The runes along his arm flared and calmed at her touch.

Her breath caught in her throat as they climbed. She knew she'd seen a flash of green reflected against the far wall. For years she had longed to see the magical lights that painted the night sky in the northern climes, but the festival each year occurred during their quiet season.

"What are you looking for?" Marcon asked from behind her, his smile buoying his voice.

"Wait and see," she insisted. A violet light flashed along the stone alcoves carved into the side of the library. It should be late enough that the students would be absent.

Iellieth dashed into one of the rounded outcroppings that the mages used for their studies during the day. The window bore a wide seat, much like the window ledge in her room at home. Iellieth sat on her knees atop the window seat and peered up through the glass. She gasped as the brilliance of the night sky overwhelmed her vision.

Bright green lines that faded to turquoise rippled across the inky expanse, broken through with splashes of magenta and lavender. The corners of her lips lifted, following her inner rays as they woke to the undulating waves outside. The twirling lights brought back the energy she'd felt the night of her initiation, the sense of belonging and connection her conclave imparted. Her heart sank in her chest. Their chance of safety was stronger without her. Could she face them after Mara's death?

The lights lulled her back into the present. Iellieth sighed, scooting closer to the cool pane, her breath condensing in a light fog on the glass. "I've always wanted to see these."

Marcon's shoulders jumped as she looked up at him. He returned his gaze outside. "Why have you not seen them before, lady? You have journeyed here every two years, have you not?"

"For the festival, yes. But it's the wrong time of the year. Whatever fae magic causes them, it's not active during those first few weeks of spring when we're here. They must be casting charms elsewhere." The colors danced across the sky, a tide rolling out along the landless indigo ocean sprinkled through with stars. "It's even more beautiful than I had imagined."

"Breathtaking." Marcon's voice rumbled low just behind her, and a tingle ran up her spine.

Iellieth shivered. She should have added a sweater to the shift Kazimir had given her to wear between dress fittings.

"Here, lady." Marcon slipped out of his navy jacket and

draped it around her shoulders. Its warm glow surrounded her, like a hearth after a stroll on a crisp autumn evening.

"Thank you, Marcon." She pulled her hair free from the neckline of the jacket and tucked her ears beneath her locks lest anyone recognize the redheaded half-elf from Linolynn. "Should we go save Dimitri from Quindythias?"

A pained look flickered away from Marcon's face as she glanced up at him. His lips curled into a smile. "Yes, I think we should."

The elf and the librarian weren't on the main floor of the library. Iellieth and Marcon returned to their room to see if Quindythias might be waiting for them. He wasn't there. Iellieth glanced through the books he'd scattered across the table to see if he'd left a note. The door behind her slammed open, and she yelped in surprise.

Quindythias marched into the room, a roll of parchment beneath his arm. "Time to make a plan, my friends." He strode around the table, grasping one side of the parchment and tossing the other at Iellieth. Marcon caught the edge just in time.

She leaned away from the bright-eyed elf. "What are you—"

"We need to develop our plan of attack." Quindythias gestured to the desk by the window. "Grab a quill and ink from over there."

"Attack?" Iellieth sat up taller, looking over the rough sketch of the Arcanium, Hadvarian Palace, and Grand Reserve sprawled out in front of her. "Where did you get this?"

"Alright, heist if you like." The elf leaned down over the parchment, his fingers drumming against the tabletop as he grinned. "We'll start in the converted ballroom." He pointed at the lower floor of the Arcanium. "All we need to do from there is somehow get upstairs, steal the piece, sneak back out, spend a few more hours at the party—assuming we're enjoying ourselves —and then head back to Red's Cross. Any questions?"

Iellieth set the quill and ink he'd requested beside his confiscated map. "I have several. First, I still don't understand where you got this."

Quindythias marked the Arcanium's lower floor and Master Yugo's room with an *x*. "Your friend Dimitri doesn't use very complicated locks in the map room downstairs. It was only safe for me to conclude that he wanted me to take one of the spare copies after he left me alone."

"You stole this from Dimitri?"

Quindythias smirked. "I was going to give it back, but now I might keep it as a memento to remember the trip by, especially after we improve this copy with our notes." The elf frowned at her. "There's no need for you to look so offended. I only picked the lock. A pre-heist! I didn't hurt anyone."

Iellieth turned to Marcon.

"He does have a knack for, well—"

"Accessing. Unauthorized. Places." The elf's grin widened with each word. "Now, if we can refocus on the task at hand. Marcon, as you're not the sneakiest personage in our esteemed trio, why don't you be in charge of creating a distraction."

The champion nodded slowly.

Iellieth said, "Since Kazimir is so interested in Marcon, perhaps he could rope Kazi in on the distraction?"

Quindythias's eyes brightened. "Wonderful! Marcon, he'll play quite well off of your 'strong and silent' nature, so ask him for a dance or see if you can start a jig."

Marcon's lips compressed. "I doubt the steps have remained the same in our absence."

"You can always suggest that he start one of the Hadvarian line dances and teach it to you," Iellieth added.

"And what will you do, lady?"

"Ah, I know," Quindythias answered before she had a chance

to speak. "Iellieth, the crescent moon pendant on your wrist allows you to, umm, transform, is that right?"

Her eyebrows knit together. "Yes, but—"

"Perfect. You can come with me." He circled the base of the stairs that she and Master Yugo had climbed earlier that evening. "Be something small but not too small, and I'll store you in my pocket." His expression wrinkled in distaste. "No bugs and nothing slimy. I have a lovely silk vest for tomorrow."

Quindythias made them rehearse the plan several times before he allowed anyone to turn in for the night. Iellieth's idea for incorporating Kazi into their plans inspired Quindythias to involve Master Yugo as well. "While Kazimir is busy with you, Marcon, I will woo Master Yugo, and he can escort me upstairs." This, he assured them, was the most dependable part of their plan. "Once we get up to Master Yugo's room, Iellieth, you in tiny form will creep over, turn back into your normal-sized self, grab the piece, and dart out while I create a second temporary distraction, and then I'll follow you."

"And this secondary distraction will be . . ."

"Very successful," Quindythias answered. He sighed at her look of reproach. "I promise that Master Yugo won't come to any lasting harm, whatever approach I decide feels most fitting in the moment."

She grinned. "Very well, I trust you and your in-the-moment judgment."

After a round of role-play in which Quindythias asked her to play first Master Yugo and then Kazimir, Iellieth snuggled deeper into the down of her pillow. The galas she'd been forced to attend growing up would have been much more engaging had they held the promise of an adventure at the end. She wrapped her hand around her father's amulet. He had no way of knowing, almost twenty-three years ago, that he'd left Mamaun with the key his daughter would use to unlock a path to find him. She smiled, trying once more to imagine what he was like. Maybe some small part of him had sensed that leaving something behind would allow his love to return to him, just in a different way than he had originally intended.

The clouds overhead parted, and against the inky backdrop of the star-studded sky, the dancing emerald and amethyst glow of the northern lights played across her face and hair as she fell asleep.

CHAPTER 15

"And so Verdigris smiled at the swirls of life in the world around her, knowing that even though she left the other titans behind, her roots would form a world more beautiful than any they had yet imagined." Persephonie grinned at the crowd of delighted children. "Her lover, Izadra, wrapped Verdigris in her arms"—Persephonie hugged herself tightly—"dividing the titan into three as she wished, and thus the Shadowlands, Brightlands, and all the realms that we know as Azuria came to be."

The children gasped as they neared the end of the story. The various classes of the city mingled all around her, sharing smiles and seats, swept up together in the magic of the tale. Juliet sat erect at Persephonie's side, pleased to have such an enthusiastic audience.

She waved her arms high overhead to encompass the shape of the world tree. "The angels fluttered around the celestial spheres of the goddesses and gods." Persephonie paused as the children settled themselves, shushing those who had missed the stories of the day before. "And the demons aided the fiends below. But"—she sat up straighter, hands upraised by her shoulders—"the three aspects of Nature wondered, who would help those who walked the lands in between to find their path? Who would guide the residents of the Brightlands, Shadowlands, and Azuria on their way?" Persephonie leaned forward, and the children held their breath. "And then," she whispered, "the guardians appeared." Persephonie's eyes flashed, and she flicked the tips of her fingers out from her palms, creating a shower of violet and rose sparks overhead. The children squealed, squinting up at the cascade of colorful light.

A dark shadow fell across Persephonie, standing between her and the early morning sun. "Do you have a permit, storyteller?" The silhouetted guard tapped a heavy wooden baton against the heel of his beefy hand.

The older children looked up, eyes wide in fright. They grabbed their siblings and pulled them away from the circle, sandals pounding as they disappeared into the maze of city streets. The few remaining watched their new friends in confusion—they had not been taught to fear the guards.

"Why don't you all head home a little early for today?" Persephonie said as she stood, bending down to wipe the dust from her wrapped skirt. "We will learn more about the guardians next time." The children joined hands and scurried away, casting glances back at her over their small shoulders.

Two other guards flanked the first. They wore full beards and linen tunics rather than armor, thick hair coating their partially bare chests. The one on the right grazed his upper lip with his tongue, a growl gurgling from the base of his throat. Oversized canines protruded beneath his lip.

Persephonie's heart pounded in her chest. Her brothers had described werewolves' human bodies after their transformation, especially those more advanced in a pack. But the city wouldn't have gone so far as enlisting them to patrol the streets. It couldn't be safe.

The guard on the left pushed back his sleeves, revealing more thick hair. His large, protruding nose crinkled as he sniffed the air over her head, his sharp teeth glistening in a twisted grin. "You found a good one, Eustace." His lips curled back in a snarl. "One of theirs."

She slid back toward the tiled fountain behind her. If they truly were werewolves, she couldn't outpace them, not if they were allowed to transform. "You can't run from them," Velkan had said, kneeling in front of her brother Stefan, trying to calm him down after he and Felix were nearly killed by one of Lucien's packs. "Their instincts take over. They see blood and you, nothing else."

He'd glanced over at her as she approached, hands tight around her waist, trying not to cry at the sight of her brothers, wanting to ensure they hadn't been bitten. It was one of the first smiles from him that she'd received since they'd ended the romantic part of their relationship a few months before.

What she wouldn't give to have him and Felix at her side now, blades drawn, wearing the dark garb and face coverings they used to disguise their identity as saudad inside Azuria's more inhospitable cities.

The guard in front ran his eyes over her, tracing the path his hands would follow if he could catch his prey. Persephonie suppressed a shudder, hand gripping the dagger hilt poking out from the back waistband of her skirt to steady herself.

"Are guardians part of the Pantheon Supreme?" The more human-seeming guard tossed the question over his shoulder to the barely disguised lycanthropes.

"No." The toothy werewolf-guard's canines flashed as his grin deepened. "No, they are not." The rumble from the back of his throat struck Persephonie in the chest as she tried to calm her breathing. The street around them had grown eerily still. Andelce Hevra's citizens were well practiced at averting their gaze to avoid bearing witness to the unpleasantness that maintaining order entailed.

She reached out to the water spirits behind her. *Would you shield me, if only for a few moments?*

The fountain burbled in reply. *Will that be enough?*

The guards' gruff voices pulled her back to their empty accusations as her mind raced, sprinting ahead of her feet to plan an escape route. Simply running back to the Green Owl wouldn't work this time. They could track her there too easily.

"And what is the penalty for proselytizing false beliefs to impressionable young minds?" the first guard continued, his eyes lingering on the exposed skin of her neck and chest.

She pushed down the bile that rose in the back of her throat at the man's close inspection. Juliet poked her head around Persephonie's ankle and hissed at the three men. Her tiny paws stood firm on the cobblestones, reminding Persephonie she wasn't alone.

"There is a difference between proselytizing, as you call it, and telling a story, is there not?" The crease in her brows deepened as hooves cantered closer down the empty street. Had they already called for reinforcements?

The first guard turned and scowled at the approaching stallion, its dark mane flowing back toward its rider, sunlight gleaming in the rolls of muscles beneath its chestnut coat. Juliet glanced up at her and rubbed her head against Persephonie's leg. A wave of ease steadied the torrents of energy crashing within her.

The horse showed no signs of slowing, and the other two guards turned, hands upheld toward it.

"Halt!" the first guard finally cried.

The rider pulled back on the stallion's reins, and they slowed, swerving just in time to avoid the guards. He swung himself from the saddle and the horse continued its trot, coming to rest by his side.

"Just the fellows I was hoping to see." The rider's coppery brown eyes shone above his tawny beard, russet hair tied low at the base of his neck. "Here"—he handed the reins to the quietest of the werewolf guards without looking at him—"get Anelius some water." The werewolf guard clicked his tongue to the horse, trying to coax him toward the cool spray of the fountain. The rider stepped past her, long strides taking him to the fountain's edge. He bent over and splashed water onto his flushed face, sighing as the cool droplets settled over skin the color of pale sand, the damp fabric of his tunic clinging to his chest.

The other two guards leaned away from the man, their eyes fixed on his every movement, as though they prepared to flee. Juliet's tail danced as she watched the newcomer.

The man brushed his hands off, flecks of water darkening the cobblestones. He shot a bright smile in her direction, the grin accentuating a scar that slashed through the hair on his upper lip. "What seems to be the problem here, gentlemen?" He stood a few feet away from her, arms tucked behind his back, relaxed, with feet shoulder width apart.

"She was misleading the children, sir," the first guard who had stopped her began, his eyes struggling to meet those of the man beside her. Why did they give him so much deference? He carried a long rapier down by his side, and a dagger hilt poked out of his boot, but he wore no discernable markers of authority.

"Misleading which children?" His right eyebrow rose as he glanced around, theatrically searching the empty square for invisible children. "Well, they're certainly skilled at hiding, which entails its own troubles, I'm sure."

Persephonie's fingers loosened around the dagger at her back.

"She was telling stories about guardians," the second protested. In this man's presence, the wildness in his eyes receded, and a hesitant desire for praise took its place. Was this how they'd tamed the werewolves into service?

"The guiding spirits of Azuria and her neighbors? How marvelous!" The man clapped his hands together, his shoulders low and at ease. "What a pity I missed it. I was quite fond of those tales myself as a lad." He turned to Persephonie. "This was before the new laws, mind you. My mother was a gifted storyteller."

Persephonie stared back at him. She risked a small nod of encouragement.

"Gentlemen, I thank you for your service to the city, but I'm sure there are other concerns more worthy of the council's finest, aren't there?"

The human guard put up a hand in protest. "But, Patron Ignatius—"

That name was familiar. Where had she heard it?

"I'm sure my father will be pleased to hear he has such diligent guards patrolling the streets." A warning crept into the man's voice, and the guards flinched as though they'd been slapped. "However, I am sure a warning is sufficient in this case, is it not? Though I question whether the law goes so far as to forbid storytelling, however limiting it may be in other respects."

The Green Law forbade nature-based magic and the worship of deities outside those included in the Pantheon Supreme. But it was natural for her to weave Cassandra's tales for others. Without them, how would the children know how their world came to be?

"Very well." The first guard grimaced and cast a threatening glare in Persephonie's direction. "See that you keep your mouth shut from here forward, girl."

"Ah"—Patron Ignatius raised a finger, and the man jumped back—"is that any way to address such a pretty visitor to our fair city? What will our lovely guest here think of us?"

"Filthy traveler . . ." the guard grumbled under his breath to his companions in rapid Torstran. The words fell too quickly for her to catch and reassemble, but the man beside her reddened, a twinge in his jaw catching as his eyes narrowed.

Datha's voice echoed deep within her, soothing the cold stab of fear that seeped from the center of her spine at the guard's slur. "Though we may not be welcomed in every place, Sephie, we carry our worth within." He had laid her hand on her heart as he said it, completely enveloping her hand in his. "And there, it can never be taken away."

Patron Ignatius strode over to retrieve his horse's reins, snatching them out of the guard's trembling hand. He walked slowly to stand over the other two. "I'd proceed more carefully if I were you, Eustace." The werewolf scowled but said nothing, motioning to his companions that they should depart. The patron crossed his arms, glaring after their backs as they slunk off down the side street.

Persephonie sighed and sank onto the lip of the fountain, cold water seeping through her skirt onto the backs of her legs as the werewolves disappeared onto a side street. The water spirits danced behind her, soothing her with their gentle song.

"Are you alright, miss?" Patron Ignatius said, turning back to her. The glare from the sun shaded the expression of his eyes.

Ignatius. The senator behind the Green Law, the one forbidding the magic that flowed through her veins, who outlawed the worship of her heart goddess, Cassandra. This was his son.

Persephonie sprang up and away from the fountain, Juliet ready at her feet.

"Yes, thank you," she said quickly, pinning her skirt up to the side to help her hurry away.

"Wait, please." He held out a hand, confusion crinkling his face. "I don't intend you any harm." The coppery glimmer in his brown eyes tugged at her, pleading. "What is your name?"

Her mother's stern gaze burned in the back of Persephonie's mind, but this man had helped her to escape the guards. Why do so if he meant ill? "Persephonie, Patron Ignatius," she whispered.

His smile widened. "Call me Rennear."

Voices rose up beyond the fountain as Andel-ce Hevra's citizens returned to the deserted square. If her mother learned that she'd been speaking with the son of a senator, especially that of Senator Ignatius . . . "I really must be going." Persephonie stumbled toward the voices, narrowly avoiding the shimmering rim of the fountain.

Rennear hurried after her. "Wait, Persephonie—"

Juliet looked back and forth between them, her ears twisting toward the senator's son.

She would return to the tavern; that would be safe for now. And if not, Otmund would know what to do. She could wait there until the guards who had stopped her had retired for the day and then make her way to Aylin's home. Her mother would know more about Rennear Ignatius, and if she ever ran into him again, she would know the threat he posed to her and those like her.

Rennear caught her elbow before she could disappear into the crowd. "Not that way." He glanced down the alley. Her eyes followed his. At the alley's end, the three guards who had accosted her shouted at a merchant cowering before an overturned fruit stall. She leapt back away from them, directly into Rennear's chest. He let out a soft *oof* in surprise.

The patron led her back over beside his horse. The surrounding crowds on the city streets paid them no mind, going about their business again as though they hadn't vanished from this courtyard a short while before.

"Where is it you're trying to go?"

"Back to Green Owl, Rennear."

His eyes sparkled, and he stared down at her without answering, a half-smile caught on his lips.

CHAPTER 16

Iellieth spent the morning with Dimitri and a new store of
novels he'd been saving to share with her while she waited
for Kazimir to whisk her away to prepare for the ball.

"I have been particularly intrigued by this one," Dimitri said,
handing her a slight volume bound in dark blue leather. "In the
author's depiction, the sea functions as both setting and charac-
ter, shaping events and individual stories as she herself is shaped
by forces stretched through time, like the line of the coast or the
breath of the wind." His dark eyes gleamed. "It made me think
of you."

Iellieth glanced away and back at her friend. "I don't know
what to say." The book's cover was smooth and soft. "Thank
you."

Dimitri nodded. "Certainly." He pushed his chair over to a
stack of books on one of the round tables spread across the main
floor of the Reserve. The librarian peered at the covers,
searching through them and grumbling about the assistants
mingling their own stacks with his.

"Ah, here it is." Dimitri seized a garnet-colored book from

the middle of the second stack and rolled away from the table, turning back to Iellieth. "This is a beautifully rendered tale." Dimitri opened the leather binding and traced the gold script on the title page. "It is a rewriting of the legend of Hugh and Lilia, back at the beginning of the world." He placed the book in Iellieth's hand, and she flipped through the embossed pages. The scribe had used a delicate hand as their model for the text, the letters forming thin sepia scrawls down the page.

"Those names are familiar." Iellieth frowned and bit her lip, her memory pacing in front of her rounded bookshelves back in Io Keep, its long fingers trailing over the spines stamped in silver and gold. "Oh! That was one of the stories Katarina and I worked on for a short while." Iellieth sat up straighter, pleased by her recollection. Something had halted Katarina's study of that particular folktale, but what had it been? That time was early on in their studies together, but the memory blurred. Iellieth pushed the book toward Dimitri, but he held his palms out, directing it back to her.

"Please, I would love for you to have it." He reached behind the counter and pulled out an identical copy. "Did I tell you that we have a new scribe who has bewitched up to six quills at once?" He grinned as he held out his hands with the fingers narrowed to a point, waving them through the air like a musical conductor as the scribes did for their magical incantations. Each scribe had only to read the words, and their enchanted quills would record the texts for them.

Dimitri shook his head. "She is truly extraordinary. Ah!" He gestured toward the entryway of the Grand Reserve as Kazimir brushed aside the student who tried to greet him at the door. "Your escort is here." Dimitri winked at her, smirking at the primping and preening she was sure to endure beneath Kazimir's watchful eye.

"I've come to escort her away from this dreadful place,"

Kazimir exclaimed. Several scholars scowled, torn from the reverie of their studies.

Dimitri's laugh echoed through the large lower chamber. "And if I were to say the same later today?"

"She would never consent to leaving one of my galas early." Kazimir glared in Iellieth's direction as though she'd threatened exactly this and forced Dimitri into service as a messenger of ill tidings.

"No, that would never happen." Dimitri cast a quick look at her over his shoulder—he'd helped her do precisely that on multiple occasions during the Festival of Renewal, though admittedly never during one of Kazimir's special events.

The socialite's eyes brightened as Marcon emerged from behind one of the stacks.

"I was just going to come and look for you," Iellieth said to Marcon, pushing herself off of the desk she'd been leaning against. She turned back for the novels the librarian had left in her care. "Would you take these for me and put them with our belongings? If past experience is any indication, Kazi has the entire rest of the afternoon filled with preparations until the gala begins."

"That's right." Kazimir strutted forward and bowed delicately to Marcon before returning his attention to Iellieth. "No sense wasting those pretty eyes of yours on books. We have relaxing, grooming, and primping to do!" His voice grew louder as he listed their activities, gesturing excitedly with the importance of their plans. Swirling winds of irritation swept around them from the shelved reaches of the room.

Marcon's brow furrowed as he watched Kazimir. He took the books from Iellieth's hands and tucked them under his arm. "And how will we find you, lady?"

"I'll meet you at the entrance to the Arcanium. Kazi will arrange it and ensure you're in the right place at the right time."

She glanced at her friend, who gave her a dramatic wink. Iellieth smiled. "He will insist on it, actually. More elegant and exciting that way," she added with a whisper.

Marcon grinned. "Then I will see you tonight." He raised her hand and kissed her knuckles, his lips sending a sparkling surge of warmth down her arm.

Iellieth's mouth parted to speak—*what was he*—but Kazimir swept between them, pulling on her other wrist and tugging her out of the library. "We're running la-ate," he exclaimed in a singsong voice.

She glanced back to Marcon and Dimitri. They watched her go with puzzled smiles.

⚬✦⚬

KAZIMIR GUIDED HER OUT OF THE GRAND RESERVE AND through an enclosed courtyard that overlooked the cottages spread across the plateau below. Sparkling frost clung to the dark rooftops and curling tendrils of smoke rose from chimneys. "I apologize for yanking you away from your handsome friend," Kazimir teased as she stopped to stare down at the city, "but we have so much to do this afternoon." His shoulders squeezed toward his ears, lifting up with his smile. "You can pretend to be as bored with the pampering as you wish, but I think you'll enjoy it."

"Kazi, I wasn't trying to make you feel as though I didn't want to spend the day with you. Won't you be occupied with preparations for the gala this evening, though?" Iellieth's borrowed heels clicked against the marble flooring as she hurried to keep pace with her friend.

"I'll be in and out, but I've set aside my best stylists to help ready my party's brightest star." His grin flashed wider.

"You can't possibly mean me." A chill ran down Iellieth's

spine. She'd already explained to him that she was here under a disguise, at least until she could uncover what had transpired between the queen and King Arontis. "Kazi, my presence—"

"Is a secret." He waved his hand absentmindedly. "I know, I know." Kazimir stopped suddenly outside the door to his hall and whirled around to face her, raising an eyebrow. "Never you fear, Lady Lilith. What would you say to . . . a masquerade ball?"

The gilt-framed white marble doors swung open to unveil a world of swirling colors. Young men and women darted across the wide entryway, trailing feathered scarves and trying on gem-colored masks dripping with crystals, beads, and feathers.

Iellieth took a half-step back, her eyes wide as she tried to take in the twirling tapestry unfurled before her. "Kazi, I . . ."

"Am speechless!" He clapped his hands together and spun to observe the first private act of the elaborate show he'd arranged. Kazimir sighed, lowering his shoulders, and gestured for her to follow him. "The idea occurred to me shortly after your arrival last night, and I have been incredibly busy bringing it all together in time. I mean, if anyone *else* had tried to pull this off, it would have been impossible, but for myself . . ." He chuckled and shook his head. "Let's just say it may be my greatest achievement to date."

Kazimir glided ahead of her, weaving in and out of the dancers, performers, and costumers. Pieces of his monologue of self-praise drifted back to Iellieth—his red-and-gold gala the year before, the time he commissioned his entire cast of performers to be painted as frozen glass statues . . .

A tall woman in a peacock mask stood posed dramatically, one hand outstretched behind her, the other draped in front, as the costumers meticulously affixed feathers to her closely knit garment formed from a fishnet.

Iellieth followed Kazimir through the crowded hallway and another set of white gilded doors that he clicked shut behind them. Running water trickled nearby, and the heavy aroma of candles lifted by heady floral perfumes trailed through her senses. Tension she hadn't realized was there melted off the tops of her shoulders.

"Much better, isn't it?" Kazimir whispered. "This way." Golden half-columns dotted the three long hallways that opened from this arched antechamber. The passageways, though their ceilings were lower, retained the rounded arches common to Hadvar's architecture. Kazi took the central hallway and disappeared into the third doorway.

Around the corner, a series of steps led to a steaming bath covered in violet and sapphire tiles embedded in the floor. A bowl of sun-warmed herbs and dried rose petals sat at the pool's edge, alongside stoppered bottles of bath perfumes. "I believe the scents will be to your liking, but test them first." Kazimir smiled. "I'll have Venetta in to attend to you shortly."

"Kazi, this is—"

"I know, I know," he interrupted, "just right." His eyes sparkled. "You're welcome." Kazimir slipped out of the room.

CHAPTER 17

Briseras scowled at the small hamlet clustered in the valley below. What if the accounts Everett had collected were mistaken and the werewolf pack simply hadn't bothered to raid these cottages? They huddled closely together, trapped between the shadows of the mountains and the forest—perhaps they didn't have any strong hunters or foragers who would make a useful addition to the lycanthropes.

Everett thumbed through his journal, his eyes bright as he gazed down on the thatched roofs. "They can help us, Briseras. I know it."

She adjusted the strap of her crossbow. "Because they have stories?" Since the day Rajas had taken her away from Haven, Briseras had studied the foul creatures that roamed Azuria and how to eliminate them. Caldara's peasants, like their counterparts she had been forced to consult on the other side of the world, would tell local versions of the legends with a few details unique to the region. But in her hunts, Briseras had found that the creatures held fewer secrets than lore or villagers liked to believe.

The folklorist sighed and slid his satchel off his shoulder. He settled onto the ground beside it, his journal open on his lap. "It's not just that they have stories but what the stories *reveal*."

Vera poked at the bag with her nose. In addition to an over-abundance of books and journals, Everett stored dried meat in his bag. He'd won the black wolf over by sharing some with her on their first day together.

Briseras squinted at the two of them. For three days straight, Everett had read her selections from his journal, accounts he'd gathered from remote villages across the mountain range that had led them here. After that first meeting when he disrupted her pursuit of the pack, she had been ready to dismiss him, but one tale had caught her attention—a ring of settlements that went untouched by the ravenous creatures, where only a few people disappeared year after year.

Her pulse had quickened, and her instincts hummed. That was where they needed to go.

The folklorist had been more than happy to sketch out a map of the settlements. They formed a near-perfect circle that, by the neighboring villagers' accounts, the lycanthropes avoided.

"What lies in the center of this area?" Briseras had asked, her fingertip pressing into the still-wet ink. She brought the spreading mark closer to her face as the liquid black seeped into her umber-toned skin. *This is all you need to know about these creatures*, she wanted to say. *Their touch ebbs and taints. They are a pestilence that must be eradicated, not understood.*

Everett's enthusiasm had nestled beneath a chink in her closely guarded core, but she would find a way to remove him once they reached a place of safety. The folklorist patted a spot on the ground beside him. "You should eat something before we travel down to the village."

Briseras frowned. She'd lost track of the number of times she'd been labeled a harbinger and banished from a village. Ignorance saw little difference between a threat and that which chased it, especially when death fluttered at the heels of each. Her own full stomach would do nothing to alleviate the distaste she would undoubtedly leave in the villagers' mouths. Surrounded by a semblance of a society, would their certain fear of outsiders, their sense that something about her was wrong, dangerous, drive Everett away as well?

By their second day of travel, she perceived that to him, she remained a puzzle to be solved. His carefully ordered world was one full of possibility, of nuances locked behind doors to which stories held the key. But she knew the truth. Scant few stood in the ether between life and death, cursed and free. She was one of only a handful of the living who could attest—there was nothing intoxicating about beings that walked in the shadows of myth. When pierced by one of her arrows, they bled like the rest.

Everett held up a red apple for her, returning her awareness to the mountainside. "Will you let me do the talking when we get down there?" His teeth tore through the thick crust of their stale traveling bread, the sound of muscle ripping from flesh. "I've been through this area before. The herbalist, Hannah, knows much of the surrounding region. If anyone can tell us more about the werewolves' ring and the longer history of disappearances, it's her." He took another bite and propped his hand on his knee. "I've been wanting to speak with her more anyway." Everett swept the remaining hunk of bread from side to side, indicating the settlement. "They warned me away from her on my first visit here. The villagers all say she's a witch."

Briseras raised an eyebrow. Her mother had been captured and sent to Haven on similar charges. She hadn't realized that those who dealt in spirits were active in Caldara too. "And still you chose to speak with her?" Where she'd grown up outside of Andel-ce Hevra, there were few brave enough to risk the council's ire by associating with practitioners of witchcraft. Rajas had been one such person. Perhaps the folklorist was braver than she'd first thought.

"Of course." He washed down his last bite with a gulp from his canteen. "In my experience, it's those on the outside who tend to have the most useful information." A smile flashed across his face as he looked at her.

"Take me to this Hannah, then. We shall see."

❦

EVERETT LED BRISERAS TO THE HERBALIST'S COTTAGE ON THE far edge of the village, tucked into the shady embrace of the encroaching forest. Otto had swept down to join them, gliding onto her shoulder as they reached the doorway.

She sat silently with the elderly human woman, Hannah, while Everett searched through the jars and clay pots that covered her counters for a special tea. Unless it had powerful warding properties, Briseras didn't see why one selection of dried and ground leaves mattered over another. At the folklorist's urging, while he continued to look, Hannah told her about the ring of villages that remained untouched by the werewolf pack.

"But why would they avoid this region? Is there no one satisfactory here for them to hunt?" Briseras studied the herbalist. She was an unlikely target for the pack, though a village of people like her would have had little chance at survival. There had to be at least a few capable hunters among them. Unless . . . "The concoction he's searching for, it is one of protection, isn't it?"

The old woman smiled. "It is." Golden light flared behind dark brown irises as her gaze met Briseras's. "You know much of these plants, do you not, Shadow-Touched?"

She said it as a name and a spell at once, an attempt to intuit

Briseras's motivations. Though the priests had forbidden her mother's practice, she continued to work smaller castings, the incantations sounding no different from mumbled speech to those not trained to listen. Briseras drew herself up taller, resisting the herbalist's charm. The old woman had sensed enough about her already.

Vera crouched at her feet, a warning growl prickling in the back of her throat.

"What's that, Hannah?" Everett rushed over and stood between them, looking back and forth at Briseras and the witch.

"I mean no harm to your friend who lives between the realms." Hannah withdrew a glass pendant from beneath her tunic. Rosemary, sage leaves, and a sprig of cinnamon rested inside the vial. "Just as she means no harm to me."

Briseras dragged her thumb across the dagger hilt hidden at the end of her sleeve. "That is yet to be determined."

Everett knelt in front of the old woman. "Hannah, we came seeking your help. It's not a trick."

She clutched her pendant in her fist. "I had to be sure." The golden glow faded as she turned from him back to Briseras. "There is a verdant glow about you, as well as a grasping shadow. How?"

Briseras crossed her arms and leaned back against her upright wooden chair. "Neither pertains to the creatures we seek."

The wrinkles around the witch's eyes crinkled. "Do they not?" She giggled to herself. "I would not be so sure, Shadow-Touched."

She refused to grant the old woman the satisfaction of a response. If the herbalist wished to share nothing more with them than trivialities Briseras preferred to keep hidden, they should leave. A few hours of daylight remained. She could find the pack's trail and return to her original pursuit. Briseras glared at the door.

"A dark castle lies deep in the forest." The old woman patted Everett's hand on the arm of her chair and struggled to her feet. She hobbled to each of her windows in turn and drew the heavy curtains closed. "Inside, the risen blood of an ancient evil paces during the day and stalks beyond the estate's borders at night. By his orders, the werewolves do not enter this domain. They save our blood for him." The few candles dispersed about the room flickered to life, their narrow flames sputtering as though they struggled against a sudden draught.

"What is this risen evil of which you speak?" Briseras gripped the curved wooden arms of her chair. Her hunter's senses roamed wider, bounding across the lots nearby, darting deeper into the forest. Vera's ears pricked up at her feet.

The golden glow returned to Hannah's eyes. The old woman's hand trembled as she raised it and pressed her fingertips to the base of her neck . . . to the same spot where Briseras bore the four white scars of a vampire's bite. "I believe you already know." Gold blotted out the ring of brown in the old woman's eyes, and the cabin around them faded. The tang of ash burned Briseras's nostrils. "You first sensed him weeks ago, when you bid farewell to the one who is dear to you." The golden orbs narrowed. "Rajas."

Briseras sprang to her feet. "That's enough." Asking about the lingering nature of Ophelia's healing after Malthael's bite was one thing, but she wouldn't discuss what had transpired between herself and Rajas. Vera leapt up after her, head lowered and teeth bared. "We're leaving."

Everett bumped into a small wooden table, and several jars toppled beneath his hands. His brow knit in confusion. "But, Briseras, we just arrived, and—"

Otto's croak rattled against the windows. A flurry of herbs burst into the air as he flapped his wings.

She grabbed Everett's arm and pulled him toward the door.

Hannah lunged after them, her eyes wide and searching. Her hands groped to catch Briseras. "The ring of protection will not long last, Briseras Ravisthinia. You cannot leave. He has been waiting for one such as you. Once you step across, it begins. You condemn us to our death."

A brook babbled beneath Hannah's words. It had been too long since Briseras had encountered someone with her mother's magic. Hannah was casting a spell to bind her to the cottage or to entwine Briseras's fate with that of someone else. The nature of the spell mattered not. Briseras struggled free of Hannah's incantations and propelled herself over the threshold.

The witch's voice rose to a shriek. "This valley and all who dwell in it will soon die. You alone can return the creature from thence he came. Then, in the castle black as night, you will meet your destiny."

Briseras slammed the door shut in Hannah's face. She yanked Everett, addled and pale, after her into the dark of the forest.

Unable to teach her daughter spells outright, her mother had taken special care to teach Briseras to resist their power, hoping that one day, her daughter would learn the magic of her birthright. "The spirits will overtake you if you let them," she had explained. "But you are strong, Briseras. They will not be able to subdue you." The priests had burst in moments later. She would never forget the leer of delight on their faces at catching her mother teaching witchcraft. They'd yanked Briseras out into the square and pressed a searing poker into her palm. She tightened her fist against the memory's scar, burning flesh, her mother's screams melding with her own.

Everett fell against a thick trunk, clutching his chest as he drew a deep, ragged breath. "What was that?" He clung to the bark.

"I'm not certain, but we broke whatever charm she was attempting to cast. She's frightened of something she's foreseen and has convinced herself that its coming to pass is connected to us." Briseras scowled. She *had* broken free of Hannah's spell, she was almost certain.

His eyes searched the forest, waiting for the elderly woman to spring out at them from the undergrowth.

They'd delayed long enough. When she tried to guide them deeper into the shelter of the trees, Everett grabbed her arm. "Briseras." He held tight, panting for breath. "I'm sorry. I had no idea that would happen."

Briseras peered at him more closely. She'd seen that look in a creature's eyes countless times before. But this time, the gazer wasn't frightened of her . . . Everett was afraid *for* her. Her pulse slowed, and Briseras smiled. "Stay with me long enough, and you'll grow to expect it." She clapped him on the shoulder and wrenched her arm free. "We need to keep moving."

The folklorist hurried after her through the trees, digging through his bag of stories to record the encounter. She shook her head. Darker forces loomed. If the witch was right, a vampire awaited them, drifting in the mist of the days soon to come.

CHAPTER 18

Iellieth leaned her head back against the tiled edge of the bath. The harried sparks of magic that had flickered at her fingertips since the revenant's attack fizzled, unwinding and stretching back through her hands and forearms, sinking deep into her muscles. They would come to her aid if she needed them. But for now, they grew their roots deeper.

She closed her eyes and drifted back to the similar preening experience she'd had during the festival two years before. So much had changed since then, and yet—her jaw clenched—the chilling grasp of her memories remained. The familiar cadence of nagging recollections drowned out the relaxing scents of the bath. She should have known the duke had something special planned. He'd left her alone the entirety of their trip, hadn't pushed suitors on her or hosted special luncheons or dinners. Kazimir had supervised her preparations for each night's gala instead of Mamaun, and she'd spent the afternoon before the final ball relaxing in a hot water pool almost identical to this one. But that night, the last evening of the celebration, the duke kept appearing before her, constantly whispering in the ear of some Hadvarian nobleman or other, a cruel glint in his eye when he spotted her watching.

It was the curl of her stepfather's lip that had done her in and driven her outside where the true object of his aims waited for her, perfectly arranged. Iellieth shivered despite the pool's heat, trying to rid her body of the memory of her encounter with Lord Stravinske.

She shook her head and inhaled deeply, inviting the herbs to traipse through her senses once more. Rising slightly, she let the cool air lick across her shoulders, and she glided over to the bottles of perfume beside the sunken tub.

"Iellieth," a tenor voice whispered from the doorway.

"Ah!" she shouted and slunk back into the water. Dark eyebrows flashed in self-satisfied delight as Quindythias strolled into the room and perched atop the pile of towels balanced on a golden stool. "What are you doing here?" Iellieth wrapped her arms around her chest and scowled up at the elf.

"I came to see you, of course." He crossed one knee over the other and propped his chin on his hand. "Not to *see* you, see you. Though you should relax. It's nothing I haven't seen before."

She had no idea how to respond.

Quindythias sighed. "Anyway, did you know that this is a masquerade?" He grinned and leaned down.

Iellieth's shoulder struck the edge of the pool as she inched away from him. "Yes, Kazi told me. I was going to try to find you . . . later." *When I wasn't naked and in a bath*, she wanted to add. "Have you figured out how this changes our plan?"

"Yes, though I welcome your input, especially if it agrees with what I've already decided."

She laughed in spite of the awkward situation Quindythias had suddenly conjured. "I'll do my best." Iellieth squinted up at the elf, working through the new opportunities a masquerade presented to them. "Have you seen Kazimir's mask by any chance?"

"I doubt it," a smooth feminine voice answered.

Both she and Quindythias froze as a woman with deep blue skin and curled sapphire horns appeared from the side passage. Iellieth had seen a few negata at the balls in Hadvar but had never had an opportunity to speak with them before.

"Pardon," the woman said, "I didn't mean to startle you."

"No, that's alright," Iellieth stammered, "I wasn't sure when someone was coming, and he . . ." She couldn't think of an appropriate reason for Quindythias to be visiting her bath or recall his secret identity.

Quindythias sprang to his feet. "Lord Havastrias Shade, at your service." He bowed. "A close personal friend of Lilith's."

The negata's extra set of canines sparkled as she smiled. "I can give you more time if you like." She lightly crossed one of her arms over the other and leaned against the gleaming tiled wall.

"No, that won't be necessary." Iellieth pushed herself over toward the stack of towels. "We were simply planning a surprise for Kazi at the gala but weren't sure, umm, how best to pull it off."

Quindythias rose and took several steps back as the woman drifted around the sunken pool, her hips pressing against the edges of her black shift dress. "What sort of surprise?" She chuckled at the rapid exchange of glances between Iellieth and Quindythias. "I'm Venetta. Here"—she lifted Iellieth's slip off the stool and opened a large, fluffy towel. Venetta met her at the pool's edge and turned her head to the side.

"Thank you," Iellieth said. The negata wrapped the towel around her and picked up another for her hair. "We thought it might be fun to engage in . . . an identity swap." Her eyes brightened as the idea began to come together.

Venetta laughed. "That does sound intriguing." She raised an arched brow as she studied Quindythias. "Lord Shade, will you be participating as well?"

"Yes," Iellieth interjected for him. "He would like to disguise himself as Kazimir for the masquerade."

Quindythias frowned at the two of them. "But he and I don't look anything alike." The elf laid his hands on his stomach and thrust his hips forward, trying to create the impression of Kazimir's round belly.

"Not yet." Venetta grinned. "Come along, we've much to do before the masquerade." Venetta ushered them out of the bathing chamber and down the right-side hall. She exchanged Iellieth's towel for a silk robe and procured one for Quindythias as well before escorting them to a private salon that overlooked an enclosed garden.

Iellieth grinned at the green plants that gazed up at the sun, dreaming of their native southern climes but contained by glass overhead.

"I appreciate the view too," Venetta said from close behind Iellieth's ear. She unwrapped her hair and directed her to one of the two leather chairs in the center of the room. "It took a while to persuade the other costumers that we should have it, but we eventually prevailed."

Before Iellieth could ask whom she was referring to, a second negata drifted out of the side chamber, pushing a cart laden with hair implements, shimmering metallic pots, and thin brushes. "My brother, Elric." The familial resemblance was readily apparent in their facial features, though Elric kept his hair short and swept back behind his horns, and his coloring was more cobalt than indigo.

Elric rubbed his hands together as he studied them. "What

promising work we have cut out for ourselves today, no?" His bark of laughter echoed across the circular room as Venetta relayed the plan for Quindythias to impersonate Kazimir for the evening. The plants sighed, breathing in the sudden flash of energy.

Quindythias warmed to the idea of his disguise beneath the negata's careful attention. Elric mumbled under his breath as he applied costume paint to Quindythias's skin, transforming his deep brown glow to Kazimir's lighter bronze.

Venetta's voice was low and husky as she swept Iellieth's curled locks into an elegant twist to reveal the line of her neck and her pointed ears. "Lucky for me, Lilith, your appearance this evening won't require any special magic."

Iellieth smiled at the compliment. "Do you think we could keep my ears covered, though?"

Venetta narrowed her dark, gold-rimmed eyes. "Are you ashamed of your elven heritage?" She traced the tip of Iellieth's ear and stared at her, head and horns tilted to the side.

"No," Iellieth answered quickly, "but I'm trying to . . . hide from someone." She bit her lips together.

Venetta's scowl deepened. "Is this the other person you came here with?"

A muffled rebuttal burst from Quindythias's closed, painted lips, but a sharp look from Elric quieted him.

Iellieth shook her head. "No, not Colabra, or Lord Havastrias here." A smile she couldn't help spread across her face. "They take care of me. We're . . ." *Friends*, her mind answered, but that didn't seem to adequately describe their relationship. *Companions who are bound to one another.*

"Hmm. Shall we say a curious set of travelers who wish to go undetected for now with clever disguises?" Venetta raised an eyebrow.

She sighed. "Yes, that's perfect."

"Very well, ears concealed." Venetta released the clips holding back Iellieth's hair. Waves of red curls spilled over her shoulders. The negata's lips pursed as she observed her client from arm's length away. "I know just the thing." She stepped back and set to work.

CHAPTER 19

U nder any other circumstance, Iellieth would have refused the dress Kazimir had selected for her for the masquerade ball. But she had no retort when he smirked and pointed out that it was a dress *Iellieth Amastacia* would never wear. He was right about that, and he refused to accept that it was one Lilith—he had a clear vision of Quindythias's improvised identity for her—wouldn't have worn either.

The gown was made of rippling obsidian silk, a windswept ocean beneath a cloud-dampened sky, with all the stars blotted out above. The bodice fit snugly around her chest and ribs, hugging past the curve of her waist to the top of her hips where the gown released, the dark sea set free to roam as it wished. Tiny straps looped over her shoulders and curved around to the back of the gown, joining the plunging line of the dress beneath the small of her back where the lacing began. The neckline was lower than she would ever have allowed Mamaun to select for her, perfectly mirroring the curve of her breasts and falling away at the center with additional thin strands joining together around a circular golden clasp.

The negata, fascinated by her stories of the druids, had painted her right shoulder and arm in a swirling floral design reminiscent of many Iellieth had seen in the camp, only in black rather than green, brown, or gold. She had left her hair loose, arranging the long waves into graceful cascades that drifted over her shoulders, teasing tendrils at the bare stretch of her back.

Elric grinned as he finished painting Quindythias's cheeks, giving them a light flush. "Lord Shade, er, Kazimir and I, will leave the final reveal for the ballroom, shall we? See if you can distinguish which Kazimir is which?"

Quindythias winked at her as he rose. "I'll be the taller, more handsome one, obviously." He hunched and angled his hips forward once more, affecting an overexaggerated impersonation of Kazimir's walk. "See you soon, Lilith." He waved as he waddled out of the room.

Venetta smiled after him. She added a final swipe of dark liner to Iellieth's lids before she placed a jeweled eye mask made of gold filigree over her eyes and the bridge of her nose. The mask was similar to the dagger sheath Scad, her closest friend in Linolynn, had made for her. Intricate branches laden with tiny strands of flowering vines intertwined along the length of her mask. The golden limbs ended in narrow, leafy tines. As Venetta tucked the mask's pins into the waves of her hair, Iellieth thought about the alabaster wolf she'd found in the catacombs beneath Io Keep. She carried it in Mara's bag, hoping it would somehow help her recover her missing friend.

The negata added slender, dangling earrings, each ending in a blood-red ruby, to match her amulet, which rested against the center of her chest. "Stunning," Venetta said, stepping back to admire her work. Iellieth turned toward the large oval mirror, her peridot irises gleaming more brightly even than the gold and red jewels in her ears.

The real Kazimir appeared in the doorway and clapped his hands together. "I just *knew* the two of you would get along! Lilith, you shall be my masterpiece this evening. Well, besides myself of course." He tittered and gave a short, signature bow, puffed lavender sleeves sweeping out and away from the plum, violet, and gold of his ensemble.

"Kazi, I can't—"

"Agh, I know, I *know*. But come"—he swept forward to collect her and take her over to the Arcanium—"one of your intriguing companions has been waiting for you for some time. I don't know where the other has gotten to."

Iellieth and Venetta exchanged a significant look. She seized the negata's hand and thanked her for all of her assistance and care that afternoon. Venetta closed her eyes and bowed her head, smiling in reply.

"Come along, come along," Kazi urged, stamping his small velvet shoes.

Iellieth grinned and followed his lead to join the grand masquerade ball.

Her heart rate quickened as they reached the end of the gilded hall that led from the palace to the Arcanium. Marcon would be waiting on the other side of the arched doors.

She steadied her breathing as Kazimir nodded to the attendants. The moment he and Elric were finished, Quindythias's curiosity would have carried him toward the myriad possibilities of one of Kazimir's balls. The elf had assured her that she needn't worry about him running across Kazi at the gala. "People like your friend and I, we tend to draw a crowd. It's those like you, who draw attention without obvious onlookers, who need to worry about standing out."

A trio of Hadvarian noblewomen to her right tittered as they adjusted each other's masks. Slowly, the doors swung open. Quindythias could have been wrong about her drawing attention to herself. And beneath her mask, it was at least less likely that Lord Stravinske or one of her other suitors would recognize her. A slight hush fell as she and Kazimir stepped into the onyx entryway. Iellieth's stomach flipped. Many of the faces had turned to stare at her.

The glow of Marcon's olive skin caught her eye to the left, and she spun toward him as he stepped out from the crowd, his gray eyes bright behind his midnight mask.

"My lady"—he reached out for her hand and bowed—"would you allow me to escort you this evening?" The low rumble of his voice sent a flurry of sparks swirling around her stomach.

"Yes, Colabra, I would."

He smiled at the false name. The room around them remained still. Marcon laid his fingers gently against the base of her spine and guided her out toward the converted halls of the Arcanium.

Whorls of music wrapped the pair of them in their embrace, sweeping down the marble corridors and pulling them nearer.

Iellieth's breath hitched at her first sight of the glittering world Kazimir had conjured inside the onyx halls of the Arcanium. Colored glass illuminated by orbs of light covered the dark walls. The orbs swirled—the glass panes held running water, joined together as a multicolored aquarium, shimmering over the top of what had been ominous, almost oppressive, and now sparkled with light.

Her lips fell open as she gazed around. Marcon's eyes caught the light as he stared down at her. "Will you dance with me, Lilith?"

The back of her tongue was dry as the energy held at her core sparkled upward in gouts of glittering flame. This was nothing like the stuffy balls she'd attended before, the gold and ivory horrors of the past five years with greedy suitors lurking behind every decorated column. Here, beneath the twirling lights and the bejeweled sea, she could be anyone she wished . . . and with whomever she wanted to be. "I would love to, Colabra."

Polite applause rippled out from among the guests as Marcon led her onto the dance floor, the muscles of his arm pressing against the lines of his coat.

His hand was a warm pressure against her back as he swept her out onto the floor. The looming weight of their heist drifted away from her to dwell among the glimmering panes of rainbow glass. She spun out and back in, watching the smile across his wide lips as he waited to receive her and hold her close.

Her hair drifted over her shoulders, following its own slower current as they danced. The sparks of magic around the room coalesced inside her, bursting out from the points where her skin met his, escaping with a laugh or smile, blurring the world around them.

Above her, the dark ceiling beckoned, watching, waiting.

Iellieth froze, a stab of ice sinking into her side. The sparks fumbled against one another, their rhythm lost. Marcon slowed their dance to a stop. Iellieth shuddered.

Lord Stravinske was here. He'd seen her.

Tears clouded the bottom of her eyes as she looked up at Marcon. His smile faded. "What is it, lady?"

"We need to go outside. Now."

THE COLD TWILIGHT OF THE BALCONY ENVELOPED IELLIETH AS she pulled Marcon after her toward the railing. Each step brought her nearer to the stretch of forest beneath the plateau and cast a wider blanket of stars above. She gripped Marcon's hand, her anchor in the storm of energy reeling inside her. Would the swirling lights of the night sky come to her aid if she needed them?

Other couples drifted across the terrace, lost in each other's eyes. Clammy fingertips crawled along Iellieth's skin, an embedded memory.

Each breath came in short gasps. A leering smile. Black eyes against a black sky. A sneering voice, laughing at her.

"Lady." Marcon's voice called her back. A tear escaped and trickled onto the branching filigree of her mask.

"He's here . . ." Her eyes danced over Marcon's face, searching for a ledge that would snatch her out of her freefall. "The one I told you about, but I left out . . ." Her breath rasped, and the words clawed against her throat, banding together against her. *But I left out what happened the last time I saw him, on a balcony much like this one. I couldn't risk you seeing me the way all of them did. For so long, as nothing. Or a pretty thing to be used. And I cannot bear that life anymore.*

Marcon pulled her into his chest, his hand holding the back of her hair. His body swept around her like a shield of golden wings.

"Excuse the interruption." A slimy voice wriggled against the sparkling night, its ooze blotting out the stars.

Lord Vladislav Stravinske had found her. A mindless cold melted around Iellieth's heart, obliterating her magic in a torrent of black energy that burbled across every recess and cranny of her being.

And in the absence of the sparks, a foul entity pressed its consciousness against hers, a frigid shoulder slamming into her, alone in the dark.

She shut her eyes tighter, but the seething tendrils remained. Beneath the jagged recollections of the assault, the threatened marriage, the disbelief and denial, there was a flash as soiled yellow eyes opened, casting light against a sickening, gray-green face. Layers of fungus swelled, forming skin over the open cavity of a decaying throat. Lucien, the lich who murdered Mara, grinned at her from out of the shadows of her mind.

"Time to turn around, my sweet," the airy baritone hissed all around her, slithering through her nasal passages and clogging her breath.

Marcon's arms tensed in their shield around her. Could he hear Lucien? She buried her head deeper into his chest, burrowing away from the prickly mind that latched on to hers, its barbs piercing her hands as she shoved it away.

"Don't be so rude to our mutual acquaintance, my dear." The yellow eyes narrowed as he smiled, and the shadowy mage leaned down to whisper in her ear. "I arranged this treat just for you."

CHAPTER 20

Persephonie settled into the worn wood of her favorite booth in the corner of the Green Owl. The mottled stained glass window cast shimmering specters in amethyst and ruby across the polished tabletop, winking in the emerald glass of Otmund's goblets. Juliet leapt onto the booth seat beside her, curling up for her midmorning nap.

Rennear signaled to Tess as he slid opposite Persephonie into the booth. They nodded that they would be over shortly.

"If I may be so bold, Persephonie, why were you headed to this particular tavern?"

"I work here and live upstairs. Otmund said to always come straight back if I ran into trouble outside."

Rennear studied the colorful glass panes and quiet patrons with heads bowed over steaming cups of coffee and tea around the tavern. "Have you encountered trouble often in the city?"

Persephonie grinned. "You might say that it stays on the lookout for me." Tess approached with a tray of coffee, eggs, and fresh-baked bread. "I do not understand how I keep doing things wrong." She shook her head. "Is it not usual to tell stories to the children? How will they know where they are from?"

Rennear thanked Tess for their food and turned back to Persephonie. The half-elf lingered beside their table, staring at him. They flashed their eyebrows to Persephonie before spinning away back into the kitchen. Rennear seemed oblivious to the entire wordless exchange.

"Children learn the origins of the city in school," he explained. "Well, the ones from the higher classes do. The others learn trades, and stories, I suppose, from their parents."

"Why do all of the children not learn the same things?" She frowned over her coffee. The fresh tang of smoke sharpened the beans' earthiness. "And I am not certain the schools are helping them so much. They knew nothing of Verdigris." The saudad immersed their children in stories from birth as part of the mantle of their people's culture and memory.

"Ah, but is it not enough for them to learn the storied history of the city, the greatest civilization in all of Azuria?" Rennear waved his hand grandly as he spoke, but the gleam in his bronze eyes separated his thoughts from the city's official teachings. "And of course, they must learn the tales of our great heroes, and the Pantheon Supreme."

This narrow subset of deities kept recurring around her, like a boring, unwelcome ghost. They could not be so narrow-minded as to believe in only a select few gods whose values represented their own and nothing more. "Do you have children?"

Rennear sputtered into his coffee. The fine lines at the corners of his eyes and sharpness of his jawline indicated that he was older than she, a few years shy of or past his thirtieth year. He wore a plain golden band on his thumb and a thick wolf's-head ring on his right middle finger, neither of which was a partnership band. "No. Much to my father's dismay, I have not yet performed that particular rite of passage."

"Your father, Senator Ignatius. I have heard a few stories about him too, though I would not tell them on the street." Her heart shuddered, thinking of the druids slaughtered from the conclave to the north of the city and the druid elders murdered in its prisons. So much death, and all at the hands of people like his father, destruction enacted in the name of their gods and maintaining their power. Rennear was without an aura of cruelty, something she suspected would not be true of his father.

"Yes." Rennear scowled. "His reputation constantly precedes me. But I hope, Persephonie, that you would be willing—"

Otmund's burly silhouette appeared beside their table, his arms crossed over the front of his apron. "And who have we here?"

"Ren—, erhm, Patron Ignatius, Otmund." Persephonie half-smiled at him, assuring the tavern keeper that she was alright.

"Rennear is fine, sir." Rennear pushed himself out of the booth and rose to clasp Otmund's forearm.

"I meant the fox that she insists on bringing into a fine establishment"—he glanced at Juliet, her pointed face hidden by her tail—"but it is an honor to meet such an esteemed captain of the guard, sir."

"Thank you." Rennear nodded and settled back into the booth across from Persephonie.

Many of the bar's regulars glanced toward their private corner, eyes narrowed at the back of Rennear's head.

He drained his cup of coffee and pulled a few coins out of his pocket to cover their breakfast.

"Rennear, you don't have to—"

"Please." His eyes glimmered over a sad smile. "I'm sure I've cost you enough in future tips sitting here. This can at least make it up to Otmund." He rose, adjusted his jacket, and bowed his head to her. "It was a pleasure meeting you, Mistress Persephonie. I hope to hear your story about Verdigris in its entirety someday soon." He drummed his knuckles on the tabletop and made his exit from the tavern.

Once outside, he untied his horse's reins from the post and hoisted himself into the saddle.

"The son of Senator Ignatius, eh?"

Persephonie jumped at Otmund's voice suddenly behind her. "How are you so sneaky today?"

He raised an eyebrow, pleased with himself.

She sighed. "Yes, Otmund, but he is nothing like that man."

"Oh? And how can you be sure?"

"I have a sense for these things." Persephonie nodded her chin, settling the matter.

Otmund leaned closer to her, the dark hairs on his arms springing out from the base of his sleeve. "And what would your mother say if she knew?"

Persephonie slumped against her booth. She hadn't yet discovered anything of interest for the Untamed during her shifts, though being accosted by guards during her morning storytelling seemed significant. "What if we just don't tell her?"

He glanced over her head and smirked. "Good idea."

A bright green, sparkling dragonfly floated above her, crackling with natural magic. "Hmph," Persephonie scoffed. During her training, Yvayne had often teased her about her "effervescent aura," though the druid had appreciated the intriguing shapes her magic took when she wasn't accidentally charming a dray of squirrels. She grabbed Juliet in one hand and pulled the edge of her skirt in the other, sliding out of the booth. "It is not *my* fault that there is too much latent energy in the air here. If there were more druids, or if the ones that *are* here were allowed to practice, you wouldn't have a magical dragonfly appearing in your pub all of a sudden."

Otmund's eyes shone in the low light as he pulled the beige towel from his shoulders and polished his fingers. He chuckled as she stormed away and up the back stairs.

❧

"YOU MET WHOM?" HER MOTHER'S HAZEL EYES, SO SIMILAR TO hers without the breath of sky blue, as Datha would say, blazed back at her, her lips pressed thin and white.

"Rennear Ignatius. I was just telling a story in the square, and then—"

Her mother gripped her shoulders. "Do you have any idea what you risk consorting with someone like him? What they would do to you if they found out who you were?"

Images flashed before her—mangled bodies left in the were-wolves' wake, Yvayne's description of the smoldering druid camp, Datha's arm bleeding after a close altercation in a mountain village. Yes, she knew. But Mama would never believe her. Aylin had somehow convinced her mother that the only dangers in the world manifested within the walls of the city.

Esmeralda grimaced and turned away, pacing back and forth in front of Aylin's scratchy couch.

"He knows where I work, that is all." The sun smiled on the plants of the balcony, and they lifted their leaves to catch her beams, but the light failed to show the way across the chasm between her and her mother.

Mama stomped into the kitchen, pulling a box of tea down from the shelf. She clunked the kettle into the sink, filled it, and banged it down onto the stovetop. She raised her voice to be heard over her own clanging. "If Cassandra shows you more regarding this man, you are to tell me. Do you understand?" Her eyes burned against the back of Persephonie's head.

"Yes, Mama, I will."

The hall door squeaked open and Aylin stepped inside. A slight frown crossed her features upon seeing Persephonie before she forced a smile and greeted her and Esmeralda.

Her mother left the kettle to boil and crossed the room to kiss Aylin and take her hand. "I hope all proceeded as you had hoped in your meetings this morning?" She led her partner into the sitting area, to a chair across from Persephonie.

Aylin nodded, but her lips remained pressed together.

"My daughter had some . . . excitement of her own today as well." Mama placed her hands on Aylin's shoulders. "Would you like to tell her, cher'a, or shall I?"

Persephonie leaned back against the hard, itchy couch and scowled at the floor. "I met Rennear Ignatius, the senator's son, today."

Aylin's eyes widened, and Mama bobbed her head in triumph. "Perhaps you might help her see the potential dangers of this acquaintance?"

When neither Persephonie nor Aylin spoke, Esmeralda crossed her arms and looked impatiently between her partner and daughter. The kettle whistled, and Mama groaned and went to pull it from the stovetop.

"What precisely did he ask you, Persephonie? Does he know who you are?" Aylin rested her elbows on her knees, staring at her. "Who your mother is?"

Persephonie sighed. Even if she repeated the conversation in its entirety to them, they would still not believe that Rennear had helped her and had no intention of harming her or anyone she knew. "I was telling a story to the children by the fountain, one that made a few of the nearby guards angry. But Rennear arrived before they were going to arrest me, and he made them leave me alone." Aylin's expression hardened further with each word she spoke. "After that, he took me back to the tavern. That is all that happened."

With a huff, Esmeralda thrust a steaming mug into her hands, stomped away, and returned with a cup for herself and Aylin. "I think he is using her," Esmeralda said, her free hand gesturing toward Persephonie's face.

Would Mama ever see her as something beyond a helpless child trying hopelessly to fend for herself in an unfriendly city? She took a sip of tea to delay her reply. A red flame of pain flared as the bitter liquid scalded her lip. Persephonie winced and set it to the side. "Using me for what? To somehow harm the Untamed? How would he go about doing that?"

Aylin shook her head, her gaze sweeping out to the sunlit terrace where rolling waves of voices crashed softly amid the sea of sounds below. "It will be difficult for us to determine his precise motivations for some time." She turned back around, and her eyes flashed as she studied Persephonie. Calculations wove together in a sticky web behind her golden irises. "I am impressed, I suppose, that he was able to identify you as a target so quickly, but that's not to say we cannot respond. A senator's son may be precisely the sort of connection we need."

"Connection? To what?" Persephonie tucked her ankles beneath her knees and leaned forward. Esmeralda sat on one of the wooden chairs, and Aylin took up her mother's pacing.

"Following his movements could give us insight into what his father is planning, where he is going to strike next."

"Strike? What are you anticipating?" Persephonie's brow furrowed. Listening for information at the tavern was one thing, but using Rennear to spy on his father . . . "I thought they had reached a truce of sorts because of the Green Law? Tess told me—"

"Don't be naïve," Aylin snapped. "If they have the opportunity, they will destroy us. We just need to make sure they're not handed their chance."

The hairs rose on the back of Persephonie's neck. Esmeralda

stood abruptly between them, balling her hands into fists. "I do not believe we need to ask that of her, Aylin. You're putting my daughter in a precarious position, and she's already new to the city. That is danger enough. She just needs to be cautious going forward."

"You're right, I'm sorry." The false smile returned to Aylin's lips. "Forgive me, Persephonie." She took a few small steps forward and wrapped her arm around Esmeralda's waist, laying her chin on Mama's shoulder as she pulled her in close. Her eyelashes fluttered up toward her partner's. "I was only thinking of you, darling. Keeping an eye on Patron Ignatius and his movements wouldn't hurt anything. I'm simply asking Persephonie to take a few small steps to set your mind at ease."

Aylin's empty eyes locked on Persephonie, a blank mask hiding the face of her mother's lover.

"Anything to help Mama." Persephonie glared at Aylin. This time, she noticed the swell of latent energy before it erupted as a sparkling creature above her. She directed it to appear over Aylin's shoulder instead.

The crimson butterfly ignited suddenly, flaring into existence. Aylin jumped away from the sizzle of magic behind her head. Mama ducked, but her arms lowered from around her head once she recognized one of her daughter's creations.

Persephonie smiled to herself as she sent the butterfly fluttering around the room, sparks of energy raining in thin, shimmering curtains from its wings. *That took care of the mask.* After a few moments, she waved her hand and dismissed the butterfly.

Otmund was expecting a larger-than-usual crowd due to the approaching festivities, and she needed to depart. Persephonie rose up on her toes and kissed Esmeralda's cheek to excuse herself for the afternoon. "I love you, Mama." Her people had long known the charm behind these words, a magic that most others had forgotten. Mama wouldn't stay cross with her over the sparkly trick, even if Aylin did.

The stale magic in the air had dispersed, though a cloud of latent energy compressed around Aylin as she recovered. "I will see you before the festival, I'm sure."

Persephonie nodded to the elf and made her exit. The woman across from her was powerful, but so long as Aylin aimed to protect her mother, Persephonie could let her unsubtle manipulations go.

Esmeralda's concerns about her meeting Rennear, the possibility of him using her the way Aylin wished to, left a lingering pressure at the base of Persephonie's neck. The light that flashed behind Rennear's eyes as he looked at her had been real, she knew it. "What they said, it's not true," she whispered to herself. Her heart fluttered in reply.

CHAPTER 21

"Have you spoken much to our new acquisition, Captain?" Kriega leaned against the railing of the quarter deck, sunlight bouncing off her light brown eyes.

Teodric straightened his waistcoat before turning to her. "Can't say that I have, Kriega, though I have noticed he spends a good amount of time on deck." He hadn't mentioned Darcy's revelation of knowledge about his family—their arrival in Nortelon, his father's disappearance—his first day aboard. Teodric had since avoided private conversations with the man, though they could not be prevented forever.

This morning, like the three before, Syleste's charge had brought a wooden chair from his room out onto the deck and sat reading and observing the crew. At times while steering, or speaking to one of his deckhands, Teodric felt a stab of ice at the base of his neck. Inevitably, he would find the pale blue eyes fixed on him. The man's lip would curl in acknowledgement, and then he would return to his book.

"Do you know what she wants with him?" Kriega openly glared at their guest.

"No, but I doubt it's anything for you to be jealous over."

Kriega pushed herself up from the rail. "It's not jealousy, Captain"—she spat out his title—"but you'd do well to show more concern. He's been asking about you."

He ought to be more careful with Kriega's feelings where Syleste was concerned. Though the admiral's infatuation with him had long ago fizzled out, it remained a sore spot between them. Even before he'd stepped aboard the *Dominion*, Kriega had been fighting the impossible battle for Syleste's unwavering affections, a desire as hopeless as trying to bottle the wind. He knew she'd been hurt by the admiral moving her onto another ship. If she could just see that they were no longer rivals, perhaps she might stop fighting long enough to recognize the opportunity to break free of Syleste's clutches. But for now, he should content himself with the fact that their other interactions remained surprisingly amiable. "What do you mean?"

The half-orc's eyes flashed. "Got your attention now, have I? He watches you almost as closely as Keever's assistant watches him." Kriega nodded to their new crew member, Genevieve.

Teodric shook his head. "That's circumstantial. When she's not in the kitchens, you won't let her work out of your sight till you're sure she's acquainted with the ship, and he's always on deck outside his quarters." A swell lifted the bow, kicking up a teasing breeze that trailed its fingers through his hair. Though he wasn't anticipating their destination—the very thought of returning to Syleste's island sent his stomach into convulsive knots—there was no match for the freedom of open water sailing a ship of his own.

His first mate crossed her arms, unconvinced by his explanation.

"Very well, how about this? Let's invite our guest to dinner tonight, and we'll see if our cook's assistant feels up to helping Keever serve." Darcy would guard his words more carefully at a crowded table, but he doubted the man could resist flaunting his special hoard of knowledge. "We'll need to invite Hallix as well. He seems to have been drafted as Darcy's close confidant."

"Or guard." Kriega raised an eyebrow. She ground her lower jaw back and forth as she thought the matter over, her tusks scouring their imprint across her lower lip. "Agreed. Athena will assist our new hand, and we'll give Ambrose the deck."

"See to it, then." Teodric nodded to her, waving Athena up to take the helm. "I'm taking a turn below."

❦

"CAREFUL NOW!" THE GOBLIN SQUEALED AT GENEVIEVE, THE high peal of his voice nearly causing her to drop the tureen of thick gravy he'd filled with a wave of his hand. She'd only stumbled slightly, Jade intervening to help her steady her footing on the rolling ship floor.

"I-I'm sorry, Keever. I've got it." She brushed a strand of hair back behind her ear, waiting to follow the chef up to the captain's quarters. Keever had been in a foul mood all day after learning of the captain's special dinner that evening. Recalling what Athena had told her when she first stepped on board, Genevieve suspected the goblin's irritation had almost as much to do with being asked to go above decks as it did the insult of being asked to prepare an elegant meal at the last moment. From what Mariellen had told her about the workings of magic in the world, whatever their origins, the energy for creation still had to come from somewhere.

"Don't know why the captain stuck me with you," Keever mumbled under his breath. "Work just fine alone."

She let the barb pass. Most days he was content with her

help, though he would certainly never say it. For the last week, she'd insisted that Athena teach her everything she could about the work needed above decks so she could learn more about the man who had acquired her conclave's sacred dagger. She'd discovered little more than his name thus far—Darcy—but tonight would be special. Despite his ambivalent pretenses, the man was anxious for the admiration of others. Beneath the glow of attention, unguarded conversation, and free-flowing wine, what truths might emerge? And afterward, when no one was watching, she and Jade would get the dagger back.

Keever levitated the silver roast pan with its gleaming slab of meat and followed it up the stairs. Genevieve trailed behind, carrying a large silver tray laden with soups for the first course as well as a gravy tureen and green vegetables dripping with butter. Crew members nodded to the goblin as he passed, grinning at his mumbled insults. Much to his dismay, Keever's magical concoctions made him one of the most popular members of the crew. "No one knows where his stores come from," Athena had whispered to her late one night after Genevieve's fruitless search of the kitchens for the marvelous apples he'd baked for dinner. "Don't ask him, either, or he'll become very cross."

A faint smile played across the goblin's expression once they reached the captain's quarters as the officers lavished praise upon his food. Genevieve suspected that Keever only pretended to despise everyone's compliments and actually invested a great deal of energy and effort into his creations, just as much as each dish would have required were he cooking by nonmagical means.

She had delivered the captain's dinners and breakfasts a few times over the last week, though the wood-paneled cabin seemed to be the one place besides the kitchen that the cook was willing to visit without too much fuss. "Captain Teodric is a good man," he'd said with a scowl on her second day. Genevieve had been so taken aback that she'd been unable to respond.

That goodness was evident this evening as well. The captain watched Keever carefully after they delivered the entrees. "Master Keever, would you prefer for your assistant to remain here so you can return to the kitchens? I'll send her down promptly if we need anything."

The goblin scowled for a moment as he considered this. "Stay here and serve," he barked at Genevieve. She bowed her head, and Keever grumbled brightly to himself as he stomped out of the room, loud enough for everyone to hear but without his usual scornful tone. "Exposed right as it's turning dark. No regard for my safety, no. We could all be snatched at any moment." A small giggle accentuated the door clicking shut.

Athena's eyes glittered with delight on the opposite side of the room. Her friend stood at ease with her arms tucked behind her back. Genevieve attempted the same stance, but the floor rolling beneath her feet made such a proposition uncomfortable. The meal began with a round of toasts and the clinking of crystal goblets filled with berry-red wine. When she'd been in the captain's cabin previously, the table where they now sat had been covered in maps with a few pages of correspondence and a bottle of ink. Now, it was draped with plain white linen, and dining implements had taken the place of the detailed maps depicting a wide array of realms unfamiliar to Genevieve. The captain sat at the head of the table, with Kriega to his left in front of Athena, and Darcy and the man she'd seen in the bunk room, Hallix, on his right, each with their back to her.

Darcy threw his head back and drained his goblet. Her stomach boiled as he turned to her and shook his empty goblet, ignoring the uncorked bottle in front of him on the table. "Something fuller bodied?" His piercing eyes darted from her to the row of wine bottles resting on a table beside a large leather armchair by the windows.

The captain nodded to her. "It's alright, Genevieve. The

second from the left should appease our honored guest's appetite."

Genevieve hurried over to the bottles. Their conversation hadn't yet progressed to any subject of note, but she didn't want to miss anything if it did. She uncorked the bottle and returned to the table. Though her teachers Mariellen and Sheffield had expressed their doubts, rumors abounded in the conclave as to the methods their enemies could use to detect their druidry. Touch was one of them. And though Darcy hadn't yet proven himself outright to be an enemy, he had acquired the dagger somehow and had used it to murder someone in Andel-ce Hevra.

Careful not to make contact with Darcy's skin, Genevieve took the goblet from his hand and refilled it. Without a word, he turned back to the table.

Genevieve repositioned herself at the end of the table. In the dancing candlelight, she could see everyone's faces while pretending to monitor the trays of food before them.

The keen-eyed first mate remained quiet through the soup course, though her gaze often drifted between Hallix, Darcy, and, Genevieve had to admit, herself. At the captain's bidding, Kriega carved the roast, after which her eyes glazed over with boredom. The only moments when she seemed moderately engaged were when someone mentioned Syleste, the admiral Captain Teodric answered to. Aboard the *Amber Queen*, the officers reminded Genevieve of her conclave's elders, balancing one another's strengths and shoring up weaknesses. But the way Athena described Admiral Syleste, the hierarchy sounded crueler, more stark, much the way she'd imagined the Council of Andel-ce Hevra behaving.

In contrast, the captain's warm brown eyes seemed to grow more intrigued by his dinner guest by the moment. Her success in uncovering Darcy's secrets had been limited thus far, but Captain Teodric appeared pleased at the information he was gleaning from Darcy. The sallow-skinned man spoke at length about his history with the admiral, bragging, as Genevieve had hoped, about his many exploits, though she couldn't link any of his tales with the concerns of her conclave.

"Patron Ignatius, you say?" the captain asked. "He's a powerful man, is he not?"

"The most powerful member of the council, yes." Darcy's eyes glittered as he studied the captain. "Do you merely pretend ignorance when it comes to other courts besides Linolynn's, Captain?"

A note of warning glowed in Teodric's eyes. "I know better than to believe life at court to be a game, Darcy."

"Or perhaps you haven't yet learned to play." A cruel grin stretched across Darcy's mouth, but the mirth failed to penetrate his eyes.

She narrowed her gaze. The Council of Andel-ce Hevra had murdered her conclave's elders. If this man was connected to them, if he viewed their politics as a game . . .

"Genevieve," the captain called her softly from the sudden pounding of her heart, "might we have another round?" A flicker of concern crossed his brow as he watched her. Could she confide her plight to him and seek his aid? Would he understand her desperation to recover her conclave's dagger, to remove it from the hands of one so foul, or would he think she'd stepped aboard under false pretenses?

Her hands shook as she refilled the goblets. Hallix stared at her and smirked.

The time ticked forward slowly as Genevieve parsed Darcy's every word for clues about the dagger or her family, but he had steered the conversation carefully away from Andel-ce Hevra and back to the admiral and her wishes. Kriega sent her below to fetch dessert and coffee while Athena made the after-dinner drinks.

By the time she returned, the mood in the room had shifted. She slid the coffee tray onto the end of the table and stepped back. The first mate's interest had revived, and she sat tall in her chair, glaring openly at Darcy.

Captain Teodric frowned. "Was that why the admiral ordered that we bring you back?"

Genevieve's heart flew into her throat. She had missed it! What had Darcy revealed?

"Part of the reason, yes. But Admiral Syleste believes a critical piece in her larger plan is finally ready to make its move, and she requested that someone of my specialty return to provide greater assistance." Darcy leaned back in his chair, propping his intertwined hands on his thin belly.

"And this mysterious larger plan?" Kriega's upper lip curled.

"I'm not at liberty to say at the present." His head rose up even farther from his shoulders as he straightened self-importantly. Jade dug her toes into the deck of the ship and growled.

Kriega snatched a glass of whiskey off of the tray in the center of the table. "Then keep it to yourself."

Athena's eyes widened as they met Genevieve's.

Darcy chuckled, replenishing his goblet of wine and ignoring the amber liquid sloshing in front of him. "But it's so much more tantalizing to tease about what one knows. Take our captain's infamous departure from Linolynn, for instance." He swung his goblet toward Teodric, sloshing wine across the table. Darcy snapped his fingers at her, pointing at the spill.

Jade's growl nearly ripped free from Genevieve's throat. Darcy was too self-absorbed to notice the captain's face flush at the insinuation behind his words. He had failed to take into account the backward roll of Kriega's shoulders, the tendons flexing beneath her fists.

And he had no idea what was waiting inside of her.

He snapped again. "Hello there." Genevieve and Jade whirled

to face him. Jade's rage bristled along Genevieve's spine as though her hair could stand on end. This time, the growl did escape.

Athena shouted from across the table as Hallix shoved himself back and leapt at Genevieve. His spine twisted, a writhing spasm that yanked at his shoulders, neck, and face as his transformation began.

Genevieve rolled to the side, dodging the werewolf's careening body. As Hallix reeled back away from the wall, he struck Darcy's chair instead. Darcy's goblet shattered as he fell to the floor.

Inside her chest, Jade howled, and Genevieve surrendered control.

Rage thundered through her body, and the transformation tore through her. Jade's muzzle ripped out of Genevieve's skull with a scream. Claws exploded from her fingertips and her fangs lengthened. Together in their shared form, Genevieve and Jade gnashed their teeth at Hallix and the man sprawled on the ground behind him.

They lunged at the other werewolf, diving for his neck. Hallix was much larger than they, but his instincts had been dulled by time, softened as he tried to blend between human and lycanthrope—she and Jade were one, like the lycan of old.

Their momentum threw Hallix to the floor. Shouts and smashed crystal ricocheted above. They spun, driving the other werewolf beneath them.

"Stop!" The voice of the captain.

A burst of energy rippled through the room. Sun-warmed leaves and the scent of rain-dampened earth streamed in. What was calling the nature spirits? Genevieve and Jade raised their head from Hallix's throat.

The spirits swarmed toward Darcy . . . toward the white bone dagger gleaming in his hand.

Before they could dive away, Darcy plunged the blade into their flesh.

She and Jade howled as they fell back and away from Hallix. Darcy ripped the dagger free and flung their blood across the floor.

Genevieve returned to her human form. Her screams mingled with Jade's cries. Blood poured from her side as she pushed herself onto her elbows. She rounded on Darcy and met his cold blue eyes.

For a moment, his gaze bore into hers.

His expression twisted.

Darcy's shout of pain tore through the cabin. His yellow teeth twisted in horror. A bright green light shone out from his palm and fingers where he'd clutched the dagger. He shrieked and yanked his hand against his chest, trying to blot out the light.

Mariellen's voice flared in her mind. "Those who would use our ancestors' magic against us will soon find the grave themselves." The blade of bone had been formed from the leg of their conclave's first varra and was intended for only their most sacred ceremonies, to be wielded by the head elder. A non-druid using it against the sole remaining member of the conclave was bound to have dire consequences.

Darcy paled as sweat dripped down his face. He grimaced. The whites of his eyes shone around the ring of bright blue as he held his wrist and screamed. The ripe scent of decay filled the cabin, and the flesh of his hand fell away, leaving nothing but bone behind.

The werewolf beside her shifted, but not quickly enough to dodge the wooden club that swung toward his head. Kriega knocked Hallix unconscious. His body returned to his human form, slumped across the floor. The half-orc breathed heavily and stomped toward her. On the other side of the table, the captain stood with his own blade drawn, blocking an anxious Athena.

Genevieve and Jade scampered away, burrowing into the corner by the armchair. Jade whimpered, wanting to lick her side clean. Darcy's screams rent the air. A heavy fist pounded on the captain's door. "What's going on in there?"

Kriega towered above her, club raised.

"I'm sorry!" Genevieve's hands shook. Darkness pooled along the edges of her vision. "I can explain."

"You were supposed to all be dead!" Darcy shouted at her. His eyes blazed as he looked between her and the dagger. He snarled, "How did you survive?"

Genevieve glared at him, shoulders thrust back. "You've no right to speak of my conclave, murderer." She spat out the last.

"How did you survive?" he mumbled a second time. His skeleton hand shook as he reached for the dagger, discarded on the floor beside him. His eyes rolled back in his head, and he collapsed to the ground.

Genevieve sprang forward after it, but Kriega caught her and pinned her against the wall. "You don't understand." Genevieve struggled, but Kriega was too strong. Jade whimpered again. They were losing too much blood.

The captain appeared over the half-orc's shoulder. He raised a hand. "Genevieve, be calm." The spirits stilled, and the scent of Ophelia's glade trickled through her nose—damp leaves, a sprig of sage. This man would help them, even if he did not yet know how.

Genevieve slumped against the wall. The edges of the room blurred. Kriega and the captain moved aside as Athena rushed forward. Blood burbled against Genevieve's fingers as she clutched her side. Her voice emerged as barely a whisper. "Elenai."

Strands of black hair trickled away from her face.

For a moment, as she brushed her hair aside, they were all there, in the conclave, around her.

She wasn't alone.

Mariellen's eyes welled, and she clutched Sheffield's hand. Ophelia laid her hand against her chest. "We're so proud of you, my girl."

The huts were gone, but the conclave remained. Generations of druids surrounded her. Yvayne's purple wings beat beside Ophelia, rippling the other druid's mossy robes.

Sariel stepped forward from behind them and bowed his regal head. The breeze rippled through the daimon's thick silver fur. "You've done well, druid daughter."

Yvayne smiled and leaned against his side. "For a time, the way is dark, but the sunrise still lies ahead."

Mariellen and Sheffield stepped forward, their lips trembling as they strove to find the words. "Trust, sweet Genevieve," Mariellen whispered.

Sheffield beamed down at her. "We will never leave your side." He knelt down to address Jade beside her. "She's counting on you, still." Jade rubbed her head against Genevieve's leg. The circle of faces gleamed in her emerald eyes.

"I want to be here when she wakes up." A soft voice drifted nearer on the ocean breeze.

"Very well." Lower, lyrical, warm. "But allow Kriega to speak with her first, Athena."

"Yes, Captain."

Genevieve shut her eyes and returned to her home.

CHAPTER 22

A flare of violet light severed the binds as indigo faery wings blazed against the shadows surrounding Iellieth. "Keep fighting back, *si'retta*." The sharp edge of Yvayne's voice ricocheted around her, bolts of lightning striking the dark plane, the nether-space from which Lucien had lashed out, sinking hooks through her mind, her skin. "I will hold him off."

Iellieth's mind cleared, the cold evening air licking against the small of her back. Lucien was gone. She shivered and raised her hands to her cheeks, securing the golden mask against her face before she stepped back from Marcon to address Lord Stravinske.

"Is there something with which we can help you, sir?" Iellieth pursed her lips as she spoke, adding an Elvish lilt to her Caldaran accent.

Stravinske smirked at her address. How had he allied himself to Lucien? Is that what made him a mutual acquaintance? "Hmm, I wished only to meet one of the most beautiful visitors to our court this evening and her . . . escort." The smirk deepened into a sneer as his eyes flashed. "I am *certain* you're already aware of who I am, but allow me to introduce myself regardless." He bowed. "Lord Vladislav Stravinske, at your service."

Heat radiated off Marcon, forming the sense of a shield around her. His body tensed, ready to strike at the slightest provocation.

"A pleasure." Iellieth curtsied. Marcon might have inclined his head, but she doubted he would have taken his eyes off Vladislav for even that long. "My name is Lilith, and this is my escort, Colabra."

"Lilith," Vladislav said with a chuckle. "Pray, which version of the guardian's tale do you hold to heart? The one where she joined with the fiends, or the one where she abandoned the darkness for a realm of perpetual creation?"

"Both." Iellieth narrowed her eyes. She and Katarina had spent a summer collecting and cataloguing Lilith mythology, her tutor spending most of that time lamenting the single-mindedness of the debate as opposed to scholars adopting a more complex and nuanced view of the guardian.

"Intriguing, I'm sure." His tone grew colder as he took a step forward. Against her will, Iellieth moved back, bumping into the solid wall of Marcon behind her. Vladislav stroked his thin goatee, jaw jutting forward. "Lilith, Lilith . . . now where have I heard a name like that before?" His dark eyes glittered. Silence seemed a safer answer. Iellieth leaned back into Marcon, wrapping her hand around his forearm.

"Your man doesn't speak much, does he?" Vladislav's voice wriggled around her, sending ripples up her spine. Marcon's hand tucked around the front of her hip, holding her in place. "The strong and silent type, I understand." The Hadvarian nobleman took another step forward.

A deep growl resonated from Marcon's chest. Vladislav faltered, then smirked. "How beastly. Now where would a noble-woman from . . . hmm, the *Realms*, is it, Lilith"—his upper lip curled—"have met such a companion?" He took another step, bringing him almost within arm's reach of her.

Her heart thudded against her chest, and her fingertips itched for the return of her sparks. She felt only fizzles on the night air. The magic of the Arcanium wasn't hers to use; its wide eyes blinked out at her from inside the halls of learning. The forest howled, a memory far away.

"Let's interrogate another situation, shall we? What if her majesty were to learn that we have a hidden enemy lurking in our midst here at her celebration? What do you suppose might happen, not only to the intruders from Linolynn"—he spat out the name—"but also to those aiding and sheltering them within these very walls?" Vladislav's dark eyes burned into her skin. "The court of your pathetic little kingdom has already moved north to launch an attack against her majesty's forces. How long do you think their soldiers will last? One day? Two?"

His revelation broke Iellieth's spell of silence. "Relocated north? Where?"

Vladislav laughed. "That kind of information will cost you." His eyes swept down her body. Marcon's forearm tightened beneath her grasp, his hand clenched into a fist. "But they, like you, will find that many surprises await them in these northern mountains. Powers more magnificent than you could ever dream."

The black cloud that had floated over Mara in her final moments returned to shade Iellieth's vision—but so did the ring of green fire that had surrounded her mentor.

A low-throated melody drifted over the wind as the waves of light shivered into existence against the sky behind the Arcanium. The song of the mountains, and the answering harmony of the sea of light. Her magic was here too.

Iellieth narrowed her eyes and straightened. "I doubt that we would be the only ones to be surprised." She raised an eyebrow as the magic roared back to life inside of her, torrents of energy rising and cresting through her limbs. She took a deep breath, sparks dancing off the ends of her fingers.

She closed the distance between herself and Vladislav, their bodies separated by half an arm's length. "Tell me, Lord Stravinske, why is it that a shadow mage spoke to me of your existence?"

Stravinske's eyes widened, a mix of curiosity and alarm. "I've made some powerful friends in your absence, Lady Amastacia." He studied her face, her body, his eyes crawling like shiny roaches over her skin.

Marcon's flaming spirit simmered behind her, radiating waves of warning.

"Then why has that powerful friend abandoned you in your time of need?"

The self-assurance flickered on Vladislav's face. "What do you—"

His voice broke off as Iellieth leaned nearer, her green eyes fixed on his. She brought her lips together, blowing a narrow stream of air directly at his throat.

The mountain winds joined her breath, a howling lament of burning ice. The dancing lights laughed in the distance, flipping over themselves, enjoying the show.

Lord Stravinske choked, his eyes wide as he raised his hand to his throat. Blue-white crystals formed over the convulsing bulge of his voice box, icy fingers gripping his throat in sparkling tendrils. "That should be familiar," Iellieth whispered. She readied herself to exhale the ice again.

Vladislav must have seen the crackle of the mountain song in her eyes. A strangled cry emerged from his frozen throat. He spun, slipping on the cold marble, and sprang away from them, darting toward the crowded ballroom.

Marcon's heat was beside her, his hand tight against her waist. "Lady, are you alright?"

Iellieth nodded, dazed. Could he really be dispatched so easily? Her swirling thoughts froze, flakes strained against their drifting nature. "He's going to tell the guards."

The champion nodded and whirled away after Lord Stravinske, a blur of heat rippling off him in his rage, the markings of the runes swirling and dark.

Vladislav knew he was being pursued. He paused for a moment inside the door and whispered in the ear of a figure in black leather armor. The dark-haired woman he'd spoken to slipped past Marcon as he slammed his hand into the door following the Hadvarian nobleman, who had taken off at a run across the mezzanine ballroom.

Iellieth slowed her breathing, the kiss of the cold air granting her clarity. The woman Stravinske had spoken to glanced around the balcony, her eyes shimmering an impossibly bright blue, visible even from across the terrace. Iellieth stepped forward, holding her arms against herself to prevent her shivering.

She walked as though she was going to take a final turn around the balcony and then slip inside. The figure angled away from her, slinking through the shadows toward the opposite edge. Iellieth held her head high and picked up her pace. The woman appeared and disappeared behind the columns. None of the other couples on the balcony paid her any mind.

The woman began to sprint toward the edge. Iellieth picked up the length of her dress and ran after her. Where could she be going?

Her heels clicked against the marble terrace, rushing after the mysterious figure. Iellieth tucked around the columns, following the woman's path and staying close to the Arcanium's outer walls. She lost sight of the woman for only a moment, and she was gone. "No!" Iellieth cried under her breath.

She continued running, sliding to a stop at the edge of the balcony, but there was nothing beyond her save a shadowy, frost-covered lawn and evergreen hedges.

The woman had vanished.

CHAPTER 23

Yvayne's sword carved through the bonds Lucien had wrapped around Iellieth. The shadow energy burned across her hands as she severed the mage's connection to the half-elf.

In the dim netherworld between the planes, Lucien turned to her, his robe trailing the ground. "You cannot protect her forever, Yvayne. The stakes for my mistress are too high, her power too great." His laughter surrounded her, a grating swarm. "Her soul will be mine before the end. You will see." Lucien lifted his fingers to his lips, slurping his decayed skin as though it dripped with animal fat. "Fhaona's power was invigorating, to be sure. But hers . . ." The yellow orbs closed as the mage sighed, his throat resonating with pleasure. "Hers will be the last piece I need."

Yvayne's eyes turned black. She screamed at Lucien, rending through the air with her blade of purple mist. The mage stumbled away and disappeared in a swirl of smoke.

Yvayne twirled the blade between her hands, blood pounding. Had Alessandra made Lucien the ultimate promise, then?

That consuming Iellieth's soul would grant him the privilege of standing by her side as a near-equal. She scowled. That oath hadn't always worked out well for Alessandra's allies in the past.

The screams she'd heard from the mountaintops as Alessandra ripped her lieutenant Braemorn's soul from existence settled back around her. She had known the dark goddess for far longer than Lucien had haunted this world. Like so many others before him, his self-assurance might be his undoing.

Yvayne exhaled, returning her spirit to the world of Azuria. The branches of her private conclave greeted her return, whispering their greeting against the breeze. "I missed you as well." She smiled out across the clearing. "Our charge remains safe for now." The trees swayed, their relief a quiet song. The druid shook her head. The faeries would be up all night scheming if the melody didn't quieten, and they all had work still to do.

She strode through her glowing entry hall and paced the dense moss of her library. Faeries swirled overhead, drawn to her swirling waves of energy. Yvayne spread out her hands, steadying herself, and searched the mountains to the east for the half-elf's spirit.

The world tinged garnet, the shade of Iellieth's hair, and scarlet roses blossomed across the floor of her home, rapid vines swirling to life around the logs and stumps. They filled her tree home with their ancient floral scent, a hint of blood, musk, and sun-kissed gemstones.

Yvayne turned back toward her doorway. The man who'd been approaching Iellieth and Marcon as Lucien appeared, the one he claimed, hadn't impressed her as one of the mage's more competent servants. She turned on her heel, facing the far wall of the library. However, his presence had unearthed deep-laid rivers of fear within Iellieth. Lucien was resorting to personal attacks earlier than she'd anticipated at this stage in their conflict.

She should have asked the half-elf more questions while she was here. Alessandra was undoubtedly aware of the girl's enhanced powers. Their dormancy through the early years of her life had been one of her soul's defense mechanisms for survival. Had Alessandra pushed Lucien to eliminate Iellieth before the seed of hope had a chance to take root? Or was his own desire for revenge choking his sight?

For years, she'd assumed the pirate queen Syleste would be the greatest challenge they faced from one of Lucien's minions. She and her ship drifted out in the waters of the Infinite Ocean, biding their time. But if they were part of some sort of concerted effort on the mage's part, what might that mean for Iellieth and her chances of recovering the pieces of the planar seal?

Beneath her questions, a ripple of discomfort fluttered, its wing weakly waving for her attention. There was something larger at work in this scheme in Caldara. Lucien wouldn't hedge all of his plans behind the selfish efforts of Vladislav Stravinske.

A realization struck the base of her spine. She had missed a player along the way. Yvayne stumbled through the events that had transpired thus far. What in Caldara had she missed? Her eyes narrowed. She caught a glimpse of a swirling cloak around the corner of a long stone hall in her mind's eye. Its silhouette disappeared out of sight by the time she rounded the bend.

IELLIETH'S BREATH TURNED TO CRYSTALS ON THE CRISP evening air. Beads of cold settled against her amulet's chain along the base of her throat, pulling the throbs of energy inward. Marcon might need her inside.

She picked up her skirts and jogged across the marble back onto the mezzanine floor of the ballroom. Though she'd spent hours beneath the sparkling rainbow of lights already, stepping back into their midst still halted her where she stood on the edge of their glittering glow.

Stravinske had darted around the staircase before she lost sight of him, but she'd taken long enough following the woman that any trace of disturbance among the revelers on the upper floor had disappeared.

A golden hallway light beckoned on the opposite side of the sweeping mezzanine. Beneath her, pairs of dancers twirled in the magical lights. She spotted Kazimir, swirling in all of his lilac and purple with one of Dimitri's older students, the young man's black hair striking against the red of his coat.

"Lady!" Iellieth skidded to a halt at Marcon's voice. He appeared from around the corner of the hallway and caught her by the elbow as she tipped backward to avoid crashing into him.

He was breathing heavily, gray eyes a tossing tempest. As soon as she was righted, he tucked his arm behind his back, tugging at his sleeves.

"Marcon, what happened? Where is . . ." Her voice trailed off as she peered over his shoulder. There were no Hadvarian noblemen lurking in the shadows.

"We need to move away from here." He guided her away from the hallway. His sleeve was sticky, and the velvet was no longer soft.

"Wait, Marcon, what—"

He spun around to face her. "That man was a threat to you, Iellieth. What would happen if he reported our being here to the queen?"

Iellieth's head spun. She grasped Marcon's forearm to hold herself up. So Lord Stravinske was gone. He would never threaten her again. For two years, she had wondered what his absence would feel like, if his utter removal were even possible. She had expected it to seem more . . . freeing. But this? The swirls of energy inside her dove around the edge of an abyss. Her lips pursed as she met Marcon's eyes. "I'm scared. What does that mean, for us? Are we still . . ." *On the right side? Good?* None of these felt right. Who were they to decide the lives of others?

"Dance with me." Marcon swept her into the waltz, drifting through the water-lit ballroom. They joined the couples near the balcony exit, the cold air prickling over her skin.

Marcon held her close as they danced. The line of his jaw crossed the top of her hair, and the enchanted runes that crossed his neck flared toward her, flowers opening in a burst of pollen. His voice drifted down, a rumbling harmony beneath the music that she alone could hear. "We only take lives when absolutely necessary, lady. That is what separates us from those we stand against."

The lights around her whirled, glinting off necklace jewels and sequined dresses. Marcon spun her back into his embrace, the length of his hand flush with the small of her back. She leaned her head into his chest as his answer trickled through her, filling the emptiness that had opened at her core. What he said rang of truth. But did that make it right?

"It's not as clear-cut as it often seems in stories, lady. And there are times when the steps we take are wrong."

She stiffened. Was this one of those times? "But, Marcon—"

He shook his head, a small, sad smile on his lips. He drew her hands together between his and led her over to the stairs. They paused at the railing before they descended. "If there ever comes a time when you don't question someone's death, when it doesn't bother you, then you can start to worry." He laid a kiss on the back of each of her hands. Lord Stravinske's blood had darkened the navy velvet of his cuffs. "Iellieth." Her eyes swam to meet his. "I made the decision. Not you. Until you trust your own judgment, will you trust me?"

Will you trust me to help you decide who should live and who should die? The cold returned, spreading frigid tentacles through her abdomen. Marcon's gaze flickered away, hurt.

"I trust you." She bit down on her lips. "I don't want us to have to keep making those sorts of choices." Iellieth closed her eyes, wishing the world would be made new as she reopened them. It wasn't, but Marcon still stood before her, solid and calm.

"You need to meet, umm, Lord Shade soon."

Iellieth grinned. She wasn't the only one who struggled to remember Quindythias's spontaneous identity. "Lord Shade looks remarkably like Kazimir this evening. But we have time for one more dance"—she stood on her tiptoes to whisper—"and then the heist. Or maybe two."

Marcon smiled in return, following her lead back into the press of pairs gliding across the ballroom floor. He sighed as she leaned into him and ran his fingers through the ends of her hair.

CHAPTER 24

A rush of cold air enveloped Persephonie's skin as she stepped out of the crowded tavern into the quiet side alley. Guests shouted over one another on the inside, trying to be heard above the din of the enthusiastic gathering on this first festival day leading up to the Hunt at the end of the week.

"Excuse me, miss." A man in a low-cut black linen tunic stepped into the alley mouth ahead of her. "Your name wouldn't happen to be Arelle, would it?" Ridges of tanned muscles rippled beneath the man's shirt.

"I, ehm, yes, my family name is Arelle." Persephonie tried to prevent her voice from shaking as she answered and stepped back deeper into the alley. It was against the nature of a saudad to deny her heritage.

"I thought so." The man lumbered closer in the moonlight, two other figures jumping in and out of the shadows on either side. "Your mother has those hazel eyes too, doesn't she?"

Persephonie opened her mouth to answer but thought better of it, turning to run instead.

She yelped as the man seized her wrist, twisted her arm behind her back, and pinned her against the wall. Her heart thudded in her chest, her thoughts swirling. How had he crossed the length of the alley so fast?

"I'm upset you don't remember me." His grip tightened, and she cried out again as he grabbed the back of her hair, scratching her face against the mottled brick. "If I'd realized then whose daughter you were, we wouldn't be having this starlit conversation tonight."

He had to be one of the guards who had stopped her in the square. Ice shot through her body. *He was one of the werewolves.*

Persephonie struggled to get away, but the iron grip only tightened. Muffled laughter rang out from the alley around her as the other two looked on.

"Since you're still a stranger here, let's start with a lesson, shall we? I'm sure you've heard the version the Untamed like to tell." His voice rumbled in the back of his throat as he pressed his face closer to hers. "Would you like to know the truth?"

Her eyes squinted against the pain, but she refused to answer or cry out again.

The werewolf sniffed the nape of her neck. "Do you know what they did with the druids who slunk out of the forest across our borders?" He chuckled at her shudder as she tried to jolt away from him, succeeding only in deepening the scratches down the side of her face. The stones' jagged teeth were nothing compared to the fangs gnashing so near to her skin. Had Felix said that they could they transmit their poison while in human form?

His claws dug into her arm, breaking the skin, and a warm rush of blood trickled down her hand. She whimpered, her vision blurring, as he squeezed her arm again. With a crack, the bone of her wrist snapped beneath his grip. Persephonie screamed.

"After those monsters exploded innocent priests in the city, we had to find a way to make an example of their kind. It was easier to use the ones from the forest"—his hot breath condensed on her skin—"and we chopped off their hands to prevent the flow of their magic."

Persephonie's heart pounded in her ears. The enchantress from her cards floated before the spread of stars above, looking down on her, inviting her spirit up and away. A tear trickled down the side of her face, vanishing into the scrape of brick against her cheek. She should have let Datha convince her to stay with him and their people. Here, she was nothing more than fodder for the fires that raged across the cursed streets.

The werewolf tugged her head back, fully exposing the skin of her throat. "When that didn't prove to be enough, we put them in cages made of black stones and listened to them shriek, like they'd been lit on fire by the very proximity." His other hand trailed down her neck to her chest.

She shut her eyes against his voice and struggled to free herself. Flickers of her magic sizzled against the air, but something kept them from catching. A pressure built in her lungs. The spirits around her had fled.

"But I have a different idea for you," the guard snarled, whipping his head to the maw of the alley, his sharpened claws piercing the skin of her chest, pawing at her clothes.

A streak of red fur flashed past in the moonlight, leaping across strewn barrels and bounding to her side.

Claws clattered on cobblestones, and the werewolf screamed, staggering away from her. Juliet's thick tail tore through the air as he waved his hand, trying to fling her off but only serving to drive her teeth deeper instead.

Cassandra had been watching over her.

Persephonie spun around and shoved the man as hard as she could in the chest. He stumbled backward, his head cracking against the brick wall on the opposite side of the alley. His two companions sprang forward from the darkness, hulking forms lurching in the low light, midway through their transformation.

The werewolf in the alley entrance froze and jolted upright, groaning as a gleaming blade pierced through his chest, catching starlight in drops of blood. His body crumpled, splatting against the cobblestones. A dark silhouette stood tall behind where the body had been.

"Watch out!" The man in the entryway pointed behind her.

Persephonie ripped the dagger from her waistband, turning it blade outward, and spun around. The third figure lunged toward her, sinking his chest onto the glittering blade in her uninjured hand, his eyes opened wide in shock.

His weight tugged on the blade, pitching toward her with a moan. Persephonie gasped and stumbled backward. The man from the entryway appeared beside her, hand wrapped around hers and arm across her waist. In one motion, he tugged her and the blade free, sending the werewolf's corpse to crash into one of the storeroom barrels lying outside the tavern.

"Persephonie—"

Loose strands of russet brown framed Rennear's anxious face, peering at her as he panted in the moonlight.

The cellar door behind them burst open and Otmund sprang into the alley, an upturned wine bottle in hand. "Back away from her!" he yelled, advancing on Rennear, who took two rapid steps toward the alley mouth.

"Wait, Otmund"—Persephonie held her hand out, halting the tavern owner—"he's helping me."

"Helping?" Otmund took in the scene of bloodshed around them, the three bodies scattered across the alley. "I heard a crash, but—"

"Are you alright?" Rennear said softly, his fingertips resting on her shoulder.

"I—" The throb in her wrist called her attention downward, and Persephonie raised her hand. The imprint of the werewolf's grasp still clung to her skin in a dark, swollen bruise, her hand at an unnatural angle at the end of her arm. Persephonie's knees swayed, and Rennear caught her elbows, steadying her.

He turned to Otmund. "Take her inside. I'll deal with this."

"How did you—"

"I'll explain soon, but you need to shelter inside the Green Owl for now." His coppery eyes pleaded with her. *Trust me.*

Persephonie nodded behind creased brows, and Otmund reached out for her, helping her down the stone steps into the kitchen's side entrance. "We'll get Tess to look at that arm for you. Come along, Juniper," he called to the fox.

"Juliet," Persephonie whispered.

"Ah, doesn't matter," Otmund grumbled, shaking his head. Juliet's paws clicked after them, and thunder boomed overhead. The enchantress had returned to Cassandra's side, and she would send a cleansing rain in her wake.

Rennear stood watching her as the tavern door closed, silhouetted between stars and lantern light.

CHAPTER 25

I t was time. Marcon split away from Iellieth, his eyes creased in worry as he went in search of Kazimir, and she hid, waiting to intercept Quindythias impersonating Kazimir. Marcon had decided to ask the socialite to join him for drinks on the terrace as opposed to attempting the complicated Hadvarian jigs. Quindythias and Kazi would still be prevented from running into one another, and, as Marcon had added, "I won't draw an undue amount of attention to myself, either."

In some respects, the masquerade had made their plan easier, so long as Master Yugo believed in the façade. But she couldn't dismiss the nagging tinge of worry that Kazimir and Master Yugo would find one another, completely sidestepping their scheme for getting upstairs. Iellieth shook her head, trying to imagine Quindythias's reaction if Master Yugo passed him over for the actual Kazimir, or if Marcon accidentally tried to woo him instead of the Hadvarian. She pressed her fingers to her lips to hide a grin.

As she crept around the corner, Iellieth willed the finely dressed nobles to pay her no mind as she slipped toward the side staircase that led up to the dormitories. Quindythias's laugh as the fake Kazimir burbled from the nearby drinks table. She needed to hurry.

Iellieth hid from sight in a dark alcove beneath the stairs. With a deep breath, she clasped her palm over the crescent moon pendant at her wrist. She searched for remnants of the spirits of nature inside the ballroom and called them to her aid. They were faint, silenced by swishing gowns and neglect, but they whispered back to her, heeded her cry. Their energy swam out of the onyx walls and flickered away from the gemstones decorating Hadvar's nobility.

"Allow yourself to take in the fullness of the world around you," Yvayne had advised when they practiced transforming into smaller creatures in the woods outside her home in the Frostmaw Mountains. "Recognize the breadth and depth of the life that surrounds us all, and let your own sense of self dissipate." It hadn't come as easily as her wolf transformations, but she eventually found the pattern and could reliably transform into a squirrel or mouse.

But this would be her first transformation in a time of great need. They didn't have a secondary plan for if she wasn't able to change her form. Iellieth floated the worry out to sea, picturing instead Yvayne's smile as the druid informed her that she had managed the smaller form but had kept her hair color—a garnet squirrel.

Iellieth exhaled and willed herself to shrink, morphing her form into that of a tiny mouse.

The ballroom had been loud before, but here along the edges, the room caught all the echoes of conversation and funneled them into her large, rounded ears. A multiplicity of sounds bombarded Iellieth from her new, shrunken position. Her nose quivered, taking in the wafted aromas, the oaky wines, the crisp fruits, and the mouthwatering warmth of the bread.

She could not stop her spine from quivering, her entire form occupied by the intense danger of the situation, of being spotted, of being stepped on.

She moved her ears back, listening for the adjusted tenor of Quindythias's voice as he drew nearer. Iellieth darted farther behind the column so that he would have the easiest chance of scooping her up on his route upstairs. The soles of his polished shoes clicked across the onyx flooring. *Heel, toe, heel, toe.* Master Yugo's right foot dragged as he walked arm in arm with the impersonator of his lover.

Four massive feet thundered around the corner. Her tiny reflection shimmered back to her in the shine of Quindythias's shoes. A garnet mouse this time. She sighed. There would be time for more practice later and at least in this case, she would be easy to spot.

Towering far above her, Quindythias wrapped his arm around Master Yugo's. The fake Kazimir threw his head back, a storm of laughter and flashing smile, waving goodnight to one of Master Yugo's students and leading the mage toward the stairs.

Quindythias patted the mage's elbow, gesturing absentmindedly with the other hand while he spoke. Their footsteps shook the floor. He called Master Yugo's attention to a small detail in the room and glanced along the floor, searching for her. Iellieth waved the tip of her red tail in the air. Quindythias's eyes widened for a moment, and he smirked.

Her stomach knotted, seeing the two of them together. Would this create a rift in Master Yugo's relationship with Kazimir? Or would he understand? Quindythias had assured her that he would make a gracious exit and not damage the mage's pride or feelings, but he refused to confide the particulars to her.

Master Yugo glanced from the glittering room to the modestly hunched fake Kazimir on his arm, his eyes shining as he looked up into Quindythias's smiling, masked face.

Quindythias swept his hand to the side as he glided across the floor to stand beside her. His dramatic gesture flung champagne from his low-rimmed glass, spilling globules of sticky golden bubbles across the floor.

Master Yugo's gaze followed the line of liquid, his face turning away from Iellieth's quaking frame on the floor. He called one of the servants over to mop up after Kazimir's accident. Quindythias pulled out a silk handkerchief, waving as though he would clean it up himself. The fabric fluttered delicately out of his hand, winding its way down to cover Iellieth's position on the floor.

Her body froze, and a warm hand wrapped around her and the handkerchief. Quindythias's altered voice giggled contentedly from far above her as she careened through the air. The elf opened his pocket wide to receive her, and she and the handkerchief plunked into the pocket.

Iellieth wiggled against the constricting fabric, clenching and releasing her paws as she righted herself. Her form still trembled at being carried through the air. What would have happened if she splatted to the ground as a mouse?

Quindythias gave the pocket a gentle tap, throwing her back against his chest. She held back a squeak and poked out her claws. *Focus, mouse self.* She could rebalance in this shifting pocket. The sway as Quindythias walked was how she had imagined sailing on the ocean would be, though, her wriggling nose added, the pocket smelled much more of flowers than the sea.

The slippery fabrics of the handkerchief and the pocket shifted again, and she lost her balance. Her sharp claw slipped, piercing through the fabric into the skin of Quindythias's chest.

"Yeow!" he cried out at the sudden shock, and Iellieth withdrew her paw, falling backward once more. "Ha! Silly me," Quindythias said quickly, shielding his pocket and seemingly grabbing his heart as he turned back to Master Yugo.

Perhaps they should have practiced tiny being transportation. Her body trembled, and she worked to calm herself as they started once more toward the stairs.

An undercurrent of musk reached into her nostrils beneath the floral of Kazimir's strong cologne. Her nose tickled, a sneeze wriggling to be set free. Her whiskers quivered as she tried to rub out the smell, worsening the sensation.

"Shall we retire upstairs?" Quindythias asked, his voice mercifully covering her loud exhalations of the cologne.

"You are sure you do not mind leaving the party early?" Master Yugo's deeper voice was soothing, his care for his former partner coating each word in thoughtfulness and concern.

"I am quite certain," Quindythias intoned from the back of his throat.

"Well, in that case . . ." Master Yugo swept the pair of them toward the stairs. They exchanged pleasantries as they walked, Quindythias clearly enjoying his role and the attention. Iellieth pushed on the outside of the vest pocket to open it slightly and peer up at her friend. A thin streak of his dark brown skin remained along the base of his neck, but otherwise, with his large mask, he had achieved a remarkable resemblance to the socialite.

Iellieth's mind began to wander as they talked. What was Kazimir like in private situations? How different was he when he felt free from needing to perform to a particular audience? When no one was watching?

Master Yugo was thoughtful and kind—she doubted she could have asked for a better companion for any number of her friends.

Quindythias's heart sped up, jolting her attention back to the conversation booming above her.

"Kazimir, I wanted to speak to you about our last conversation on a fanciful night such as this."

Quindythias inhaled sharply. His heart pounded against her wide mouse ears.

"Yes . . . about that . . ."

Iellieth pulled herself up from the top of the pocket, her nose, eyes, and large ears emerging from Quindythias's vest, partially shielded by his jacket.

Master Yugo paused on the stairs and laid his hand on Quindythias's. "I am sorry for having upset you, but I hope that you now understand. I cannot tell you how relieved I was to find a few moments alone with you this evening. I understood from our exchange yesterday that you might still be upset with me."

Quindythias smiled back. "No, certainly not. I was relieved that you were willing to put up with my flights of fancy." He brushed his free hand to the side.

Master Yugo stared up into Quindythias's masqueraded eyes and leaned forward. Quindythias took the cue and met the older man's lips, sharing in a passionate kiss.

Iellieth's heart warmed at the sight, and her mouse tail flicked back and forth. Though it was pretend, their conversation felt real. She grinned. Quindythias had found the companionship he was searching for after all.

Master Yugo pressed into Quindythias, leaning into her slight mouse form. They could crush her between them! Iellieth gasped. She turned her paws into the elf's chest. *Quindythias! Too close!*

He winced and rolled his shoulder away from the mage. She took a full breath of air and plummeted back to the bottom of Quindythias's pocket. If they had crushed her, would she have simply reappeared between them? Yvayne had indicated that possibility if she experienced enough strain in an animal form. Iellieth curled into the silk-lined bottom, head tucked around her rump.

"Well"—Master Yugo spoke after a few moments, his voice lower than usual—"may I escort you up to my quarters?"

"What an enchanting proposition," Quindythias-as-Kazimir purred. "I thought you'd never ask, and then I would have been forced to insist, which is, of course, *so* very unlike me."

Master Yugo chuckled amiably and resumed climbing the stairs.

Iellieth's pulse slowed once more, and the click of their footsteps soon grew louder than her pounding heart. She shook her fur. Her mouse paw brushed across her furry chest, where her amulet would usually be.

The echo of their footsteps sharpened. They must be near the top. She clawed against the outside of the pocket and pulled her pointy nose and large ears free from the top. Two and a half flights of stairs later, they arrived in front of Master Yugo's door.

This is it. Iellieth pressed her paws against the line of Quindythias's pocket, but the movement was too slight for him to notice. She let out a tiny mouse sigh. After they had recovered the seal piece and made it to safety, the two of them could develop an ear-signaling system for future adventures. Quindythias averted his masked eyes as Master Yugo stepped toward his door.

"One moment please, my dear," the mage said. "If you'll wait just here for me." He squeezed Quindythias's hand and stepped to face the middle door, murmuring the incantation she'd heard the evening before with his hand pressed against the stone surface. "There we are." Master Yugo glanced back over his shoulder, his features crinkling as he smiled.

A chilling wind rushed across the landing, tinged with smoke. Thunder rumbled in Iellieth's mind. Something wasn't right. The night before—

The stone door shot to the side with a crash. Master Yugo

whirled around, his body angled half in front of Quindythias-Kazimir.

An arrow flew out of the darkness and pierced the mage's throat. He stumbled back, gurgling as he tried to catch himself.

Quindythias shouted and caught Master Yugo before he slumped to the ground.

A second arrow struck the wall where Quindythias had been a moment before. Iellieth curled up in Quindythias's pocket, cringing away from the *thud* of two more arrows striking Master Yugo's body.

Quindythias groaned, extricating himself, his hand reflexively over his pocket to cover Iellieth. He darted clear of the doorway's range and leaned his back against the wall. His heart pounded against her enlarged ears. "This wasn't part of any of our sub-plans," he whispered.

Iellieth's mind whirled. Why would someone be in the room, waiting to attack Master Yugo? Unless . . . *Cheep, cheep, cheep!* She scrambled against the pocket silk, trying to get the elf's attention.

He pulled her out and cupped her in his hands. There was no time to communicate "agents of Alessandra here for the seal piece" in mouse body language. She stuck out a tiny arm and pointed at the room instead.

"Got it." Quindythias hugged her against his chest and somersalted into the room. "Yah!" he shouted, flinging a dagger at the black-clad figure crouching by the low ledge that lined Master Yugo's wall. She was directly in front of where Iellieth had left the seal piece the evening before.

The woman cried out as the dagger pierced her shoulder. There was a flash of gray, tucked tight against her waist, as she reeled back. Iellieth squeaked. The assassin's head darted toward the shattered window on the opposite side of the room. The undulating form of a floating rug drifted just outside, a sharp red against the dark glimmer of the Hadvarian sky.

She couldn't get away, not with the seal piece, their one hope for restoring Marcon and Quindythias to their full selves, for protecting everything her friends had fought for. With all of her might, Iellieth flung herself from the elf's hands and flew toward the figure. She called on the energy that she'd struggled to steady during her conversation with Vladislav, balling it together in the center of her chest. The tide pressed, condensed, and exploded within her, waves roaring out to her extremities.

Be the wolf, Yvayne's voice echoed in her memory.

The slain form of Master Yugo, the thump of the arrow striking his body, filled her mind.

Iellieth's feet crashed onto the stone floor of the mage's bedroom. The silk of her dress tangled around her ankles, and she rolled toward the assassin.

Her transformation had failed.

A demented grin stretched across the woman's face, tugging at the scar that crossed in a crescent moon from her eye down to the side of her jaw. "That was unexpected." Scarlet drops fell from the gleaming dagger in her hand, Quindythias's blade ripped free from her shoulder.

Iellieth ground her teeth together and grabbed her father's amulet. Already, it had begun to pulse in such close proximity to the seal piece. "Dark as night, thick as shadow, pure as shade, I summon thee," Iellieth chanted in Druidic. "Piece of seal, element pure, come to me."

Indigo light flared from the arcane runes surrounding the seal piece. The assassin yelped in surprise, and Iellieth sprang forward, wrapping her hands around ancient stone.

The woman growled and tried to yank the seal piece free of Iellieth's grasp.

Iellieth pulled herself closer instead, falling onto the floor, arms around the stone, with the assassin snarling above her. *If only I could have been the wolf.*

The assassin reeled back, blue eyes gleaming, dagger raised.

Iellieth swung her knee around, catching the woman in the side.

With a gasp, the assassin fell to the floor beside Iellieth.

A flurry of knives appeared between them. "Iellieth, go!" Quindythias shouted. Kazimir's mask lay discarded behind him on the floor. Wind whipped through the room, tugging at the assassin's long, dark hair.

The woman spun on her heel away from Quindythias's attack and threw herself toward the open window.

Iellieth scrambled to her feet, slipping once on the hem of her dress. She grabbed the inky silk and sprinted for the door.

Behind her, glass crunched beneath booted feet, and Quindythias shouted a stream of Elvish curses.

Her heels clattered on the stairs, and the elf slid out onto the landing just behind her. "She escaped through the window." His dark eyes flared. "Time to go."

Iellieth nodded, her heart pounding in her throat.

Footsteps thundered up the stairs below them. Guards shouted.

She glanced back at Quindythias. "Time to disappear." The seal piece vibrated in her hands. *"Aiya'ne."* With a solid thrum, dark purple shadows poured out of the seal piece and darted down the staircase ahead of them. For a moment, the torches lining the winding stone stairs trembled and then extinguished. A soft purple glow lit her hands, Quindythias's face, and the few stairs ahead of them.

"Well done." Quindythias nodded to her, impressed. "Let's get Marcon and get out of here."

CHAPTER 26

"Ow!" Persephonie jerked her hand back from Tess's careful touch. They looked back at her, eyes burning. "I'm sorry, Tess." She blinked away tears. "If I could just—"

"You cannot cast anything tonight," Otmund murmured under his breath, hurrying back into the kitchen's warm glow.

Rain pounded against the tavern walls as though it were trying to drown out her memories of the attack while Tess bound her wrist to help set it back in place. How had those men found her, and why? Rennear had said he would explain, but how had he known they would be there?

Juliet stared back at her, amber eyes glowing.

"You knew," she whispered to the fox.

"Persephonie, did you hear me?"

She jumped and shook her head at Otmund.

"I think we need to get you upstairs to rest, my girl."

"But—"

"I'll send him along once he's finished with the business outside."

Tess winked at her, and Persephonie blushed. "It's not . . ." She sighed, shaking her head. They wouldn't believe her regardless.

Otmund escorted her to the back door and upstairs to the sitting room on the third floor. He checked her room and the hall to set both her and himself at ease before excusing himself back downstairs. The din from below was no match for the rain.

Persephonie curled up on the olive sofa with brown and gold flowers, pulling her favorite cream-colored blanket around her shoulders. Her hand traced the eye of Cassandra on her golden bangle. "Why didn't you tell me?" she whispered, closing her eyes and waiting for an answer.

The scrape and clatter of carriages came and went beneath the sound of rain as she rehearsed the events of the alley over and over again. Was what the werewolf said about the conclave's elders true? The statue that she and her mother had seen, of the kneeling priests . . . how could they blame the conclave for the actions of the Untamed? Mama had dodged her questions whenever she pressed about the more radical elements of her organization. Was this why?

Rapid footsteps ascended the stairs behind her, and Persephonie's neck and shoulders tensed as she craned her head around.

"Juliet, hello." Rennear inclined his head to the fox, thrusting his wet hair back and out of his face as he took in her and the room. It was certainly nothing compared to the fine furnishings of a senator's house, but Otmund had more interior space than anyone she had ever known besides Varra Yvayne. Rennear's brow furrowed as he stared at her on the sofa. The scrapes on her cheek must be starting to swell.

"Would you like me to add more logs to the fire? Are you chilled?" He hurried toward her but stopped at the edge of the rug.

"I am alright, but you should see about drying off." She glanced at the puddle forming around his feet. "There is a coatrack there in the corner by my room." She gestured to her door. "You can spread your jacket out on that and put it in front of the fire."

"Thank you, Persephonie." He crossed the room in a few long strides and picked up the forest green coatrack, placing it in front of the fire and draping his sopping doublet over the prongs. He added his cravat and vest as well, the pitter-patter of their collected drops accenting the rushing downpour outside.

His linen shirt clung to his skin. "May I join you?"

"Please." She patted the cushion next to her, scooting her feet in to make more space for him. Her breath faltered as he sat facing her, taking her hand in his.

The copper in his eyes flared, but he turned away, shoulder squared to the wall. He released her hand to watch the black torrent raging against the windows. "I want to explain every-thing to you, how . . ." He sighed and dropped his head in frus-tration. Rennear's eyes burned as he looked back at her. "I'm sorry."

"Why?" She leaned forward. Perhaps he had misunderstood. "Rennear, you and Juliet, you rescued me." She reached for his hand again, his fingers warm in hers. "If you hadn't . . ." A lump in the back of her throat cut off her words, and tears gathered in her eyes, their shimmer blurring her vision.

Rennear caught the first one to fall from the top of her cheek, fingertip tracing her skin before he tucked a stray lock of hair behind her ear. "Don't think of that for now." His voice was low, each tenor note tinged with concern. "May I see your wrist again?"

She slipped free of the blanket and held out her bandaged arm for his inspection.

He slowly unwound the bindings, frowning at the claw marks

on her arm and the dark blue hand that still gripped her wrist. "I can fetch a healer for you."

Persephonie pulled away from him, wincing as she did so. "Not them." She clutched her hand to her chest. Not the horrible priests who condemned those who were like her for being who they were, for being different. Who severed hands from limbs to staunch the flow of magic, as though that would stopper someone's connection to the world around them.

"They won't hurt you."

The werewolf's words came floating back to her, and the elders' screams echoed over the storm's wails. "Yes, they will." She huddled back against the couch corner away from him. He still had much to explain. "How did you know where I would be? What was happening?"

Rennear cast his eyes over to Juliet, curled within the ring of her tail on the saffron armchair. "If I told you that I had a sense that something was wrong, would you believe me?"

She nodded.

"And if that sense was louder and clearer than it was on the day we met?"

Another nod. *Tell me what is truly going on*, she wanted to say but waited.

"Hold tight, little one," Cassandra's spirit whispered to her, "the truth will come in time."

He returned his stare to the window. She would try a different approach.

"Those men, they are gone?"

It was Rennear's turn to wordlessly answer, his jaw twinging as he did so.

"They are dead?"

"Yes." Rennear's voice emerged from the back of his throat, a glowing ember.

"Where did their bodies go?" Her voice tiptoed across the sofa, resting its fingers against his arm, asking to be let in.

"To the morgue. I handled everything with the guards." Rennear met her gaze once more. "Your name won't appear anywhere in the investigation, which should be brief if it's pursued at all." He stood and started to pace in front of the fire.

"And no guards will be back tonight?"

"No one will bother you."

Persephonie sighed. This still wasn't the clarity she had hoped for, but her wrist had throbbed for long enough. She laid it out on her lap, meaty fingertips visible over the pale gold of the underside of her arm. "Otmund said I should not, but if they are not coming back . . ."

His pacing slowed, head tilted as he watched her lay her fingers against her wrist and close her eyes. "Where the spirit and soul combine," she began her prayer in Saudad, "allow a return to what once was, to a time before. Fate's change, beneath Cassandra's gaze"—and ended in Druidic—"Elenai." Healing spirits fluttered to life around her, and she released them to their work.

Rennear gasped as translucent droplets of purple light swirled around her hands and soaked into her wrist, tiny wings fluttering as the spirits worked their way into bruised muscle and twisted bone. With a faint glow, the marks faded, and her hand returned to how it had been before, leaving only the dried blood drawn by the werewolf's claw behind.

Hesitantly, she raised her eyes to the bronze orbs staring between her face and her wrist. "How?" He exhaled slowly. "It's healed now? You're no longer hurt?"

She twisted her wrist in front of her, the movement fully restored. "My wrist is healed, yes." The horrible memories still groped at her, tugging her back into the past. "Other things take more time."

Rennear knelt beside her, gingerly picking up her hand and wrist as though she were spun from glass. "I never realized that magic like yours . . ." His voice trailed off, and he bowed his head over her hand and kissed the inside of her wrist; her pulse leaped up to meet his lips. "Will you forgive me, for taking so long to arrive?"

"I still do not understand. How could you have possibly known?" Her hair fell over her shoulder, and she brushed it back again. "You are saying that Juliet came to get you? I am still not certain how she knew that something bad was going to happen."

The fox breathed deeply, probably dreaming of a cozy den in the Brightlands or of splashing in puddles on the morrow.

"Persephonie, I . . ." He sat back on his heels, face turned to the fire. "You know who my father is. And what the guards who attacked you are." His fingers trailed through his thick russet hair. "But what you don't know . . ." Rennear's jaw tightened, his teeth grinding as he glared at the floor. When he looked back at her, he stared for a long moment before speaking. "I'm a were-wolf too."

CHAPTER 27

Ten days passed beneath the cover of the trees as Briseras and Everett traveled from village to village around the "ring of protection," as Hannah had called it. The settlements formed a rough circle around the Nocturne estate, a black castle that few in the region had ever laid eyes on. Each village bore its own tales of the frightening figure who dwelled within the castle and, of more interest to Briseras, a string of disappearances that spanned the last five years.

They had returned almost to their starting place, one village removed from Hannah's. Briseras scowled at the herbalist's warning and desperation. Putting faces to so many endangered lives . . . but endangered by what? She couldn't allow a stream of superstition to divert her from ridding the region of the true threat to their well-being, the vampire who lived within a few days of their homes. But since Hannah's second binding spell, Briseras had been unable to shake the foreboding sense of dark clouds gathered on the horizon. She paid scant heed to her own role in Hannah's warning. Since the age of fourteen, she had been on the path of destiny. Her mother would have said since birth. Yet still, each dawn, the witch's words hovered over her, and she awoke choking on the stench of decay, a scent that drifted away moments later, leaving only the foul memory in its wake.

"Have you finished compiling the villagers' timeline of the disappearances?" she asked. With an accurate account of the vampire's feeding, she could estimate the creature's strength, age, and habits, as well as discern whether or not it was working alone.

Briseras crested the rise that held the last of the settlements. Vera sniffed the air. They had seen smoke rising from this hillside not two days ago. But something had transpired here in the interim. No one stirred over the stone paths that wound between the small homes.

A soft breeze whispered over the eaves. With it rose the cloying odor of rot. But this time, unlike from her dreams, it lingered.

"Shouldn't someone be here?" Everett whispered.

"Just follow me." Briseras led the way down the deserted street. The villagers were either paranoid or dead. In either case, they'd draw less attention by moving purposefully.

She slid silently past the first several cottages and winced at a sudden knocking behind her.

"Anyone there?" Everett rapped his knuckles against the front door of one of the homes she'd passed. No answer came from inside. "Hello?" He knocked again.

Briseras sighed. Civility absorbed so much time. She strode forward, raised her knee, and pummeled the door with her foot. Its latch sprang open, and the door swung inside.

The hinges' squeak echoed across the floor as a rat scurried for cover. The creature bolted from the cabin, and Everett jumped back. "What?" Briseras shrugged. "If whoever's house this is minds, I'll fix it." She crouched through the low opening before pulling back her hood. Mottled rays of faint sun strained against the musty interior.

It was unlikely that the homeowner was still around to protest at the intrusion.

Everett peered through the dim light into the home's interior, leaning in from the outside.

Ripped, olive green curtains lay on the floor beside smashed pots and a broken table. A faint trail of blood led from the cottage deeper into the village. She met Everett's wide, frightened eyes. A single nod. "Werewolves."

Briseras strode into the center of the deserted village. A damp chill clung to the air. Somewhere nearby, they would find a scene of carnage. "Stay alert," she fired over her shoulder to Everett.

He frowned at her, turning back to his black leather-bound journal. "You asked after my timeline, and I'm trying to find it for you."

"Never mind that now." She leaned through the smashed windows of the homes in the center of the village. No survivors thus far.

Just like Hannah had said.

The folklorist carefully stepped around shattered glass and leaned closer to examine a broken doorway. "Is anyone left?" His mouth fell open as he studied the ransacked village.

A large paw print had pressed into the mud between the scattered stones of the street. The pack had arrived just after the rain the morning before.

Everett held up a clump of fur from one of the cobbles. Congealed blood held the hairs together.

The breeze shifted again, and a putrid stench brought Briseras over to the well on the far edge of the stone courtyard. Dried blood had stained the rough bricks of the top of the well, and the foul odor drifted up from its depths. They'd need to refill their canteens elsewhere.

"Should I come over there?" Everett raised his voice from across the courtyard.

A metallic tang, cold, called Briseras to the village meeting house. She brushed her hair back from her face. Beads of fog clung to the strands and bound them together. Pebbles settled into the mud beneath her feet. Her crossbow waited, pointing at the ground, ready.

The wooden doors to the long meeting house were closed despite claw marks across their surface. That's where they would find the bodies.

"Before we go in there, Briseras, I wanted to tell you . . ." Everett cleared his throat, wandering nearer and watching his feet. "For the longest time, I hadn't wanted to believe that James was gone." He met her eyes. "Thank you for that. Setting him free. I didn't know that was what I needed."

His demeanor toward her had warmed further after their encounter with Hannah, and in the days since, only one of the four villages they'd visited had forbidden her to return. Two weeks after they'd returned James's ashes to the earth, Everett was beginning to mend. The timing was fortunate. They had work to do.

"Closure helps." Briseras nodded and kicked open the heavy wooden doors.

The broken doors groaned on rusted hinges, banging back and creaking as they continued to sway. Everett gagged, throwing himself away from the smell.

"Found the villagers." Briseras grinned at him, then cast her eyes back over the piles of misshapen bodies left in the monsters' wake. "Take a look at their wounds."

"Are you sure?" Everett's hands shook as he held his fists up near his chest, frowning at the nearest set of corpses.

She turned away, shaking her head. From all the accounts they'd heard—save Hannah's warning—this settlement should have been safe from the werewolves' attacks. But the pack had done more than feed and glean here—they'd decimated the village. Why? Did they have the vampire's permission, or was this part of a larger conflict playing out among the creatures?

Briseras grimaced. If Hannah had been wrong about the vampire or had manipulated Briseras's hatred for their kind, then all of their information gathering of the last week and a half was for nothing. The tracks they had followed, the trails of information and where they led . . . useless.

Expired torches hung in the iron sconces on the walls. Villagers' bodies were draped over the long central table. Others had been cast aside, splintering the smaller carts and tables that lined the log-paneled room.

Her boots echoed against the planks. She had been right in her first reckoning of when the attack had taken place. They'd missed this assault by a day, two at most. The bodies were cold but not yet swollen beyond study.

Briseras sniffed the still air. Before she'd met Everett, months had passed across these mountains without her being able to pin down the clue that eluded her. She'd separated from Rajas in search of it, telling herself that she had to uncover what was driving the pack. With Everett, after Hannah's revelation, that mission finally moved a step forward—she knew, at least before today, what held the lycanthropes back.

The tales they'd gathered over the last ten days each began with small disappearances—one person here, a lone traveler there, a few children lost in the woods. Beyond the ring of protection, as the pack appeared, its size grew rapidly through midnight mass conversions. They raided a village, infected the strong, ate the weakest, and saved the rest for their next passage. But they'd never left a scene of carnage like this one, massacring every last adult and child.

Briseras shuddered at the sensation of cold breath across the back of her neck. Her shoulders tensed as they did each time she repeated the varied descriptions of the alpha. In most accounts, the lycanthropes followed a gray-green, decaying man in flowing black robes. Probably a lich of some kind. But in a few, rare tales, the ones Everett had gathered along the borders of the untouched ring surrounding the Nocturne estate, the lycanthropes followed a well-dressed nobleman in a purple coat with high, deathly pale cheekbones.

A set of fine leather boots gleamed beneath the shadows. The body lay amid a few others that had been mauled. One was missing a leg, the other had taken a fierce bite to the arm and face. Briseras shifted them to the side. The corpses *thump*ed to the ground as she dug for the wealthy man's body. There was something special about this one. If she could just see his wounds . . . Her hand seized the corpse's shoulder.

"Stop!" a woman yelled from the open doors behind her.

Briseras set her jaw and slowly turned her head. They didn't have time for this.

Misty morning light silhouetted the woman's thin frame. She held Everett by the hair, a curved black dagger pressed against his quivering throat. Ice-blue eyes burned beneath her white hair, and rich azure inks marked her fawn-colored skin. A ripple of mist swirled around Everett, restraining his hands and ankles and covering his mouth.

Briseras released the body and raised both hands in the air, crossbow pointed at the sky.

"Lower the bow." The ice-blue eyes flashed.

"I don't think so." Briseras narrowed her gaze. Who was this intruder, and why was she investigating the village so soon after the werewolves had been through it?

"You've no business here," the woman snapped.

Everett struggled again. A dark line of blood appeared beneath the dagger. He whimpered at the cut.

Briseras began to lower the crossbow. She could shoot the woman on the way down.

"We're here to help," Everett cried, choking out the words from beneath the fog spell.

The woman's face spun toward his. "Say that again." The mist drifted away from his mouth.

Briseras exhaled slowly and continued lowering her bow. She took careful aim with the woman's gaze averted.

"I said we're here to help." Everett's voice quavered as he spoke, looking back and forth between them.

Twang.

The woman screamed as Briseras's arrow embedded itself in her wrist. She dropped the blade, and blood spurted from her arm.

"Oof." Everett, his arms and ankles still bound by the spell, fell hard on his shoulder.

Briseras sprang onto the tabletop, tucking and rolling down its length as she dodged the strewn bodies. The next arrow clicked into place, and she pointed it at the woman's neck, towering above her. "Back. Away. From. Him."

Tears dripped from the woman's icy eyes as she stared up at Briseras, clutching her hand to her chest.

"Now!"

She took two stumbling steps back. Everett tried to scoot toward Briseras across the floor.

"Wait," the woman begged. "Please."

Briseras tilted her head.

"You're from here, aren't you?" the caster asked with a quick glance at Everett.

He froze in place and turned back to her. "Just over the mountain." There was a similar lilt to their accents.

The woman took a shuddering breath. "Please, I can explain." She stared up at Briseras.

Vera appeared from behind them, and Otto croaked overhead.

"You're late," Briseras called to them.

The wolf's golden eyes gleamed against her fur. She didn't react to the woman with animosity.

"Very well." Briseras sighed and gestured with her crossbow. "Have a seat. And release him."

The fog dissipated from around Everett's body, and Vera padded up to his side, nuzzling his head.

⁂

BRISERAS SHOWED EVERETT HOW TO HOLD THE WOMAN'S ARM steady so she could remove the arrow. He sat down promptly after, holding his forehead in his hands.

The woman called Lavinia muttered an incantation over her pierced arm. The blue-tinged mist returned and wove around the wound.

"You're a witch, aren't you?" Briseras asked.

"I prefer healer." Her blue eyes glowed brighter, wrinkling at the corners. "What gave it away?"

Everett chuckled nervously and hugged his stomach. "We had an unfortunate encounter with an herbalist a few days ago." He inclined his head toward Briseras. "She's been even more on edge ever since."

"You knew Hannah?" The brilliant blue gaze settled on Briseras, shimmering with questions.

"We met her." Briseras studied the woman before her. Lavinia's traveling pack was small. She had journeyed from nearby, ostensibly alone. How had she so exactly timed her own inspection of the village?

Lavinia frowned. She scratched at the worn wood of the tabletop. "Would it sadden you to learn that she's dead?"

"What?" Everett sat up. He winced as he grabbed his forehead, his face growing paler. He still hadn't recovered from the witch's spell mingled with the decaying bodies and blood.

"Her village looks exactly like this one." Lavinia's voice was soft, her eyes downcast.

"She said something of that nature." Briseras rose and began to walk the length of the room. "It was a desperate prophecy, or a warning. We dismissed it at the time. She kept . . . prying at me. But other things she said about the region, they couldn't wait." She wanted to leave out the herbalist's interest in her, but so long as Everett didn't repeat the connection between the deaths and what Hannah said about her destiny, it shouldn't do any harm for Lavinia to know some of what had happened.

Slowly, the witch raised her head. "My sister and I grew up on the hillside just above the Nocturne village, a day's ride from here or where Hannah lived. We were orphaned in our adolescence, our mother to sickness." Lavinia cleared her throat, her expression straining against her story. "Our father disappeared." She rubbed at the dark circles beneath her eyes. Briseras had missed them in the light of the fog spell. "Three nights ago, my sister, Saige, disappeared. I searched our homestead, the village, and the hillsides around the estate, but I couldn't find her. There were times when our father bid us to reach out to Hannah, to help us with our magic, as well as with the witch who lived in this village. I told myself that there was a chance Saige had ventured out here without me—" Lavinia's voice broke and she crumpled, sobs shaking her shoulders.

Everett glanced at Briseras in alarm before scooting closer to Lavinia and wrapping an arm around her. Briseras returned to examining the bodies while the storm of grief passed.

"Can you tell us more about what you found in Hannah's village?" Everett prodded.

Lavinia stared out of the open double doors into the still town center. "There were only a few bodies, not like this. I didn't see Hannah. But on the street, there was a man lying next to a slain horse."

"What did the body look like?" Briseras asked, glancing up from her perusal of the corpses.

Lavinia gasped at the question, but Everett squeezed her shoulders tighter. "She asks that about everyone."

Briseras shook her head and returned to her work.

"His neck had been ripped open," Lavinia whispered.

"Oh?" Briseras waded back to the pile she'd been investigating when Lavinia interrupted. She pushed one thin body to the side, straddling another to pick up the man who'd first piqued her interest. "Like this?" She grunted as she raised the heavy corpse up by the shoulder.

"Ugh," Everett cried. His hands darted over his eyes.

Lavinia's brow furrowed as she approached Briseras and her prize. She squinted at the body.

A solid chunk had been torn from the man's throat, severing the jugular vein. Briseras dragged him closer to the table, his feet bumping over his fellows on the floor.

"Mmph." She shoved the weighty torso onto the table and went to stand beside his neck. "If you look here"—she ran her finger along the edges of the wound, tracing the four dramatic gouges and peering closer—"these bite marks, they're not from a werewolf."

Lavinia squinted at her, each word hesitantly following the last. "How can you tell?"

Briseras pulled a thin metal gauge from her bag to measure the gashes. "See these top two, the deepest ones? They're over-sized for a werewolf bite and too precise for their claws." Her eyes flashed. *Finally.*

Lavinia's lips parted. "So what you're saying . . ."

Briseras nodded. "Go ahead."

"I don't want . . ."

Briseras raised an eyebrow.

"A vampire," Lavinia whispered.

"Exactly." Briseras clapped her hands together. She rubbed the gauge against her pant leg, compressed it, and stashed it back in the pouch on her hip. The next shot was loaded and ready in her crossbow. "Shall we? You can tell us more about Hannah's village and yours as we go."

Lavinia stared at her, lips pursed. "I, uh, I still haven't found my sister, and . . ."

Everett shook his head at Briseras, trying to stop her from something—she could never tell what.

"Look"—Briseras leaned her hands against the table—"there are two likely scenarios at work here, and neither is good news for your sister. If you're saying she wouldn't have run away, then either she was taken by the pack in the middle of the night, and they left you, or the vampire took her. The second scenario seems more probable to me, depending on how long it had been since you last saw her and when you discovered she was missing." Briseras didn't stop to allow Lavinia a chance to offer clarifying details. They'd have time for that on their journey to the estate, where she should have gone ten days ago instead of gathering further evidence. She'd fought a vampire before. Briseras gestured to Everett. "He's been helping me collect accounts. There's something else at work. The pack is a newer evil. Someone else has been here longer. A vampire." She rose to full height and crossed her arms. "Too many disappearances, over too long a period for it to be otherwise." And now they finally had proof. The deep bite of a vampire feeding. Hunting the pack would have to wait a few days more.

"Where did you last see your sister?" Everett asked.

Briseras stifled an impatient groan. What did it matter? They knew where they had to go.

Lavinia looked down at the floor. "We were sleeping in our cottage. Something . . . a noise woke me in the middle of the night. I went to check on Saige, and she was gone."

Everett started to speak, but Briseras cut in first. "Well, what's it going to be? Do you want to let the bloodsucker continue picking off strays like your sister, or are you going to come track down the vampire with us?" Not everyone had the opportunity to avenge their family. If this woman truly cared for her sister, she would come along. Otherwise, she would just slow them down.

Lavinia scowled.

"Suit yourself." Briseras shrugged. She adjusted her quiver and nodded for Everett to follow. "Let's go."

"I can guide you to the Nocturne estate," Lavinia said. Her eyes searched Briseras's expression. "It's a day from here if you know the way." She adjusted the bandage on her wrist and pulled on her glove. "Saige . . . she suspected something similar. I think that might be part of why she disappeared."

Briseras bit the inside of her lip. Too large a party led to squandered time.

"There were . . . boot prints, outside our house." Her gaze narrowed. "But the trail didn't go far." Lavinia sniffed and pulled the collar of her coat tighter. "She can't just be . . . gone."

Everett crossed the hall to Lavinia and wrapped his arm around her shoulders again, murmuring something in their soothing mountain tongue. They glanced up at her, and Lavinia spoke. "If you find the creature, the vampire, responsible for this, what are you going to do?"

Briseras grinned, her own enlarged canines emerging from beneath a rare smile. "Kill it." Vera growled happily beside her.

CHAPTER 28

Iellieth and Quindythias sprinted past one of the apprentice mages' dormitories. Torches sputtered out one by one as they ran down the hall. Two young men appeared in the violet glow that surrounded the seal piece, rubbing sleep out of their eyes. Their mouths fell open, but Iellieth shouted over their protest. "It's just an effect for the masquerade!"

"We're calling it 'the magic of romance,'" Quindythias added. He dove into a narrow alcove and pulled Iellieth after him. His voice dropped to a whisper, and he waved for her to follow him down the hall. "The plans I took from Dimitri indicated the entrance to a secondary stair up ahead. It should take us to the opposite side of the ballroom. If we hear anyone coming, kiss me. They won't bother us."

"Quindythias, no. I don't think that's a good idea." His tone sounded serious, but she couldn't see his expression to be certain. "Has that ever helped you evade capture before?"

"Havastrias, darling Lilith." He spun around with a wide smile. "And yes. Thrice."

Iellieth sighed. "Well, let's try another strategy this time. I think you should wait for me outside the ballroom while I find Marcon. You don't have your mask—" She gasped and stopped short. They'd left the mask identical to Kazimir's on the floor of Master Yugo's room with Master Yugo lying just outside, murdered. She shut her eyes. The situation was cruel enough already—what if Kazi were implicated in the attack?

"You're right." Quindythias cupped his hands around the outside of hers, supporting the seal piece. "Try to put the rest from your mind until we're safely away." He lowered his eyes. "That may seem selfish, and I know I'm often eager to make light of a serious situation, but here in your hands, you hold the future of Azuria." With a deep breath, he met her eyes. "This is something the three of us share together. Don't let our enemies distract you with blaming yourself for deaths they've caused."

She nodded, pressing her lips together. "Thank you, Quin—ahem, Havastrias."

"Of course, Lilith."

When they reached the stairs, Iellieth whispered to the seal piece in Druidic, asking it to dim its magic. Quindythias wrapped some of his additional Kazimir padding around the stone and followed after her. "I'll meet you here," he said. "Do not tarry, but try to look natural."

Iellieth smoothed the front of her gown and glided back out into the transformed Arcanium. She peered over the heads of those nearby, searching for Marcon's tall silhouette among the crowd. A few dancers whispered and stared—her dress had wrinkled and torn in her fight for the seal piece. She wrapped her hand over a spot of dried blood on her arm, either hers or the assassin's, she wasn't sure.

All across the gala floor, guards stood at attention. Had there been so many before? Her breaths rang hollow in her ears. *Where was Marcon?*

She nearly crashed into a young couple in her hurry. They

leapt to the side, clutching their chests in surprise. *There.* Marcon was standing serenely behind one of the refreshment tables in the side ballroom. She picked up the top of her skirt and scurried over.

His glance found her, and he stood taller to see over the crowd. Marcon pushed through dancers to meet her halfway across the ballroom. "Lady, what is it?" He peered past her shoulder for Quindythias. "Where's—"

"You have to come with me," Iellieth panted. She pulled on his arm, and he hurried after her.

"What happened?" He spoke low, worry coating his voice.

She glanced back. The ballroom blurred in smears of brilliant colors. Master Yugo falling, drowning in his own blood. The assassin's cruel smile.

Iellieth's lips parted to speak, but it was all too much. She shook her head. They had to meet Quindythias and leave. They'd return south to Red's Cross.

"Where do we need to go?"

She pointed out the archway where Quindythias would be waiting.

"Follow me." Marcon kept hold of her hand and blazed a path through the sea of revelers. Without a word, Kazimir's elegant guests parted for the two of them, yielding to the determined set of Marcon's broad shoulders.

Iellieth held his hand in both of hers and followed quickly behind, avoiding meeting anyone's eye.

Quindythias waved them over as they approached and dashed off down the corridor on the opposite side of the stairs.

A breathless quarter of an hour later, Quindythias threw their belongings into her bag. "Ah!" she yelled, arm extended. "Put those down." Quindythias frowned over the set of books he'd found and was prepared to steal from Dimitri. "He'll have enough to deal with."

Her shaking hand ran through her hair. Would she ever have a chance to scour the halls of the Grand Reserve? The Soul Shepherds and their records would have to wait a little while longer.

Marcon held her leather jacket out to her. "In case of pursuit." His eyes glowed.

She shrugged into it, wrapping Mara's magical bag over her shoulders. She tucked the seal piece inside. The two champions ushered her from the room, flying back down the stairs.

A groggy Dimitri stared up at her from the main floor as they sprinted down, and Iellieth's heart seized in her chest. What dangers had they brought upon Dimitri, upon Kazimir, by their sudden arrival? By their actions since? "Dimitri, I—"

"Shh." The librarian reached out for her hand, taking it between his, and held her gaze. "You may have missed this in the stories, so allow me to tell you now." He smiled and leaned back in his chair. "An important part of your new life is allowing others to step in the line of fire for you, Ellie." The words read like an ancient prophecy spilling from the page of a beloved tome. "And as you do so, you'll find them—and yourself—stronger than you now believe." He turned to Marcon and nodded. "Go. I'll stall them as best I can."

The champion bowed his head to Dimitri and urged them out into the night.

She caught a final glimpse of her friend, his comforting silhouette dark against the glow of his library around him. He raised a hand in farewell, his blessing a warm aura around her.

Quindythias crouched and ducked onto a side street, gesturing for them to follow. How many cities would the three of them sneak out of like this? When escaping Linolynn, she'd had a vision of Hadvarian soldiers swarming the streets. The image recurred to her now—only this time, they would pursue her and her two companions rather than the people of Linolynn.

Iellieth lowered her head and crept away after Quindythias.

Below the plateau, the dark glow of the Stormside Forest beckoned. Her fingertips grazed the seal piece in Mara's bag, and her amulet warmed. They could lose the guards among the trees. The darkness would help them.

CHAPTER 29

Genevieve turned her head aside from Kriega's glare. She couldn't control who in the crew passed her, or what they said, but she didn't have to acknowledge their presence. The half-orc leaned against the wall and slid down, legs stretched out in front of her, and continued to stare.

If Genevieve ignored her, maybe she would go away.

"I've been in the position you're in before." The first mate's voice was softer than she had ever heard it. "He won't keep you locked in here forever."

"I'm relieved to hear it." Genevieve crossed her arms.

"On our old ship, with the admiral, it would have been a different story. But the captain has a soft spot for people in need."

"I would have guessed that you wouldn't like that about him." Genevieve finally turned to face Kriega with a scowl. "You don't look at it as a weakness?"

She shrugged. "We all have things or people we care about that make us weak. If the worst charge we can level against the captain's habits is wanting to help people who are vulnerable, then I've certainly seen more dangerous patterns for a leader to have. And in this case, I think it worked out well." Kriega grinned in the half-darkness outside the ship's prison cells. "I like having a werewolf or two on board. If you had told me sooner, I might have put you on a security patrol instead of scrubbing the decks."

Genevieve smiled in return. "How do you know that I would have been any better suited to that?" Jade's spirit nuzzled against her. They had managed well enough as new acquaintances of the ocean.

"Just a feeling." She crossed one ankle over another. "I'm sure Athena will come and keep you company. But let me know if anyone gives you any trouble down here."

There were only two people on the crew she suspected would try to cause her any harm. "Are . . . *they* allowed down here?" Jade's hair stood on end, a growl bristling in the back of her throat.

"Ha! Don't you worry about that. Darcy's barely left his room since the skin of his arm rotted off." Kriega looked thoughtful. "Any idea what caused that?"

She should lie and say she didn't know, but that might make it all the more difficult for her to acquire the dagger later. And she had been certain, as she slipped into unconsciousness, that her ancestors believed Captain Teodric would help her. She just needed to find out how. "I might," Genevieve whispered.

Kriega whistled. "I didn't anticipate you saying so, but you did seem the least horrified of anyone in that cabin. That's usually a telltale sign to me. Hmm, well in that case, should we anticipate the flesh will keep decaying and falling off? It's up to his elbow now."

Genevieve hugged her knees against her chest, and Jade's

ears pricked up. *All the way to his elbow. How long till the rest of him rotted away?* "I know that using the dagger in the way he did will spell his demise unless someone intervenes."

"Understood." Kriega frowned, but Genevieve wasn't certain which part of their conversation troubled her. "And just so you know, Hallix is even further below decks than you. Captain's not happy about someone who should *know* to disclose their lycanthropy being aboard and saying nothing." Kriega ran her tongue over her teeth, regarding Genevieve from the corner of her eye. "You want that dagger back, don't you?"

A knot swelled in Genevieve's throat. Jade perked up her ears. "More than anything."

Her brown eyes flashed. "I'll see what I can do." Kriega pushed herself up off the floor, the taut muscles of her legs swelling to steady her as the *Queen* swayed. The half-orc's footsteps pounded up the stairs and up onto the deck.

"Do you really think she meant it, Jade?" She tried not to picture the spread of rot and dried blood up Darcy's arm. The druidic artifact didn't entail an easy death . . . She glowered at her knees. The deaths of the elders, of her conclave, hadn't been easy either. Didn't Darcy deserve to slowly rot away after whatever he had taken part in that brought the dagger into his possession?

She still didn't know for certain what role he had played.

Genevieve closed her eyes, recalling the faces of her mentors, Mariellen and Sheffield. Even after what they'd endured in their final moments, would they have condemned another to slowly rot away?

A set of lighter footsteps approached. Athena's blonde hair caught the lantern light outside Genevieve's cell. She still wasn't sure what to say. Would Athena be upset that she'd befriended a werewolf?

"I brought you some extra fruit from Keever," she said, holding out a ripe plum. "He won't admit it, but he's very upset you've been locked away here." A small smile crossed her face. "And I am too."

Genevieve sighed and slid over to the bars next to Athena. She took the fruit from the sailor's hand, their fingertips brushing in the exchange. Keever would have grumbled at the request if Athena had made it or found another way to be upset by it if he'd thought of it on his own. "Thank you," she said softly. She blinked quickly to dismiss the sudden swell of tears. *First Yvayne, Sariel, Ophelia, and now Athena, Keever, and Kriega.* The process would take time, but just like an acorn planted in the forest, her conclave was beginning to grow.

⚜

TEODRIC CROSSED HIS ARMS AND RESTED HIS CHIN ON TOP OF his wrists, staring at the shard of bone and the broken horn handle on the other side of his desk. He had ordered Ambrose to reroute their course to Nortelon in hopes of saving Darcy's arm, but the chances of avoiding an amputation . . . or worse appeared low.

But why had the broken dagger attacked Darcy? He chuckled to himself. The more useful question was—How did the dagger *know* to attack Darcy? Genevieve's wound, conversely, had all but disappeared.

There was a familiarity he couldn't place to the magic he'd felt swarming around her. He had never imagined himself calm and collected in the face of a werewolf, especially on so small a space as a ship, but he'd known she didn't mean him, Kriega, or Athena any harm. But the sense was more than that. It was like being back in Linolynn, taking a stroll through the Arboretum, or playing a ballad he'd learned as a boy—a sense that the stars had aligned, and he was precisely where he was meant to be. He thought that feeling had forever vanished with the disappearance of his father.

Athena had reported some of Genevieve's mumblings in her sleep, names that meant nothing to anyone save the speaker. Had she fled her family? Did they turn her out after her transformation? He'd met several survivors of werewolf attacks during his years in Nortelon. A haunted absence filled their eyes when they spoke of it—the way he imagined he looked when he tried to remember Syleste's island. Most of them were among only a few survivors. They'd fled south to avoid the roving highland packs.

"I've heard the most curious report," his father had said one evening when he returned home from the meeting house in Nortelon. He had waved Teodric into the library after greeting his mother with a kiss and asking after her day. "Perhaps it is more of a concerning request than a report proper." He hurried over to the collection of maps and withdrew a faded depiction of Tor'stre Vahn. "One of my appointments today was with a young diplomat from Andel-ce Hevra who had been sent from the city to see about extending the southern reach of their patrols." Frederick had smiled and clapped him on the shoulder. "He reminded me of you—bright, charming, with his own view of how the world ought to be."

His father had gone on to explain that behind the cleverly worded request, the message functioned as a warning to the modest port city of Nortelon that Andel-ce Hevra intended to extend the reach of its empire further and would be employing regiments of werewolves to do so. One of their senators, a man with a great deal of influence in the council, had worked diligently to train and win over the creatures for the city's cause, promising them equal citizenship after a set period of honorable service. Frederick had been unsure at the time how widely known such a tactic was, but he had wondered aloud—If one man could alter the ages-old reputation of the highland packs, what could several like-minded diplomats accomplish toward the goals of preventing wars or of establishing fair and equal trading practices?

Teodric missed his father's optimism. Even after the king turned his back on them and allowed Duke Amastacia to expel him and his family from Linolynn, Frederick still believed in the possibilities for a better world, for second chances and new beginnings. In sun-soaked moments, he hoped to be such a visionary for his crew, but storms were frequent on the high seas of the Infinite Ocean, especially for those sailing under the greedy banner of Admiral Syleste.

He rose and tucked his arms behind his back, crossing to the window. Kriega had organized a special watch to be kept over Hallix below. Rumors circulated among the crew as to what had happened, but as of yet, none of them knew there were two werewolves on board. When he had lived in Caldara, werewolves were little more than folklore, the frightful, sometimes misunderstood figures of campfire tales who held no bearing over daily life. They were as distant as the fae.

But in Tor'stre Vahn, where most of his crew originated from, the same could not be said. The packs made travel dangerous, especially for families with healthy adolescent children. Several of his deckhands had lost older siblings to lycanthropy. In kinder cases, their parents cared for their infected offspring as long as they could, turning them out to find their way into the wilds two days before one of the moons was full. Other parents killed their afflicted children, either from fear or to spare them from a painful, dangerous fate.

Would most of his crew take pity on the two werewolves on

board and see their infection as no fault of their own, or would they be frightened to the point of mutiny? Hallix had sailed aboard the *Dominion* for several weeks—had Syleste known of his lycanthropy? How could he have avoided transformation during that time? Teodric was certain that the cells would hold Genevieve and Hallix during their change. There were still a few days before the full moon. He would find a way to tell the crew and prevent their panicking before then.

Teodric returned to the desk and leaned his palm against the edge. At his request, Kriega had swiped Darcy's papers from his room. The man was barely conscious and in no position to explain the significance of the dagger or how it fit into whatever work he'd been doing for Syleste. Before returning Darcy to her, he needed to understand what the weapon might do in her hands and what else Darcy had been hiding.

Darcy kept several ledgers that Teodric had piled at the corner of his desk. Beside them, he stacked the loose pages scattered among Darcy's belongings. Teodric sifted through the individual sheets first. Several pages in, he froze.

Adhemar, he read across the top of the page.

Linolynn: Confirmation of departure, abandoned tacks inquiring after reason for departure

Nortelon: father, Lord Frederick Adhemar, disappeared three years; mother, Lady Aurelia Adhemar, mad

Teodric scowled at the wall separating his cabin from the deck. His hands clenched. It was fortunate for Darcy that he was under Syleste's protection.

Dominion: list of names of those who were aboard versus those who had been acquired since

His and Kriega's names joined Hallix on the first list. Darcy had recorded Athena and Genevieve on the second.

He flipped through several more sheets, and a small, folded

piece of parchment fell from the middle of the pile. He unfolded the page and immediately dropped it.

It drifted, a feather on the breeze, onto his desk.

His hands shook as he stared down at the single word, transcribed in Darcy's angular handwriting.

Iellieth

CHAPTER 30

The first tendrils of dawn trickled across the sky above the Stormside Forest, and Iellieth collapsed against a fallen trunk. She laid her head on her arms, breathing heavily. "Have we lost them?" She tilted sideways to squint up at Quindythias with one eye. The elf braced himself against a tree, straining on tiptoe to see if they were being pursued.

Marcon tensed beside him, scanning the forest for Hadvarian soldiers. "I believe so, lady. At least for now. After you have a few minutes to rest, can you disguise our trail?"

Iellieth sighed deeply and nodded. "I think so." The sparks coursing through her veins had slowed, spent, like she was, by the long night of travel and the cold. Guards had caught sight of them as they escaped the city, and Iellieth had led Marcon and Quindythias beneath the boughs of the forest, though she'd exhausted most of her magical reserves covering their tracks through the woods. Once they had lost their pursuers, they could find a path south to Red's Cross. Red would hold the seal piece for them while they made their way across the Infinite Ocean for the second seal piece.

"And what if you use the seal piece?" Quindythias raised an eyebrow. "It served us well last night?"

"It is why I led us here." She pulled the stone from her bag and traced over the runes. "I didn't hesitate before because I didn't see that we had very many other options in the moment, but now . . . Red was afraid that using it would draw creatures of darkness to us, that its magic works like a beacon. He did say that the creatures it summons wouldn't necessarily be harmful." She studied her companions. Quindythias was unperturbed by the potential danger, but Marcon watched her closely, his brow contracting as she began to pick twigs from the tattered silk of Kazimir's gown. "Do you think Kazi will be implicated in the attack against Master Yugo?" Over and over, she had pictured her friend receiving the news of his lover's death, his face contorting in pain and confusion, and his dismay as guards dragged him away.

A warm hand pressed on her shoulder, and Marcon knelt next to her. His runes were darker than they had been, a reflection of the strain of fleeing through the night. "He'll find a way out, lady. Have faith, like Dimitri said." He half-smiled. "It is a shame to ruin a dress that looked so beautiful on you."

Heat blossomed across Iellieth's chest and face. She glanced away, and Quindythias stomped closer. "A dress that is slowing us down more than anything." He crossed his arms standing above her. "Let me see your feet."

Iellieth grimaced, pulling her swollen ankles in toward herself. They had chosen a snow-free path whenever possible, but the earth was still frosty and slick from snowmelt.

Quindythias frowned. "You need to get into your boots while you still can." His face softened. "I know you don't want us to get caught, but we both need you to be well."

Beside him, the furrow in Marcon's brow deepened.

"Alright, just give me a couple minutes then."

While she slipped her leggings on under her dress, Quindythias dug in her bag for her boots and began loosening their ties. Marcon rose to fill their canteens from the shallow brook nearby.

"That's much better, thank you." Iellieth grinned up at Quindythias and held out her hand for him to pull her up.

"Marcon, she's ready," the elf called.

Iellieth chanted to the forest under her breath, asking that their footsteps and tracks be obscured. The leaves twitched behind them, swirling to cover any trace they'd scrawled onto the surface of the earth.

Her voice grew hoarse as the morning wore on, and the sparks at her throat and fingertips dwindled. She swallowed the final gulp of the springmelt Marcon had procured for her. "It's no use. I have to use the seal piece if we're going to continue on without leaving tracks."

Marcon set his jaw and glared at her magical bag. "I will shield you, lady, from whatever follows the magic's trail."

"Agreed." Quindythias crossed his arms and nodded, eyes skipping over the forest as though daring a threat to suddenly appear.

Iellieth exhaled slowly and withdrew the seal piece from her bag. Her amulet warmed the moment the stone met the air, and the runes along the back and sides of the piece glowed a deep violet. A Druidic incantation rose to her mind unbidden. As she turned the spell over in her mind, the runes darkened to indigo, and a swirling abyss began to take shape within the stone. "Blacker than night and thick as blood," she chanted, "umbral shroud, bringer of dawn, encircle us here in your embrace, hide our steps, remove our trace." Iellieth shivered and lowered the stone. Marcon and Quindythias stared back at her. How was she to tell if the spell worked?

Beads of indigo light dripped off the stone in her hand and

whooshed toward the forest. They splashed onto tree trunks, a soft violet glow emanating from beneath the branches as they dissipated. The wind picked up behind her. Leaves rushed past on swirling breezes that lifted strands of her hair and tugged deeper into the forest.

"I think something heard you." Quindythias raised his voice over the rush of wind and the groaning trees. "What should we do?"

Dark clouds gathered overhead, and the shadows around them deepened. The violet glow in the forest ahead beckoned to Iellieth, and the hairs along the back of her neck rose. Whatever was approaching didn't mean them well. "We need to run."

Iellieth's ankles throbbed as she pounded her swollen heels into the earth. She held the seal piece out in front of her as she sprinted beneath the cover of the dark purple trunks. Waves of energy ebbed out from the stone and into her hands, her arms, enveloping her in ivy tendrils of its magic. They tugged like velvet marionette strings as she dashed away from the gathering gloom overhead, the two champions just behind her, fleeing from whatever had sensed her spell. But the ominous clouds followed their steps, pursuing them deeper into the Stormside Forest.

"Where are you going?" Quindythias shouted, his voice barely audible over the haunting wails of the storm swirling around them.

Iellieth slipped on the damp forest floor as a rotted trunk careened to the side just ahead of her. Marcon caught her around the waist as she fell and pulled her into his chest. He swung them both to the side to avoid the tumbling branches. "Is this what you intended to summon?" Even directly beside her ear, the howling winds snatched his voice, pulling it away from her and into the storm.

Thunder rumbled overhead, and the glow around them

intensified. A shadow loomed in the darkness over Iellieth's shoulder. She turned slowly, stepping around Marcon. With the second peal of thunder, two orbs of red light flared in the swirls of darkness that surrounded them. "Marcon?" Iellieth inched away from the two glowing eyes, and the champion interposed himself between them.

Flashes of silver twirled through the air beside her as Quindythias stepped forward and stood beside Marcon.

Iellieth rifled through the deep reserves of her magic, searching desperately for the energy to fight the creature that had attacked them in the forest on the way to Red's Cross. The seal piece hissed in her hands, shooting motes of indigo into the trees. Red's words of warning came drifting back to her. *Not all creatures of darkness are to be feared*, the gnome had explained. *Some will have ill intentions toward you, but not all. As a Shepherd, you must learn to trust your own magic, and the magic that answers your call.*

The creature of shadow bristled as it stalked forward. The jutting limb of a young sapling, turned amethyst by the stone, sliced through the revenant's arm as it passed, carving a violet tear through the shadow flesh.

Scarlet eyes glared at Quindythias and Iellieth in turn before the creature fixed its stare on Marcon.

"Who are you?" the champion growled, tightening his grasp on his longsword.

Sizzling words whooshed from the creature's mouth. The revenant stepped forward, pushing flaming tendrils of hair from her face. She answered again in her language of smoke. Marcon's shoulders lowered, and his head tilted to the side.

The revenant's coal-red eyes softened to the orange of the sunset, and the swirling smoke of her face and neck stilled, condensing to ash. Marcon leaned closer.

Had he discovered who had been sent from his past to

destroy him now? Or had the creature placed him under some sort of spell?

Iellieth tightened her grip on the stone. *Send the motes of light into the revenant.* It shuddered in her grasp, but the seal piece obeyed.

The revenant squealed and hissed as the first drops of violet condensed across her skin. For a moment, where the lights struck, warm copper skin appeared beneath the covering of smoke and ash, and flying tendrils of hair turned to a rich, rippling brunette.

The orange eyes flared crimson once more, and the revenant shrieked at Iellieth, hurtling forward in a cloud of smoke.

Quindythias's daggers sliced through her sides, tearing at the smoke that held her together. Marcon roared as he leapt forward. His longsword slashed through the creature's chest, revealing a core of molten shadow.

She stumbled away from him at the impact, eyes softening as they widened in surprise. The revenant clutched at her core, rasping cries of pain falling from her lips as she sank to the ground. For a final moment, she locked her gaze on Marcon before she lifted her heart upward and flew away in a swirl of shadow and smoke.

The wind died down, but the violet glow remained. Marcon stared at the spot on the ground where the revenant had fallen, his brow knitted tight as his chest rapidly rose and fell.

Iellieth rushed to his side. "Are you alright?" She held the stone to her stomach and laid her free hand on his arm. "Did you recognize who it was?"

Quindythias glanced at them each in turn but said nothing. He jogged across the clearing to pull his blades from the trunks where they'd embedded themselves after striking the revenant.

Marcon still wouldn't meet her eye.

"Do you both know but just don't want to tell me? Who is she?"

Finally, he raised his gaze to hers. "Lady, I wanted to speak with you after the ball. There's something—"

The wind whistled past them again, and the stone's magic pulled Iellieth back in the direction they'd been traveling before the revenant appeared. Her amulet glowed warm on her chest.

"What is it now?" Quindythias grumbled as he hurried over to meet them.

Though they'd slowed the pace of their drifting, the motes of light urged them forward once more.

AS NIGHT FELL, THEY FOUND A SMALL GAP IN THE TREES WITH a large boulder to shield them from the winds. Iellieth collapsed gratefully onto the log that Quindythias acquired for her just outside their clearing, and Marcon knelt over a stack of kindling to make their fire.

The flames caught and cast their warm glow across Marcon's olive skin. On the other side of the campfire, Quindythias looked through their rations, muttering to himself about all the things he was going to eat when they eventually discovered a habitable, civilized location. Marcon brought a second log over. "May I?" he asked, gesturing to the dirt and leaves directly beside her.

"Of course." Throughout that afternoon, when she wasn't occupied with trying to follow the path carved by violet runes and drifting lights or the exhaustion in her limbs from their flight from Hadvar, her mind drifted to the revenant and whoever it was she might have been.

They sat in silence for a short while. Marcon's runes light-ened in such close proximity to the blaze. His eyes were earnest, searching, as he turned to her. "There's a part of my past that I have been . . . unsure of the proper time to discuss. But at the ball, I wondered if I had in fact waited too long." He cleared his throat and looked at the loose clasp of his hands propped between his knees. "There was a young woman at the orphanage with me, Lorieannan. We grew up together, fell in love, and then I left to join the war." The reflection of the flames danced in his eyes as his gaze drifted off and away through the past, as it had so often in Mara's hut.

Iellieth pulled her arms tighter around her waist. The air around her hummed. Her breath caught in her chest.

Marcon squinted at the fire. "I was gone most of the time, which led to difficulties between us. After a particularly heated argument, one of many, she said she was leaving. I stormed out and returned to my regiment." His jaw pulsed. "But she decided to give me a final chance. She was in our home outside the city walls the night our forces were routed, when the swarms of undead attacked the city. I searched for her, treading my way upstream through the bodies." He sighed deeply and lowered his head.

Iellieth's throat constricted.

"When I found her, she'd already been taken, become one of them." His voice was haunted, hoarse, and careful. "I called out to her, desperate for a way to bring her back to herself, to right what I had done. Lorieannan lurched toward me and seized my arm, her expression radiating with rage and hunger." He ran his hand through his hair. "But I was luckier than she. One of my allies, a dwarf named Tali, saved me. She prevented me from being overwhelmed by them, or worse. Tali turned them all to ash." His jaw twinged again, and his eyes squinted at the lingering pain. "It was then that I swore my vengeance, and Ignis answered me."

Iellieth shivered, her head reeling with the loose, tumbling bursts of energy around her. The cold eked out from the center of her being. The inner voice that she hadn't heard for so long returned. *Everything he's done since then, the entirety of his life before and the continuing source of his power now, is retribution for the death of his love. Lorieannan.*

"What are you two talking about?" Quindythias peered at them over the fire, a slight pout tugging on his lower lip at being left out. Iellieth's shoulders jumped. The elf frowned at her, puzzled, and picked up the bundle of flowers he'd gathered over the course of the afternoon. "Marcon, will you sketch these for me?"

He nodded. "I was just telling Iellieth about Lorieannan." Quindythias's eyes widened and flashed over to her. She turned her head quickly to avoid meeting his gaze. "The walls around Hadvar reminded me of Respite, and then—"

Iellieth rose, and Marcon stopped speaking. "I'm, umm, going to get some more wood for our fire." She forced a smile and spun around. So long as neither of them followed her, she would be fine.

Quindythias's voice reached her through the trees, but the hum around her ears was too loud for her to catch what he said.

The forest withheld its embrace as she paced through the woods. Her thoughts had scattered around her, like acorns in autumn. Had she done something wrong at the ball? Tears prickled against her eyelids, but she blinked them away.

The air shimmered around her. New breaths stuttered in. She released them slowly, forcing calm. The voice in the back of her mind scoffed. *What did you expect? This can't come as a surprise.* It didn't matter. She'd misunderstood, that was all. Iellieth shoved away the memory of the evening before, the swirl of the ballroom, the two of them together, before Lord Stravinske, before the heist, before their escape.

In the weeks after Teodric had been sent from Io Keep, she

silenced her screams with a pillow, determined the duke would gain no further satisfaction from his cruelty. She taught herself to stop waiting for a return that would never happen. But since then, she had . . . had learned not to think about it. To let it float away on the wind when it fluttered nearby. She could do that again.

A fallen limb snapped beneath her boot. She bent down to pick it up and begin her gathering but pulled back her hand in surprise. A bundle of dried branches and twigs rested together just beyond her fingertips, as though the trees had gathered them to help her. "Thank you," she whispered and scooped them up into her arms.

A shape shifted in the shadows beyond her hand. Slowly, Iellieth rose to her feet. She peered into the forest.

The figure took a step closer, and the silhouette crystallized. Iellieth shouted and fell back as a giant black wolf emerged from between the trees.

CHAPTER 31

Persephonie sat back, absorbing Rennear's tale of his early turning, his forced transformation. "So your father wanted you to be like them . . . for power?"

Rennear lowered his eyes. "Over the werewolves and over me, yes."

"But you were just a little boy."

"My mother died when I was young. She was the only one who could hold back his ambition. But without her guidance, I and everyone around me became leverage."

He must have been so frightened, a young boy left at the mercy of werewolves and his monstrous father. "Is that how you knew something was going to happen to me? Why you . . . apologized for taking so long to arrive?"

Rennear shook his head. He struggled to meet her eyes. "I wish . . ." His expression darkened. "I wish you could believe me when I say that had I known, I would have acted much sooner than I did. It was more a feeling, an instinct, that something wasn't right."

He stood up from the settee and ambled over to the window,

rubbing the back of his neck. She waited for him to speak, but he crossed his arms and stared out into the drumming dark of the rain.

Juliet growled faintly in her sleep, her paws twitching, perhaps chasing a faery across a rolling azure field. The cold wooden floors arched to support Persephonie's silent feet as she tiptoed across the room. Rennear jumped as she laid her hand on his arm, his face a tempest of hope and hurt. "I do believe you." Persephonie squeezed his forearm, his muscles taut beneath her touch.

His hand trailed through her hair, thumb tracing the line of her cheek. The strain left his expression, uncertainty ebbing into the void of its wake. "What is this?" Rennear's fingertips traced the three thin scars along the base of her neck.

"The remnant of my childhood experience with werewolves," she whispered. Rennear's hand shot back like he'd been stung. "My Datha, he emerged from the woods just in time and pulled me up and onto his horse. They chased us through the trees. He and I managed to escape. My friend was not so lucky." Her toes dug into the wood beneath her feet. The old spirits resting in the grain pressed up to meet her, certain that all would be well.

His bronze eyes darkened, sifting through her tale. "I'd never hurt you, Persephonie."

Under the wrong conditions, would he have a choice? The other werewolves, that day in the square, responded to him as their alpha. But under the stern gaze of his father . . . She peered up at him. "What are you doing tomorrow?"

"Hah"—Rennear smiled—"anything you ask of me." The light behind his eyes returned.

"Otmund told me about a concert."

PERSEPHONIE TRADED HER EVENING SHIFT WITH TESS AND spent the morning serving coffee and daydreaming about the night to come.

A shimmering black carriage arrived outside the tavern, splashing back the glow of lantern light. Rennear stepped out as the driver pulled the horses to a stop, and Persephonie ducked beneath her windowsill just in time as he searched the windows in the upper stories, looking for her.

She adjusted the ties of her pale green dress a final time and added one more golden bangle to the mix on her arm. Her long, dark hair had taken its curls well, and she grew a few flowers to weave through the tresses. The scarlet buds accentuated the hint of auburn in her hair.

The Hunt leered from the end of the week, promising an afternoon of horrors. But the city's other celebrations in antici-pation of the cruel slaughter were supposed to be spectacular. Otmund had told her that this was to be a special event, the first of its kind for many years in the city.

Her cards rested on the low black table painted with suns and moons, waiting for her return. Knuckles tapped against her door. Persephonie grinned and dashed down her narrow hallway, and Rennear swept her out into the night.

He held her hand and led her to the center of one of the stadium benches in the concert coliseum. Rennear inclined his head, pointing to their seats, and followed her along the velvet-lined bench.

Her heartbeat raced and her stomach fluttered as Rennear wrapped his arm around her, hand clasped between her waist and hip. He told her about the other wonders he'd seen in the Andel-ce Hevran auditorium—circus performances as a young boy, dramatic reenactments of famous battles—his eyes never leaving her face as he spoke.

The magical lights dimmed, and the show began. A woman

emerged from the side of the tent. Her skin was a deep sapphire blue, and the gills along her neck rippled as she glided forward. Persephonie tapped Rennear's leg, leaning forward. "I've never seen one of the mer-folk before," she whispered. "She's so beautiful."

Rennear smiled. "I've met a few, though it's been several years." Rennear put a hand on Persephonie's arm and nodded to the center of the tent. A trio of faeries swirled together and took one another's hands. They stretched out with their tiny chests, backs to one another. Their dragonfly wings fluttered against the lantern light, creating a shimmering prism of light.

"How are they here? Are they in danger?" Persephonie glanced around, ready to defend the faeries from the same enforcers who would persecute her and her mother.

"There's a special dispensation since they're with the theatre," he answered. "They've a fierce protector in the conductor, and they're free to come and go as they like."

The mermaid sighed deeply and rolled back her shoulders. She turned to take in her audience and then, with a deep breath, she began to sing. The first notes set out on their own across the tent before the carnival bards joined in. The mermaid smiled as the melody unfurled from her lips, and then, somehow, a second voice joined hers in harmony. The audience emitted a collective gasp. The sound came from the mermaid herself, endowed with a double set of vocal cords.

The intense harmony dipped into a minor key with a freefall. The mermaid's crescendo brought back, for a moment, the campfires of Persephonie's childhood—her younger brother sitting close beside her while Felix rushed back and forth behind them, determined to not miss a single note of the music. Their muster's rich guitars and blends of alto and tenor had spiraled together and enraptured her as the mermaid did, an octave higher, this evening.

A knot twirled into being at the base of her throat. Though it had been only a few days, she missed Datha and her brothers, her people. Before she could swallow it away, Rennear bent down and kissed the tip of her ear where it peeked through her curls. She inhaled sharply, turning to him, eyes bright.

He must have been watching her while she watched the singer. Rennear gazed at the features of her face in turn. His eyes fluttered down to her lips as his fingers slid back to the nape of her neck. She leaned into him, joining the heat of her lips to his.

Rennear gripped her waist, hugging her closer as her tongue found its way between his lips. With his other hand, he traced the line of her jaw, and her senses swirled.

⁂

PERSEPHONIE DRIFTED THROUGH HER SHIFT AT THE GREEN Owl the next morning, turning over every detail of their evening together.

"I think someone's waiting for you," Otmund said, nodding toward the red-leafed autumnwood tree outside. Rennear sat on the bench beneath it, his foot tapping against the side of his knee.

Persephonie's stomach fluttered. "He could be just sitting out there." She shrugged. "You never know."

Otmund laughed. "Sometimes, you know. Why don't you run along early? You've messed up enough orders today as it is."

"That's not true. I—"

"It is. And we're not busy." He shook his head, suppressing a smile. "Off you go."

She grinned back at him. "Thank you, Otmund." Persephonie hurried through the tavern and emerged, squinting, into the sunlight.

Rennear sprang up when he saw her and crossed the courtyard to her side in three quick strides. He wrapped an arm around her waist and pulled her close, planting a full kiss on her lips.

Persephonie leaned into him, the fluttering intensifying.

He pulled away and looked down at her. "I don't know what sort of spell you've cast on me, but I have been thinking about you all day, Mistress Persephonie. Are you free this afternoon and evening?"

"Yes." Her smile widened at the prospect.

"Wherever you would like to go, I would be honored to escort you."

He sat in the parlor upstairs and entertained Juliet while Persephonie changed, and the three of them emerged into the bustle below.

Persephonie took Rennear's proffered hand, her footsteps skipping across the courtyard. "There is a wonderful bakery in Holdenfield, Shadow and Sugar, where we could go."

"That sounds delightful," he said.

She led the way, guiding them through her favorite streets in City Center South toward the more modest neighborhoods of Holdenfield. Rennear squinted at the smaller buildings and increased greenery of the area.

"You do not often come through this part of the city, do you?" Persephonie asked.

"Not often, no. Most of my patrols keep me in City Center or in Glory Home."

"Where all of the priests live?"

He nodded. "They appreciate the additional security, after recent events." Persephonie bit her lip. She hadn't expected the subject of the druids to come up so soon. Rennear's eyes had drifted away. His expression fell. "I haven't talked to very many people about it, but I was there, the day of the attack."

Persephonie's heart leapt into her throat. "You saw the

attack on the druids?" She stopped walking and looked up at him. Had he been involved in the raid of their conclave?

"No, no, the attack on the priests." Rennear's eyes creased, contemplating what she had said. "Oh, Persephonie, you can't think I would have had anything to do with that. Even given what I am . . ." He lowered his head, running his tongue over the front of his teeth.

She caught his hand again. "I was just confused by what you were referring to. Are you talking about the attack they made the statue for?"

"Yes." They continued walking, with him avoiding her gaze. "I was on duty that day, in the vicinity." His jaw tightened. "I heard their screams from blocks away. But by the time we got there, it was too late."

"I am sorry you had to see that," Persephonie said softly. She hadn't told him of the horrors she and her people had witnessed in the wake of the werewolf pack's rampage over the last several months in Caldara. "My mother told me a little about the attack."

Rennear frowned just as the sticky-sweet aromas drifting out of Shadow and Sugar reached her nose. She tugged on his hand, pulling him and Juliet into the small brick bakery. "Colette," she called as a bell jingled on the door, "I brought new friends to meet you."

Colette was a beautiful negata with crimson skin and burgundy hair who had been her mother's lover the last time she visited the city. They had been at the height of their romance then, doting on one another and laughing constantly. It was the happiest she'd seen Mama in years. As summer turned to autumn, the flame of her mother's passion cooled. Shortly after that, it seemed, she'd met Aylin, and her infatuation with the elf and the Untamed began. But Colette would still want to see her.

"Persephonie, my darling," a sultry voice called. Colette was, as usual, clothed entirely in black, though shinier than usual for the celebrations. The negata slipped out from behind the counter and clasped Persephonie's shoulders, placing a kiss on each of her cheeks. "I did not even realize you were in the city, or I would have made the cinnamon cookies you enjoy so much." Colette's smile dimmed as she took in Rennear's strong silhouette beside her and Juliet's pattering at their feet.

"Such strange guests you bring with you today." Colette winked. "I have been hoping to see your beautiful mother, but I believe she is too busy for me." The negata swept aside Persephonie's apology for Esmeralda before it could leave her lips. She sauntered back behind the counter and began floating ingredients across the kitchen. The powdery confections swirled together into a wooden mixing bowl, Colette too absorbed in her own mixing spell to notice that Rennear's eyes were wide at seeing unsanctioned magic used openly.

"I wanted them to meet you," Persephonie answered, squeezing Rennear's hand before releasing it to help Colette.

The baker waved absentmindedly, and a table and four chairs drifted from the walls to the center of her shop. With a flick of Colette's wrist, a black lace cloth appeared across its surface. Persephonie murmured into her palms, shaping the drifting energy of the city into winding purple flowers to decorate the table.

"Will I have the pleasure of seeing your mother during the festivities, by any chance?" The negata's emerald eyes glimmered as she raised an eyebrow.

"I will encourage her to stop by and see you. But you do know, Colette, that Mama is seeing a new partner?" Persephonie bit the inside of her bottom lip.

Colette nodded slowly, twirling her fingers above strands of icing over the lavender cake. "Yes, I am aware." She sighed, her shoulders dropping as she floated the cake over to the table, gesturing for her and Rennear to sit. Juliet hopped up on a chair too, wide amber eyes gleaming at the treat.

The negata picked up her fork and pointed it at Persephonie, emphasizing each word with a tiny stab through the air. "You steer clear of her, Persephonie." She shook her head. "And I don't say that out of jealousy. Ever since she received the 'blessing of Apollo,' as she calls it, her grabs for power have become more extreme. Not enough of her own people see her fervor for what it is, but make no mistake, Aylin is dangerous."

Mama had mentioned the guardian Apollo promising to watch over the Untamed. In the past, he had served as an ally of Cassandra, though she couldn't recall when she'd last heard of the guardian taking an active interest in events in Azuria. Colette's eyes still burned with her warning. Could she set the negata's mind at ease? "I know that there have been some members of the Untamed who are suspicious, but—"

"Wait, *the* Aylin of the Untamed?" Rennear leaned forward, a piece of lemon-iced lavender cake poised precariously on his fork.

Persephonie's brow furrowed. "I do not know how many Aylins there are." She looked away from both of them, the tingling bite of the lemon turning sharp in her mouth, the sweetness fading too quickly. Was it a common name? "What are you both trying to tell me?"

"Aylin has a fierce reputation, Persephonie, and not in a positive way." Colette's lips pursed, and she turned to Rennear for confirmation.

"We think she may be responsible for the attacks in the city. The priests I mentioned on the way here. I've looked into it myself." Rennear's brow furrowed as he watched her closely, lowering his voice. "It was her attacks that led to the deaths of the druid elders, and—"

Persephonie's chair screeched as she pushed it back,

springing up from the table. "The deaths of the elders and the conclave were because of cruel leaders in this city. People who hate and are afraid of those like me." A cloud of violet dragonflies erupted over Persephonie's head. There was too much stale magic in the city, too few to wield it. She took a shuddering breath, trying to calm herself, but Esmeralda's warning echoed back to her—*How do you know he's not using you?* "People like your father." She spat the words out, choking on the unshed tears at the back of her throat, the memories of the faces she would never see again.

The blacks and purples of the sunlit shop blurred, and Persephonie stumbled outside into the full light of the street. The burbling music of the fountain was muffled, as were the voices around her. The bell on Colette's door jangled, and Rennear yelled after her, his call somehow far away. She should have known better. He was just trying to get to her mother, to Aylin —no different than Aylin's plan for using Persephonie against him and his father.

But their accusations were false. They had to be. Her mother would never be with someone responsible for putting innocent people in danger, for attacking young acolytes on the street. Regardless of the cruelty against the druid conclave, against the natural-magic wielders in the city, there were lines they wouldn't cross.

She ducked onto a side street and disappeared into the crowd.

CHAPTER 32

"L ady! Iellieth!" Her friends' voices rushed toward her through the trees.

The giant wolf tilted its head to the side, teal blue eyes swirling with light as the creature stared down at her. "I mean you no harm, little druid," a smooth, feminine voice spoke inside her mind. "You summoned darkness to aid you, and here to help I am."

Iellieth scooted back on her elbows and heels, the branches the forest had bundled for her cast to the side. "How—? Who—?"

Sparkling teal eyes smiled in reply.

Quindythias and Marcon crashed into the clearing. "Gah!" Quindythias reared back when he saw the wolf.

Marcon bellowed and jumped forward, his longsword shimmering in his grasp.

"Wait." The voice was calm and soothing. The two champions froze, Marcon in mid-leap, Quindythias poised to throw a dagger.

Iellieth scrambled to her feet. "Who are you?" She scurried to stand between her friends and the wolf. "They're with me. Have you truly come to help us?" Iellieth reached to pull the seal piece from her bag, but she had left it back at camp. Her magic was utterly spent.

The wolf chuckled and nodded her head to Iellieth's companions. "Very well, little druid, your friends are free."

Quindythias's eyes remained wild and wide. "Can you—" He pointed from his ears to the wolf and turned to Iellieth.

"Yes, I hear her in my mind. Do you?"

He nodded.

The wolf laughed again. "Though there is much that one who lives so long as you could forget, Champion of Air, I would have thought telepathy would be something to remember."

The elf's mouth bobbed open and closed. He jutted his chin into the air and crossed his arms. "I do remember. You caught me by surprise is all."

"And you, Champion of Fire?" The giant wolf turned to Marcon. "Do you recognize one like me well enough to tell the little druid who I am?" She stepped closer, and Iellieth gasped. Starlight glimmered along the wolf's dark coat, lending her fur a deep, amethyst glow.

Marcon peered at the wolf, whose eyes were on level with his own. "You are one of the daimon, are you not?" She inclined her head, and he turned to Iellieth. "Lady, the daimon were some of the first creatures to walk the world that you now call Azuria. There were here in the first days and dwelled alongside the fae."

Eyes blue as the autumn sky shimmered at the two of them. "You speak well, Marcon Colabra. Few of my people now traverse this plane, little druid. We were forced to retreat from the surface of your world, some to the Brightlands, others to Shadow. But a few of us remain."

The daimon's voice struck a familiar chord in her mind. "You helped me in the forest, didn't you?" Iellieth grinned. "The spell that I heard—that was you!"

The wolf bowed her head in reply. "My name is Nova, little druid. Much of the conjuring today was the seal piece's answer to you. But I did help, in the beginning, and I influenced where in the forest the stone led you. Darkness is powerful in any realm but is especially so in the Stormside Forest. There are groves you should not visit until you are ready." Nova swished her long, sparkling tail and plodded slowly back to their camp.

"What groves?" Iellieth chased after her, and the wolf's amusement rumbled in her mind.

"Rest now, little druid. Answers will rise with the sun."

❧

A COLD, WET NOSE NUZZLED IELLIETH'S CHEEK THE NEXT morning. She startled, but Nova's teal eyes quickly brought a sense of calm.

"I believe I have heard of the daimon before. It came to me while I was sleeping. At one time, people believed that daimon were guiding spirits, right?" Iellieth bit her lower lip. She hadn't meant the question to sound as though the daimon were mythical creatures, placed on the planes to help other civilizations rather than developing their own. "Was that just because they weren't seen very often?"

Nova chuckled and shook her giant wolf head slowly. "You needn't fear offending me, little druid. My people, like many of those first on the planes, appeared only to those we wished to show ourselves to, similar to your Yvayne."

Iellieth's brows knit together. "But how did you—"

The wolf bumped her with her nose again, playfully pushing

against her arm. "Her protective scent wraps an aura around you, little druid. For millennia, she has lived in these mountains, but very few know of her." Nova's eyes flashed. "There are other creatures of legend who dwell in this forest, near the roots of the mountains, who were forgotten but should not be. Come, let us take a walk. We will return for your companions."

Marcon scowled as she told him Nova's plan.

Quindythias approached and squeezed his shoulder. "Let her go. What's going to happen with a daimon to protect her?"

The side of Marcon's jaw clenched as he looked between her and the daimon. He reached out for her hand and ran his thumb across the base of her fingers. "Lady, about last night, I . . ." Marcon sighed and squeezed her hand. "Be careful." Unspoken words swirled in a dark gray cloud behind his eyes. He raised his gaze to Nova. "Don't take her too far."

A smile caught the edges of Iellieth's lips. His concern was embedded deeper than the memory of his runes flaring when he journeyed away from her in search of the werewolves. She was certain.

Quindythias raised his eyebrow to the wolf. "Don't do anything too exciting without us." He winked and went to join Marcon by the fire.

Nova led her away from the camp and back into the depths of the forest. Her ears remained perked, twisting to the side occasionally as they walked. "You carry much, little druid."

"What do you mean?" She hurried forward to catch back up to Nova. Even the daimon's slow strides easily outpaced her own.

"The crescent moon you wear, for instance." The starlight speckled along Nova's fur winked off of the golden crescent pendant on the back of her wrist. "Something has happened that separates the two of you. A rift."

Iellieth clutched the pendant to her chest. So something had broken between her and the necklace Yvayne had given her. Had the magic changed its mind? Had her failure to transform a second time in Hadvar made her unworthy of the transformation?

Nova stopped and slid her hind paws around to stand in front of Iellieth. The daimon lowered her head to look straight into her eyes. "Rifts are meant to be mended, little druid," Nova whispered, her voice soft and warm in Iellieth's mind. The blue eyes bore deeper. "The magic chose you, Iellieth. It is part of who you are, down to the very glimmer of your soul. But it can only be as strong as you believe yourself to be."

Her failure to transform, that had endangered her and Quindythias's lives and allowed the assassin to escape, perhaps it was not the end of the story. A spark of magic warmed across the back of her hand, releasing the spicy tang of cinnamon into the damp spring air. Soothing, a promise.

The wolf lowered to sit down. "Come here."

Tentatively, Iellieth stepped closer. Nova inclined her head, and she moved closer again. After the second nod, Iellieth closed the distance between them and leaned into the wolf's warm chest. Nova's heart beat solidly against her ear. Iellieth trailed her fingers through the glittering fur, and the weight in her own chest lightened.

"Some rifts are born from miscommunication, but they can be mended with openness and time."

Nova's fur was soft beneath her fingers. No tangles marred the long, ebony strands. She inhaled deeply, a rush of pine and midnight stormclouds.

"Others come about through extreme loss, one so profound that it can sever the soul's connection to the self. Each lives on in its shell, but these are the hardest to mend, though the breach will always remain." Nova sighed, and Iellieth relaxed into the sound, closing her eyes. The chill of her encounter with Lord Stravinske, the horror of their escape, finally left her body so near to the daimon's warm fur. "It is a breach of this sort that the forest needs you to mend."

She stumbled back from Nova. "What do you mean? How can I mend a rift in the forest?" Iellieth shuddered at the memory of Mara saving her from Lucien by rending a crevice through the forest in the moments before her death. Would she ever be powerful enough for such a task? Her heart sank to the pit of her stomach. Was Nova asking her to return to the ruins of her conclave?

"Little druid." The calm waves of Nova's voice tugged her back to shore. Iellieth met the daimon's blue eyes. "It is a different rift of which I speak. One part of the forest chokes beneath a corruption that has smoldered there for centuries. Recently, this smoky weight has coalesced into flames." Nova nuzzled her head against Iellieth's torso, and she wrapped her arms in the wolf's fur. "The forest needs you to remind her of who she once was."

Iellieth squinted at the wolf as she raised back up to all fours. "But, Nova, we need to travel to Red's Cross and then to the Realms." Her heart fluttered at the prospect, and she trailed her fingers over her father's amulet. Finally, she would have a chance to meet him.

Nova's eyes darkened as she surveyed the forest. "That which creeps beneath the trees will find you before your journey's end, little druid. It cannot resist the call of darkness." Her tail swished through the lower tree branches, and the boughs flared with the same violet glow that the seal piece had conjured. The daimon's voice took on the tenor of an incantation or a prophecy. "But if you will tend to the black oak and remind her that not all is lost, you will loosen Lucien's grasp on your home-land and allow the spirit of this forest to once again roam free."

Nova's eyes glimmered at this last—there was something significant, something the daimon hadn't yet revealed about this forest spirit.

Before Iellieth could ask what it was, the daimon continued. "The black oak's heart broke upon her mistress's death. She waits for one to bring her healing and to remind her of who she once was, why she allowed her roots to grow deep, and where she fits in the branches of the great world tree. Can you help her, little druid? Can you show her what it means to love again?"

Was it Dimitri who had told her a story like this once, about a tree who helped a young woman to find her true love, though he lived far away? The roots of the story stretched in the depths of her mind. The tree sent an acorn with the woman to guide her and to connect them, regardless of the miles that stretched between. But when tragedy struck the couple, the young woman died, and the tree was heartbroken. Maybe it had been Mara who told her this story of how black oaks and dark patches of otherwise healthy forest came to be? "Nova, I don't know how."

The daimon's urgings continued on as though Nova hadn't heard her. "Purge the evil from within the tree, and send the corruption back to the darkness from thence it came." The wolf narrowed her gaze. Her tongue darted out of her mouth to catch the scents that drifted nearer. "When a single corruption takes root, others follow. A darkness moves behind the war that shadows your homeland. Uproot the evil that grows thick nearby, and you will save your home from the darkness of war."

Questions whirled through Iellieth's mind, their shapes blending together in a flurry of waving branches. A few leafy outlines remained distinct. "Can you show me how to find the black oak?"

A soft growl of assent rumbled in the back of the daimon's throat.

"And you suspect that we'll run into this . . . corruption, this enemy, on our way back to Red's Cross either way?"

Nova's lips curled back. Her sharp white teeth shone in the dappled sunlight. "Even now he hunts for you, little druid. He knows not that your heart is strong enough to have found me or that you know of the tree."

Iellieth's pulse quickened as her internal breeze flickered through the trees nearest them, increasing to a howl that leapt deeper into the forest.

The daimon dug her feet uneasily into the earth. "It is time for you to return, little druid." She lowered to her belly and bid Iellieth to climb onto her back.

With Iellieth's fingers locked into the daimon's twilight fur, the wolf darted back through the trees, hurtling Iellieth toward their campsite. "The tree will find you—she is drawn to those who carry the light such as you."

"But, Nova—"

The wolf silenced her with a growl. "It is in your blood, like the first Shepherd, little druid. She sought out more than the souls of the lost champions. The Shepherd guided spirits of water and earth and those of the trees. Greater powers than you yet understand dwell within you. Trust that they will show you the way."

Nova skidded into their camp, and Marcon and Quindythias rushed over. "That was fast," Quindythias said with a smile.

Iellieth's lips pursed as she examined the camp. Though she and Nova had been gone for over an hour, very little had changed at their site. The coals still gleamed in the fire.

The daimon continued to shift her weight from paw to paw. When she didn't lower down, Marcon reached up for Iellieth and slid her from the wolf's back. Nova's starlit coat shimmered brighter, but the outline of her fur began to fade.

Iellieth gasped and reached out for the daimon. "Nova, your

fur—" She glided her hand across the wolf's coat. It turned to mist beneath her fingers.

A wolf-shaped cloud of smoke glimmered before them a moment longer. "I am the forest spirit of darkness, little druid. Only you can set me free."

CHAPTER 33

For two days, the seal piece guided them through the forest, casting its glowing orbs into the trunks ahead until they reached a shadowed ring of towering oaks. The stone stilled in her hand. Its internal glow remained, the same deep violet as the trees' impossibly dark leaves. They were unlike any oak Iellieth had ever seen. Their lobes' bristle-tipped teeth were sharp, as though the leaves could draw the blood of any who walked past.

Soft pulses of energy lit the runes of the seal piece. They matched the beat of her heart. "This is the grove Nova spoke of," Iellieth whispered. She took a step forward and shivered at the sudden cold that stood sentry among the trees.

Over her shoulder, Marcon's hand tightened around his sword. "And what are we to do now that we've reached it?"

"We need to find the black oak at the center." She had asked the forest for its help as they traveled, for any sign of Nova, but the trees remained silent. Was the daimon's spirit trapped within this circle of trees? Bound in some way to the black oak she spoke of?

Carefully, Iellieth led them forward. No wind moved through the indigo leaves.

"It's creepy in here," Quindythias muttered. He tiptoed through the forest with blades drawn, eyes darting side to side.

Iellieth held the stone out in front of her. To Marcon and Quindythias, it would look like she was following the pull of its energy just as she had to guide them here. She wouldn't tell them that it was a force from within the trees that pulled her and the stone nearer. It hooked a tendrilled finger through her magic and tugged, reeling her and the seal piece in on the tide.

"I still don't understand why we're going to see this tree instead of traveling to Red's Cross." Quindythias frowned when she didn't answer. He addressed Marcon instead. "We could have avoided whatever it was the wolf was worried about catching us."

"Perhaps. But I trust her, and we follow where she leads." Marcon's gravelly whisper lodged in Iellieth's stomach, glowing warm against the cold that gripped the grove.

The pulse of the seal piece beat faster. Iellieth picked up her pace, jogging ahead. She ignored the shouts of protest her companions sent darting after her.

Iellieth broke through the press of the ring of trees. A towering black oak, unseasonably bare, stretched to embrace the gray sky at the top of a small rise.

They'd found it.

The branches shifted, angling toward her. The seal piece turned to ice in her hands. Iellieth winced and dropped it on the ground.

"Only you," an airy alto sighed within her mind. The tug against her increased, and she stumbled forward.

Shing. A sword swept from its sheath behind her. "Lady!" Marcon's arm wrapped around her waist and tugged her back.

She cried out as the force intensified. It dragged her and Marcon toward the base of the oak. Branches whipped at his face, trying to force him to release her from his grasp. Quindythias's muffled shouts rang out from the edge of the surrounding trees.

Marcon groaned after a sharp *thwack*, and his grip around her loosened. The voice in her mind squealed in delight, and the branches attacked him with renewed vigor.

"Stop!" Iellieth leapt at the trunk, hand extended. It had said it wanted her to come forward. Her fingertips pressed against the bark, its rough, dark surface scraping, till her palm was flush with its skin.

The branches throttling Marcon stilled.

The tree hummed in response to her touch, a satisfied exhale that rustled through branches and roots. "More," the voice wheezed. A pulse of stagnant, twisted energy burst from its bark and struck her palm.

Iellieth yelped and jumped back, clutching her hand to her chest. Marcon limped closer, his jaw set.

Her hand quivered. Green-black mold rippled across the surface of her palm and fingers. The champion swore and grabbed her wrist. Her arm seized as a bolt of pain flared to life from the tips of her fingers up to her shoulder. She screamed.

The mold burbled thicker, obscuring her skin. Black spots prickled at the edge of her vision.

"Iellieth, we need to get away." A familiar, low voice urged from her side.

The black oak grew larger, expanding to block out the thin light, stretching its limbs to consume the forest around it. The screams and cries of the surrounding trees shook the earth. Iellieth's legs trembled, and she fell to her knees.

The low voice called out to someone else for aid. Warm hands tugged at her, but they weren't strong enough.

Her blackened arm stretched out in front of her, the dark tree drawing her closer. It would consume her too.

The world turned to shadow as the oak whisked her into its embrace.

Two golden eyes, twin flames, parted the darkness. "Why have you come here, Iellieth Amastacia?" The alto voice rang clearer here, drifting nearer on a breeze.

Cold lumps of dirt crumbled beneath her hands. Iellieth crawled back away from the eyes. Her shoulders struck a rounded wooden wall. "Where are we?" she whispered. Where were Marcon and Quindythias?

The glowing eyes followed her movements. In a slither of vines, a twisted form took shape before her, lit by flickering purple light. The shape was feminine, a gnarled body made of decaying bark and held together with ivy binds.

Iellieth gasped. *A dryad.*

"Take my hand." The dryad extended a twisted branch toward the earthen floor.

"Are we inside your tree?" Iellieth huddled away from her. Her arms shook at the effort of resisting the dryad's command.

"Take it." Another shock of burning energy struck Iellieth's back where it rested against the inside of the tree's trunk. Her arm—covered in the same decaying bark as the dryad—shot forward, and the dryad caught her moldering hand in her branch.

Images flashed before Iellieth's eyes. A young woman with flowing dark hair smiling at a strong oak tree. The shy skip of the dryad's heart as she revealed herself to her admirer for the first time, drawing the woman with her into the embrace of the tree. A perfect acorn pressed from delicate twig fingers into a soft mauve palm. Her sorrow caught on the wind as the woman left her behind to float away across thick gray clouds. Sobs turned to screeches as a cloaked figure severed the frail bond between the woman and the dryad. Silver-brown bark decayed to a rotting green and then foul black mold as the dryad walked through her grove, utterly alone.

A hot tear trailed down Iellieth's cheek. "What happened to her? The woman?"

The dryad took a shuddering breath. "A blood sickness took her away from the sun." Golden eyes crinkled at the tear. She caught it on a tiny leaf at the end of her finger-twig.

The leaf turned from black to green. The dryad stared at it in wonder.

"Nova sent me to help you."

She shook her head. "I am beyond helping."

Iellieth braced against the inner trunk with her free hand and pushed herself up to standing. "She said there's a corruption in the forest that keeps you in this state . . . or that prevents you from healing from your loss." The dryad studied her with an ancient gaze but didn't speak. Iellieth took a deep breath and clung to Nova's words. She could almost see the smile of the daimon's teal eyes in the darkness around her. "Some wounds, some losses, will never entirely heal, but we can still move forward." Iellieth tightened the grasp of her decayed hand around the dryad's. "We can still live."

A new set of visions flickered through Iellieth's mind. As the dryad's arms turned from silver to black, as the sadness strangled the life from her leaves, her very touch befouled the world around her. Streams dried up, rocks turned to dust, burbles of acid struck the trees of her grove, turning them to tall black husks. Nova bounded into a clearing, her fur covered almost entirely with stars. The daimon whimpered at the dryad's touch, and shadows rippled over her fur, blotting out her glow. "I see why Nova sent you, druid with hair of fire and eyes of earth, but it is too late. No power you possess is great enough to defeat the darkness that grows inside my heart. The creature who stalks my lands—" The dryad sighed. "My roots grow too deep, they stretch into lands of shadow, and I cannot free myself."

Iellieth cast her eyes around the trunk. Marcon and Quindythias's voices couldn't reach her here. Did time pass the same outside the tree, or would it be like her conversation with Nova, where only a short time had passed for them but several hours for her? Iellieth shuddered. What if it were the opposite? Her breath caught. Marcon would never leave her inside a tree, but what would happen to him when he tried to pull her out? Could they be pulled into another plane? They'd be turned back into statues if they were separated too far from her . . . or if she died inside this tree.

Nova's warning about the creature hunting for her through the forest flared in the back of her mind. The daimon had said she should remind the tree of what it was to love and be loved. Would getting rid of the other corruption be enough to do that?

"Nova told me about the other creature lurking in the woods, the one whose corruption grips you."

The dryad's eyes flashed. "And . . ."

"What if I got rid of it for you?"

She released Iellieth's hand and crossed her arm-branches over one another. A cruel laugh burst from her lips. "You. How would you manage such a feat?"

"I, umm, I don't know yet. But would you allow me to try?"

Golden eyes narrowed further. "Why would you do such a thing for me?"

Iellieth took a step closer. The dryad's leafy hair shuddered in surprise, but she did not otherwise react. "I waited many years for a freedom that never came, at least not in the way I'd first envisioned it." Iellieth's heart warmed, and the pungent odor of decay lifted from the space around her. Somewhere beneath all of this rot, a black rose bloomed. She inhaled deeply, clinging to the whiff of hope—she might be breaking through the thick bark walls after all. "There were others who had been waiting for me, and I for them." The words came faster. Warmth flooded her body as she thought of Marcon and Quindythias, wherever they were, trying to find her. "I thought freedom would mean traveling on my own, going wherever I chose."

Her pulse pounded in her ears. *Yes. Yes. Yes.*

"But that wouldn't have been anything more than a different sort of cage." A second rose blossomed as the dryad's lips parted. A light flared behind her golden eyes. "You already knew this, before you lost the one you cared for . . . and after too. But I think you need to allow yourself that freedom again, the one that comes when we attach our fate to the ones we love, no matter what." The dryad stared back at her, as though seeing her face clearly for the first time. "If you'll give us a chance to free you from the creature's corruption, to . . . to send it back to where it came from, then you could once again care for this forest the way you used to." A final deep breath. "You could find a way to love again."

The dryad bowed her head, and wind rippled through her hair. "May the cycle of darkness and light guide you, Iellieth Amastacia." The wind howled louder. Thick bark scratched against her skin, and light exploded all around her.

Iellieth squinted against the sudden change. A tongue of pale green flame splashed onto her hand. She shouted in surprise.

Damp grass, lavender flowers, and thyme swept through her senses. The scents pulled at her, dragging her to the earth.

No. The dryad had let her go. She wasn't returning inside the tree. Iellieth struggled. She kicked against the earth's tug. Her foot made contact with a thump, answered by a sharp cry and an Elvish curse.

"Stop fighting me, lady." The low voice growled from beside her ear, burning coals and soothing fire. "Iellieth, open your eyes."

Their faces blocked out the weak rays of the sun. Anxious eyes, pale gray and scowling, darkest blue, peered at her. Her breath rose and fell, wheezing in her chest. "Where are we? We have to go before—" Iellieth surged forward again, but Marcon's arms refused to release her. *Oh.* "You pulled me away from the tree," she said softly.

He nodded.

"And you kicked me!" Quindythias stuck his hands on his hips and thrust his chest forward. The lower half of a boot print stained the shoulder of his leather coat. The runes along his dark skin had intensified, almost to solid black. Marcon's, too, were a deep brown against his olive skin.

Iellieth crumpled forward. Marcon seated her gently in the grass and knelt in front of her, clutching her hand.

The burning along her arm had cooled. A thin green liquid dripped off her fingers and onto the earth. The source of the herbs. "Mara's tincture," she whispered.

Marcon's eyes smiled.

"Thank you." His thumb trailed across her palm, rubbing the last of the clinging droplets into her skin. "There was a dryad in the tree. She . . . spoke to me and showed me what happened to her. The creature Nova warned us about, it's hurting the dryad too." But how were they to find out what it was?

"I thought I heard someone in the forest." A tenor voice pierced the air. Marcon and Quindythias whirled around, blades drawn. Lord Victoro Nassarq, one of the nobles from Linolynn who she'd known almost all her life, stood tall and pale beneath the sunless sky. "Lady Amastacia, what a surprise."

CHAPTER 34

Briseras's footsteps stole softly over the narrow mountain trail leading south as Lavinia guided them to her family's homestead, positioned above the Nocturne village. Through their travels, the forest was unnaturally still. Vera's uneasiness rippled over to Briseras, but neither she nor the wolf could trace the source of their disquiet.

At Everett's careful prodding, the witch spoke about her family and what they could expect at the Nocturne estate. "We grew up just outside the village, and Saige and I would go there often to trade, especially after our father disappeared. It's a place afflicted with many tragedies—other disappearances, illnesses, misfortune. But despite all of this, we've rarely seen Lord Nassarq, the master of the estate. He's reclusive and leaves the village to mind itself."

"Sounds vampiric to me," Everett muttered.

"Don't jump to conclusions on a hunt." Briseras narrowed her eyes. "It swiftly becomes too convenient to twist evidence and fit it around the story you've written in your mind than to follow the actual trail."

"I'm a folklorist, Briseras. I'm meant to uncover and recreate the story."

Briseras suppressed a sigh. "Not when you're hunting with me." They'd gone over this before they found evidence of a vampire, but all of that effort would still be wasted if they pursued one nobleman who was guilty only of aloofness and not of consuming his populace.

Everett frowned and fell silent.

"What stories have you heard about vampires, Everett?" Lavinia asked. He stood up straighter, and the two exchanged the tales they'd heard growing up in the mountains, debating some of the nuances they attributed to differences between villages or regions.

Briseras and Vera walked ahead of them, ears perked for sounds of danger.

Near dusk, tall black turrets appeared against the sky, rising like fangs. Red and orange light undulated behind their silhouette, blood oozing from a wound.

"Can we make it there by nightfall?" Everett bent down to massage his calf.

"It's just over this rise," Lavinia said softly. "Dark creatures roam the estate borders after dark. It's best if we wait here till dawn."

There was a longing behind her quiet suggestion, as though a night spent in her home might return all she had lost. "Very well. Take us to your cabin," Briseras said.

As the last rays disappeared over the horizon, Lavinia jogged across a wanderers-grass field and into a three-room stone cabin with a thatch roof. It stood alone on the edge of a hill, overlooking the valley beyond. Just beneath the ridge, the pinnacle tops of the Nocturne estate blotted out the low stars.

It had been a few years since Briseras had hunted a vampire in earnest. "I'll be outside." She stepped back out into the night as Everett helped Lavinia to put her cabin in order for their short stay. They would build a fire in the hearth and warm some of the dried meat stored in the smokehouse behind the cabin.

Briseras walked to the edge of the hilltop, Vera at her side. Otto's silhouette cut a path of disappearing stars above them. Seeing Lavinia returned to her home after her sister had vanished brought back memories of Haven and her mother. The spirit-remnants of her past swirled around her. She closed her eyes to protect the scars on her heart.

"You must promise me," her mother had said, kneeling before her the day Rajas was to take Briseras from Haven, "you must promise that no matter what you hear, about me or anything else, you will not come back here. Whatever they say" —her mother pulled the black necklace from around her neck and looped it around her daughter's head—"my heart beats with yours." She tucked the beads beneath Briseras's tunic. They were warm from her mother's chest, and they eased the chill Briseras couldn't suppress. Her mother pulled her in close. "Never forget, my child, as long as you live, so will I."

Briseras had nodded, wanting desperately to believe her mother in that moment, the last time they would ever see one another. The rebellion began the morning after she and Rajas left. It was subdued by nightfall. She had never learned how long they'd kept her mother alive afterward or how they'd punished her. She had long suspected that Rajas, her teacher and guardian thereafter, had shielded her from any reports that made their way to the camp from the ancient holy city. Growing up among the terrors of the priests, she had plenty of examples of punishments to choose from. But at her core, she knew that even what she'd endured fell short of what her mother's torturers had done in those final days.

She had kept her promise and had never returned to Haven.

Half a world away from the fortress just outside Andel-ce

Hevra, Everett and Lavinia's voices called her back to the chilly mountainside. Their words bounced back and forth as they climbed up the hill behind the house, moonlight glinting off of the witch's hair as they approached the smokehouse.

If Lavinia's account was correct, there would soon be shadowy patrols circling the base of the black castle. Lamplight gleamed from its tall windows, tongues of flame burning bright on the mountainside. Here in the darkness, she couldn't deny that the vampire they hunted was stalking them in return.

Once a vampire's fangs had pierced mortal flesh, it was easier for those few who survived to sense their nearness. The feeling condensed like chilled breath against her neck, the tingling of trapped prey in the moments before it surrenders to its predator. Those final heartbeats when it still believes it has a chance to fight.

Briseras pulled the cold in and around herself, an additional layer of armor. Everett and Lavinia would stand a better chance of survival if she split from them now and pursued the creature alone.

She started down the hill just as the pair emerged from the smokehouse.

"Wrong way, Briseras," Everett called.

Lavinia's voice followed. "We can't eat this pork shoulder by ourselves."

The chill left her, leaving raw and exposed her desire to spend the evening with her two unlikely companions. Otto swooped down to join her, and Vera whimpered, golden eyes staring at the cabin. With a pang she wasn't willing to investigate, Briseras turned and climbed up the hill. After tonight, she would find a way to part from them. They should be safe to spend a final evening together.

Everett's cry woke Briseras in the middle of the night. "Lavinia's gone!

IT DIDN'T TAKE LONG TO FIND THE TRAIL BENEATH THE bright light of the moons overhead. No sign of a struggle in the cabin. Lavinia's boot prints led down the hill, straight toward the Nocturne estate.

The folklorist bowed his head, clutching his hair in his hand. "Do you think the vampire took her too?" Grief-stricken eyes met hers. "Like her sister, Saige?"

"No, Everett." Briseras's voice was low. Her stomach churned. She'd dismissed that possibility during their search. "I think it unlikely that the vampire entered the cabin without our knowing and stole Lavinia away from her bed. That may be what happened with Saige, if she was telling the truth about that . . ."

"Wait, Briseras, what are you saying?"

"That she betrayed us." Briseras removed her flask from her jacket and poured a swallow of whiskey into the lid. The burn in her throat matched the crackling fire in her mind. This was why it was better she travel alone. No betrayal, no tricks.

Everett shook his head and turned to a clean page in his journal. "I don't believe that, and I don't think you should either." He held up a finger to prevent her interjection. "But, let's do this the Briseras way, like you did the day we met Lavinia. There are only a few options for what could have happened, aren't there? If she lied to us—"

"The most likely scenario."

He glared at her. "*If* she lied us, or betrayed us, as you said earlier, then it's most probable that she intended to do so from the beginning."

Briseras nodded. "Agreed. It would help explain why she happened upon the village we were investigating shortly after a werewolf attack and why she left the more probable scene of her sister's capture."

"Hmm, alright." Everett bit down on his lower lip and trimmed his quill. "Would Lavinia have entered the Nocturne estate by herself?"

She leaned back against the wooden beam beside Everett and stared up at the thatched ceiling. "I would have."

"Not everyone can be you." Everett elbowed her. "And you don't have to admit it, but I know you prefer for the world to be that way."

A smirk pulled against the side of her lip. *Perhaps.*

The quill scratched in the silence between them as Everett made a note. "This line of reasoning doesn't entirely add up. Lavinia sets out to lie to us and bring us here . . . and then leaves us in the cabin while going to the estate herself? Why?" He scribbled furiously for a moment, flipped back a few pages, and frowned. Slowly, he met her eyes. "Do you remember what Hannah said to you about your destiny?"

Briseras sighed. "Yes."

"Maybe that's the missing piece."

"What do you mean?" She leaned over to look at Everett's page, but he pulled the book back.

"If Hannah was right and it's your destiny to go into the estate, maybe Lavinia is part of why that's supposed to happen." He squinted at his notes. "And maybe Lavinia knew that, and she was trying to help you." Everett brightened. "Tonight could have been a shift in her plan. Let's say she was supposed to bring you to the castle, but something made her change her mind. She went instead."

Briseras leaned over and adjusted her boots. The glimmer of truth shone around Everett's words. "What would have made her change her mind?"

"I don't know." He smiled.

"How are you so optimistic at this moment?"

Everett shook his head and held out the journal page he'd

hidden from her. The outer edges contained names scrawled in the folklorist's angular hand. Among them, she read *James*, *Hannah*, *Lavinia*, and, in the lower right corner, *Everett*. A series of lines and arrows riddled the center of the page with a few notes about the werewolves and the vampire. In the center, where most of the arrows led, a single name: *Briseras*.

She met Everett's gaze.

His voice emerged in a whisper. "I know you probably won't believe me. You prefer to see yourself on the fringe. But, like I told you, it's my job to recreate the story. And this one that we're in, it's yours, Briseras. Everyone else around you can see it, but you don't want to." He squeezed her knee. "Lavinia arrived in that village because some part of her sensed that the help she needed was there. Or, if you're right and she betrayed us, because a vampire sent her there. I'm not certain the why really matters because that was before she had a choice."

Briseras cleared her throat. "And after?"

"After she met you, she changed her mind about the path she was going to follow. She went to Nocturne alone." He laid his quill in the fold of his journal. "If you think she went to the castle to tell the vampire about us, then we need to move, right? But wouldn't you have already sensed that?"

She grinned. The thought had occurred to her, but they were close enough to the vampire's domain for him to sense their presence. If he had truly wanted to bring them into his lair, he or his servants would have arrived already. "We still can't be certain the vampire lives in the castle."

"Hah. Sure."

Briseras took a deep breath and slowly exhaled. Everett's words thawed a hole in her chest. First he wriggled through the gap in her armor and now this.

"I know we just met her, and that you've only recently met me, but . . . I have a sense about Lavinia, just like I had one about you. I think there's something we missed, or something she wasn't able to say." He leaned his head back against the wall and swung his eyes over to her. "Will you trust me long enough for us to find out?"

The steady rhythm of Briseras's heart sped up. Over the last ten days, possibly even several months, she'd avoided what now stared her in the face—she was frightened of encountering another vampire. This time, Rajas wouldn't be there to intervene. Ophelia wouldn't be nearby to revive her. It would be Everett and Lavinia who relied upon her instead—the folklorist whose easy trust had guided her to this point, and the witch, whose deception or self-sacrifice, she still wasn't sure which, had created the need for this ultimate confrontation. "The vampire wants us to venture into his lair."

Everett pursed his lips. "How do you know?"

"If you're right, and Lavinia played a part in a scheme to draw us here or she wanted us to help free her sister from the vampire, he has two choices—hunt or be hunted."

The folklorist nodded and waited for her to continue.

"A good predator—and vampires are excellent predators— knows their prey." She narrowed her eyes and rose to her feet. The missing piece Everett had talked about began to take shape around her. "In this case, if we're assuming that we are the prey . . ."

"He knows that you'll come hunting for him."

"Exactly." Briseras ran her tongue over her extended canines. She should have more quickly suspected that someone would want to complete the transformation Malthael had initiated. Briseras smiled. "Let's give him what he wants."

BEFORE SUNRISE, SHE AND EVERETT LEFT LAVINIA'S CABIN. They created a deliberate trail leading away from the estate. Once in the forest, they walked upstream along a creek bed, occasionally leaving tracks. At midmorning, they made camp to solidify the appearance of their retreat from Nocturne.

Briseras cut a slice out of a bright red apple. "Thank you for what you said about me killing James." She hadn't regretted it at the time or since, but Everett's spoken understanding had created a similar sense of freedom to what she knew his lover now possessed. "I will be honest with you in turn. Until last night, I wasn't planning on taking you with me into the estate."

Everett took a deep swallow from his canteen. "I know." He wiped his mouth clean with his sleeve, revealing a smile. "I was going to give you this to help you on your journey." The folklorist held out his journal toward her.

"You do not wish to accompany me?" Briseras pushed the journal back toward him. The feeling was understandable. She must have misread his wishes.

"No, I do." He slid the journal away from the palm of her hand and dropped it onto her lap. "I'd like for you to keep it, though, just in case."

"In case of what?"

Vera picked her head up off her paws, observing the woodland.

Everett shrugged. "We all find ourselves needing something we didn't expect. Maybe the journal will do that for you."

"I'm not going to start writing down everything that happens to me." Briseras scowled at the book.

The folklorist laughed and drew another journal, this one a light brown, from his bag. "I didn't expect that you would." His expression grew more serious. "Just hold on to that one for me, for a little while at least."

"Very well." She tucked it into her bag and crunched the final slice of apple between her teeth. "Are you ready to head back downstream?"

"Lead the way."

As midmorning fell into afternoon, Briseras led them down the creek and deep into the dense forest that surrounded the northern side of the Nocturne estate. As the light began to fade, the glow of torchlight and voices reached them from inside the castle. They crept down to the cemetery that abutted the wood. This was where they would make their entrance. Briseras leapt over the graveyard fence and sneaked behind a large mausoleum. In blocky script across its front: MOART ETERNA, "death is eternal."

The din from inside the estate rose and fell, most likely from a large gathering taking place. Briseras dodged tombstone to tombstone, guiding them to the base of the estate's walls. Around the side, in deep shadow, a door to the lower levels hung ajar. She secured her hood and gestured toward it. Everett stayed close behind her, followed by Otto and Vera.

Heavy moisture in the lower chambers dampened the echoes of their boots and Vera's claws. Briseras crouched against the dark stone walls, the low light from her torch the only guide as they slid deeper into the castle's cellars.

"How much farther does this tunnel go?" Briseras swatted the cobwebs away with her torch. They'd been traveling for nearly an hour, winding ever deeper and down. Did the tunnel lead beneath the mountain?

Vera's eyes glowed copper-green in the torchlight.

"Hopefully not much farther." Everett's face was pale in the gleam of the fire.

After a second cramped, crouching hour, the light ahead changed. The stone tunnel opened a black maw into a cavernous room. "What would be down here?" Briseras whispered. Their steps slowed.

Vera's ears stood erect beside her, muscles taut, ready to lunge at the slightest provocation.

Briseras stilled, inviting the shadows nearby to shield them. *Little more than moss, little more than earth*—Rajas had taught her the incantation early on in her training. Tracking came easily to her. Concealment less so.

"How did you—"

She covered Everett's mouth with her hand. The time for excessive noise and questions had passed. "Stay close behind me."

The light from her torch dimmed, a low green-blue flame clinging to the wood. With her back to the wall, Briseras crept to the end of the tunnel. Her breath swept out from her chest.

The tunnel opened into an ancient cathedral, the swoop of its arches disappearing into the darkness around them. Heavy iron sconces hung down between rows of black wooden pews. How many thousands would the sanctuary hold at any one time?

They walked down the center aisle, the colossal space absorbing any sound they made before it could fly back to them. Flickering at the edges of her sight, spirits flared briefly to life. "Little more than moss, little more than earth"—Briseras's chanting intensified. "Spirits go and spirits come, drift away and be undone."

Shadowy hands pulled at the edges of her being, like she had felt as Ophelia returned her to life. "You will see them, and they you," the druid had said. "But it will not be easy for them to extinguish your light—nor your shadow."

The figures made of licking black flames shrank back into the netherworlds where they dwelled, and a blanket of cold ensnared Briseras's shoulders. The icy fingers of death clung tightly to this space. A horror had unfolded here in ages long past.

From the middle of the expansive chamber, an altar rippled

into physical form, emerging from the surrounding dark. Everett grabbed her arm, but she shook free.

Briseras calmed her breathing further. Once in, once out, and then a minute would pass. Once in, once out, and stillness again.

Five black steps swam into focus beneath the altar as she approached. The shadows shifted.

She and Everett stood at the base of the stairs. Briseras fixed her eyes on the onyx slab above. "Stay here." Whatever secrets this chamber contained, she would find them on top of the shining black altar.

The cold weight grew heavier as she climbed the first stair. Her breath crystallized in front of her face, the frozen particles falling to the floor.

There was a scroll, wrapped around a bone, in the center, between two black candelabrum. She had to know what it said.

By the third stair, the weight was so great she fell to her hands and knees. Vera whimpered and slunk beneath her, supporting Briseras's chest with her sharp, angular shoulders. Everett and Otto huddled together at the base of the altar.

Together, she and her wolf slunk up the final two steps, and Briseras clawed her way to the top. With shaking arms, she resisted the weight.

She took a gasping breath as her head emerged, like one drowning beneath the frozen surface of a river, a lone rapid allowing the body to break free.

The broken seal on the rolled parchment bore a black wax skull. Briseras unfurled the document, revealing an ancient script written in dark red ink. It had been many years since she had deciphered such a text, and this one was bristling with ornamental flourishes. Across the top, the parchment looped around what she could now see was a human arm bone. Briseras shuddered.

The arcane letters described a foul ceremony of some kind.

It spoke of a return and of life eternal. At the bottom, the writer had sketched out an intricate box and a chalice. The ink smelled of iron—it had been written in blood.

There, along the bottom of the scroll, a name in a looping script: *Lord Victoro Nassarq.*

Everett's suspicion had been correct. Lavinia must have known as well. They'd yet to encounter any sign of her.

A creaking sound interrupted the silence on the opposite side of the chamber. Long, low moans drifted forth, the shambling of many footsteps. Vera's hackles rose, and a growl prickled at the back of her throat. "We must go." Everett nodded, poised to run. The vampire's servants would attempt to surround them soon.

CHAPTER 35

Captain Teodric knelt in front of Genevieve's cell, a crease of worry across his brow. "I know it's a lot to ask of you, Genevieve, but he will die otherwise."

Three days had passed since her transformation, and Darcy's condition was slowly worsening. Kriega and the captain were anxious to save him, more to avoid the wrath of their admiral than out of any sense of obligation for Darcy himself. Genevieve sighed. With Darcy's death, she would lose the only hope she'd found thus far of uncovering who had organized the attack against her conclave. "I will, but only on three conditions." Over the course of her imprisonment, she'd had plenty of time to think. "The first, that Darcy answers my questions about my conclave." She smiled. "The second, that the dagger returns to me. And the third . . ." Genevieve took a deep breath. "You will take me to Caldara before you sail to the island where the admiral is waiting for us."

"Hmm." Teodric rubbed his stomach like she'd just struck him. After a moment's pause, he nodded. "I will make the first promise on Darcy's behalf. I am certain he places his own life above any other allegiance. What do you need to attempt to heal him?"

Genevieve's features scrunched together. She thought back through the remedies Mariellen had taught her, but none of them were intended for reversing an affliction brought on by a sacred artifact of their people. "Our healing comes from the roots of the old forests," Mariellen had said. "They run deep, like our magic, like our ancestors."

"It is not something I have attempted before, Captain." She couldn't lie to him, not when she was so close to regaining her conclave's dagger and embarking on the first part of Ophelia's quest—to make her way to Caldara. "But if you can take us to an ancient forest, he may stand a chance."

Teodric scowled for a moment, and then his features brightened. "Are you familiar with the legend of Isla de Como, Genevieve?"

She shook her head.

"It's said to be guarded by the spirit of an ancient dragon." The captain's eyes flashed. "Does that sound old enough to work?"

"Yes, I believe so." Her stomach tingled. He still hadn't answered her other two demands.

"The island is on the way to Caldara. The admiral won't be pleased at the change in plans." A shadow crossed over his face. "But such, I've found, is life on the sea. Very well, we sail east."

"And the dagger, Captain."

Teodric grinned. "Will you agree to let me hold on to it until after you've healed Darcy? That way, it will appear as though its return to you is contingent upon his return to health."

"But is it?" Genevieve frowned.

"No," he whispered, "but let's keep that secret between us."

"Agreed." Her stomach flipped as she tried to picture what the healing would entail. Would she be able to intuit it from the forest, as she had seen Mariellen do on several occasions? "Unless . . ."

The captain stopped and turned back to her. "Yes?" He raised an eyebrow, waiting.

"Unless I need the dagger for the healing." Internally, Jade's head lifted up from resting on her paws, suddenly interested in Genevieve's plan. Was her inner wolf trying to tell her that she'd struck upon part of the process for healing Darcy? She grimaced, imagining needing to cut off the rotted bones and sinew from Darcy's shoulder to protect the rest of his body.

"That sounds a reasonable request to me, Genevieve." He winked and strode away to climb above decks and reroute their course.

How true do you think the legend of the ancient dragon he spoke of is, Jade? The wolf's tail swished. She didn't know how to read that response.

Genevieve leaned back against the wall of her cell and crossed her arms over her knees. Ophelia had said that she bore a special kind of druidic magic that hadn't existed in the world for generations. She already thought of the ancient druids who sought to understand lycanthropy as incredibly brave. Would their daring have extended beyond connecting to their inner wolves and pushed them to encounter one of the great, ancient creatures, the perfect blend of wisdom and ferocity? She closed her eyes, imagining herself and Vera in their wolf form, bounding over a rocky hill toward a dragon's lair. A mist rose from its depths and swirled all around them. In the darkness beyond the rounded opening, a great many mysteries waited to be revealed.

CHAPTER 36

A raven flew in meandering circles over the small, abandoned village. It was the first creature Iellieth had seen since Lord Nassarq found them in the woods. The nobleman had insisted they accompany him back to his estate, declaring the Stormside Forest no place for a lady of the court and her companions. "Besides," he added with a grin, "you wouldn't want to miss an opportunity to see your stepfather, would you?"

Iellieth clutched her fingers into fists. "No," she lied through gritted teeth, "no, I wouldn't."

She pulled Mara's shawl tighter around her shoulders at the stare of the empty houses. The chill she'd felt from inside the black oak returned and had yet to release its grasp.

Their boots crunched softly on the pebbled path through the center of town. Quindythias meandered closer to one of the cottages but shook his head as he walked away. Where had everyone gone?

"It's a beautiful estate, is it not?" Lord Nassarq raised his arm overhead, his eyes never turning to the homes that huddled beneath the shadow of his grand estate. The black castle, Nocturne, jutted up from the roots of the mountain, glaring down at the spread of forest and cottages beneath its feet. The tallest points of the dark edifice pierced the clouds, shearing curls of mist from their wooly coats. Beyond its turrets, some of the highest peaks of the Frostmaws glittered against the gray sky, snow-capped even in mid-spring. Iellieth shivered.

Quindythias squinted up at the towers as Lord Nassarq strode toward the gatehouse that barred entry to the winding road up to the estate. "I cannot believe what passes for civilization these days."

No figure emerged to greet the castle's lord, but a shadow stirred in the murky depths of the small stone structure with the flick of the nobleman's wrist.

Oversized ravens leered from the tall gray pillars on either side of the gate, sharply contorted depictions of the graceful figure that circled above. Their black eyes seemed to shift to follow her wherever she stepped.

"Terribly lifelike, aren't they, Lady Amastacia?" His wide lips stretched into a sharp smile as he gestured for them to follow him up the path. "Pardon the carriage dust." He glanced at the twin furrows through the wide gravel path and the faint film coating the gray stones that bordered the road. "I am thrilled to be hosting the king and his court," he said flatly. He spun back toward his estate with a swirl of his dark blue cloak.

Dusk fell as they climbed the path to Nocturne.

Two glowing lanterns observed their final turns along the path, staring like eyes of fire from the face of the estate's edifice. Lord Nassarq extended a gloved hand to Iellieth. "Please, allow me to escort yourself and your friends inside. Duke Amastacia will wish to know of your arrival."

Iellieth's stomach sank lower. "I wouldn't be so sure of that." Nassarq tucked her hand into the crook of his elbow. She jumped as servants emerged from the shadows and pulled open the iron doors. The corner of the nobleman's mouth twitched, and he patted her hand. She shivered again as Lord Nassarq led her over the threshold of his estate. Standing tall beside her, Marcon released the hilt of his sword but kept a narrow gaze trained on their host.

Nassarq's polished shoes clicked against shining marble of his entry hall. His boots had remained impeccably clean despite the journey through the woods and up the gravel path. "Will you tell me once more how you and your friends came to be in the woods outside my estate?" Lord Nassarq ran his tongue over his front teeth as he stared down at her. "I want to ensure we have an identical story to report to your stepfather."

Quindythias's eyes burned against the base of her neck. *Say nothing more than you have to.* He had repeated these instructions to her over and over again in their few weeks together. "We . . . heard about it in Hadvar." It had been easier to dodge this question in the woods.

A fit of coughing erupted behind her, bouncing off the distant arch of the stone ceiling overhead. What was she supposed to say if she couldn't even say that?

"Hadvar, really?" The nobleman lifted an eyebrow. "And why shall we say the queen allowed you out alive during a time of war?"

Shouts of laughter reached them from around a corner at the end of the hall.

Nassarq's upper lip curled as she made him no answer, like he had caught a whiff of a displeasing odor. "I'm simply surprised no one tried to stop you, Lady Amastacia." His voice had a longer, deeper drawl than she remembered.

The fury burning in Lord Stravinske's eyes tore back through her, white flames of terror licking at her spine.

"That man will never bother you again," Marcon had assured

her that long, first night of their escape. Immediately after, he'd checked his sleeve, tucking the dagger he kept there tighter into his sheath.

She could still feel the scratchy press of the blood-coated fabric against her back in their final dance together.

For a moment, that same burning hatred flared in Lord Nassarq's eyes. It was less personal, still calculating. He looked on her as prey.

Who's to say they didn't try to stop us, she wanted to reply but settled on something vaguer. "We're just extremely lucky, I suppose." Iellieth faked a smile and stared ahead. Above her, Nassarq's expression soured.

She suppressed a sigh of relief as the clamor of the court became clear in the grand hall to the right of the long entryway. Iellieth released the nobleman's arm as a familiar figure emerged from the hall and poked his head forward.

"Ellie?" Basha's voice rolled across the dark stone walls. "Ellie, is that you?"

Iellieth laughed as she ran forward and threw her arms around the dwarf's neck. "You've no idea how glad I am to see you!" Waves of relief crashed against her heart. Whatever malignant force haunted Nova and the dryad in the forest and whatever malice brewed in Lord Nassarq's mind faded away in Basha's presence.

The stormguard chuckled and patted her on the back. "There, there, glad the three of you could make it." He nodded to Marcon and Quindythias over her shoulder. "I've got them from here, Lord Nassarq. The king's been looking for you."

The nobleman nodded, his expression unchanging. His eyes lingered on the stormguard a moment too long before he swept into the grand hall behind Basha.

Iellieth peered anxiously over the dwarf's shoulder. If King Arontis was in the hall, her stepfather would be as well.

"An odd one, that," Basha whispered to her once Nassarq was out of hearing. "Oh well. If the king trusts him, then so do I." Basha shrugged as though he was concluding an internal debate. "So, Ellie, what brings the three of you here? Your mother and Katarina, they've stayed behind in Io Keep, not wanting to join in the war council." The dwarf leaned closer again. "Though between you and me, your stepfather could use a clever aide like the duchess to help him back into the king's good graces. More children disappeared while you were gone, and the duke hasn't been able to uncover what's happened to them. The king placed him in charge of the search, thinking he'd be able to bring about results quickly. But there's been no trace. Rumors are starting to spread among the people, and the citizenry grows more anxious by the day."

"More children?" Iellieth's brow furrowed. "And what about Scad?" Her stomach turned at the idea of her stepfather being responsible for her friend's safe return.

Basha shook his head. "No word yet. They thought they might have found something"—Basha's voice dropped lower—"down in the tunnels, you know. There were a few holding cells we hadn't been aware of, and some additional routes, but nothing beyond that."

Scad, where are you? Iellieth bit the inside of her lower lip. "And, umm, when did everyone arrive?" Marcon was the only one who caught the hitch in her voice. He stepped closer behind her.

"Here, I'll show you to some unclaimed guest rooms." Basha gestured down the long stone corridor. "Let's see. Lord Nassarq and some of his carriages left about a week ahead of everyone else, not too long after you, come to think of it, and the rest of us arrived early yesterday."

Sparks danced in the back of her mind. "When did you find the empty cells beneath Io Keep?"

The stormguard turned off the main hallway onto one that

reached through the southern portion of the estate. "This whole place is cold and shaded, but I think you'll be most comfortable where there's a chance of sun." He peered into the various wings on the hall to discern which were still free. "You know, for as many carriages as he sent ahead, there aren't as many servants as one might think."

"Basha, did you hear me? The empty cells?"

"Ah, yes, sorry, Ellie. Here you all go." He directed them onto a narrow hall with an adjoining living space and two small bedrooms, each with a tall arched window looking at the wooded valley below. "You know, it's odd." The dwarf's eye twitched, and he frowned. "Now that you mention it . . ." His eye twitched again, and Basha swayed on his feet.

Marcon leapt forward and caught the dwarf under the arms, and Quindythias slid a wooden chair over to catch him.

"Ooh, Ellie, I'm sorry." Basha laid a hand on his chest. "That was . . ." He shook his head. "Humph. I can't recall exactly." The dwarf squinted and rubbed beneath his eye. "Shortly before we left, but precisely when, I don't know." Basha peered off into the cloudy sky outside the tall window, his gaze drifting over the leagues they'd traveled to arrive here along the kingdom's borders. "The lads said it was like they'd stumbled on a set of passages that had been right in front of them the whole time, and they'd just . . . missed them somehow." He scratched at his beard, brow furrowed. "A terrible cold, they said . . ." His eyes grew unfocused again, and Basha swung his head back around to her. "That's all I've got for you, Ell." He stood up and clapped her on the back. "Happy you've returned."

The three of them stared after the dwarf as he wobbled out of the room.

Iellieth motioned Marcon and Quindythias over, keeping her voice low until Basha's footsteps faded down the hall. "There was a passageway like that, when we were trying to find you," she said to Quindythias, then turned to Marcon. "Do you remember?"

"I do, lady."

"That's where I found this." Iellieth withdrew the wolf figurine from her pocket. Her trinket, now talisman, that would lead her back to Scad.

"I don't remember the stormguard being so absentminded." Quindythias peered over her head. "It seemed almost as though he . . ." The elf frowned. "Well, as though he couldn't find the memories, like they'd been removed or tampered with."

"I know people can be charmed, but can their memories be altered?" Iellieth's eyes grew wide. She'd read such accounts in stories, but for them to be truly possible . . .

"It is possible for memories to be changed, lady," Marcon said. He followed Quindythias's gaze after Basha, as though they could find the answers inscribed on the air behind him. "But it requires very powerful magic. Is there anyone in the court who could wield such power?"

Iellieth shook her head. "No, there is no one like that among the nobility, or who would have easy access to the king. We have a few healers who could attempt to aid the king should something befall him, but Linolynn's precautions do not extend beyond that."

Marcon narrowed his eyes at the door and pulled her and Quindythias closer. "There's something foul afoot in this castle. I sense it." His nose wrinkled, trying to sniff out the evil inside the dark stone walls. "We need to be on guard."

Quindythias smirked as he twirled a dagger through his fingers. "Good. I was starting to get bored in the woods." They both turned to look at him, and he threw up his hands, the blade poised between his two smallest fingers. "What? I don't see why we can't have sophisticated society *and* some adventure."

A cold breeze blew against the base of Iellieth's neck, and the catacomb that had called to her beneath Io Keep flashed before her eyes once more. Whatever lay ahead, it seemed almost certain that Quindythias would be granted his wish.

IELLIETH STARTLED AS A YOUNG PAGE APPEARED IN THEIR doorway to announce dinner. She sighed. Still no sign of her stepfather.

The crease faded from Marcon's brow as she met his eyes. He'd been watching her. "You are worried about seeing Duke Amastacia again, are you not?"

"I am." Iellieth lowered her gaze. "I don't want to still be concerned about his influence over me. But I don't know how to make it go away." Even with the shadow of Lord Stravinske gone forever, the duke still lurked in the corners of her mind.

Marcon smiled and squeezed her shoulder. "It will take time, lady." He shrugged and patted the hilt of his longsword, the grin remaining on his lips. "We can always do some persuading if you want."

Quindythias sat up straighter on the bed across from her. "Yes! He would never bother you again." His toes tapped against the floor as his scheme developed. "We just need to get him in a room alone with the two of us—he doesn't need to know that you're involved at all. Oh! We can wear masks, and then he won't know who we are." He pursed his lips, considering, and then the tapping resumed. "How many scented scarves did the two of you pick up while we were in Hadvar? I wanted to get more, but I only managed three or four."

Iellieth laughed and held up her hands. "No, none of that will be necessary, though I'm very grateful to have two such willing, capable, and . . . creative protectors." She set aside the amusing picture of her stepfather's outrage at being tied to a chair and accosted by two "ruffians" in whichever ridiculous masks Quindythias had also secretly acquired in Hadvar. Despite Marcon's teasing, he wouldn't lightly abide the duke's bullying her. They'd need a clear, specific plan for their intervention in the inevitable encounter with her stepfather on top of the general reconnaissance for illuminating whatever dark force lurked nearby. Nova had said that freeing the black oak from the corruption would also somehow stop the war. Did whatever was connecting them dwell inside the castle? Or would they have to sneak back out to the forest to find it?

She exhaled slowly, focusing back on the task at hand. First, at dinner, they needed to see if the strange memory magic affecting Basha had splashed over onto anyone else. If they could uncover enough connections, they might be able to follow them to the source of the darkness that Marcon sensed. And if nothing turned up, they could borrow horses and leave for Red's Cross at first light.

Deftly, Quindythias knotted the ties of her dress as she finished explaining their information-gathering plan for dinner. "I think it will work best if we split up. Lord Nassarq was doing *something* odd in the woods earlier. His brother and sister-in-law should be here, Duke and Duchess Jorgan. The running of Nocturne passed to Lord Nassarq upon his brother's marriage, though I think the estate technically belongs to the Jorgans now . . ." Iellieth squinted up at the ceiling. The entailments of the various noble estates had never held much interest for her. "It probably doesn't matter." She shook her head and scowled. Undoubtedly, they would have assigned places in the elegant dining room and would need to make the best of them. But the seal piece—and Lord Nassarq—had led them here. There had to be a reason.

CHAPTER 37

S he had been right about the assigned places in the dining hall at least. Iellieth frowned down at her plate, avoiding the cold gaze of her stepfather across the linen-covered table from her. The duke had been waiting for her outside the doors to the candlelit hall, completely unavoidable.

His grimace of distaste at seeing her in her travel-wrinkled gown made Lord Nassarq's occasional glare from beside the king's right hand seem like a friendly smile in comparison. Duke Amastacia had crossed his arms, sneering at her down his long nose as Marcon's stance stiffened beside her. "I see you continue to insist on debasing yourself with these . . . companions."

Iellieth stood taller. "I do." She had promised herself that no matter what he said, he wouldn't distract her from searching for the dark creature Nova had warned them about.

"Come," he snapped. "You can remember your place long enough to accompany me." His eyes flicked over to Marcon and Quindythias, but he said nothing to them.

Marcon's warm hand found hers and squeezed before she followed a step behind her stepfather into the dining hall.

It was strange to see Lord Nassarq in her stepfather's place beside the king, and the demotion had done nothing to improve the duke's mood.

Near the middle of the long table, Marcon, Basha, and one of the lieutenant stormguards stared at a small crystal fortress they had made from their neighbors' unused white wine glasses. The lieutenant stroked his barely existent beard as he slid regiments of forks and spoons toward the propped-knife battlements of the delicate fortress.

Farther down, a burst of laughter erupted from the priests at whatever tale Quindythias was recounting for them. The elf's arms flailed about before he clutched his throat dramatically, mimicking being strangled before he embarked on a seated reenactment of a fistfight.

The king sat quietly at the head of the table, his attention only stirring when Lord Nassarq leaned closer to whisper in his ear.

"I shall write to your mother this evening and assure her that you look well." Duchess Jorgan's voice pulled Iellieth from her study of the room. Iellieth smiled and nodded her thanks. "She had asked me to inform her if the change of scenery helped alleviate my son Pierre's nightmares, but I'm afraid they've only gotten worse inside these dreary walls." The duchess shook her head and leaned toward Iellieth's stepfather. "Shall I write anything on your behalf, Calderon?"

He glanced up at the two of them. "That won't be necessary."

"Very well." She settled back into her seat and turned to whisper to Iellieth. "He's been quite cross since my brother-in-law replaced him as the king's closest advisor."

The duke's glower darkened. Duchess Jorgan wasn't whispering quietly enough for him to be unable to hear her, but he wouldn't risk the slight to his pride that actually acknowledging he could hear her insults would inflict.

"It began at the Festival of Renewal, I believe," the duchess continued. "Calderon was running around after your mother, who was practically hysterical in her worries over what had happened to you." Iellieth's stomach flipped as she recalled her own fears that Mamaun had mis-transmigrated as she had. "I told her you would turn up eventually, and here you are, back again!" Duchess Jorgan waved her hand at the simplicity with which Iellieth's weeks of absence from the castle were resolved. What had Mamaun told the other ladies of the court after Iellieth's brief return and second disappearance?

Her whisper lowered to true conspiratorial tones. "Anyway, your stepfather was practically begging that sallow-faced suitor of yours—I could never keep track of them—to wait on you to miraculously appear, and he wasn't ready at all to assist the king on his negotiations with the Hadvarians, so my brother-in-law stepped in." Her eyes shone as she regarded Lord Nassarq. "It was *he* who discerned the Hadvarians' hand in the attacks through the mountains and the dangers they pose to those of us with northern estates."

"But they weren't behind those attacks," Iellieth added quickly. "It was a huge pack of werewolves. I saw them myself."

The clatter of silverware around her stilled. She'd spoken louder than she had intended.

The duchess tittered beside her. "Oh, dear, don't be ridiculous! Werewolves, honestly." She pressed her napkin to the sides of her lips to accentuate her giggles but calmed as Lord Nassarq's gaze fell on her.

"That is quite enough, Odette." He shifted his leer to Iellieth, his eyebrows rising over dark, glimmering eyes. "Lady Amastacia knows and sees more than most give her credit for."

Iellieth's insides churned. The cold calculation in his voice didn't sound like a compliment. She leaned back against her chair, pressing her fingertips beneath her thighs to quell the sudden swirl of her magic. But what exactly was it responding to?

When the servers whisked away her plate to make room for the dessert course, she sneaked away to join the children's table at the far end of the hall. Maybe there was a connection between Pierre's nightmares and the corruption they were trying to find.

"Aren't you too big to sit at our table?" The two Jorgan children, Eunice and Pierre, blinked up at her.

Iellieth grinned. "Yes, I suppose I am. But I'm not enjoying the company of the people at my table. Do you have room for me here?"

"Yes." Pierre nodded. "Then my uncle can't take that seat."

"Your uncle?"

The boy's large eyes whirled away from hers, and he stared at the tabletop.

"He spends a lot of time with Pierre," Eunice said, "but he's not very good at playing with us. Uncle Nassarq tucks Pierre in every night, but he still has nightmares."

Pierre sniffed and nodded.

"I hate having nightmares," Iellieth said, laying a hand over the little boy's. His skin was clammy and cold.

"I didn't have them as much when I stayed with Eunice." Pierre's shoulder quivered as he drew himself up and toward his sister. "But Uncle Nassarq said we had to stay in our own rooms now."

"And why is that?" Iellieth leaned in closer. Pierre's hand locked tight around her thumb as a dark shadow extended its wings across their table.

"Lady Amastacia, a word?" Lord Nassarq towered above her.

Iellieth shivered. "Yes, of course." She stretched her lips into a smile for the children. "Excuse me," she whispered. Their faces were nearly as pale as their uncle's, and Eunice gripped Pierre's shoulders, holding her little brother close to her.

Nassarq indicated the side of the grand dining hall. The center of the room glowed with bright lanterns and candles and cast the edges beyond the pillars in shadow. The nobleman stood behind one of the slate columns, becoming one with the darkness. "I see that you have befriended my niece and nephew."

"Yes"—Iellieth intertwined her fingers behind her back, wrapping and unwrapping her grasp—"they're very sweet. I thought I might share my dessert with them."

"Your stepfather seems displeased at your sudden arrival at my estate."

"He is, I believe." She considered the man in front of her. Though Nassarq had spent most of the last several years in Nocturne and away from Io Keep, the nature of her relationship with the duke shouldn't have been a surprise. "If I may be so bold, despite finding us in the woods, it does not appear that you are entirely thrilled with our arrival either."

"My apologies for giving you that impression." He swept into a low bow, arms extended to the side. "I am intrigued by your arrival, as a matter of fact." His eyes darkened as he stared down at her. "A beautiful young woman such as yourself will certainly prove to be an interesting guest inside the walls of my castle." Lord Nassarq caught her chin beneath the crook of his pointer finger despite her instinctive flinch away. "Your two companions are most curious as well." A note of warning rumbled beneath his voice. "And capable, too, though they are not quite the companions I would have selected for a . . . magical noblewoman." His gaze flickered down toward her hand.

Her magic pulsed in protest. Iellieth tucked her arm and Yvayne's pendant behind her back. She tugged her chin free but resisted the urge to step away from him. "I'm not sure I take your meaning."

He chuckled, this time glancing at her amulet. "Ah, but I am certain that you do."

Her heart pounded in her chest. *Stop giving things away*, Quindythias's voice whispered in her mind.

The solid stomp of heavy bootsteps approaching from behind her alleviated the need for her to respond.

Marcon's hand was warm against the small of her back, immediately offsetting the chill of Nassarq's words. Heat radiated from the champion beside her as he glowered at Lord Nassarq. The nobleman's dark eyes never left Iellieth. "Lady Amastacia, if you'll come with me," Marcon finally said. He angled his shoulders to interpose himself between them and shield her from the nobleman.

Lord Nassarq's upper lip curled, and he inclined his head a fraction of an inch. "I look forward to our next meeting." The chill returned, and he swept away, disappearing into the shadows of a room adjacent to the banquet hall.

Iellieth shivered and stepped closer to Marcon. "Thank you."

His gray eyes never wandered from the nobleman's back, and he continued to glare at the doorway even after Nassarq was gone. He spun to put himself between her and the door and took her hand. "Are you alright, lady? What was that about? It looked like he was threatening you."

"It felt more like an invitation," she said quickly. Marcon's eyes narrowed. "Or maybe a challenge? He mentioned the two of you and said that he was . . . intrigued by my being in the castle." Iellieth chewed her bottom lip, combing through the conversation for the exact source of the unease coursing through her veins. She pulled her hand from behind her back and twisted the crescent pendant to catch the candlelight. "He knows about my magic."

"That sounds like a threat to me," Quindythias said, appearing on the opposite side of the pillar, licking the residue of a sticky pastry from each of his fingers in turn.

"It's like he wants us to go looking for something." She

scowled. "Maybe we should accept the offer." Iellieth raised her eyebrows. "He apparently watches his nephew while he sleeps, so we know where he won't be tonight."

They both scrunched up their faces. "Where does that passageway lead?" Marcon nodded at the narrow wooden door through which Nassarq had disappeared.

"After everyone leaves the dinner, let's find out." Iellieth rose onto her tiptoes to see over Marcon's shoulder and lowered back down. "There was something else strange about talking to him. My magic, before you got here . . . it kept reacting."

Marcon frowned, looking from her to the door, but Quindythias had already started talking excitedly about the next phase of their plans and the various scenarios that might open up before them. "We'll definitely need to change into something more appropriate." He shook his head at the two of them. "Neither of you are fit for sneaking around like that." The elf threw his hands out in front of him. "Then, we'll creep back here, follow him down the hall—should we wear cloaks, too, or is that just expected at this point?"

Iellieth grinned as the magic thrummed through her body. It glided toward her from the black silhouette of the forest beyond arched panes of glass. She didn't need to pull the seal piece from her bag to know that its runes would glow violet in response to whatever power awaited them in the depths of Nocturne.

Quindythias plopped a hand on her and Marcon's shoulders to guide them out of the hall. "I for one am really enjoying this castle," he said as they left. "So many hidden places to explore."

Cobwebs hung heavy in the ceiling corners, barely strong enough to contain the darkness that pressed behind them.

CHAPTER 38

The journey to the Brightlands was easier, in many ways, than its counterpart venture into the realm of shadow. Vaxis still dwelt among the jubilant fae, and she would know how they might best be persuaded to make a stand for their world once more.

They had retreated after the fall of Eldura, surrounding themselves with frivolity, color, and ease. Dark whispers wound through the wood, old sicknesses threatened the living bark, and yet they refused to intervene. Even the waters grew stagnant, choking mosses gathering along the rivers' borders. And still the fae celebrated, as though they had not, over theirs and their ancestors' long lives, lost almost all they had ever known and loved, accepting these simple pleasures in return.

Shadows crept across the Brightlands. A time would come when they could no longer pretend they had not a wakeful, watchful enemy, one who would negate the very forest they called home.

"Vaxis?" Yvayne called through the trees. She tiptoed around the shallow pond outside the fae's cabin, but not carefully enough. Fuchsia fronds burst out of the depths and encircled her ankles, tugging her toward the bank. "Vaxis?"

A crash rang out from inside the stone structure. Yvayne hissed at the grasping flowers, and a layer of mist rose up and covered the water. The fronds slithered back away from her and retreated beneath the surface. Yvayne scrambled forward and pried open the wooden door.

A fae with burnt orange skin, burgundy hair, and dancing emerald eyes stared up at her from the floor, her lips twisted into a large smile. Books, scrolls, and an overturned side table lay scattered around Vaxis. "I didn't realize you were coming by!"

Yvayne hurried forward and pulled her up. "I am a bit of a surprise. What happened?" She bent to right the table and began stacking the books on top of it.

Vaxis giggled and brushed herself off. "Either one of my accidents or that table has turned on me." She scooped up an armful of the scrolls and carried them to the dark wood desk against the wall, already covered in similar collections of parchment. "What brings you to see me?" Vaxis leaned in close to Yvayne, her face only inches from the other fae. She grinned, seized Yvayne's elbow, and led her into the kitchen. "Tell me while I make tea."

The fae fluttered about her cabin, dashes of herbs bursting into the air as she clattered among the shelves. A kitchen faery yawned and stretched, scowling as Vaxis relocated her to the top of a carved cookie jar. Tiny supports stretched off one of her wings. Vaxis had always been a gifted healer.

Yvayne relocated a spellbook, a box of matches, and a sprig of dried lavender to the crowded table and sat just as a forest-green fox bounced into the room, purple eyes alighting on her. "It's nice to see you, Amethyst." She pranced over, wound about Yvayne's feet, and then settled onto the fae's lap. "Matters have begun to move apace in Azuria." The fae fox's soft fur rippled beneath her fingers. "I came here hoping to enlist your aid."

The fae frowned and shook her head.

"Wait, Vaxis, there's more that you need to hear. This time—"

Her friend spun around, orange arms crossed. "I can't bear it again, Yvayne." She shook her head again. "And don't tell me it will be different this time. You've said that before, but it never is." Vaxis's breath quickened. "My sister Mercedes, Brendan, countless others . . ." She hugged her arms tighter, her large eyes searching Yvayne's expression. "How many more must we lose?"

"Mara," Yvayne whispered. Vaxis's eyes flooded, and she turned her face away. Yvayne carried Amethyst over to her friend and laid her in her arms. "You sit. I'll make tea."

Vaxis sniffled and carried the fox to the kitchen table, settling onto one of her wooden chairs.

Yvayne sighed. "I know we have all been through a lot." Her friend nodded. The weight of the dead pressed upon Yvayne's shoulders. She placed the kettle on the stovetop, pulled Mara's emerald ring from her finger, and knelt on the floor at Vaxis's feet. "Take this, for a moment."

Burnished fingertips trembled as Vaxis took the ring from her hand. The emerald flashed, and her friend's eyes drew far away. It would show her what Yvayne could not.

Vaxis had spoken true—it was right that they should question the pain and the loss. She sensed Lucien's movement in the Shadowlands. He was regaining strength, amassing followers in greater numbers, and preparing the next phase of Alessandra's plan. In the past, Yvayne had resisted asking for aid, not wishing to endanger others. But the circle couldn't go on repeating.

A sharp breath above her returned Vaxis to the room. Yvayne squeezed her knee. "Did you see her?"

"Which one?" Vaxis frowned. "There are three of them."

"Three?" Yvayne rose. She waved her hand over the flame on the stove, extinguishing it, and poured the hot water into their leaves of tea. The liquid turned dark purple and faded to red.

"Yes." The light had returned to Vaxis's eyes. "Three." She grinned. "They can help one another, and we can help them." She jumped out of her chair.

"Vaxis!" Yvayne chased her down the hall, skittering around the golden squirrels. She nodded to Ember, the elderly currant-red daimon in the corner who had adopted Vaxis as a young pup. The tiny scarlet leaves that hung from his coat resembled exactly the two floating at the top of her tea. That could wait. "Who did you see?"

The fae yanked a knitted tunic from the back of one of her chairs and thrust her arms through, and she and Amethyst strode out the door. Yvayne dodged the table they'd covered upon her arrival and pulled the door shut behind her. Vaxis took her hand and skipped along the edge of the lake. "Iellieth, Genevieve, Persephonie. Iellieth, Genevieve, Persephonie." She skipped around again and again.

Yvayne clenched her teeth waiting for Vaxis's raptures to ebb. The enthusiasm would pass, and then they could formulate a plan. She wanted to scream. Why could no one respond with the appropriate urgency?

"You're irritated with me." Vaxis spun mid-bounce and stopped in front of Yvayne. She leaned closer. "Where are they? What do they need from us? Who should I help? Oh! The first one, she looks exactly like—"

"Rowan." Yvayne nodded as her heart migrated to the base of her throat. The one they—she—had pinned so many hopes on before. "I need you to help me . . . find her." Vaxis had more reliable access to the realm of spirits than she.

"I can do that." Vaxis's voice was soft. "Amethyst wants to know who is the fox with Persephonie."

"Ah." Yvayne settled onto one of the rocks. Vaxis sat directly beside her and leaned her head on her shoulder. She must be lonely here, even among the Brightlands fae. "Apollo sent one of the vulpine to watch over her."

Vaxis shook her head. "Guardians. They never learn. We will keep an eye as well. Would that help to ease your burden?"

Yvayne lowered her head. "I want us to be proactive this time, to do more than simply respond to Alessandra's attacks. How can we do that?"

Her friend gazed up at the silver clouds gathered overhead. The shapes rolled, stretched. Four legs grew, a long neck, a sparkling pink horn. "I don't know." Vaxis shrugged, staring up at the unicorn. "But I am certain we can find out."

CHAPTER 39

The festive streets blurred as Persephonie pushed her way through, her feet carrying her back to her mother's apartment.

She caught sight of Esmeralda's hair first, the strands of dark brown shimmering garnet in the afternoon sun amid the busy kiosks. Persephonie's lips turned down against her will, and the restraint she'd maintained on her way across the city fell away. She burst into tears on her mother's shoulder. "You were right, Mama, I should have listened."

Esmeralda stroked the back of her hair. "Come, sit, and tell me what happened." She pulled Persephonie away from the booths and sat with her in a shady corner beneath the apartment window.

Persephonie dabbed the tears from her eyes and the trails of salt from her cheeks. "Rennear and I went to see Colette, and then we were going to go to dinner. But"—her lips pursed again —"but they both accused Aylin . . ." Persephonie shook her head, unable to voice the charge aloud.

Esmeralda leaned down, her head angled sideways. "What did they say, cher'a?"

She took another shuddering breath, trying to calm the torrent of her thoughts. "Rennear"—her chest constricted—"he tried to blame Aylin for the attacks on the druids. He said it was part of the city's revenge for Aylin harming the priests during their prayers when they couldn't defend themselves." Persephonie covered her face once more, her fingers cooling the heat from her cheeks. Her breathing slowed.

Esmeralda caught her wrists and lowered her hands. "So now you see their manipulations?" Her eyes were wide, questioning, not angry.

Persephonie nodded.

"They twist everything around, cher'a. They had planned their attack before Aylin executed hers."

Her body tensed. "What did you say, Mama?"

Esmeralda's brow furrowed. "Their attack on the druids, it was premeditated, planned long before the Untamed took any true steps against them."

This couldn't be true. What was her mother saying?

"Aylin hoped that making the first move would send a strong enough message to save the druid conclave, that it would stave off any attack. She had no idea that—"

"So what Rennear said is true?"

"In a sense, yes, but—"

Persephonie sprang up, her narrowed gaze taking in the market around them. A beam of fluffy red fur streaked through the shoppers as Juliet came bounding into the square. Persephonie opened her arms wide and hugged the fox tight to her chest. She glanced back at her mother, who sat rooted to her bench, staring after her. The shadows from her visions had revealed themselves, ones Mama had willingly embraced, an outcome she hadn't foreseen. Persephonie spun away and carried Juliet back to the Green Owl.

⚜

HER HAND SHOOK AS SHE LAID OUT THE READING. VIOLET sparks crackled overhead and rained down onto Persephonie's shoulders. She had to focus. A heavy knock rapped against her door, sending shivers down the scarves she'd hung behind it. She wiped her eyes, a line of kohl coming away on her fingertips as she rose to answer it. Otmund usually yelled for her from the parlor.

Rennear stood with his hand raised on the other side, fingers curled as he prepared to knock again. The top part of his hair had fallen out of its tie and lay on either side of his face.

Her heart pulsed, and Persephonie caught him around the neck, pulling his face down to hers. A growl rumbled low in his throat as he kissed her back and pressed her against the door-frame. She rolled her hip, angling the two of them inside. Rennear swung the door shut behind her and stumbled back onto the array of floor pillows near the entrance to her room.

Buffeted by the howls of unspent magic after seeing her mother, Persephonie clung to him, a craggy shelter in a storm. The threads of his linen shirt scraped against her palms, his chest tensing beneath her touch.

He bunched the silk of her dress, pulling her closer. Gusts of energy swirled around her, tossing her about in the leather and spice of his scent. His hand trailed the line of her throat and ventured out across her collarbone. "I'm sorry," Rennear whispered, his voice low. His breath was ragged, copper eyes glowing.

Persephonie shook her head and wrapped her legs tighter around his waist. Her mother's revelation about Aylin unleashed a squall of questions that she wasn't prepared to answer or try to solve. In this moment, before the chaos and cruelty of the Hunt, she and Rennear could be together. She kissed him again, and Rennear's hands locked behind her, holding her hips closer, anchoring her to the present.

He slid the thin straps of her dress over her shoulders, the fabric falling to her waist. She gasped as his thumbs grazed the floral lace covering her breasts, his tongue following shortly thereafter.

Persephonie leaned down to his ear. "Would you like to spend the night with me?" His pulse thudded beneath her palm.

Bronze eyes glimmered in the candlelight, burning bright and solid beneath her. Rennear sat up on his elbows so that his bare chest was nearly touching hers. He nodded and cleared his throat. "I would, Persephonie."

Rennear wrapped his arm around her waist and cradled the back of her head, laying her down against the floor pillows. The brush of his skin brought her magic to the surface where it trickled and diffused away from his touch, shivering up to the surface elsewhere.

He slipped her dress off her hips. Her lace undergarments sighed as they caressed and left her skin. Rennear's tongue stroked against her, at first gentle and teasing. Her breath caught in her throat. He tilted her hips up, tasting her fully. Her body answered in waves of its own.

Later that evening, the air above her was still. Rennear dozed, breathing softly, a wolf resting in his den. Flashes of their time together trickled past, memories caught on a cool, cleansing breeze.

His eyes fluttered open, searching for hers in the dark. He sighed. "Persephonie, that was . . . you've left me speechless."

She snuggled back against him, tucked firmly into the sheltered harbor of his side. There would be storms again on the morrow, the omen of a crimson sunrise, but tonight, her soul could rest soundly, travelers' promise of a red night sky.

PERSEPHONIE AWOKE THE NEXT MORNING TO A RUSH OF COOL air. She winced and snuggled back against Rennear. "Apologies, my darling." His voice rumbled low as his lips skimmed the back of her neck. "I didn't mean to wake you."

She turned and brushed the loose strands from his face. "Do you really have to take part in the Hunt today?"

His lips compressed into a thin line as he looked away. "I do. I'm sorry. It's not that I want to, but . . ." His hand pressed against the bare skin of her back as she scooted away from him, hugging her closer instead. "Do you think I would not much rather be here"—his eyes gleamed—"with you?"

She dropped her hand to the tendons of his neck, following the prickly line of his jaw. "I do think you would rather be here." The crisp air splashed over her shoulder as Rennear twisted, pulling her on top of him, her gem-colored blanket remaining on the bed beside her. She gasped and burrowed into the warmth of his chest, which rumbled with self-satisfaction.

"Let's continue your negotiations from here."

"Hmm"—Persephonie's lips curled to the side—"are you sure that's wise?"

"No." He twirled a curling lock between his fingers. "My role in the Hunt is to ensure that things don't get out of hand. To protect pretty saudad and their foxes, or members of the Untamed out for a stroll." Clouds rolled in and obscured the light behind his eyes. "There have been . . . incidents in the past, where people were harmed during the festival for even the slightest inkling of natural magic." His voice grew softer as his eyes drifted away. "They were just in the wrong place at the wrong time."

Her mother's arms returned around her as they sheltered at a friend's house through the entire afternoon, cringing at the slightest sound of voices or movements outside. She'd heard other stories over the years—an innocent herbalist on her way home from the apothecary's, a satyr she had befriended the autumn before, several young girls with flowers in their hair holding hands on their way to the alternative celebration on the city outskirts.

He must have witnessed these attacks firsthand. The ghosts of his memories flickered between them.

Persephonie took his hand. "I understand why you need to be there." She lowered her lips to his, the dark berries of the wine they'd shared still blossoming on his tongue.

Rennear's hand slid across her hips and rooted her in place once more. "May I show you why I'd rather be here instead?"

❦

AFTER RENNEAR HAD LEFT TO JOIN THE RANKS FOR THE Hunt, there was a soft tapping at her door. Persephonie set the slip she'd been folding on the end of her bed and went to answer it, Juliet clicking at her heels.

"Mama, I did not expect to see you today."

Esmeralda's lower lip quivered. "I needed to talk to you."

"Should we go for a walk?" She pulled a shawl from behind the door to ward off the dampness of the early morning.

"I was hoping you might still join me in the Sessorium today," Mama said as they stepped outside. Families and friends met on the streets, walking arm in arm. They carried baskets on their way to City Center where the Hunt and the procession following it would take place.

"That is kind of you. Otmund said we'll be closed till late tonight when the crowds make their way back here. But what about Aylin? I though the two of you would be spending the day together?"

Her mother scanned the rooftops, squinting up at the pale blue sky. "We had a quarrel last night, after you and I spoke."

"Mama, I—"

"No, cher'a, a moment, please. Your . . . horror at Aylin's actions, against those of the Untamed, was justified. I don't know how it took me so long to see it clearly. And I have neglected you on your visit thus far, for which I am also sorry." Her mother took a deep breath and slowly released it. "If you think that Otmund might have room for one more, Aylin and I are spending some time apart."

Persephonie stopped and wrapped her arms around her mother, and Esmeralda leaned into her hug. She brushed the tears from beneath her mother's eyes, and Juliet wound herself around their feet. "I would love to spend the day with you at the green festival." She wrapped her elbow through her mother's, and they continued down the street. "Are you worried about seeing Aylin there? Will that be uncomfortable for either of you, so soon?"

"No, cher'a, she won't be attending today."

The nagging pressure at the base of Persephonie's neck returned, and Juliet stopped, ears erect, head tilted toward the crowds gathered for the Hunt. "Where will she be?"

Esmeralda shrugged. "I do not know. She was agitated when she came home, muttering about something coming into fruition. Things grew more heated as we talked about you. I brought up the festival today, and she said she was obligated to celebrate in other ways."

"In other ways? Did you see her this morning?" Persephonie's heartbeat quickened. Energy crackled above her, and the pit of her stomach sank. Aylin was plotting something.

Esmeralda frowned. "She said she wanted to witness the city's true nature for herself." Aylin's words sounded strange coming out of her mother's mouth.

"Did you tell her about our fight? About what I said about Rennear suspecting—" Persephonie gasped against the oozing cold that spread across her chest. That was it. She'd provided the proof Aylin needed for taking her next action against the council. Against Rennear.

"I did, Sephie." Esmeralda's eyes widened. "Gods, do you think that she—"

"Yes, Mama." Persephonie clutched her mother's arm. "Now what would she do with this information? Please."

Esmeralda's eyes darted back and forth, shallow breaths rising and falling. "She . . ."

"Would she be planning another attack?"

Mama nodded wordlessly. The color fled from her face.

"Where would it be?"

"The guards chase the animals into Tempus Market. It surrounds a square on three sides. If someone wanted to save the animals and obliterate the guards . . ."

Persephonie took her mother's trembling hand in hers. "We have to stop her."

Juliet yipped and darted toward the crowds, thick tail bounding behind her.

"Wait!" Persephonie called, jumping after the fox. She was headed straight for the Hunt.

CHAPTER 40

"What were you discussing with Stormguard Basha?" Iellieth whispered to Marcon as they followed Quindythias down the hall.

"He wanted to consult someone with an outside perspective about their strategy for an attack against Hadvar." Marcon glanced around the hallway. "Since we had recently been in the city, he was even more anxious to hear my thoughts."

Quindythias tapped his foot impatiently as he waited outside the door to their room. "Are you two almost ready? The castle isn't going to investigate itself."

Iellieth recounted her conversation with Lord Nassarq in detail while she dug a spare set of clothes from her bag. Quindythias insisted on calling them "snooping costumes," but they were really nothing more than darker leathers and tunics.

Marcon scowled after she finished. "Amid all the talk of war at dinner, I heard a strange theory." He pushed Quindythias away to prevent him from stuffing strips of cloth between the fastenings of his chain mail. "It will be fine." He held the elf out at arm's length. "King Arontis declared war in part because of the disappearances through the mountains. We know that they are caused by a large werewolf pack, but the king seems reluctant to believe it." His frown deepened. "One of the lieutenants, though, who's been stationed in the mountains for some time seems to think the disappearances through the Frostmaws and those in Linolynn might be connected." He shook his head.

Iellieth sat beside him, her fingers entangled on her lap. "Did he say what sorts of disappearances people reported? Was there a special reason he thought there was a connection?"

His jaw twinged, tightening and loosening, before he would look at her. "He did, lady. Beautiful young women, at first, though there were some outliers, mostly lone travelers, but that, as he said, is not necessarily uncommon in these woods. Later on, the targets grew younger. Little boys and girls, disappearing."

"Scad is seventeen," Iellieth whispered, holding back the swarm of images of what might have happened to the missing young women and children, the grief and fear that must plague their families. "I thought his vanishing might be connected to all of this, but—"

"He could be one of the outliers," Quindythias added brightly. He shrank back at Marcon's glare.

Iellieth untwined her fingers and squeezed her nails into her palms. "There's only one way for us to find out, isn't there?"

Quindythias nodded eagerly, but Marcon was slower to agree. "What is it?" She laid her hand on his knee.

His lips pursed. "The sort of monster that would do such a thing . . ." Marcon shook his head. "I can't shake this press of darkness, lady." His voice grew softer still. "And I don't want anything to happen to you. It is enough already that you bear the weighted bond that allows us to live."

Iellieth clutched her amulet, tracing its golden edges. "You're thinking about the revenant, aren't you? You're worried she's here."

Marcon sighed and lowered his gaze to the floor. "I am, lady."

Quindythias squatted down in front of both of them. "We'll just keep a sharp eye, like I've taught you both." He hopped up, midnight blue leather armor clinging to his lean frame. His eyes flashed against his dark skin. "And this time, if she's here, we'll find her before she finds us."

Iellieth turned Marcon's words over in her hands, studying them closely. But the doorway where Lord Nassarq had disappeared after the champion arrived continued to interrupt her thoughts. The threshold called, as the black oak had. Something lay in wait for them behind the veil.

❧

THE MOONS HUNG HIGH IN THE SKY, THEIR LIGHT FLICKERING through thick clouds onto the cold stone floors of the empty dining room as Iellieth, Quindythias, and Marcon sneaked back through the chamber and into the dark passageway where Lord Nassarq had disappeared earlier.

"Wait just a moment." Iellieth darted back into the dining room and pulled three scarlet peonies from the arrangements. She held the petals in a beam of moonlight, whispering a Druidic incantation over them. Slowly, the petals began to glow, their edges dripping with the incandescent magic of the moons.

She tiptoed back to the two champions. "Here." She held out a peony for each of them. The flowers lit the underside of their faces, casting their eyes in shadow. "They'll light our way, and we can drop petals to mark our path if we need to."

Marcon grinned and lowered his flower. "Very clever, lady." He wrapped his free hand around hers. "Quindythias will lead, then you, and I'll shield us should anything approach from behind." They must have discussed this while she was enchanting the flowers. "Whatever happens"—he glanced at

BETH BALL

Quindythias and returned his eyes to her—"we stay together. Agreed?"

"Agreed." Quindythias's smile sparkled in the milky blue aura of light.

Iellieth tilted her head, studying him. "You did a lot of things like this before, didn't you?"

"All the time." His eyebrows and shoulders rose. "Ready?" The elf whirled around dramatically and flung himself against the gray hallway wall. He raised the peony, winked, and twirled again, creeping down the hall.

Marcon shook his head while watching his friend and gave Iellieth's hand a squeeze before releasing it so she could follow.

The hallway sloped down, its quiet interrupted by occasional drips and the scurry of tiny feet. "Rats," Quindythias hissed. Iellieth suppressed a shudder. The walls curved several feet over her head to form a rounded ceiling, but a nameless weight pressed down against her shoulders, urging her to crouch if not to run.

A set of wide, flat stairs curved around a bend and out of sight. Quindythias motioned them to the wide side of the turn, his silhouette poised to take on the slightest disturbance.

Should they have checked the children's rooms before they left to ensure Lord Nassarq was there? What if he were down here, somewhere, beneath the castle? And why would he have sneaked down here before? The questions flickered through Iellieth's mind, tall and strong one moment, a flame quivering against a shallow breath the next.

She lost track of time as they continued on. Her right shoulder started to cramp from hunching over. Quindythias slowed ahead and signaled for the three of them to stop.

Iellieth inched over beside the elf. "What is it?"

He raised his head above hers and motioned for Marcon to

come and stand beside them. "I think we're finally out of the tunnels, but where exactly we are instead, I don't know."

The scent of old wax swirled against the damp musk of the catacombs beneath Nocturne. Whatever basement chamber they'd found was well made, though its walls seemed wiser, more cunning, and older than the castle that stretched into the mountains above.

"It feels like one of the old hideouts in Eldura," Marcon whispered. "But whose?"

"Let's find out." Quindythias resumed the lead but held up a hand behind him, urging Iellieth to stay back so the three of them could spread out. He peered around the corner and gestured wildly once more. Iellieth hurried forward, her footsteps echoing across the hallway. "Shush!" Quindythias glared at her. "Look." He held his flower out beyond the corner they'd hidden behind. Its glow shimmered outward but fell away as the tunnel opened up beyond it. "A crossroads."

Iellieth plucked one of the glowing petals from her peony and released it, fluttering, to the floor. They'd need to know which way they'd come to escape and climb up to the light once more.

The crossroads opened onto four separate passageways. The doorway across from theirs seemed equally nondescript. The other two were wider and taller, marked with large columns carved in runes she couldn't read. Marcon scowled darkly at the pillars but said nothing. Quindythias chose the one on the left, and she and Marcon followed.

It started as only a quiet whisper at first, a tittering giggle, but the hairs along Iellieth's spine prickled upward immediately as though a blade of ice had sliced down her back.

The sound stopped. Her own hushed breath echoed in her ears. There was a rush of footsteps down the hall ahead of her, and Quindythias cried out, flinging his peony into the air.

In its moonstone aura, two dark shapes swarmed the elf, clawing on to his shoulders. Quindythias shouted and writhed.

Marcon's bellow echoed from behind her, and his sword roared to life, a streak of flame barreling toward his companion. He spun the sword up and behind his shoulder, sprinting past Iellieth, and slashed across the nearest of the grappling forms.

Iellieth crouched where she was and set free the bolt of energy that had sped to her fingertips at the jolt of noise and movement. It struck the second figure, which went careening off of Quindythias's shoulder, and the elf fell to the ground, moaning.

Marcon leapt over the two prone forms. A child, or what had once been a child, hissed up at him, its eyes squinted against the firelight, sharp teeth bared against its pasty white skin. The champion spun and swiped, severing its head from its body. Across the expanse of its neck, its skin and tendons turned to ash.

Iellieth's stomach heaved, but her chilled hand against her throat calmed her reflexes. She slid forward to Quindythias's side, catching his head and shoulders in her lap. Beside them, the second child-monster sizzled, its body disintegrating away. "Shh, shh," Iellieth urged, "elenai." The healing energy floated from her fingers and off her lips, cerulean sparks settling over his shoulders and the base of his neck, knitting the wounds back together.

His shaking calmed, and his large, elven eyes stared back at her, lit by the light of Marcon's sword. Quindythias twitched away from the growing pile of ash beside him. The child's black eyes reflected the firelight, and long fangs hung from the skeletal remains of its skull.

"Marcon?" The champion stood poised above them, sword raised over his shoulder, ready to strike. Fire glittered in his gaze, more fearsome than any of the illustrations in Red's book had managed to capture. "What was—"

"Vampires, lady." His eyes flashed over to her and back at the chamber around them. "They're weak because of their age."

"Someone must have made them," Quindythias grumbled from her lap, groaning as he pushed himself up. He shuddered. "And recently. But how'd they get down here?"

The puddled remnants of Quindythias's flower leaked beads of moonlight as they crept down the hall, the shimmering liquid reflecting the sweeping ceiling overhead. "I don't know. Here." Iellieth dug a torch from her bag and pressed the end of it to Marcon's sword. "Since we've lost the element of surprise, we should at least have light." The torch roared to life, and she handed it to the elf.

Twenty paces down the narrow stone hall, four reinforced wooden doors glowed in the light of Marcon's sword. As they crept closer, Iellieth could make out a small, square opening reinforced with iron bars carved into the top of each door.

"Prison cells," Marcon whispered.

One door was cracked open. Sparks of energy flared through Iellieth's being. "We should have asked, how did they get out?"

CHAPTER 41

Iellieth peered around Marcon's side as he investigated the open door of the first of the four prison cells. The champion barred the opening with his foot, his sword raised at his shoulder. Four empty sets of iron manacles hung from stone walls streaked with blood, but no vampire children hid within.

A heavy cough echoed from the cell across from them. Iellieth spun. She'd know it anywhere. One winter holiday, they were both sick and kept warm by the fire together. "Scad," she whispered. Iellieth sprang across the hallway and yanked against the locked door.

Quindythias slid up beside her and handed her the torch. "You asked how I got in the map room in Hadvar?" He pulled a small dagger from the bandolier at his waist and pressed the hilt. Two metal pins sprang out of the base of the knife. The elf held up the picks with a flourish and bent to spring the lock free.

With a whispered cry of victory, the door creaked open.

Iellieth darted inside. "Scad, are you—*agh*!" A solid arm caught her around the waist and yanked her back into the doorway.

"Lady, he could be already turning," Marcon urged. She struggled to free herself, but it was no use. The champion scowled down at her.

"He's not, he's my friend." Iellieth tugged again, her feet scraping the damp stone floor.

"Ellie?" Scad's voice flitted out of the darkness. A second coughing fit wracked his body.

Quindythias took the torch from her grasp.

The fire along Marcon's sword dimmed. His jaw ground side to side as it went out entirely. Gray eyes blazed against the darkness. "Together." His voice rumbled low in his chest, and he kept an arm grasped tight around her as he walked them into the room. Marcon leaned over her, keeping them in step. "If his eyes are red or black, we leave. Do you understand?"

Iellieth bit her lip and nodded. How did Marcon know so much about vampires? Had he used a similar test to determine whether or not Lorieannan was beyond saving when he found her, in the moments before someone arrived to help him and turned her to ash?

Her questions extinguished as the torchlight fell on Scad. Iellieth's throat constricted at the sight of her friend. He was alive, but badly hurt. Dark slashes marred the sides of his throat. A slumped woman with white hair was chained behind his back. Marcon ordered Quindythias to check on her. Iellieth held her breath.

Scad raised his head, squinting at the torchlight. His eyes glowed a warm, dark brown.

Iellieth cried out in relief and sank to her knees. Marcon released her, and she crawled to Scad's side. She whispered his name. Scad blinked against the light as she neared, as though he couldn't believe what his eyes were seeing. A knot swirled in her throat as she wrapped her arms around his thin shoulders. Iellieth's voice broke. "I found you."

His head slumped to her neck. A muffled sob turned into a cough. He was sick. "You can't be here," Scad croaked. "It's too dangerous. He'll know."

"We're here to get you out." She ran her hands through the back of Scad's grimy hair. Tears welled in Iellieth's eyes as she took in the gashes covering the sides of his neck. The scars had layered so tightly over one another it looked as though a great beast had gnawed on her friend and spit him out—how different was the appearance from what had actually happened?

Weakly, Scad shook his head. "No, Ellie. He can't find you here." Another deep cough. Scad's tear-brightened eyes burned. "Please. That's why he took me. He wanted you to come."

"Who?" She cupped the sides of Scad's face.

"Lord Nassarq."

Iellieth's heart pounded in her chest. Lord Nassarq was a vampire. But why did he want her? She shook her head. "That doesn't matter now. Come on, we're getting you out of here."

"Light blue, almost white, not red," Quindythias said beside her. He gently laid the woman's head back on her chest. "Iellieth, if you have any magic you can spare, I don't think she'll make it otherwise."

"Yes, alright. Scad, one moment, and we'll leave." She shook her head at the question in his eyes. They didn't have time now for her to explain. "Quindythias, free their hands. Can we leave the way we came?"

He nodded and crouched down in front of Scad.

Marcon angled the torch for her so she could look in the woman's face. "Do you know anything about this young woman?" His voice was soft as he addressed Scad. Quindythias's tools clinked softly inside the stone cell.

"Elenai," Iellieth whispered. Cobalt sparks fluttered around the woman and settled across her face and chest. Her throat wasn't marked by slashes and bite marks the way Scad's was.

Instead, dark bruises swelled beneath remnants of azure paint that dotted her pale skin.

"Her name's Lavinia. She was here for a little while, and then she left. He brought her back . . . not long ago, but I don't know when."

The woman's breath deepened as the magic began to take hold. Iellieth held the woman's hand in hers, waiting to see if she would awaken. Three of her fingers bent the wrong way. Iellieth shuddered.

"Are there others?" Marcon rose from his kneeling position in front of Scad.

"You mean besides those two who attacked me?" Quindythias scowled and rubbed the back of his neck, insulted that he'd been ambushed by tiny vampires.

"He eats the little ones, Ellie." Scad dropped his gaze. "We heard them. H-he took them down the hall. They screamed . . . and then nothing."

The young woman stirred.

"Lavinia," Scad whispered, "they're here to help us."

The woman groaned weakly.

"Got it," Quindythias proclaimed. The chains rattled as they dropped onto the wooden bench and clattered across the stone floor.

Marcon pulled in his lips, his eyes bright reflections of the fire. "We need to keep moving."

Iellieth wrapped an arm around Scad's waist to support him. Quindythias crouched and picked up Lavinia.

"Who are you?" Her voice carried the lilt of the Frostmaw Mountains.

"A handsome elf in a snooping costume, here to rescue you."

Iellieth wouldn't have recognized it when they first met, but there was an edge to Quindythias's bravado here in the catacombs. He was frightened too.

"Is there anyone else?" Iellieth pulled Scad with her as she rose on tiptoes beside Marcon to look through the barred opening in the door beside Scad's prison cell. "Basha mentioned dozens of missing children—"

Marcon's arm shot out to stop her. "Don't look in there, lady." The champion's jaw clenched.

"Are they—"

"Trust me."

Iellieth gulped and nodded. She hugged Scad closer. His ribs jutted into her side.

Footsteps echoed down the hall the way they'd come.

"It's him." Scad tried to pull himself away from her. "Leave me here, Ellie. Run."

Iellieth stumbled as she held him back, and Marcon caught them both. With one look at her, the champion scooped Scad up into his arms.

Marcon and Quindythias looked at her. They were depending on her to find a way out. She exhaled slowly, calming the torrents of energy. "Aiya'ne," she whispered. With a prayer for their aid, Iellieth sent waves of magical energy out from herself. "Follow me." She hurried down the corridor. The sparks swirled behind her and around her friends. She could do this.

Soft tremors of energy rose up from the stones beneath her feet. She felt more than heard the distant echo of the daimon with the star-studded coat. "It is time, little druid. Do not lose heart." The magic coursing through her veins jumped with her pulse.

After a few turns, the waves coalesced in front of an arched doorway at the end of the hall. "In here." The iron handle clicked open. "It's not locked." She led the way into the large underground chamber.

A giant four-poster bed dominated the room, its black frame cloaked in crimson satins and velvets. Iellieth cringed away from the bed. A small body lay unmoving at the foot of the mattress. Dried blood coated the collar of the child's tunic.

Her eyes were wide as she turned back to her two companions, Scad, and Lavinia. The woman in Quindythias's arms spoke first. "It is better than the alternative. The child does not have to live through the nightmare of the cursed life. There was something coming?"

Iellieth nodded. "Someone."

"I heard your prayer to the spirits. It was not possible for us to escape the one who stalks these halls, but the spirits have provided us a chance to prepare."

The calm of Lavinia's tone and her lack of horror at the room's contents crashed against Iellieth in a rough wave. The evidence of Nassarq's evil followed quickly behind, tugging her toward a dark undertow. She pressed her fingers to the sides of her temples. Lavinia was right. Even if they escaped the tunnels, the problem of a vampire stalking the court remained. They needed to prepare.

A large black wardrobe stood beside the bed. "We'll hide the two of you in there. And then, Marcon, will you . . ." She nodded to the child's still body.

"Yes, lady."

Velvet cloaks, silk tunics, and leather breeches hung inside the wardrobe. Marcon set Scad down first, and Quindythias put Lavinia opposite him.

Iellieth knelt on a plush rug in front of Scad and took his hand. The sparks swirled around her, and her pulse raced. They didn't have much time. She dug into the pocket at her waist and withdrew the wolf figurine.

Her throat swelled shut again as the memories of finding it flocked to her. He had been so near. What might he have been spared if she'd found him sooner? She pressed it into his hands, and he let out a small gasp of recognition.

"Ellie, how did you find this?"

She couldn't bear to look at his face. "I'm so sorry," she murmured. "But it will all be over soon, and I'll take you back home."

"Ellie." Scad's eyes grew wider, his voice pleading. "He can't find you here."

Iellieth shook her head. "Whatever happens, don't leave this wardrobe until he's gone." She tried to swallow the knot in her throat, but it held fast. Scad squeezed her hand tighter.

Quindythias stood behind her. At Lavinia's nod, he closed the door in front of her. Iellieth pried her hand free from Scad's and shut the wardrobe door.

"How can we be certain Lord Nassarq will be here?" She'd read countless legends about vampires. But what would drive one to investigate its own lair?

A cold voice prickled against the air around her. "Invading my private sanctum is a good start."

CHAPTER 42

J uliet darted in and out of the groups of onlookers. From several blocks away, a cloud of dust floated into the sky as the pounding hooves thundered closer. The screams of oxen, lions, and people intermingled, the tang of bloodlust in the air.

"Juliet!" Persephonie called, pushing her way past a clot of men clamoring over one another beside a tobacco shop. Her mother squeezed through after her.

The crowd grumbled as the Hunt drew nearer, some jeering about the fallen empress whose legacy as a shape-shifter had inspired the chase of innocent animals through the city, leading to their slaughter in Tempus Market, where the council was said to have overwhelmed her and all the wiles of her natural magic. Others scooted back from the packed streets. It was a delicate balance, bearing witness to the annual celebration without risking being trampled to death in the spectacle. The Hunt entailed a score of accidental deaths in addition to those that were planned each year.

"There's one now!" several voices cried at a flash of fur across the packed square.

"Juliet!" Persephonie shoved her way through, her heart cantering in her chest. Her eyes bounced back and forth, seeking the gaps between couples and families. If she could just get to the street edge, Juliet would see her, and—

"Got her!" a man cried, holding up Juliet by the scruff of her neck, the fox's feet a wild flurry as she tried to escape.

"No!" Persephonie's hands shot forward, a beam of magenta sparks striking the man in the chest. He froze, his expression half-excitement, half-horror as he dropped the fox and crumpled to the ground.

Persephonie scrambled forward and grabbed Juliet, flinging her shawl around the trembling vixen. "Shh, you're alright." Sobs lapped at the base of her throat, but she held them back as she clutched Juliet tighter to her chest, trying to still the fox's panicked breathing.

Several people crowded around the man she'd struck, helping him to his feet while others gave Persephonie a wider berth.

"Ow!" She jerked her head back as Juliet's claws pierced her chest, drawing scratch marks across her bare skin. "What is it—"

"Persephonie!" Mama flew up beside her, hands clasped around her shoulders. "We have to go."

The thundering of hooves grew closer.

"You!" the man she'd attacked shouted, pointing at her.

Others rounded on Persephonie and Esmeralda, blotting out their view of the packed streets that opened onto Tempus Market. Juliet had led them to the apex of the Hunt.

The crowd gasped as a stray arrow flew down the street, twanging into the wooden siding of a blacksmith's shop. Their pursuers halted, jostled by the milling swarm pushing them in multiple directions.

A heavy hand fell on Persephonie's shoulder and pulled her away from the fracas.

She jerked away from the firm grasp, and her eyes flew up to find Otmund staring down at her, his jaw set in the direction of the men who had yelled at her and Esmeralda.

"Otmund!" Persephonie flung her free arm around his solid waist, careful to avoid pinning Juliet between them. The tavern owner clapped her on the back, and her mother sighed beside her.

"Don't know why the two of you think I'm a witches' guardian rather than a bartender," he grumbled.

Persephonie shook her head against his chest. "Druids, not witches, Otmund."

"Ah." He waved his hand, the difference negligible. A darting shadow crossed over their faces, something running past overhead. "What the—" His eyes shot up to the roofs.

A brown-clad figure with green hair crept over the rooftops across the street, angling toward the market. "Aylin," Persephonie whispered.

The crowd cheered as the first animals, a pair of elk and three purple foxes, burst into view.

"Otmund, lift me up." Persephonie tugged on the tavern owner's sleeve. They had to hurry. "Mama, take Juliet." She handed the scrambling fox to her mother, and Otmund followed her to the blacksmith shop.

"You sure about this?"

Persephonie reached up the wall, her foot raised. Otmund knit his fingers together and boosted her onto the sloped surface. She scurried up onto the clay tiled roof, Aylin a block ahead of her on the street opposite.

More shouts echoed up from below as the animals stampeded by. *You can do this, Persephonie.* She whispered a prayer to

Cassandra as she scurried over the rooftops trying to catch up to Aylin.

Spirits foul, spirits fair,
by shadow, light, or on the air,
meet me here, by fate's decree
I summon thee, of aid to me.

Energy crackled overhead, and thunder boomed in the distance. Clouds swarmed and darkened over Aylin. She was conjuring as well. Sparks flew beneath the elf's feet and lifted her onto the roof of the market. The three-story structure surrounded the square.

The eastern wall of the market held a series of leaning ladders and narrow staircases. Persephonie tucked her head, sprinting for the nearest one, ignoring the slip of her shoes on the tiles damp with morning condensation. The red of the clay roof was stained to that of blood.

Shrieks and a deep bellow resounded from the street below. A powerful ox slid into the statue of Tempus in the center of the city, another combatant slain by the fearsome god of war.

"Aylin!" Persephonie shouted as she scaled the final ladder and rounded the corner on the back side of the market. People streamed into the square below, shielded from the stampeding beasts locked in the center of the square by a line of horses and spear-wielding riders. The trapped animals shrieked against their living cage.

Rennear's russet-brown hair shimmered near the entrance to the square, Anelius's sweat-covered coat gleaming beneath him. The crowd jeered, screamed, as a lioness leapt at one of the guards, tearing him from his horse. The stones beneath them turned red as she and her pack ripped the man apart.

Aylin grimaced from the other end of the rooftop, raising one hand overhead, her fingers twisted into claws.

"Aylin, don't do this!"

Her arm wrenched down, and she glared across the roof to Persephonie. The first patters of rain dripped down from above them.

Persephonie squared off against her. "There has to be another way."

Thunder rolled and laughter blossomed deep in Aylin's throat. "No, there doesn't." She slashed her arm across the air between them, and a streak of lightning shot onto the rooftop.

Persephonie dove out of the way, the heat singeing the edge of her skirt. She picked herself up, scrambling higher on the tiles as Aylin turned to the crush of people and animals below. The elf called on eldritch fire, angling her arm at the crowded mass.

"No!" A flare of crimson sparks burst from Persephonie's hand, intercepting the elf's aim.

Aylin shouted in frustration as her spell missed its mark. One of the posts below ignited—a pile of barrels rested near the entrance of the stall beside it. People in the crowd screamed and began pushing one another in a scramble toward the entrance.

Persephonie called a winged spirit to her aid. The elf was too quick for her. She shoved her hands out in front of herself, the giant faery wings a shield as Aylin sent a torrent of dark energy shooting toward her.

The force knocked Persephonie onto her back. Aylin clucked her tongue, using a chimney for shelter as she took aim below once more.

Persephonie groaned as she rolled over, holding on to the back of her head. Her hand came away red and sticky, and blisters appeared on her palms from the heat of Aylin's spell.

The back of her neck tingled, directing her gaze below. Persephonie gasped. Her mother clung to one of the posts near the entry-way, Juliet on her shoulder. She was calling across and over the mob streaming out of the square—shouting for Rennear's attention.

Aylin's voice rose over the din, and Persephonie heaved herself up from the tiles, sprinting toward the elf. With a cackle, Aylin sent another streak of lightning flashing into the square.

The thunder's roar deafened everything around them, and the light seared Persephonie's vision. She screamed, clutching her eyes.

Behind the spray of red, Aylin's spell burned through the air, striking the pile of barrels. Above the panic, a roar of flame.

A ball of fire erupted in the square below, sending animal and human corpses flying. Rocks and wooden beams careened through the air, ripping into rows of red-and-silver-clad guards and the citizens who had gathered in the square.

Persephonie spun toward her mother and Rennear, searching for them through the smoke. A dark brown horse crossed the sea of screams as its russet-haired rider scoured the crowds. Esmeralda waded through the press of people, making her way toward Rennear and his horse. Mama gestured to the rooftop as she went, pointing to where Persephonie stood. Rennear turned and looked up, his eyes wide as he found her on top of the market roof.

Another peal of thunder blasted into Persephonie. Its force knocked her from her feet and sent her skidding toward the edge of the roof. Her fingers scraped the tiles, digging in for purchase. Her swollen skin slipped on the damp clay.

A tall silhouette appeared above her. Persephonie screamed as her fingers crunched beneath Aylin's boot. They both skidded closer to the edge. Aylin's golden eyes blazed in fury, reflecting the flames from below.

"I'm so pleased at the turnout for this year's festivities. Did you know we have a special guest?" Her head twisted, a wicked grin crossing her face.

Persephonie's feet slipped over the roof's edge, her momentum carrying her and Aylin nearer to the inferno. The elk bellowed in fright, a bear growled.

"Ready for the finale?" Aylin whipped her hand across the sky. The clouds rumbled. Shuddered.

Persephonie clung to the clay tiles. The second-story handrail began smoking beneath her. She turned away from the elf, searching the crowd.

Rennear watched from below, pushing his way upstream against the chaos. Esmeralda peered up behind him, her hand over her mouth.

Another streak of lightning bolted for the entryway. Its roar was sharper, more metallic. Rennear spun and wrapped his arms around Esmeralda, shielding her from the brunt of the silver blast that blew them both off their feet.

"Esmeralda," Aylin cried, her hand stretched out for Mama.

An auburn ball struck Persephonie's waist, pulling her from beneath the weight of Aylin's boot. She crashed, hand tucked over her head, onto the floor below, Juliet whimpering on her chest.

Men's voices rose below, morphing into snarls. The guards' bodies writhed, convulsing on the stone of the square. Werewolves took their place, their bleeding wounds dripping silver.

"My gods," Persephonie gasped. She grabbed Juliet and ran toward the entrance. Aylin's explosion would reveal the true nature of the city's protectors—and destroy them. Silver had killed the monsters they'd encountered in the mountains. The city must have placed special wards on their own werewolves, silver triggering their transformation.

The wooden flooring of the second floor buckled beneath

Persephonie's feet. As the beams ignited she launched herself forward, diving over the fire's blaze underneath.

People screamed in the square, caught between the flames, animals, and werewolves. The transformed guards howled at the undulating pall overhead.

Persephonie's feet flew beneath her, and she skidded to a stop above where she'd seen the second explosion toss her mother and Rennear.

Growls burbled below her, and Persephonie swung herself and Juliet over the railing. She fell onto a stack of smashed crates, their edges just beginning to catch.

Someone whimpered in the darkness. Juliet landed carefully beside her, darting into the shadows.

Persephonie crouched low, crawling toward the sound.

Her eyes adjusted to the penumbral smoke. As she drew closer, two familiar silhouettes took shape in the thick clouds around her. Persephonie sighed. She'd found them.

Rennear stood with his back to her. His red jacket was ripped across the shoulder seam. The back of his coat, slashed by the explosion, hung in tatters across thick brown fur.

Mama huddled against the wall, clutching her knees. Her eyes were locked on the fully transformed werewolf before her.

Juliet bounded over to her mother, standing between Esmeralda and the werewolf, tail raised, amber eyes shining as she stared at Persephonie.

Persephonie held her injured arm against her chest and crossed the smoldering market stall. She stepped between them, in front of her mother and Juliet. The werewolf's eyes narrowed.

She took a step closer to him. "Rennear."

His lips curled back in a snarl, and his teeth shot forward, snapping at her.

Persephonie's shoulders seized, but she remained where she

was. There had to be a way for him to come back to himself. He had promised he wouldn't hurt her.

Werewolf Rennear shook his fur and snarled at the oozing, silver wounds.

She held her hand out in front of herself to show him she meant no harm. Her legs trembled as she crouched, lowering her gaze to be even with his.

A deep growl rumbled in his throat; familiar copper eyes glared at her. Saliva dripped along his teeth.

"Persephonie, get away—"

She shook her head, glancing at Mama over her shoulder. "Trust me." Persephonie reached out for the werewolf. Rennear snapped at her again, and she jerked her hand back.

The fire inched closer, and the wooden structure keened in the heightened winds.

"We need to get out into the square, Mama," Persephonie whispered. "Stay behind me."

Esmeralda tried to scoop up Juliet, but the fox bristled, her tiny teeth bared, and she jumped closer to Persephonie. Rennear growled, sniffing, his tongue darting forward. "You smell like honeysuckle and sunshine," he had told her the night before, his beard scraping against the nape of her neck. "And something else." His lips had lifted into a smile, sending goose bumps down the length of her back. "Magic."

Persephonie crossed ankle over ankle, maintaining her low crouch as Esmeralda scrambled behind her. They circled the werewolf, angling toward the market square.

Rennear matched each step she took away from him, slowly stalking her as they inched out of the market's depths and into the square's roiling air.

"Once there was a young boy in the city of Andel-ce Hevra," Persephonie whispered. Rennear's throat grumbled, his saliva flicking across her skin. "The boy's father was powerful, and he wanted to use the little boy to help him grow even more so." The large copper eyes blinked, her image shining against black pupils.

"But the little boy, he wanted something else. A better future for himself, for his city." Boards crackled overhead, and Persephonie's breath hitched as the ceiling above where they'd been began to kindle, the smoke curling down toward them. "He helped everyone he could, but tensions still rose around him. As the boy grew into a man, some of the people became more unhappy, and it was harder for the man to protect them."

Her foot caught on her skirt as her mother emerged from beneath the structure. Persephonie fell back and swore, and Rennear jerked forward. Juliet leapt in front of her, erect tail waving as she snarled and held off the werewolf. Persephonie ground her teeth as she picked herself up. She coughed against the smoke. Stories couldn't be rushed, but she wasn't sure that she could tell Rennear his in time.

"And then one day . . ." She cleared her throat against the clogging smoke, continuing to creep out from beneath the structure. She and Juliet had twenty feet to go. Rennear growled from within arm's reach. "The man met a girl who was new to the city, who was in trouble for telling a story much like this one. He protected her from the angry guards and walked her home."

The werewolf snarled, and her mother's voice picked up behind her. She caught only her name, the rest lost to the howling flames and errant screams. Persephonie raised her voice over the rollicking fire. "A few days later, the guards returned for the girl, but the man was there to stop them again. He had help" —Juliet's tail swished—"and he learned that the girl was part of the people his father had warned him against. But she wasn't as scary as he'd been taught to believe."

Persephonie took another wheezing breath. Rennear stalked forward, his head lowering further. "He told the girl that he was a werewolf, like the men who had hunted her. But she knew that wasn't his true being."

Her mother screamed at the same moment that a streak of lightning flashed, bursting into the beam on the edge of the structure, the only remaining support holding the burning ceiling in place. Inside the square, Aylin stood with upraised hands, her silver skin gleaming in the fire's orange glow. Aylin's voice rose above the flames as she prepared to call a second bolt. The brilliant flash of the first beam shimmered in her golden eyes.

The split-second distraction ripped apart the structure of Persephonie's spell. Juliet hissed, lunging into the fur of Rennear's neck as he leapt forward. His jaw locked around the fabric of Persephonie's skirt. His momentum carried them into the courtyard as the ceiling roared to the earth behind them, crashing in a squeal of wood and shower of sparks.

Juliet whipped back and forth on Rennear's neck above her, her teeth too small to break the werewolf's thick hide. Persephonie whimpered, shielding her eyes and face. Her injured arm pulsed white behind her eyes, her shoulder and back screaming as she slid across the cobbles.

Rennear's jaws released, and he crouched over top of her, the hair of his chest brushing the side of her face where she lay curled on the ground. The muscles of his forelegs bulged as he lowered further, angled not at her—but at Aylin.

The elf paled as fat raindrops splashed down. Juliet released her hold on Rennear's neck and burrowed into Persephonie's side. Esmeralda stood frozen, poised to run to her daughter but afraid to move nearer to the werewolf or her lover.

Another crack of thunder overhead.

Aylin drew her hand back, glaring at Rennear, whitened eyes flashing. She was going to kill him, and in the wake of her attack, all the members of the Untamed would be destroyed.

"By the light," Persephonie murmured, swooping her fingers in a line across Aylin's torso. The ancient spell was only for the rarest of occasions, embedded in the origins of the world.

Roots groaned beneath the city as spirits teemed to the surface, long-forgotten souls and stories streaming to life to answer her call.

A blinding flash. Lightning struck Aylin, her body a pillar of white light. Rennear leapt forward. Spectral forms swarmed between them, shielding him from the brilliant flames from above.

Green hair toppled backward. A mighty werewolf followed, snarling. Aylin's eyes remained the longest. Golden circles wide in shock.

᳄

A LOW TENOR VOICE CALLED ABOVE HER AS THE DARKNESS beckoned, tugging, pulling her under. Warm fingers brushed raindrops off her face, the voice growing more urgent, a rope snug around her waist.

A wet, cold triangle poked the bones Aylin had crushed with her boot, sending a shock of white pain through her body. Persephonie cried out and then stilled. The pain wasn't alone. Shimmering waves of purple energy lapped along her hand, her arm, covering her chest. Around the waves, green dragonflies shimmered, skimming the surface. The tugging at her legs, her ankles lessened. Water droplets coalesced across her eyelids, clinging to her lashes.

She struggled against the tide's grasp, the voices from the world above her becoming clearer.

Her eyelids fluttered. The hushed voices flared, louder, more hopeful. Her mother was beckoning her. And Rennear.

Strong arms held her tight as her eyes opened. Esmeralda

knelt in front of her, hands on either side of her face, eyes misty with tears.

Two warm amber orbs appeared beside her, glowing beneath furry ears. "I don't know how she did it, but Juliet was the one who saved you." Rennear's voice rumbled against her ear, and she relaxed into his bare chest, his skin warm against her back. Scraps of his tattered jacket hung loosely from his arms. "She poked you with her nose, and there was a flash of violet." His voice grew hoarse. "We thought we'd lost you."

"Oof." Juliet leapt onto Persephonie's stomach, her tiny paws pressing against her ribs and hips. Over the vixen's head, a bushy tail wagged. "Thank you, Juliet." The big ears perked up. Persephonie leaned her head back against Rennear. He traced the side of her face with his fingertip.

"And you saved me," he whispered, lifting her up for a kiss.

CHAPTER 43

Iellieth spun toward the door to the bedchamber beneath Nocturne.

Lord Nassarq leaned against the doorframe with his arms crossed. "I'm pleased you brought your friends, Lady Amastacia." He spoke as though they were still upstairs, exchanging polite conversation, and not in an opulent bedroom in the catacombs beneath his castle. "I invited a guest to join us as well. Perhaps you know her?" A rush of shadow swept down the hallways and materialized beside Lord Nassarq. Coals burned beneath ashen skin as the revenant fixed her glowing red eyes on Marcon.

"Bringing delectable bait is another way to summon me, if you were wondering." The vampire smirked as he glanced between her and Marcon. He licked his lips, his tongue pausing to polish his two fangs.

She didn't need to hear anything more.

A shot of green flame streaked from Iellieth's hand toward Nassarq. The vampire spun, catching the verdant blaze on his

338

cloak, and shrugged it from his shoulders. The flames licked across the velvet pile on the floor and smoldered out.

Nassarq chuckled as he turned to Marcon. "Can *you* do any better?"

Marcon sprinted toward the vampire, sword raised.

The revenant's eyes gleamed scarlet, watching the champion. She lowered and bared her claws.

Iellieth threw a second gout of fire at the shadow creature, Red's warning that she existed solely to destroy Marcon echoing in her mind.

If the revenant could kill her, both Marcon and Quindythias would return to a crystalline state. The creature roared, eyes glittering as her gaze pulled away from Marcon and settled on Iellieth. At her core, sinking ice. *The creature knew.*

With a shout of warning, Quindythias crashed into Iellieth, yanking her out of the way as the revenant darted toward them. Marcon's sword was a whirl of silver in the corner of her eye.

"I said I'd see you again," the revenant rasped. Flakes of ash fell to the floor as she angled toward Iellieth. The molten crescent of a smile split her face.

Quindythias stabbed two daggers into the revenant's chest. Her smoky voice sizzled back up at him, the words lost in a crackle of flame. Quindythias yelled back, his strikes spinning wilder.

Claws lashed out from the creature and sliced the length of the elf's arm.

The vampire's eyes widened at the scent of blood.

A heavy black arm struck Iellieth across the face. Dancing stars covered her eyes. Her cheek throbbed. A crack jolted all the way up the sides of her neck as her elbows hit the stone floor. Marcon cried out from the opposite side of the room.

Iellieth caught her breath, pushed herself up. Quindythias knelt between her and the shadow creature.

Nassarq lashed out, flinging Marcon's sword from his grasp, and wrapped his foul, white hand around Marcon's bulging throat.

"There is but one way you can save her and your friend, champion." Nassarq's voice, magically amplified, flooded the room. Quindythias held her back, his eyes locked on Marcon's.

The revenant swung again, claws extended, and dug her black fingers deep into the elf's stomach.

He screamed, buckling at the pain.

Tears blurred Iellieth's eyes. Blood dripped from the creature's claws.

Iellieth stood over Quindythias and clapped her hands together. A bright blast of green energy burst forth from her, striking the revenant's head as the force threw her backward, sliding across the cold dungeon floor. She crawled forward, reaching out for Quindythias. His dark blue eyes found hers.

She wrapped her hand around her amulet, pushing away the growing pool of blood, sticky and bright, around her friend. "Come here," she whispered.

The flash of a weak smile, and Quindythias was gone. Her amulet glowed warm against her skin.

Marcon struggled against the vampire's grasp, pulling at the thin fingers clenched around his throat.

With a sweep of shadow, the revenant righted herself, red ember eyes fixed on Iellieth once more.

She murmured enchantments to the walls, and a torrent of vines appeared, slashing out at the creature. The vines wrapped around her arm, her ankle, but she kept stomping forward, slowed but undeterred. She broke one limb free, then the next.

A deep chuckle rose up from her core. "Lucien keeps telling me how pleased he will be to see you again."

Nassarq's free hand darted out toward the revenant, and she froze in her hunched tracks. "See?" His black eyes glittered up at

Marcon. "See what you could do if you joined me?" His pale face swiveled over to hers. "You could protect her from the past that haunts you."

The revenant strained against his spell. Ash rained from her skin, revealing a tan glow. Just like in the forest, the embers of her hair transformed into sweeping waves of warm brown. Delicate facial features emerged from beneath the burns, and forest-green eyes looked from Iellieth to Marcon.

The champion's mouth fell open, and he ceased his struggle against Nassarq. "Lorieannan," he groaned. His brow creased as he stared at the half-transformed creature.

Iellieth's heart leapt into the base of her throat.

The revenant's arms lowered. Her claws shrank back into her fingers.

And a sly smile twisted across Nassarq's lips. His fangs lengthened as he leaned toward Marcon's throat.

They were going to kill him.

Iellieth clamped her palm over her left wrist, where Quindythias had refashioned the crescent moon pendant as part of her gauntlet. She cast aside the memory of her failed transformation in Hadvar. This time would be different.

Her back arched and she roared, the cry morphing into a howl as she stretched into her wolf form.

Power thundered through her veins. Her paws dug into the carpeted floors, hair standing on end down the line of her back.

Nassarq's eyes widened. He released Lorieannan.

But he was too late.

The confused, half-ashen creature lunged for Iellieth, who leapt over her, a paw drawing blood and smoke as it raked across Lorieannan's torso and sent her flying. With her second bound, she collided with Nassarq's extended arm, jaws clamping down around his elbow, her weight and momentum driving him and Marcon to the ground.

Iellieth sprang up, head lowered. A growl burbled up from deep within her throat as she stood between Marcon and the vampire.

Nassarq rolled into a low crouch.

Behind him, Lorieannan hissed as she rose to her feet. Ash and embers crawled back over her skin, reforming her into the revenant that had haunted them since they'd left Linolynn. Four slash marks glowed red across her chest from Iellieth's claws. She slunk closer to the vampire. The scarlet coals of her eyes glistened.

Nassarq glanced at the flickering creature beside him. The deep black pools of his eyes darted over her wolf form, calculating the best point of attack.

Chain mail clinked behind her as Marcon stood.

Iellieth held her ground, blocking their path to the champion.

"Lady, no!"

The two lurched forward.

In a flash, Marcon threw his body between her and them. A strangled cry broke as fangs sank into his throat. The revenant's claws dug into his body, her mouth a wide, burning coal.

Marcon stilled. Gray eyes fluttered, then locked on hers.

Iellieth howled again, her heart stricken. Could Marcon return to the amulet if she wasn't in her true form? She dove forward, transforming back into herself, and caught Marcon's head as it began to fall.

The champion disappeared. A second glow spread against her chest.

Lorieannan's claws ripped along Iellieth's side. She screamed as blood poured from the wounds. Nassarq's eyes widened. A bright pink tongue darted across his pale lips.

She'd never make it past them and to the door in time. Her eyes fell on the wardrobe beside the bed where Scad and Lavinia hid. She could lead them away and buy the two of them time to escape . . . Scad had said Nassarq wanted her. *For Lucien.* The pieces fell into place. Nassarq, Lorieannan, Lord Stravinske—they were all working for Lucien. She could almost hear the burbling sigh of his voice: *And this time, Yvayne isn't here to save you.*

Iellieth's hand curled around her father's amulet, and she whispered to Marcon and Quindythias, "You'll find a new Shepherd." The promise set her heart at ease. They'd given her so much already. She could leave them with this. The amulet glowed beneath her hand, beams of ruby light shining from the gaps between her fingers.

She filled her lungs and drew the final dregs of energy from the room around her. The torches dimmed as she called the spirits of flame and root to her fingertips. A small circle of green flames appeared at her feet, and tongues of verdant fire burst from the palms of her hands. *Just like Mara.* Swinging her arms forward, Iellieth thrust the streams of fire at Nassarq and Lorieannan. The flames around her extinguished, and she collapsed to the ground.

The revenant screamed as the blaze caught hold of her. She writhed along the floor, struggling to free herself from their enveloping grasp.

Nassarq hissed as he whirled around. Black smoke curled from his lips and settled along his burning clothes and Lorieannan, suppressing the flames. "My lord is not finished with you yet," he growled. Mottled boils, left by the fire, scarred the side of his face.

Iellieth's arms shook as she rose to her feet. Inky tendrils waved at the edges of her vision. Blood continued to drip from her side. She pulled Teodric's dagger from her boot, her last defense. "But Lucien is nearly finished with you, is he not? What else do you have to offer him?"

For a moment, fear flashed behind Nassarq's eyes. The vampire waved his hand in front of his face. His skin returned to untouched parchment, all sign of the burns having faded away. He smirked. "You are wrong, Iellieth Amastacia. Our work is only beginning."

"No!" A strained voice rose from behind her as the wardrobe doors burst open. Scad and Lavinia scrambled out onto the thick rug but stopped short as the revenant spun to block their path.

Nassarq chuckled at the diversion. With a flick of his wrist, the vampire sent Scad flying.

Iellieth screamed as her friend's body struck the side of the giant bed. Scad fell to the floor and lay still.

Lavinia ran over to him.

"I wondered if you would find him." Nassarq smiled and snapped his fingers. "Lorieannan, leave them be. We're taking her with us."

Scad stirred slightly as the revenant turned away from him. Iellieth's breath caught in her chest, and she fixed her eyes on Nassarq. *Can I stall him long enough to . . .* A tiny sliver of root curled out from beneath the rug at her feet. *To make a wooden stake.*

"You created an excellent trap for me," Iellieth said quickly.

Nassarq's lips pursed. "I was getting rather bored playing puppets with the court. Your stepfather is much less perceptive than you."

Iellieth curled her hands into fists. Was the root coming from the dryad? From Nova? Whoever it was, they needed more time.

"Is that so?" Iellieth took a step closer to the vampire. Her amulet began to burn against her skin. "Have you been playing with the court and supervising Lucien's lackeys?" She gestured to Lorieannan beside him. "I must say, that was an impressive surprise."

The vampire laughed. "Was it? I thought you would put together the war behind the war, little Iellieth. It seems I was wrong."

"I'd love to hear." She slid nearer. The root was as long as her thumb now, and equidistant from herself and Nassarq. Her skin screamed as the gold of her amulet heated. Were Marcon and Quindythias responsible? Or something else?

"Surely your champion told you about our armies of old, did he not?" He cast a fond glance at Lorieannan. "He has firsthand experience, after all. The undead are much simpler to control than the beastly werewolves running about, gobbling up town after town. A slaughter or two later, and we'd be ready to subdue all of Caldara." Nassarq shook his head, his eyes sweeping over her. "*Lucien*"—he spat—"keeps getting distracted with you." The vampire brushed his palms against one another. "But I won't. Now, where were we?"

A snarling onyx streak flew into the room from the open doorway—a second wolf. The creature clamped its jaw around Nassarq's throat, rolling and gnashing as it drove the screeching vampire to the ground.

The arc of a silver arrow pierced the revenant. A chunk of ash crumbled from Lorieannan's side. Her ember eyes were fixed on the doorway. She tumbled backward as a second arrow struck her chest. With a high-pitched howl, Lorieannan disappeared in a swirl of smoke.

A hooded figure stomped into the room. Glowing eyes of melted silver lit cedar skin beneath the woman's hood. She extended her arms, a loaded crossbow in each hand, and fired at the vampire.

Nassarq hunched, his gaze darting about to keep the three women in his sights.

"Briseras, wait!" A breathless young man ran into the room, a large black raven on his shoulder. He gasped and skidded to a stop at the sight of the cornered vampire.

Slowly, Nassarq's head tilted to the side as he surveyed his prey. "Oh, Lavinia, I should have been more patient with you. Look what treats you've brought me." He licked his lips again. His shoulders remained hunched toward the woman with the crossbows. *The strongest of the four of us.*

Beside Lavinia, Scad groaned. He lifted his head from the rug and let it fall back.

"Don't listen to him, Briseras." Lavinia's pale blue eyes contracted.

"Oh," Nassarq purred, "but I really think you should."

In a swirl of black, Nassarq lunged toward the woman with the crossbows. He snarled as another of her arrows pierced his chest and lashed out. One of the two intricate wooden weapons shattered as he struck it.

Iellieth and Lavinia sprinted after him across the room.

Nassarq seized the young man who'd entered behind Briseras and sank his teeth deep into his neck. His eyes flared red, and he ripped his teeth free, disgorging the torn flesh in a spray of blood.

"No!" Briseras screamed and dove forward. The man crumpled into her waiting arms.

The black wolf leapt at the vampire's heels as he shoved himself toward the door. His boot struck her snout, and she fell back with a whimper.

Nassarq's footsteps echoed down the hall. He was getting away.

Iellieth returned to seize the root that had sprouted from the ground. It had grown into a spiral as long as her forearm and bore the dark bark of the tree she'd promised to free from the vampire's corruption. *"Buen dita,"* Iellieth whispered to the ancient black oak. *Thank you.* She yanked it free and spun back toward her new allies.

"Ellie, wait," Scad urged from beside the bed.

"I'll come back for you."

"This way." Lavinia's white-blue eyes glowed in the doorway. Tearstains covered her bruised cheeks.

The man Nassarq had bitten lay unmoving on the floor with his hands crossed over his chest, a smashed crossbow at his side.

The one called Briseras was already gone.

CHAPTER 44

T he vampire left a blood-scented trail in his wake.
Briseras and Vera flew down the halls, Otto flapping
over her shoulder as they careened around every wind
and turn.

She'd watched the light fade from Everett's eyes.

And she would now do the same with the vampire's.

The creature retreated through the dark sanctuary. She could
almost hear his shriek of dismay at the piles of slain undead she
and Everett had left smoldering in the large chamber. But that
was nowhere near satisfaction enough. Briseras tightened her
grasp on her unbroken crossbow. Before that last encounter, the
rest had almost been too easy.

A perfect trap? And why do you think that is? Forest-green eyes
and auburn hair glared from her memories. Rajas's voice
remained with her even after their parting. Would Everett's do
the same? *There is a difference between parted and dead.* She ground
her teeth together and sprinted faster.

The vampire thrust himself into a stone mausoleum. Narrow
recesses lined the tomb's walls. Slanting candles flickered within

their depths, dripping thick wax. Were it not for the marble plinth and closed, polished wood coffin in the center of the mausoleum, the space would resemble a glowing cave. Briseras jumped after him into the room, Vera at her side, and reached in her boot for the wooden stake.

He spun and caught her around the throat. Briseras gagged as the vampire lifted her off the ground with one hand and climbed the plinth, holding her aloft above the coffin. Her feet kicked and thrashed as he lifted her higher. She pulled at his thumb, his fingers, but his grip was iron and ice.

As cold and unmoving as Everett, whom she'd led to his doom.

A slow smiled spread across the vampire's features. "That is an affecting narrative of self-blame, my dear." He drew her closer, his nose tracing the line of her throat.

Briseras swung her foot back and struck the vampire's shin. He didn't even wince. Vera whimpered from the ground beneath her, held down by a magic force emanating from the creature's other palm.

"What strong potential you have." His face drifted into her hair. "Even more than he sensed in you before." Her wolf cried. *Who was he talking about?* Briseras shouted, but the hand gripped tighter, and his eyes flashed against his pale face.

The vampire lowered her feet to the coffin lid. The edges of the room swam in her vision, the candlelight blurring. Black eyes locked her in place.

The fingers of his free hand crawled down her neck, spider's legs one-by-one, and gripped her collar. He yanked it away from her throat and revealed the puncture scars from fangs similar to his own. "You really can't blame Malthael for wanting to turn you into a thrall, now, can you?"

I can.

"Did he not have a chance to fully explain why you made

such a tempting target?" Cold breath condensed against her bared skin. "I'm curious—why didn't he manage it before?"

The twist of pain in her abdomen. A shout of dismay. Ophelia's liquid voice, calling her back from the ether and stars between the worlds.

The vampire's touch burned like ice. She choked as his grip tightened.

A flurry of movement at her ankle. The wooden stake yanked from the side of her boot.

Nassarq careened back at Lavinia's shout of triumph. The woman withdrew the blood-soaked stake from his calf and drove it through him once more, this time piercing his torso.

A flash of ruby beside her. A curling black branch, sharp on the end, with midnight flowers on top. The red-haired woman from the vampire's chamber sprang up from her other side and plunged the wooden rod into the vampire's thigh.

Nassarq shouted and crumpled, his blood pooling on the floor around them, running in rivulets from the top of the coffin.

Briseras crashed to her knees, gasping for breath.

When she closed her eyes, she saw Everett's lifeless body. Briseras screamed, yanked an arrow from the quiver on her thigh, and drove it into the vampire's thin chest.

He gurgled, seized, and fell still.

The three women stood poised, lungs heaving, around the tomb. The red rim around Lavinia's eyes, the streaks through the paint on her face, spoke what Briseras couldn't bear to ask.

She tore her gaze from the icy blue of one to the questioning green of the other.

But then the body moved. Convulsed.

Trickles of black blood oozed around the stakes. The liquid ate away at the wooden piercings, its acid dissolving them in streams of smoke. Nassarq's body shivered. Shook. Convulsed again.

"Something's wrong." Briseras narrowed her eyes at the two women. There was another force at work here in this tomb.

She raised her crossbow and fired it, point-blank, through the base of Nassarq's jaw up into his skull.

A small circle in the center of his chest caved in, and his skin and bones began to deliquesce, turning into blood. The dark red fluid pooled together, and a thin rivulet streamed off the side of the coffin. He couldn't be regenerating. The laws of undeath forbade it.

Lavinia murmured a curse, staring at the corpse, resigning it to the afterlife.

Drip, drip, drip. A thick, viscous liquid plinked against the stone floor on the far side of the room.

Vera nuzzled her palm. Bow in hand, Briseras slipped away from the melting corpse to investigate the source of the dripping. The trickle of blood from the body drained faster, and the liquid carved a slithering trail across the floor, as though it was following her.

A thin spiral of blood undulated in mid-air, occasionally releasing fat droplets onto the floor. With each moment that passed, its circumference grew wider, and the blood running off of the vampire's corpse thickened into a river, rushing toward the beckoning swirl.

Tendrils of bright red stretched across the spinning blood like cracks in a dark, liquid mirror.

"It looks like a portal," the red-haired woman whispered from the other side of the emaciated vampire.

"It is." But to where? "He's escaping." Briseras turned to them, her jaw set.

Lavinia and the red-haired woman stared back at her as the portal swirled, faster and faster, as wide now as she was tall.

The last shreds of Nassarq's body condensed into blood and dribbled across the floor, joining the whirling ring.

Vhoom.

The portal thrummed with energy as the vampire made his escape.

"No!" Lavinia screamed. She sprinted for the portal and leapt, head tucked, and disappeared through the spinning blood.

"Lavinia!" Briseras yelled. Everett had asked her to trust him, and he trusted Lavinia. She glanced at the other woman and turned to Otto and Vera. How had Nassarq conjured this loophole?

The wolf lowered her head. The raven croaked. They'd travel together. She leaned back on her heel and bounded forward. Otto flew through the blood portal. Her arms wrapped around Vera and held her body on top of the wolf's. She'd navigate the rest as they landed.

⚜

"ELLIE!" A SHARP, CLEAR VOICE RANG OUT FROM THE EDGE OF the room. "Ellie, wait!" A clammy hand seized hers, and warm, dark brown eyes swam into view. "Ellie, don't follow him. Stay here."

The floor dropped away from Iellieth as the blood portal emitted a louder throb. It tugged at her hair, her limbs, but Scad held her tight, pulling her away from the swirling interplanar door.

A dark chasm yawned beneath her feet. Iellieth swung her other hand up and sank the blood-soaked stake from the black oak into the crumbling rubble of the stone floor.

The sound of wind whistling through the trees engulfed her, and a tangle of roots spilled out of the remains of the stone. Black branches splintered beneath her, holding her up. Their pointed tips bore delicate oak leaves, the dark green of a moss-covered rock in the shade.

She and Scad stared at the bowl of branches that supported her in the middle of the hollowed-out chamber. Did the green of the leaves and the absence of the vampire mean that the black oak was now rid of the corruption? And Nova would be free too?

Below, a final roar echoed from the chasm. It shook the stone, but the roots held fast. The quiet of the tomb returned.

Scad paled as he looked around. Tucked behind the candles' low glow, iron and onyx icons surrounded the room, interspersed along shelves littered with skulls.

Iellieth nodded before Scad could say anything, and she crawled off of the roots to follow him out of the mausoleum.

They collapsed at the end of the hall. Iellieth flung her arms around Scad's shoulders, and he laid his head against hers. "I never thought I'd see you again, Ellie." Scad pulled her closer and sighed. "Who were those men you were with?"

Iellieth sighed. "I have so much to tell you." Her amulet burned against her chest, another protest rising from within. "I'll let them out so they can meet you more officially."

The two warriors exploded into view as she wrapped her hand around the amulet. Quindythias spun around the hall, daggers out, searching for enemies. Marcon released the hilt of his sword and rushed over to her, scooping her up into his arms. "You fought brilliantly, lady." He held her against his chest, his warmth beating back the chill of Nassarq's tomb.

Marcon released her feet to the floor. His hand cupped the side of her face. Gray eyes burned bright, staring into hers. "I'm sorry I failed to stay by your side."

Iellieth grinned and shook her head. She ran her fingers over the lines of her amulet, the golden bands still warm against her skin. "You never left me. I kept you both right here."

He returned her smile. "What now, lady?"

Iellieth leaned away from him to gesture to Scad. "We need to get him back to his family and to tell Basha what Lord

Nassarq said about the war and trying to control the king. And there's the young man who came to our aid, plus the children." She swallowed at the memory of the tiny body and the cell Marcon prevented her from looking inside. "But then . . ." Her eyes widened. After all this time . . . Iellieth pressed her lips together, the words choking her in their rush to flutter free. "Then, we're going to the Realms."

Quindythias skipped over to her friend and helped him up from the floor. Scad's eyes widened at the elf's tattoos and ears, and he carefully studied the broad-shouldered man who stood close beside her.

Iellieth breathed deeply, the dungeon around her a shimmering blur. They could acquire a ship and cross the Infinite Ocean. They would ask the elven council for the final piece of the planar seal before their enemies had time to regroup.

And finally, after all these years, she could find her father.

EPILOGUE

Mist rolled over the moss-covered tombs of what had been the great burial ground of the druids of Lis-Maen, transported into the Brightlands in the wake of Eldura's fall. Vaxis clung tight to Yvayne's elbow. "Are you sure you want to tell her now?"

Yvayne stared out across the cemetery. The next step in their course was clear. "She'll know how to help where I don't."

Vaxis squeezed her arm. "But you'll lose her again."

The invisible presence of her wings folded in and out. To what extent was this decision hers to make? She slowly exhaled. "That is my role." To lose, to linger. "Hers is to be reborn, to live. It's her—it's Iellieth, and those who will rise up around her—that we need."

Yvayne pulled away from Vaxis, waving aside the mist that clung to the tombs. "We have relied on me before." The grasping hand of the dead and gone seized her throat. She choked it away with their names. "Lilia, Rowan, your sister Mercedes, Fhaona, Mara . . ."

Vaxis appeared out of the mist behind her, arms wrapped tightly around her waist. "So what do we do now?"

A wreath of autumn leaves pushed aside the blanket of fog, the misty tendrils lingering on their rigid edges. The colors were as vibrant as the day she'd laid them, almost five thousand years ago. The burial song emerged from the hidden grasses. It rippled up to swirl through the fog.

"We wake her up."

BLOOD COATED BRISERAS'S HEAD AND HAIR AS SHE, VERA, AND Otto rippled through the portal after Lavinia.

The space around them compressed, and she couldn't breathe. Fierce winds from the ether between the planes drove her hood back and whistled through her damp hair. Without warning, the winds released, and she and Vera plummeted through the air toward a dark forest beneath. Briseras pivoted in midair and bent her knees. She'd cushion the fall for Vera.

Pine needles and sharp branches slashed at the pair of them. The dense forest floor rushed up to meet her, hungry for her last breath of Caldaran air.

"Mmph." She thumped to the ground, and the earth darkened.

The sound of a river was whooshing through the trees ahead of where she'd landed. Briseras groaned at the pain in her legs and side as she slowly rolled up to seated. Her ribs were bruised, but she could take full breaths, so nothing was broken.

Vera plodded over to her from a few feet away. She whimpered and rubbed her nose beneath Briseras's chin. Otto croaked weakly from a branch overhead.

The huntress wrapped her arm around her wolf's neck. "We're alright." Briseras's heartbeat slowed as she stroked Vera's fur. She glanced through her pack, a necessary habit for survival in a new or unknown location. Her breath stuttered as she seized Everett's journal.

She shut her eyes against the light fleeing his and the sudden weight of his body in her arms. Had he expected that he wouldn't live through the vampire's lair, and that's why he entrusted his journal to her?

Under earlier circumstances, she would have told the foolish griever she was with that the spirit was free now. Let it be. But something about Everett's spirit . . . was he holding on to this life? Had he truly drifted away or into the journal that he poured his heart into, contained in the bag at her feet?

Leaves covered the forest floor. They were dry, pale oranges and browns, tinges of red, the colors of late autumn. The warm spring sun had begun melting the high mountain peaks of Caldara when they entered Nassarq's foul estate. She knew of migration through planes, but not time.

Briseras leaned against the bark of a tree and pulled out the leather volume, flipping through its thick vellum pages. Everett's careful hand was interspersed with notes from others. Letters from his lover, James, had been pressed between the pages. She stopped on the entry with her name, thinking back to Everett's surety that she occupied a central role in whatever story he imagined was playing out all around them. Might there be other ways besides hers of living as one divided between life and death? Would part of the folklorist stay behind with her and help her on her journey to wherever it was the portal of blood had delivered them?

She rose to standing, taking stock of their surroundings. No sign of Lavinia. Everett had had a feeling about her, just as he had Briseras. Her blood ran cold, thinking of Everett's lonely passage from one life to the next. "Vera, we need to find her."

The river's rumble increased as she and the wolf drew closer. Otto circled the trees overhead. The water rushed through the woods, white rapids cresting over its depths. Lavinia's form wasn't draped across the riverbank.

Briseras made a small totem with rocks to mark their place of arrival. She, Vera, and Otto ducked back into the first line of the trees and headed downstream.

A lone wolf howled as darkness gathered. Vera's ears turned toward the cry, but she didn't answer.

She stepped out of the trees' covering in the fading light to ensure she could see anyone stranded on the opposite bank. The river widened as it went, the rapids calming across the shallows.

A shadow darted through the trees opposite them.

"*Tsst,*" Briseras hissed.

The wolf lowered her head, a growl percolating in the back of her throat.

A shambling form appeared on the opposite riverbank, its ripped clothing hanging in tatters off its body. Its speed increased as another followed it, breaking through the tree line toward the three of them.

Briseras took aim at the first of the creatures. Dark energy rippled through the air between her and it, pressing against her as she readied her shot. She reached for the second crossbow from her back as she fired the first. *The vampire smashed it in the castle.* She had left it beside Everett's body. The zombie creature shrieked as the arrow struck true.

Splash. The undead monster crashed into the rapids. If her shot hadn't killed it, the water would.

A second appeared from the shaded trunks. Briseras lowered her crossbow and took careful aim. She fired at the creature as it stomped through the rapids, black eyes fixed on her and her wolf.

It screeched and joined its fellow, careening downriver to be gnawed by rocks and swirling water.

She knew not where the blood portal had taken them, but a realm darker than Azuria held her now.

❦

"Yvayne?"

The silver-skinned elf squinted, brushing aside her long, garnet hair.

The fae's heart pounded in reply. How many years had they been parted? "Yes," her vocal cords rasped like they'd been drying out all this time, "it's me."

"But I don't understand." Rowan frowned, pushing herself up to seated. She laid her forehead against the heel of her hand. "How am I here? I thought . . ."

"So long as your amulet lives, you do as well." Yvayne took a step nearer. In another world, story, or time, she would have woken Rowan with a kiss. *My love, I've returned. I brought you back to be mine.* But that age for them, if it had ever truly been, had passed, vanished in the decades following the collapse of Eldura.

Rowan shook her head. "That was hypothetical. We were never certain that—"

She looked just the way Yvayne had remembered. *Turn your eyes to me, let me see their glow.* The faeries were better at these expressions than she. Maybe, given time, and plenty of focus, they could help her. "Your amulet has found your soul-heir." The elf's peridot eyes spun up, a knife through Yvayne's heart. "Iellieth is her name." Yvayne smiled as tears filled her gaze. "Her eyes are precisely the same shade as yours."

The elf's face paled, silver to ivory. Her spirit-shape shimmered as she internalized what Yvayne had said. *Don't you dare go.* "And she found the amulet? Or it found her?" Rowan tucked a strand of hair behind her pointed ear.

Yvayne crossed her arms and leaned against the barrow. "In a way. To say it took ages would be an understatement." She gazed out over the moss-covered mounds. "There were so many times I thought you would return but didn't. I've met only one iteration between." Yvayne sighed. And now to reveal what she wished could stay hidden, the barrier that had remained between them before. "Rowan. There's one more thing."

The elf's brow furrowed at the shift in Yvayne's tone.

Yvayne knelt and took the shimmering, incorporeal hands between hers. "Iellieth is a Soul Shepherd, just like you." A slow breath, in and out. "And she found him. Marcon."

Rowan's eyes flared bright. Her image flickered. The soul-bond blazed to life once more.

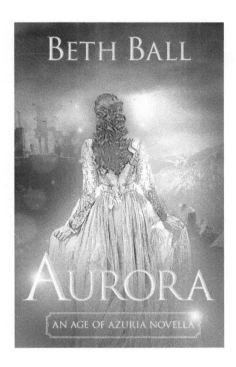

Dorric Themear has experienced the giddy flutterings of new love before. But not like this. Behind the sapphire eyes of Lady Emelyee Amastacia lies a long-awaited destiny that neither of them can sense or stop.

However, forces darker than Emelyee's husband are prepared to stand in their way.

Ridel, one of Lucien's most trusted servants, is less than enthused about her assignment to watch the lovers. If only her master had been visionary enough to see that a child cannot result if the parents are dead. She'll do her best to comply with his orders to watch and to wait —at least for now.

High in the Frostmaw Mountains, Yvayne has seen the signs of a turning of the age before. Perhaps this time, with the proper intervention, she and the druids can make a play for Azuria after all.

⁂

Visit bethballbooks.com/join to join our reading community, and you'll receive a free copy of *Aurora*, the prequel novella for the *Age of Azuria* series. Find out where Iellieth's story truly began!

Song of Parting: An Age of Azuria Novella releases February 9, 2021

Preorder today!

You can find *Song of Parting* in your favorite bookstore or purchase directly from the author at bethballbooks.com

Among the many truths they hold close to heart, story-weavers know: Across all eras, Love and Loss rest on either side of the turning wheel of fate.

Azurian legends tell such a story, of love found and lost in the early days of the worlds. Katarina Starsend, a story-hunter and scholar, dedicates her life to tracking down these tales and finding their new iterations in the world. She's in luck. A legendary fae has been reborn —and her incarnation is only a day's ride away.

Within the walls of Io Keep, a storm gathers as the callous Duke Amastacia sets his plans in motion. Soon enough, he'll be rid of his stepdaughter, Iellieth Amastacia. Seeing what lies ahead, Teodric Adhemar faces a choice—does he warn Iellieth or allow her to hold tight her illusion of freedom?

And can Iellieth out-plot the duke?

Find out in this prequel novella perfect for current fans and new readers of the *Age of Azuria* high fantasy series!

ABOUT THE AUTHOR

Beth Ball is a high fantasy author telling stories in the world of Azuria. When she's not writing fantasy fiction, Beth is a tabletop RPG designer and a literary scholar. Her academic work focuses on contemporary novels that encourage readers to find agency and empowerment in their approach to nature and their impact on the natural world, and her TTRPG adventures incorporate lots of druids.

You can find her and more stories set in Azuria at bethballbooks.com.

twitter.com/GroveGuardian
instagram.com/bethballauthor

Lightning Source UK Ltd.
Milton Keynes UK
UKHW010031141220
375092UK00011B/605/J